TWO NOVELLA S

IN ONE

BOOK

The Black Widowmaker

&

Satan's Dark Angels

By

Rick Magers

© 2007

ABOUT

The Black Widowmaker

Pearl was a happy, smiling young black girl when her mother dropped her off at school—never to see her mother again.

The day that Pearl's grandmother picked her up at school, and brought her to the small house in the Miami Florida ghetto, was the beginning of what could have been the best part of her life.

A slip of her tongue, while speaking to a pair of tough young hoodlums seals her grandmother's fate and changes Pearl's life forever.

The teenager meets the Reverend Jedediah Simon Peterson, and feels momentarily safe—false security; needed so badly.

The *Reverend* and his associate, D'Julliette, sequester Pearl in a filthy locked bedroom and begin teaching her an ancient trade.

To survive, Pearl knows that she must do what they say. The horror of her new life is met with a resilience that even she didn't know was in her. She does as she's told and hangs on to one thought—revenge.

And then she meets Yan Brodjevinski.

Pearl E. White will never be the same.

Rick Magers

TABLE OF CONTENTS

CHAPTER	PAGE
TOUGH BEGINNING	5
FATAL ERRORS	11
A NIGHTMARE BEGINS	18
TOUGH COP	23
THE DEVIL ENTERS THE NIGHTMARE	26
OPPORTUNITY KNOCKS	28
TRAINING BEGINS	31
GATHERING INFO	32
MORE TRAINING	36
DELIVERY MAN	38
THE DEVIL'S FRIEND	41
ISLAND PITSTOP	43
TRAINING/LEARNING	46
OLD PAL—NEW INFO	48
EMANCIPATION	51
CARIBBEAN CONTACTS	54
CONTRACT SEVERED	58
YAN'S RULES	62
CAREFUL PLANNING	65
ISLAND CLUES	68
RETIREMENT PACKAGE	70
CLUES BEHIND A FOGSCREEN	74
DEMONS ARRIVING	78
DICKLESS DEADMEN	82
DEADLY SURPRISE	84
EYE CONTACT	86
NEW HUNTING GROUNDS	89
HI TECH—TOO LATE	92
CHECK OUT—CHECK IN	92
TOUGHEST GAME IN TOWN	94
THE BIG APPLE	104

Rick Magers

SURPRISE DEVELOPMENT	107
NIGHTMARE REVISITED	111
BOATING—TO—YACHTING	112
FLAWED REVENGE	115
GAS—TO—SAILS	118
FIRST CONFRONTATION	120
ENCOUNTER—DE JA VU	122
EYE—TO—EYE	125
A NEW LIFE BEGINS	130
WOUNDS THAT NEVER HEAL	132

Satan' Dark Angels begins on page 136

THE BLACK WIDOWMAKER

April first 1980 wasn't a good day for Pearl E. White. She began it with three strikes against her. <u>ONE</u>: She was black. <u>TWO</u>: She was female. <u>THREE</u>: She was born.

~ O ~

1

TOUGH BEGINNING

The day her mother dropped her off at school—never to see her mother again—she asked, "How come you had to have me on April Fool's Day? My friends all laugh at me and say I a fool."

"Woman ain't got nuttin t'do wit when de baby comin into dis worl, girl." She was too young to understand, but in a few short years the diminutive young black girl would learn that her mother was telling her the truth, as she understood it.

One week after her grandmother arrived, to take ten-year-old Pearl to live with her in the sprawling squalor of the Miami ghetto she asked, "How come mama didn't give me no middle name? Juss E?"

The tiny, wrinkled, black, forty-seven-year-old woman looked down at the granddaughter, who she would soon learn love more than anything ever to come into her difficult life. "Probably that no-good Snoe White gittin back at he own mama for naming him like dat."

Rick Magers

"Was he really white like mama said?"

"Bout as white dese ole suncooked Nassau arms girl," she held out her strong-coffee-colored arms for the tiny girl to inspect. She patiently watched as Pearl quietly inspected them. "Whachoo tink girl?"

"He probably black as mama," she smiled as her grandmother hugged her and laughed hard.

"He was dat girl." She spoke in a Bahamian singsong voice, which she brought with her in the tiny fishing boat from Nassau, over thirty years earlier—the only voice she knew. "Dat de onliest White boy on New Providence Island what blacker n' dem downtown Bay Street boys." Tears ran down the old-before-her-time face as she laughed with the little girl.

"How come you talk so funny, gramma?"

"Me! Me?" She leaned down with the artificial scowl on her face, which Pearl had already learned was the old woman's way to have a little fun with her, "Ise tinkin all dis time was you what talkin kinda funny." She walked to the old oak cabinet; paint peeling on all sides, and removed an album, which was even more tattered than the simple dress she wore. "C'mere, girl." She spoke while patting the long-ago- collapsed cushions on the dilapidated couch that she and her husband bought during their first year in America.

"Who dat?" Pearl asked as she pointed at a tall black man wearing a straw hat and bathing suit. He was holding a huge sea turtle upright on the rear end of it's shell, in the sand of the beach for the picture.

"Artnell Brothius Sawyer," she looked hard at the faded photo a moment before continuing, "he my husband when we come cross dat water from Nassau."

"Where dat?"

"Million miles an a tousan years from here, girl." Her mind was rolling back across the years, and she didn't hear the little girl until she tugged on her frayed shawl. "Huh?"

"Who dis pretty lady besides him?"

The wrinkles widened as she looked down into Pearl's tiny face, "You takes a closer look, an I bet you knows who dat be, witout I tell you."

Her tiny nose almost touched the cracked and crinkled photo as she studied it. "Nope," she finally said, "ain somebody what I knows."

The old woman placed the album on Pearl's knees and stood, "You keep lookin at dat pitcher an I be bock directly." She turned and disappeared into the other room, which served as bedroom and bathroom, even though it had no tub or shower; just a broken down old box spring and mattress plus a commode and little sink—all kept as spotless as the rest of the tiny house.

When she returned, she had already removed the tattered dress and shawl. She was now wearing a large beach towel, which she considered one of her most treasured items of comfort, because it was what she always took to the

Virginia Key Beach, where she occasionally went to swim. On her head was a straw hat, which she rescued from a trash pile in Coconut Grove. She worked there as a cleaning woman, every Monday through Saturday, from seven in the morning until seven at night before boarding a bus for the return trip to her tiny refuge. With her native talents and nimble fingers she repaired the hat, so that it now looked new. It was sitting at the same rakish angle on her head as the lady in the photo.

Pearl looked from the photo to her grandmother and back again; finally blurting out, "Dat you in de picture, Gramma." She put her nose so close that it was touching as she looked at the young woman in the picture. "You was beautiful, Gramma." She said it over and over as she returned many times to the photo.

When her grandmother returned from putting her dress and shawl back on, tears that had started rolling down the wrinkles in her face were dried and she was wearing a smile. She sat beside the little girl and began telling her all about the people in the photos, as she strolled back through the pleasant valleys of her memory.

"An dis ole fella in de boat, my doddy."

Pearl held the album on her knees, leaning down to look at the black man standing in the small Nassau Dingy. "He de blackest man I ever see," she said and continued inspecting the aged, cracked photo.

"I spect he dat sure nuff," the old woman laughed, "cause if he keep he eye shut, an he mout close, you gone walk right into him in de night time."

"Ha, ha, ha," the little girl giggled, "he sure nuff be real good for playin hide n' seek wit, huh?"

The old woman turned to the final page and pointed to a very tiny, very black old woman standing next to a huge pile of conch shells, "Dat my mama."

After a thorough inspection of the picture Pearl said, "What dem ting she workin on?"

"Dem conch shells, chile. She knockin de meat out dem shell, what my doddy juss bring in."

"What dey do wit dem shells?"

"Doddy gotta carry dem ting out to Conch Island an trow em up on it."

"Why he do dat, Gramma?"

"Cause de law say he gotta. Dey doan want dem stinky ting layin roun on de lan."

"Why dey stinky?"

"Cause mama can't get all de meat out dem ting."

The curious little girl leaned closer to the photo, trying to see what the old woman in it was holding. "Is that a hatchet she got in her hand?"

"Yep, dat were her doddy ver own hatchet."

Rick Magers

"Is that what she knocks em outa the shell with?"

The old woman grinned, "No chile, dat what she knock a hole in de end wit, so she can poke her knife in an git dat sweet meat out."

"Yech! You mean they eat it?"

"Oh yes girl," she closed her eyes and hummed softly, "mmmmmm, I can taste dem sweet ting right now in my mouth memories."

The little girl stuck her tongue out and repeated, "Yech! I don't think they're sweet like bananas or mangos."

"No," the old woman responded seriously, "you right. Dey not sweet like dat but when you eat one dem ting you gone tradin away a buncha banana for juss one."

"Not me; I'll eat the bananas and you eat them stinky cronks."

"Dat a deal girl," she said with a smile as she got up to return her precious album to it's dilapidated old oak cabinet. When she returned to the couch, the little girl was silent for several moments, so she waited patiently to see what was on her mind.

"Gramma how come dem pictures all cracked an dull? We can hardly see the peoples in em."

"Dat juss de way life be darlin, cause ever ting git old no matter how hard it try not to." Pearl looked up into the old woman's face and studied it a moment before asking, "You gonna git old too, Gramma?"

"I reckon I already is, girl."

"How old are you?" The girl innocently asked.

"Mmm, well now," her grandmother mused a moment then said, "I only juss a little younger den dat school you goes to, cause it were built juss awhile before I born." She watched the expressions on the girl's face all the time, because she had noticed how Pearl pondered and questioned everything. When the girl finally spoke, the old woman smiled.

"That school is really old Gramma, cause it falling down an we get hit all the time by stuff coming off the ceiling." She looked hard once again at her grandmother then finally said, "You don't look old Gramma, at least not old like that school."

The old woman put her arm around the girl's shoulders and hugged her. "I glad you don't tink I too old darlin."

"Gramma," the little face turned up to look at her grandmother, "why ain't Grampaw Arsnel witchew any more?"

"Artnell," the old woman corrected, "he name aye-are-tee-en-e-ell-ell; ARTNELL. Art, juss like a pitcher on a wall, an Nell, juss like dem nell what holdin dis ole house together."

"Artnail," Pearl said with a big smile of accomplishment.

"Dat right, Artnell."

"Where he at Gramma?"

The wrinkled old black woman looked back into her past briefly before answering the inquisitive child. "He gone off on a boat wit a Cuban fella long time ago, an he ain ever come bock."

"Where dey gone, Gramma?"

"Me an Artie, dat what ever body call him, were down on dem dock at de Miami River when he tellin dis Cuban fella bout some crawfish trop he seen in de North Bahamas when he were snapper fishin. He tole em dat nobody was usin dem box, so dey should go pullin dem ting an get dem crawfishes." She remained silent as her granddaughter thought over what she had just heard, then hugged the little girl before continuing, "An I ain seen dat mon again after dey goin to pull dem trop."

A frown crossed Pearl's shiny black face as she looked up, "You think the boat mighta sunk and sharks ate em?"

"Ha, ha, ha," the old woman laughed, "dat always got a chance to hoppen when you out dere on dat big ocean."

After a long silence the little girl asked, "Gramma?"

"Yes chile."

"How come you din get anudder man after Grampaw Artnail ain come bock?"

"Well girl," she smiled down, "I be tinkin bout dat, time an agin, but din seem t'be no time f'dat foolishness. I been workin six day ever week at dis same people house, cleanin an all dem ting dey need all dese year, an I only got Sunday f'me." She grinned down into Pearl's innocent face, "An I sho ain gone wastin dat time on no silly man-chasin."

"Doncha git lonesome, Gramma?"

"How I gone be lonesome girl? I ridin dat bus wit plenty peoples ever mornin f'one hour, den wit dem folks in dey big ole house all day f'twelf hour, den bock on dat bus anudder hour gittin home here." She looked down with the artificial scowl that Pearl was already used to and added, "Till you comin to be wit me, I juss eat a can of soup an sleep till time t'go again. Sunday I git dress all up an go to church where I got so many peoples I doan even know all dey name."

Pearl smiled saying, "Nope, don't spose you git lonesome."

The little girl noticed what she now recognized as thought creases spreading across her grandmother's forehead. "Whachew tinkin bout Gramma?"

"How you know I tinkin?"

"Cause I Mombo lady."

A look of alarm crossed the old woman's face, "Whachew know bout dat Voodoo, girl?"

"Dem kids at dat park I go to after school till you git home, all time talkin bout dat stuff an say I so black I gone be Mombo lady."

Rick Magers

"Dat voodoo ain no ting be messin roun wit," she gave Pearl a very severe, very stern look, "even if you kiddin. You tell dem kids you gramma gone have nuff money when time you gone to college, f'you to be a doctor or lawyer."

2

FATAL ERRORS

During an eighth grade break with her friends, Pearl watched two teenage boys that had been in her school until the previous year. They casually mingled with the children selling their wares—drugs.

"Those two boys," she said to her girlfriend, in her now nearly perfect English, "have thrown away any future they might have had, just to make a few dollars now." Her 'gramma' from the Bahamas constantly insisted that she stop using island slang, each time she heard her talk use it.

"Girl, Ise only gone to school a couple year in m'whole life, an I juss doan know how to speak de way you muss to get along here in dese United States." She looked hard at the little girl, who she loved more than her own daughter, "Dat why Ise all time workin for juss a few dollar ever day." She stared hard at Pearl, "De way I talk dey know straight away I a dumb island nigger, an gone take any little ole dollar dey toss my way."

The once gangly, skinny little black girl stood in front of the old woman, who had done without many things so that her granddaughter could become the blossoming Black Pearl, as she now referred to her. She reached out and held her grandmother, as she now called her, in her brand new teenage arms. "You are not dumb, grandmother, and you are certainly not a nigger." She held the person she loved more than any other on earth, then pushed her gently back and said, "I go to school with a lot of niggers. Grandmother, most of them are as white as those biscuits you make on Sunday."

"Dat true darlin," the old woman commented, "you ain gotta be black to be a nigger."

Pearl's girlfriend was also watching the two boys, but with different eyes.

Rick Magers

"They're fools to drop outa school," she said, "but that blonde boy's a cute little devil, ain't he?"

"Yeah, he's sure cute," Pearl answered, "but know what my grandmother says about that?"

"Huh, uh," the girl grunted as she followed the blonde boy's butt across the basketball court.

"Pretty is as pretty does."

"Huh," the girl turned back to Pearl, "whaja say?"

"Oh never mind, here comes your Clorox baby."

Her friend turned to her; "I don't care where he gets his blonde hair, it's gorgeous."

The two schoolyard entrepreneurs swaggered to the redheaded white girl and Black Pearl, then casually looked them up and down, while puffing on the cigarettes hanging from the corners of their lips. "How's our gorgeous little fireplug and the April Fool doin' today?"

"Just fine," Maureen answered as Pearl just looked quietly at the two young toughs, "how're you boys doing?"

The boy with the bottle-blonde, flat top haircut, with long sides combed back, was doing the talking. He turned to his short stocky friend; always looking at the world through mean eyes, rarely saying a word. "She calls a coupla guys with foot long dicks and a thousand bucks in their pockets BOY, whadaya think o' that?"

Still nothing—mean eyes staring.

"Aw, you know what I mean," Maureen answered.

"No! I don't know whacha mean Fireplug," the bottle-blonde, New York City mimic-hoodlum spoke while advancing to stand close between her legs; dangling from the end of the concrete picnic table. "Y'mean you don't believe I have a thousand bucks here in m'pocket?" He pulled a wad of money that resembled a green jellyroll from his baggy orange pant's pocket. After returning it, he unzipped his fly, "Or don't you think my dick's really a foot long?"

When Maureen, ever searching for acceptance by the older boys, reached toward his fly, he stepped back and zipped it up. "Easy now little fireplug," he glanced nervously around, "business now and a little playin' around later, if you're still around when we're done."

As they walked to a small nearby group of eighth grade boys, his mean-eyed friend thought, *She'll laugh like hell if she ever sees that pinky-finger sized thing that Jenner calls a foot long dick.*

When Maureen was finally able to tear her eyes from Jenner's nine-inch-wide butt and artificial blonde, outdated DA haircut, she asked Pearl, "Your grandma still gonna letcha spend tonight with me?"

Pearl lit up at the reminder of her first-time-ever, all night pajama party at a friends house, "Yes, but I gotta wait'll she gets home so she knows everything's all right, then I can catch the bus to your house." She grinned wide at her only close white girlfriend, "We're gonna have so much fun, Maury."

Maureen's attention was back on the boys nearby, "What's in those little papers they keep taking out of their boots?"

"My friend Aleechia's older brother says it's a drug called coke, and is a big deal up in New York City."

"You ever tried any drugs, Pearl?"

"Nope, and I ain't gonna try 'em either, because my grandmother's worked hard to put away enough money in her little safe, so I can go to college to be a doctor." She paused as she thought a moment, "It would break her heart if I did something stupid like that."

"Ohhhh Pearl," her friend said as she nudged her with her shoulder, "ain't anything wrong with just trying something once." She jumped down from the table saying, "I'm going over and talk to them."

"Okay," Pearl answered, "I wanna go in and talk to my music teacher anyway," she waved over her shoulder and headed for the old school building.

Jenner and Arturo had finished making their sales, as the busty little redheaded girl walked up. Jenner grinned, "Come to check out that foot long dick, huh?"

Maureen just gave him her best, 'In-a-month-I'll-be-a-teenager grin,' then said, "No, I wanna see what you guys're selling that all them guys are going crazy about."

"Well, nuttin' to worry about there baby," Jenner replied as he pulled the pants leg up to remove a waxed paper packet about half as big as a stick of chewing gum. (He carried the free little 'get-em-hooked' packets in his left sock, away from the full gram packets in the right sock.) As he handed it to her he said, "Here's a little plastic straw to use it with," he stuck it into his nostril and pantomimed a snort on the back of his hand. "Like that."

When Maureen started unwrapping it, he grabbed her hand and looked around, "Wait'll you're alone in your bedroom at home, then you can put on some cool music and take a nice trip on some cool blow," he grinned at her, "you dig baby?"

"Sure," she said with a self-conscious grin, "I just wanted to see what it looks like."

"Nothing to see baby," her blonde HUNK, as she was beginning to think of him said, "looks just like the baking soda your mom makes her cookies n' stuff out of."

Cause that's what half the shit is, Arturo thought with absolutely no expression on his face.

"How 'bout that little tar-baby April Fool with ya," he made a motion at Pearl, who was almost inside the school building, "think she'd want a little to join ya with?"

"Oh no," Maureen said emphatically, "she's getting ready to go to college and be a doctor when she graduates."

"A doctor?" Jenner said.

Arturo spoke for the first time since the two had entered the fenced in school basketball court, "Takes a helluva lotta dough to go to medical school." He glared at the redhead, "Where the fuck's she gonna get it?"

Maureen was a little shocked at the abrupt change from a smiling Jenner to the intensely hostile boy with the Spanish accent, so she stammered when she answered, "Well, uh, I, uh, Pearl says her grandma keeps the money in a safe that she's gonna send her to college with." She could only stare into the short man's mean eyes a moment before turning away to speak to her new boyfriend. "Are you gonna be back here tomorrow?"

Before he could answer Arturo said, "We don't know where the hell we'll be tomorrow or any other day, why?" With the last word he leaned toward her.

It frightened the girl to be confronted by someone she had never met or spoken to, so she moved away as she answered, "No reason, I was just…

"Then just get the fuck outa here n' let us do our thing, bitch." He responded before she could even finish, then leaned closer, "Get it?"

"Well yeah, jeez I'm leaving." When she turned back after a few steps, Arturo was still staring at her—she didn't turn again.

A completely innocent statement made by her friend Pearl, then casually passed on by her friend Maureen, was the handful of verbal nails that sealed the grandmother's coffin. Pearl would eventually figure out that her casual statement about her grandmother's plan to save enough money for her to go to college, was what cost the old woman her life. It was a hard way to learn about the ghetto's ability to hear all.

As soon as Arturo was certain that the redheaded kid was out of earshot, he said quietly to Jenner, "I'm goin' around to the other door to be sure that little black bitch don't leave that way—you cover this one." He looked intently at the blonde boy then added emphatically, "Do not let her get away from us."

"No sweat man, got it covered."

Yeah, the young Cuban thought, *just like you've got a foot long dick.*

Arturo Espinosa's last partner met with an accident a month earlier, while they were picking up their next five kilos of cocaine from Emilio Espinosa, Arturo's uncle. They were on his commercial lobster boat on the Miami River, not far in from Burlingame Island where the river meets Biscayne Bay.

The two boys had no sooner entered the wheelhouse of the converted shrimper, when the seventeen-year-old, they knew only as Rican, felt a wire go around his neck. He was dead in three minutes. Before he quit twitching Arturo had untied the line on the bow, as the black Cuban who had used the wire, was untying the one on the stern. Emilio eased the boat into the river and within half an hour they were crossing the bay. By the time the boat was half way to Rickenbacher Causeway, the black and Arturo had the boys body wrapped with rusty anchor chain and secured with stainless fishing wire. "Help me get it up on this gunnel," the black said in Spanish. After the small body was laying on top of the wide wooden rail he said, "Hold it steady while I slit open the stomach so it'll stay on the bottom till the crabs n' things eat it."

As Arturo held the boy's body, the huge black man slit the stomach between the chain in a couple places. As he watched, Arturo realized the man had already quit referring to Rican as HE or HIM. All he called Rican now was IT. As they shoved Rican off the boat's gunwale, Arturo thought, *Shouldn't have stolen that cocaine, Rican.*

Emilio turned the boat and headed back toward the Miami River as Arturo hosed the blood off where the black man had gutted Rican. First he cleaned the inside, then the outside.

Pele, who was all Arturo had ever heard the black Cuban called, held the light and searched out blood spots as Arturo handled the hose. "This bother you?" The black man asked in Spanish, which was all Arturo had ever heard him speak.

The short, stocky, sixteen-year-old boy with mean eyes that everyone noticed, looked up at Pele with a curious expression on his face. He'd known Pele for five years, ever since he came from Cuba to work with his uncle Emilio, so it surprised him that he would ask such a question. "No sir," he answered, "it wouldn't be proper for me to hold the light and you to do the washing."

"Ha, ha, ha, ha," The big man bent over and laughed more before catching his breath.

Arturo just stood with the hose spraying over the side as Pele caught his breath.

"No little sailor," the man said, still laughing quietly, "I mean killing that thieving bastard."

"Shit no," Arturo said, "I'm the one who brought him into this business and what does he do? Steals from us." He spit into the water. "He's where he belongs—sleeping with the crabs."

Rick Magers

Pele inspected the outside again before speaking. "Looks okay, put the hose up and come have some coffee."

Arturo had known Jenner since they were in the fifth grade. He had never liked the way he always bragged about being such a good lover, especially after they were strip searched by the police, earlier in the year when they were accused of dealing drugs on the schoolyard. The search yielded no drugs and Arturo knew Jenner was not involved in his uncle's operation. He refused to say a word other than that his name was Jenner Lundren. When asked for more he kept replying, "Ask the school." Nothing more, and Arturo liked that very much.

The strip search did reveal one thing, though. *That poor cracker's got the smallest dick I ever saw*, Arturo thought. It was impossible not to notice because of the jokes the police were making about his small 'puppy-pecker' as they laughingly referred to his penis. Jenner didn't seem to let it bother him, but Arturo noticed that whenever he was around girls he always referred to his manhood as a 'foot o' dick.' 'Don't come sniffin' around me gal, 'less you can handle a foot o' dick.' Girls always left him alone. Arturo figured that was probably what he really wanted.

After Rican was caught stealing from his uncle, Arturo was faced with locating a new partner. The first person he thought of was Jenner. He told his Uncle Emilio, "That cracker sure ain't got much dick, but he's got big balls."

Emilio looked up from the cocaine he and Pele were packaging down in the empty freezer compartment, "You said before that he stood up for you?"

"Sure did, uncle. These three black guys from jig-town were gonna rip me off after school when I was still going, but Jenner came over and pulled out a little silver twenty-five automatic." Arturo laughed then continued, "One of those spooks just laughed when he saw the gun but about shit when Jenner stuck it in his gut and pulled the trigger."

"Goddamn," Emilio said, "what happened?"

"Son-of-a-bitch misfired," Arturo laughed again, "and that spook's eyes got bigger'n hell as he jumped back. Jenner said casually, 'This piece o' shit,' and cocked it again ejecting the bad bullet, then said as he pointed it at the guys balls, 'it'll fire now, Sambo.'"

"Guy's got guts." Emilio commented.

"I like that." Pele added.

Arturo said, "Wasn't any doubt in that guy's mind that he'd shoot him."

Emilio looked up from the pile of cocaine on the sheet of glass and asked, "Did he?"

"Didn't have time, those guys turned and ran like hell."

"Talk to him," his uncle said, "and see if he wants to work for us."

From the first day Jenner started working, Arturo noticed the Alabama boy with the mimic, New York City tough attitude, had a way of getting the younger kids to try a little cocaine then come back to buy more. The tough young Cuban knew he'd tied in with a good partner.

After waiting half an hour for the young black girl to come back out of the school building, Arturo returned to where he had left Jenner watching. Where in the hell's that cracker?

An hour later Jenner walked into the Cuban diner on Southwest Eighth Street where the two boys always went when separated. He was grinning as he pulled the chair back and sat across from his Cuban friend.

"Where you been, man?"

"That little black chick came back out on my side, so I followed her home." He waved at the dumpy waitress in orange spandex pants, green blouse and purple shoes, "Bring me a Cuban sandwich, Angelina, and a bottle of mango soda."

"Good," Arturo said with quiet enthusiasm, "where she live, man?"

"Over across the tracks north of Flagler Street in that ratty-ass section of town."

"See anybody else at the house?"

"Nope, the house was all closed up and she had to unlock the door, then open the windows."

An evil grin crossed Arturo's face. "Let's go have a look at granny's safe later this evening, amigo."

3

A NIGHTMARE BEGINS

When the tired old black woman walked the dozen steps along the cracked and grass covered cement walkway toward the tiny, shack-like hovel, which she shared with her granddaughter, two sets of mean uninvited eyes watched.

From a block away, Jenner and Arturo watched, and waited for night to draw its deadly curtain down across the stage of their malignant little play.

The two hoodlums watched, as the door opened just as the last rays of light flickered across the Miami Ghetto. The little black girl stood holding the new cardboard suitcase. Her grandmother had got off of the bus earlier at a department store, to purchase it for her precious Black Pearl's first overnight trip since coming to live with her.

Pearl stood as the old woman fussed over her dress and red silk bows, which she had placed in the two long pigtails hanging from the carefully woven corn rows on the girl's shiny, black head. Pearl finally turned and walked to the cracked sidewalk, and headed toward the bus stop.

The two young hoodlums continued watching as darkness closed in. The bus headlights flooded the deserted street momentarily, and then rolled on to the next destination, pulling a dark shroud over everything behind.

"C'mon m'man," Jenner said, "let's you n' me go see how thrifty ole black granny's been."

Another of the transplanted Alabama boy's talents was picking locks. Arturo had been impressed several times by Jenner's ability to gain entrance to anyplace they needed to get into. He stood patiently in the darkness behind, as the boy slid a stolen credit card into the crack between the door and the frame. He heard a slight click as the card shoved the primitive latch aside.

Kenner turned and whispered, "Got it."

Arturo was holding a home made blackjack, made from fishing sinkers in a short length of garden hose wrapped with duck tape. Jenner held his shiny 25 caliber automatic pistol. They silently closed the door behind them and stood waiting, as their eyes adjusted to the room's darkness. Their animal senses probed the room beyond the curtain hanging in place of a door. Jenner moved ahead and peered through. One lone bulb hanging from the ceiling on a short piece of wire lit the room.

The old woman had tired early and drifted off to sleep, with the sweater she was knitting for Pearl resting on her lap. As swiftly as a lion would grab a lamb, Arturo grabbed her by the neck and arm, and yanked her from the chair. He placed his other hand over her mouth as he dragged her to the room they had entered. "If you scream you old bitch I'll cut your throat, then we'll wait'll that little pickaninny comes home to tell us where your money's at." Arturo spoke threateningly into her ear as he held her entire frail body up off the floor. His command of English was perfect when needed. "Now I'm gonna setcha down, and if you scream you're dead." He held her a moment to let his words sink in then added, "and so will that pickaninny when she comes home."

When he set her on her feet she let out a gasp, as she attempted to get air in her lungs. Jenner punched her on the side of the face then leaned close, "Quiet you black old hag or I'll hitcha again."

Arturo had to steady the old woman to keep her from falling from Jenner's blow. He leaned close to her ear, "Now where's that money you been saving to send that kid to college?"

A few busted ribs, a bloody and broken nose, teeth knocked out, a cracked jaw, and a closed and swollen eye later she mumbled, "De money in a safe box unner de bed."

Arturo held her while Jenner went into the next room to enter the tiny bedroom. He returned with a wad of bills; the result of a lifetime of saving. "Right where she said it'd be."

"Lemme have it," Arturo commanded, "while you give granny a sleeping pill."

Jenner complied and without a moments hesitation he hit the old woman behind the neck with the side of his stiffened hand. They both heard the loud snap as her neck broke. She fell dead to the clean, recently bleached floor.

Arturo removed a plastic bottle full of diesel fuel from his baggy purple and green pants, as Jenner did the same. Less than half an hour since they entered the old woman's home, they stood across the street, a block away in the shadows, watching as it went up in flames like a pile of dry tinder—which was all it actually was.

Rick Magers

On Saturday afternoon, Pearl was happily walking from the bus stop near her home; impatient to get there and tell her grandmother all about her overnight stay at her rich white girlfriend's house. When she came around the corner she was struck by lightning—Oh God, oh God, oh God. She was screaming as she ran to the pile of ashes and little else, where her home had been standing the previous day.

The teenage girl stood beside the small cardboard box containing everything she owned in the world and cried. The front of her blouse was soaked when a police patrol car stopped awhile later.

During the time Jenner and Arturo were torching the shack the previous night, another man was also preparing to dispose of a woman's dead body. "I tole you not t'be stealin no money from me, bitch." He spoke to the limp carcass of the young girl he was stuffing into the smelly old sleeping bag she had used as her bed, during the rare times he allowed her some rest. When he finished, he turned to the two older girls sitting silently on the couch. "Put this bitch in the trunk an bote chew gitcher ass out there n' make me some money." He watched as they carried the bundle into the garage. When they returned he glared at the two young women, still in their early twenties, "I gots plenty more dem sleepin bag, so doan be tinkin bout doin no guy witout me knowin."

The two young hookers, which he paid to come from his Jamaican home, depended on D'Julliette for their drugs, food, and sleeping quarters. They were also in America illegally, and were terrified of him—for good reason. They had now seen first hand what he would do when crossed. They headed out into the Miami sun looking for tricks.

The black policeman approached the crying young girl, while the Cuban officer waited in the patrol car. "Hi, what's your name?"

Through sobs she answered, "Pearl."

"Well Pearl, I guess this was someone's home that you knew, huh?"

"My Gramma."

"Mmm, I'm sorry. Were you coming to visit or did you live here too?"

"Dis were my home." Pearl always reverted to the slang she was taught as a child whenever she was upset.

"Well," the young officer said, "I gotta tell you that we found a body in the rubble."

She turned a weary, tear-stained face up toward him, "Why dis house gotta burn down?"

He just shook his head slowly from side to side, "Guess God's the only one who knows the answer to that, Pearl." He stood and looked around—knowing no one in the seedy neighborhood would come forward to assist the child. "Did your Grandmother go to a church around here?"

"Huh?" She looked up as she tried to wipe the tears from her face.

After hearing the question again, she replied, "Yes, right cross dat road dere, an down tree block." She pointed toward North First Street.

He picked up her suitcase and touched her arm, "C'mon Pearl we'll drive over there and see if they'll help you."

"Jedediah," D'Julliette was saying into the phone, "if you wanna keep gittin dis free pussy all de time you want it, you bess gits me anudder young girl, cause dese two old ting I got now ain gone be makin some dese big money dude hoppy."

"Yes, yes, mon," the honey colored Jamaican answered into the phone, "I gone git right on dat, yes mon, I gone fine one quick."

"Is this the church that your grandmother went to?" The friendly black policeman asked Pearl.

"Yessir," she said in a sad, defeated, tone of voice—barely able to be heard.

He looked at his partner and shook his head slightly. They knew that many of the churches, which were springing up all over the city, were not what they appeared to be. The ministerial degrees that the 'pastors' displayed on their walls were usually acquired through mail order programs. 'Send $50 and be your own clergyman.'

"Yes, may I help you?" The smiling, fortyish, honey colored man spoke to the two officers standing beside the small black girl.

"Is this your grandmother's church, Pearl?" The young officer asked.

"Yes."

"Well Pearl, your grandmother's pastor and his church will help you now."

"Yessir, we certainly will." The Jamaican answered in flawless English, "The Reverend Jedediah Simon Peterson at your service, and whatever the problem is, my parish is ready to help."

After listening to their story he said, "Oh my dear Heavenly Father," and placed his arm around Pearl's tiny shoulder. "Yes, I knew her grandmother very well." Every evil word he spoke was disguised with syrup coating. "Oh you poor dear," he gently brought her head close to him and held her a moment before continuing, "you may leave her here officer and we'll see to it that she's well cared for."

Both officers knew it was against city policy, but they also knew what happened to most like her who were thrown into the overburdened system. 'Find the lesser of two evils' was a very common answer to many such dilemmas they were regularly confronted with. In this case they had found the greatest evil of all.

"I don't know," the Cuban officer said as they drove away, "he seemed like a straight up and down guy."

"Yeah," the black policeman responded, "some of 'em's gotta be legit."

A few moments after Pearl was seated at the kitchen table eating a peanut butter sandwich, the Reverend Jedediah Simon Peterson was on the phone. "Hey D'Julliette, guess what just flew in the door?"

4

TOUGH COP

Yan Brodjevinski was a damn good private detective, but he had a few faults. His worst was no patience with smart-ass young wannabe toughs. He knew that one of the black guys he was approaching had some information he needed. The skinny, very black guy sitting on the steps of the old run down apartment building took the card he held out and read it. He looked up with what Yan referred to as a 'shit-eatin-grin' on his perfect, 'never-been-punched face'. He looked at the card, then said in his best SHAFT voice, "What the hell kinda name's that, honky?"

Yan sent him his very best 'let's-be-pals' look. "It's a Polish name, what's yours? Sambo?"

The young punk came up from the steps just far enough to meet Yan's hand hammered, silver-dollar ring coming down. The first punch the kid ever took was a beauty, and split his left eyebrow right in the middle. A body would be found a few weeks later with three eyebrows. A single on one side and a double on the other. The kid went out like a liquor store streetlight; just before a midnight break in. One second on—the next out. Yan picked up his card, which had fallen from the long, skinny, manicured black fingers. He thought, *Bet he'll keep his black ass down the next time he's confronted by a scarred up old war horse like me.*

Yan smiled as he headed on along the sidewalk toward the two men standing beneath a streetlight that was due to come on any minute. It was getting close to dark as Yan thought, *Gotta make this quick n' get the hell outa here 'fore dark.* The hundred-dollar-bill he tore in half got Yan the info he wanted. "Get me the address where that bail jumpin' little asshole is, and you get the other half, and another picture of Benny t'go with it." Before leaving he spoke to the fat, young, black Cuban he'd been searching for. "I'll be right on that corner at nine Saturday morning Jorge, and don't take that bill to the bank because without this half it's no damn good." He grinned, "I left some of the numbers from yours on my half."

Awhile later he was driving toward Coconut Grove, the suburb of Miami where he moored the forty-foot boat he lived on. He pulled the rusting, 1990 Aerostar into a spot beneath one of the lights that illuminated the parking area and the 1950 Huckins Flybridge Cruiser, laying on its mooring buoy a hundred feet away.

Before Yan had the door locked he heard the old army jeep coming, so he turned the key then shoved it down into his pocket and waited for the old night guard to pull up beside him. Murphy O'Brien had secured his job as night watchman at the marina a couple of months before Yan bought the Huckins, two years earlier. Murphy had just retired after thirty years on the NYPD, and was fulfilling a dream. The two men learned a lot about each other during the two months that Yan paid dockage next to Murphy, as he prepared the Huckins to lay on a mooring buoy. Neither man had ever needed a close friend, so they just became helpful acquaintances, and liked each other ever since. Yan learned that Murphy worked five, twelve-hour-shifts a week in exchange for dockage, utilities and two hundred dollars each month—under the table and no deductions. Murphy recently bought a 36-foot Drift-R-Cruise houseboat, and was changing a few things about it so he could live aboard comfortably. The two men swapped tools, as they needed them, and offered a third hand when necessary. Murphy was off weekends, so Yan offered a beer at the end of the first Saturday they became neighbors.

"Sure thing," he said with a wide smile, "soon's I finish securing this little color telly I bought today."

Yan handed the six-foot-three-inch, two-hundred-and-fifty pounds of solid Irish muscle, a can of Rolling Rock after he was settled into one of the two folding lawn chairs on the stern. "Hope your're not particular about your beer, I buy whatever's on sale."

The ruddy, red-complexioned face spread into the friendly grin that Yan was getting used to, "Beer's beer Yan, all gets pissed against the wall anyway."

After a couple more beers Yan said, "I see you're securing everything in there, but the outdrive's been removed; you planning to put an engine in it or an outboard on it?"

"Nope, I just like livin' here on the water so I made a deal with the marina to take it out and put it in dry storage when a hurricane's coming, 'cause I can't afford to replace it."

"Damn good deal y'made there Murph," Yan smiled, "because I've already found out how much it would cost to take the Huckins out and put it in one of those dry storage hangers."

"Yeah," the old cop answered, "it'll soon be where only rich folks can live on a boat."

Yan shook his head up and down as his shaggy black hair bounced, "Especially around here," he motioned toward the fancy yachts nearby.

5

THE DEVIL ENTERS THE NIGHTMARE

Fifteen-year-old Pearl was still in shock when Reverend Peterson led her to the car in the alley behind the church. "I want to introduce you to someone who will help you adjust to your loss, my child."

She held her grandmother's preacher's hand trustingly, and followed silently. Many years as a Kingston, Jamaica bible salesman, and later a Chicago used car salesman, had taught Jedediah how to use body language and facial expressions to win people over.

Pearl sat quietly in the big black Lincoln and looked out through the tinted windows. The trip took less than thirty minutes, but when they stopped in front of the garage beside a big house, she had no idea where she was. Pearl turned to watch the Reverend when he pressed a button on something he was holding, and then turned back as she heard the garage door opening.

When the door closed back down to the floor, it was dark until suddenly several lights came on in the garage. She was momentarily startled when her door was opened and a man stuck his head inside. She turned to the reverend, who was smiling at her. "Everything will be just fine, my child. Go with Mr. D'Julliette and I'll be back tonight."

Pearl was terrified as the tall, thin, very black man took her arm and pulled her from the car. She was almost petrified as the man shoved the door closed with his foot.

After they were inside the house, she heard the garage door opening but not the Lincoln leaving. It all happened so fast that she was still unable to speak as the door closed again.

"C'mon little rabbit," the thin man said as he turned her toward a door leading to a room on the other side of the house. "You an me got some schoolin to do fore dem worn out old gals of mine get back." He led Pearl toward a bedroom at the end of a long hallway, which turned out to be her prison cell for a long time. Her life and what future she might have had was about to change forever.

6

OPPORTUNITY KNOCKS

Yan looked up from his laptop when he noticed the Cadillac pull into the parking place in front of his agency. SECURITY PLUS was painted in six-inch red letters across the window with Yan Brodjevinski—Private Detective below in smaller black letters. He had them placed so he could look through at any arrivals without being noticed.

Yan watched as a very large man got out and went to the rear door on the other side. He held it open as a tiny black woman stepped out. *Wonder if that big dude's her husband or chauffeur?* He knew the answer when the mountain of white muscle opened Yan's door for the lady, then stood outside next to it with his arms folded across his chest. *Probably has a double shoulder holster rig on and that keeps both hands close to his armory.*

Something about the old woman's regal bearing made Yan do something he seldom did—he stood. As she moved gracefully toward his desk they got into an eye contest. Her black face was a stone mask as her intense dark eyes held his. Not blinking was a habit Yan developed as a Miami cop for twenty years. When she arrived across from him she stood motionless for a moment; staring deeply into what Yan liked to refer to as, *my one-hundred-percent Polish brown eyes.* Yan was born in Warsaw in 1957, and at four moved to Miami with his family when they emigrated.

"You're not an easily intimidated man, are you?" Her voice could have come from a teenager it was so intensely independent.

Without leaving her eyes or blinking he said, "Actually I am. By guys like Igor there next to my door with both hands close to his armpits."

She finally broke eye contact and held out a tiny hand encased in a purple silk glove. "Mrs. Tamerlane Broadsword."

Her smile was sincere as she held out her hand so Yan said, "I'm the guy on the front window." He shook her hand as though one shake too brisk and it would come off in his. He released it and nodded toward the black leather and oak chair beside her, "Have a seat and tell me what I can do for you." When Yan heard her name he knew who she was, even though he'd never met her.

"I want to know what actually happened to my husband." The smile was now gone, and she spoke in a clipped business-like manner. "Police commissioner Carvajol recommended you very highly. He said I will get the truth from you"—the smile was back—"Even if it turns to molten lava in his mouth, were his exact words." She leaned slightly forward to lock his eyes again as she asked, "Is that true?"

"Only because lies are so damn hard to remember and the truth is always there, just as it happened."

"Very good," she said, still doing eye battle with the first real competitor she'd met in years. "Are you free to devote all of your time to this?"

"Missus Broadsword, I was just sitting here contemplating filling out a form at Wal-Mart to be one of those guys who greet people at the door."

"Yes, of course you were," she smiled again, "and Emil out there beside the door will be checking groceries nearby." Before Yan could get to the price of his services she removed a small device from her purse and spoke into it so softly that Yan couldn't hear what she said. He noticed the neckless behemoth move toward the car and open the trunk.

"I know that this will be a very time consuming ordeal," she said as Emil came through the door carrying a small suitcase. After placing it on the desk in front of her, he returned to sentry duty.

I wonder if that gorilla can speak?

"Mister Brodjevinski, I want this to remain between just you and I, with no news media involved," she leaned toward him again and said with emphasis, "EVER. No bank deposits you might be required to explain later, either. There is fifty thousand dollars cash in this suitcase and a number where you can leave the payphone number you'll be at so I can call you back if necessary. If I do not answer please leave the time and number where you'll be and I'll try to get right back to you." All business again she asked, "Any problems?"

"Not a one," he said as he reached across and picked up the suitcase.

"Good day then." She turned and headed for the door. Apparently she had touched another button on her little device because Emil had the door open before she got to it.

Yan studied the small lady as she entered the vehicle's rear door. She moved with grace and a self-confidence that is not learned, but born with. His mind was bringing back the headlines on the front page of the Miami Herald a couple of months earlier, as he scribbled a message on a sheet of paper then taped it to his open sign. After turning the key in the door to his office, he went to his van, which was sitting in the parking lot a short walk away. With the still unopened suitcase on the floor between the two seats he backed out then paused to look at the sign.

GONE FISHING—BCNU WHEN ICU

7

TRAINING BEGINS

D'Julliette held Pearl's arm as he unlocked the bedroom door. He shoved her into the room and turned the dead bolt. She looked at the two mattresses on the floor and the windows that had plywood nailed over the curtains. When she heard a noise behind her she turned to see the man who the reverend left her with removing his other boot. The noise was the first, zipper-side leather boot hitting the floor. As soon as the boot was off he removed his pants and silk shirt. D'Julliette then removed his red silk bikini under shorts and was stroking his penis slowly as he moved toward the terrified young girl.

"Git out dem clothes little rabbit," he growled, "I got many ting to show you, so you know how to make dem moneybag honky ver hoppy." He flashed an almost solid gold grin then added, "An me a ver rich fella."

Pearl cowered in the corner with her eyes bulging. All she could do was shake her head violently from side-to-side.

"Okay den bitch, I got some ting else what I can show you." He moved to the closet and reached through the doorless opening. When he turned he was pulling a small boxing glove on his right hand. "Dis ting doan leave no mark on dat pretty young body, but it gone make you inside parts hurt like a tooth ache." He made a fist with the glove and advanced to her. "Now bitch, you want git out dem clothes or you want I give you some help?"

8

GATHERING INFO

"**How's it goin' Yan?**" Murphy O'Brien stopped the jeep beside him and turned the engine off.

"So damn good is scares me Murph, how bouchew?"

"Wait'll you see what I bought at the flea market Sunday. I got it inside the boat n' oughta have 'er hooked up in a few days." His ruddy Irish face lit up in a grin, "You're gonna love it, man."

"What the hell is it?"

"Ain't gonna tell ya." Another grin, "I'll give you a holler when it's ready." He turned the key and started the old WW II army jeep, then roared off into the dark to make his rounds.

Yan stood smiling as his new friend disappeared into the dimly lit area near the dry storage building. He glanced around before grabbing the suitcase, which now only had ten thousand dollars in it. He intuitively reached behind to feel the Sphinx in the holster on his belt.

He'd stopped earlier at the spa he belonged to and put the rest in his athletic bag, then put the lock back on his locker door before heading to the steam room. I'll have time tomorrow to put this dough in my safety deposit box, he thought. After an intense one-hour workout, he spent fifteen minutes in the sauna then headed for Dinner Key.

It only took a few minutes to row his small dingy out to the Huckins. Once aboard, he tossed the suitcase on the couch and opened one of the cans of Olympia from the six-pack he bought on the way through Coconut Grove.

After checking both banks of batteries, Yan put his favorite CD in the Kenwood, which was operated by the inverter he splurged on when he first bought the boat. After draining the first beer he opened another and lay back to flush the day from his head.

Broadsword, he thought, *one of the richest blacks in America.* Yan took a sip as he tried to remember the story he read in the Herald a few months earlier. *Wealthy black American murdered in the Bahamas.* I'll hafta go to the library tomorrow and read up on that.

Two cold, day-old slices of pizza and four beers later Yan turned off the single 12-volt light and stretched out on the couch to let Tchaikovsky's Swan Lake carry him into sleep.

Better fire up both engines, he thought the next morning as he returned from the galley where he'd fired up a fresh pot of coffee. He flipped the switch to BILGE FANS and waited five minutes then looked at the FUME INDICATOR. "Safe," he said aloud as he looked at the readout. After turning the fans off he hit first one starter button, then the other. As the twin 440 hp V-8 Chrysler engines sat purring on idle, Yan walked onto the rear deck to relieve his kidneys. Pissin' off your porch's one o' the best percs of livin' out here.

He returned from the cabin with a flashlight and raised the starboard engine box. There was one on each side of the main cabin door. With the lid-prop in place, he shined the light on everything, including the V-Drive transmission that allowed the engines to sit so far to the rear. After lowering the port lid, he flipped the light off. "You're a coupla real beauties," he said aloud as he looked at the engines, then climbed the chrome ladder to the control station on the flying bridge. He sat back-to-the-wheel in the captain's seat and looked for Murphy. When he couldn't see the jeep, Yan pushed the button on his watch to illuminate the dial in the pre-dawn darkness. *Ten minutes after six, so he's checkin' the main docks on the north end.*

Yan spun around and turned the running and dash control lights on. Assured all were working, he turned the running lights off then flipped the masthead anchor light switch a couple times and looked for the flicker above the Bimini top. *That automatic timer for the anchor light's best damn thing I've bought in awhile.*

After revving both engines a little, he idled them again before easing each transmission into gear, one-at-a-time. *Phew! Don't get smoother'n that.* He turned both engine keys off and went below to the in-cabin-control-station. Yan sat in the soft, upholstered seat and reached down on the right side of the seat box. There was a space of a foot between it and the cabin wall. He pushed down slightly on the spring-loaded lever sticking out a half-inch. The compartment he made and installed after anchoring out, so no one could see what he was doing, fell open. There, in a leather holster was the twin to the

Sphinx he carried on the rear of his belt. Lying at the bottom was a thin leather belt with six clips. They each could hold fifteen bullets, but Yan only kept six in each so the springs wouldn't weaken. There was fifteen in the clip of the one on his belt, plus one in the chamber. Every six months he threw away the clip and replaced it with a new one with a strong spring. *Cheap insurance,* he thought. Yan then closed the compartment and went forward to shower and dress for the day. After getting fresh socks and shorts from the wide drawer beneath the starboard bunk, he removed everything else. He used the butter knife he brought from the galley to lift the false bottom. When he could get his fingers beneath the edge, he removed the entire thing. Between it and the real bottom was strapped the Israeli sub machinegun that he traded his 1952 Harley for, after retiring form the Miami Police Department, two and a half years earlier in 1999. *This Uzi,* Yan thought as he lifted it out, *will be worth ten times as much as that old hog if I ever need some fast dough.*

He removed the 40 round clip from the pistol grip and lay it on the bunk. It, like the two others strapped there, was not loaded and wouldn't be until he went to sea. He put a drop of oil in a few select places then replaced the ammo clip. He then pulled the Velcro strap across the Uzi and put back the drawer's false bottom. He arranged the socks and underwear on the false bottom then closed the drawer.

When the second cup of coffee was gone, Yan went on deck and stretched to his full six-foot-six-inch height. He carried the one-hundred-and-eighty pounds of almost perfectly distributed muscle with the grace of a dancer—which he was. He once told a friend, "I'd date a homely gal that could dance before a beauty that couldn't."

Yan knew that around forty-five was when so many guys start falling apart, and he had no intentions of letting it happen to him. When it was light enough to head to the dock he had done all of his stretches plus a hundred pushups. A fellow cop once jealously commented, "That Polack's ninety percent muscle and a hundred percent mean."

"Only when ya piss'm off," another cop responded.

Yan untied the rope that ran through a ring midway out the extended outrigger. He pulled in the dingy's bowline as he played out slack in the outrigger rope. *Hope I run into that sailboat bum who showed me this so I can thank him, 'cause it sure keeps the dingy from bangin' into the boat.*

He could smell the bacon as he tied the dingy to Murphy's houseboat. Yan bought all of the breakfast ingredients and Murphy cooked them breakfast every weekday morning. "What's for breakfast?" He said as he entered the open door.

"Sliced pig dick, chicken sperm, Georgia ice cream, and God's own Irish gravy," he turned a wide smile toward Yan, "as only a cracker Irishman can make it."

After breakfast and a little small talk Yan said, "I'm gonna take a week or so off n' cruise over to Freeport Murph, anything I can bring ya?"

"Shitchess, lemme go git a coupla rolls of toilet paper and a ball point pen to make a list."

"I might hafta get a bigger boat," Yan said smiling, "like that guy in Jaws."

"Nah, all small shit. Twenty pounds of skinned conch, twenty pounds of green turtle meat, a few o' them wild sour oranges, a bushel basket full o' whelks, a few cases of that wonderful island rum, and maybe a few. . .

"Hey Murph."

"What?" his Irish pal said smiling.

"Write all that shit down n' when I get that freighter we'll go over n' get it all, but right now I gotta go put a knot in that bail jumpin' little peckerhead's rope."

They enjoyed breakfast as they talked about the Miami Dolphins, and then as his friend stood to leave Murphy said, "See ya later, Yan."

"In a coupla hours I hope. Thanks for that Irish breakfast."

"Cracker Irish ole cock. When I was in Ireland we drank our breakfast. That's why I bought this little gem at the flea market." He pointed at a small fridge in the corner with a beer tap on the door.

"Well I'll be damn," Yan said. "Gotcher own keg o' suds waitin' on ya, huh?"

"Yep," Murphy grinned, "and any time ya want a cool one, just step right in n' help yourself."

9

MORE TRAINING

Pearl lay crying on the filthy mattress. Two cracked ribs hurt worse that anything she had experienced in her fifteen years. Her stomach was sore from the repeated punches by D'Julliette's gloved fist. Her vagina hurt so badly that it made the other pain seem light. When he forced his penis through her hymen she screamed, and that brought more punches. The tall, thin, black man who talked funnier than her grandmother, pumped away inside of her. As he began to ejaculate he thrust deeper and deeper until she thought he intended to kill her, for some reason she didn't understand. So much had happened in just one day that she didn't understand—couldn't understand. *Why did gramma have to burn up?—why didn't that nice policeman take me home with him?—why did that nice preacher of grammas' bring me here?—why is this funny talking man trying to kill me?—I thought doing this was suppose to be fun and feel good—I think I'm bleeding to death—he must have cut me down there with a knife.*

"Well I be goddom." D'Julliette looked down at his red penis and laughed. "You was a virgin. What de matter witchew bitch? You ol' enuff t'be usin dat ting two, tree year now. You one dem good Christian girl what tink dis doan start till you marry?" He wiped himself on a filthy rag then tossed it to Pearl. "It done start now girl an if you wanna stay alive you best git better you juss was. Wipe dat ting an go in dere an clean you nosty cryin face, cause preacher gonna be comin f'some dat young stuff bye n' bye."

D'Julliette locked the door behind him and went straight to the phone. A woman answered on the third ring. "Judge Handle's office."

"Dis de mechanic what fixin de judge car. Tell him call me an I tell him what wrong."

"Yes, of course, he has your number doesn't he."

"Yes, he got dat number long time now."

"Very well, he'll call you as soon as possible."

After putting the phone down she smiled thinking, *I'd love to know what that fat little bastard's up to with this Jamaican.*

Thirty minutes later, D'Julliette picked up the ringing phone. "Yes mon."

"Hello D'Julliette, Judge Handle. Whatcha got?"

"Some ting bout tirteen mon, what ain had no ting in it till I juss break de blood. She scared like a rabbit so you bring a tousan dollar mon, an you gone have fun like you ain dream bout yet."

"I'll call and tell you when I'll be by this weekend." The short, fat, baldheaded, sixty-year-old Judge replaced his private cell phone back into the drawer and locked it. His sausage & gravy swollen eyelids closed as he thought about the afternoon of pleasure he would soon be rolling around with. Saliva ran from his puffy lips as he began panting.

Rick Magers

10

DELIVERY MAN

Yan laid the pizza box that he brought from Murphy's boat on the passenger's seat of the Aerostar and headed toward the old Dade Hotel on the north side of Flagler Street. He parked a block away and walked quickly to the rear entrance. The door hadn't locked since two professional mob 'collection' men, a year earlier, threw a three-hundred-and-fifty-pound ex-wrestler through it. Yan slipped inside and went up the stairs to the second floor. He knew the layout, after making several busts during his police career, so he went directly to 208. "Twenty-four-hour pizza. Hot n' ready," Yan yelled through the door. He waited a moment then yelled louder, "Hey man c'mon, I got a shitload o' these in the van to deliver." He waited to let the guy inside think a moment and it paid off.
"I didn't order a pizza," the voice came through the thin door.
"Well, this's two-oh-eight," Yan said with an impatient tone of voice, "so if you want this pizza open the door n' give me six bucks and screw the jerk who gave me the damn wrong room number."
The Sphinx was in Yan's hand beneath the pizza box as the door opened. Before the young black man knew what was happening, he was smacked on the side of his head with the pistol, and was out before he hit the filthy carpet. "Keep your hands out where I can see 'em sweetie," Yan said to the naked, skeletal-thin white boy getting out of the bed—as he pointed the pistol at him. "Get your ass over in that corner and don't even think about trying to run or I'll put something in your sorry ass that won't feel anything like Tinker Bell's tongue."

"Oh yessir, please don't hurt me. I'll do exac…"

"Shut the fuck up and stand in that corner." The skeleton quietly complied, and Yan dragged the black man to the window with steel bars. After securing him to them with handcuffs, he turned to the boy in the corner. "Now you can get your cloths on and get the hell outa here before the cops arrive."

The Sphinx motioning toward the pile of rags beside the bed, brought the boy out of the temporary stupor. "Yessir, oh yessir," he kept babbling as he got into his pants and slipped his feet into the rubber tongs. As he left the room pulling his T-shirt over his head, he was still mumbling. "Yessir, I'm outa here. Thank you sir. Oh lordy, thank you sir."

Yan took the tiny cell phone from his pocket and dialed. The voice answered, "Yeah."

"Yan here with Chilipepper cuffed to a window, Boris, so get somebody over here t'get him 'fore the cops show up."

"Where?"

"The old Dade Hotel in room two-oh-eight and don't forget to give whoever you send, that key to open these cuffs."

"They're on the way amigo, thanks."

Yan shut the phone off without answering and looked at the still unconscious, black young Cuban. "When you skip on a murder rap you oughta go a little farther to hole up shithead." He closed the door behind him and headed toward the stairs.

The fat, young Cuban was waiting on the corner when Yan drove up. He hit the button to lower his window as the boy walked over.

"How'd it go, man?"

"Like time on a Rolex. Here's the other half of that hundred and another Ben Franklin, just like I said amigo."

"You're a good man to do business with."

"Keep your ear to the rail and we'll do plenty more." He ran the window up and drove off. He stopped at his spa to get the forty thousand, and then made a brief stop at his bank to put it in his safety deposit box.

He looked at his watch when he parked the van. *Ten-thirty-five; that shit with Chilipepper went so smooth it's spooky*. He heard the Jeep and turned to see Murphy drive up beside the van. He locked the door and turned to his friend, "How's your day goin' so far?"

"Great!" Murphy smiled, "If it was any better I'd think I died and was already in hell with my pals."

"When I see how some o' these assholes live," Yan said, "I think maybe we are in hell—theirs."

"Where you headin' now?"

"Gonna fire up n' head on across to Bimini and spend the rest of the day at the End Of The World Saloon."

"Got her all fueled up?"

"Yeah, I've only used enough to fire 'em up a few times since we came back from Stiltsville a coupla weeks ago."

"That's right, I remember. You topped 'er off that day as soon as we got back."

"You're gonna have to put some gas in the van if you use it Murph, 'cause I didn't wanna take time to stop."

"No problem. I gotta go check the docks now; have a good trip Yan." The big Irishman waved over his shoulder as he drove off.

11

THE DEVIL'S FRIEND

Pearl was terrified of D'Julliette, so she did as she was told and cleaned herself. She stood in the corner shivering and mumbling quietly. "Gramma if you up dere wit de Lord God," she began in the tongue she had learned first and reverted to whenever she became upset, "please axe him to help me." She squeezed her eyes together tightly and paused a moment. "I ver, ver scared."

Pearl couldn't possibly know it, but as the lock on the door released, all hope of help was far in her future, and would come from a source unimaginable to the young black girl. A brief moment of hope rushed through her mind when The Reverend stepped into the room. It vanished as he stared at her while removing his clothes.

"Hello child," the Reverend Jedediah Simon Peterson said with a sinister smile when he kicked his yellow silk shorts aside. Holding his penis with one hand, he motioned for Pearl to come to him with the other. "Don't be contrary child, the only way you will survive this is to do what me and D'Julliette tell you to do."

Pearl backed slowly into the corner and said in a shaky voice, "I so sore down there Father that I can't do that again. Please don't make me."

His smile took on an evil, wicked gleam as he slowly stroked his penis, "Don't you worry 'bout that child, I'm here to teach you how to use those lovely full lips of yours.

Pearl tried to back farther into the corner, as the preacher she had known and loved since she came to her grandmother's home to live, advanced. Tears began streaming down her face as he shoved her down to her knees.

An hour later the Reverend closed the door behind him and turned the key in the deadbolt. D'Julliette had used a hacksaw to remove the turning knob on the other side. He turned and walked toward the living room where D'Julliette sat laughing as he watched re-runs of The Simpsons.

"You do like I tole you?" He looked up at the preacher as he hit mute on the remote.

"Yes mon, she ain likin dis big black snake in her mouth but a couple of slaps side her head and she git goin on it."

"Be careful mon, doan cut dat pretty face cause I got big plans for dat lil beauty."

The preacher pulled a Red Stripe from the pail of ice and opened it before saying, "I gone bring Vaseline tomorrow an show her how to take dis snake if she oss mon."

D'Julliette drained his beer then said, "Take it slow an easy mon cause dat Judge comin on Sunday right when he church out. He doan wanna see no bruise on little doll baby or dem hole bruise up an bloody."

Preacher grinned, "Mon, I gone have her all ready to do whatever dat fat little judge want her to do."

12

ISLAND PIT STOP

Yan maneuvered the old cruiser south of the sandbar that prevented a direct approach to Bimini's North Island. He watched the bottom through the Polaroid's as he sat beneath the canvas top at the controls on the flying bridge. When he saw the tip of the bar on his port side, he turned left and came around to a northwesterly heading. *Lotta wannabe yachtsmen have found that bar the hard way,* he thought as watched the shallow sandbar on his left and the beach not too far away on the right, *especially comin' at night for the first time.*

Yan eased into one of the narrow slips behind Fisherman's Cafe and tied up. After turning the engines off, he walked in the back door to the kitchen. He smiled when he saw the big black lady coming toward him. "Hi Ruby, what's good t'eat today?"

"Mister Yan," she said with a huge golden smile, "ever ting in dis place de bess on dis lil island."

"That's why I stopped," Yan said with a grin, "t'get me some o' them great conch fritters you make and a big turtle steak."

"I git dat turtle fryin right dis ver second." She lumbered toward the ancient refrigerator with the cooling unit on top. After taking a package out, she turned to him, "You gone sit out front or bock here?"

"Back here if you'll ask one of the girls to bring me a cold Beck's Beer."

"I tell her directly, but ise gotta turn dis chicken firse." A minute later she yelled through the little service window for a beer.

"Randolph around?" Yan asked.

"Yep! He say he gone be right bock. Dat seaplane juss landin an bring a part for dat sorry ole truck he always workin on, so he run out soon he hear it go over."

"Yeah, Chalks went right over the top of me when I was coming in. So Randolph's gonna get that thing running again, huh?"

"Ttssstst," she popped the sound off the back of her top teeth with her tongue as she shook her wooly head, "dat silly mon talk all time bout makin dat ting run so long now dat dem tire all rot, an he lip still flappin." She grinned at Yan, "Dat ting juss he toy."

"Keeps him from chasin' these young girls."

"Ha!" She exploded with laughter, "What he tink he gone do if he cotch one dem little bunny?"

"Probably turn n' run the other way."

"Yep! Dat zackly wha he do sur'nuff, cause he be so bod scared."

"Hey mon," the skinny old man said as soon as the screen door opened, "I seen you boat comin long de channel." He put the package down, and held out a well worked and time weathered hand, "How you doin, Yan?"

"A helluva lot better now that I'm outa that rat-race for awhile." He shook his hand and smiled, "Got a few packages for you to get off the boat tonight when the custom guy's asleep."

"Junkanoo stuff?"

"Yep," Yan smiled, "about fifty cow bells, three old army bugles, four marching drums that look in great shape, and a few air horns with a case of air cans. I got 'em all at the Army Navy Store about a month ago."

"Mon, dat super-duper. I gone have my ownself de bess marching Junkanoo band dis year ain nobody ever see de like of roun here." The old man pulled out his wallet, "How much I owe you mon?"

"Being able to dock out back now n' then's good enough for me if that suits you."

"Dat a sur'nuff deal mon. Tank you ver much f'bringin dat stuff." He grinned, displaying a mouthful of gold, "I already makin dem costume for dese fella."

"Oh yeah," Yan said, "I forgot, I also bought twenty packs of crepe paper in all kinds of colors to add to the costumes."

"Oh mon," the huge lady said as she sat his plate on the tiny kitchen table, "dis gone be a pretty Junkanoo."

"Phewee," Yan said later, looking at his watch, "almost six o'clock." When she turned her back he slid two twenties beneath the plate and stood up. "Ruby, remind Randolph to get that stuff off the boat whenever he wants to after dark. I'm goin' up to the End of the World Bar for awhile." He smiled at the big woman hustling plates together for the evening crowd. "I'll see ya for breakfast."

Rick Magers

Without turning she said, "I be here cookin it."

Yan walked around to the street and headed south toward the tiny bar, which Hemingway once called, "The best damn bar in the entire Bahamas."

He heard the seaplane's engines begin to roar and walked along the side of Brown's Bar and stopped at the rear. He leaned against the building and shaded his eyes as he watched the Mallard Seaplane, owned by Chalks Air Service in Florida, begin its run to get up enough speed to lift from the water.

After the plane broke free and began to climb, Yan turned and walked back to the narrow road thinking, *I never get tired of watching those things take off from the water.*

13

TRAINING / LEARNING

The next two years for Pearl was an education she never dreamed that she could endure. During the first three months, she never one time left the room that she was first thrown into. She learned many things. If she wanted to eat she did as she was told—to avoid more beatings with D'Julliette's gloved hand. She did it without complaint. D'Julliette and the reverend taught her more about using her body to please men than most women learn in a lifetime.

One thing she learned during that first couple of months was that if she was to survive this nightmare then she must be patient. She must go along with the two monsters that arrived many mornings to give her more lessons, prior to the arrival of men to discharge their lust in her each day and night. "I gone survive dis ting, Gramma." Pearl spoke to her dead grandmother when she was alone. "I gone make dese mans wish dey never see me in dey ver own lifetime."

Pearl's second nightmare began two months after her confinement. "She know how to use dat body now," D'Julliette said to the reverend during coffee before their regular morning teaching lesson. "I gone get her ready to go out an visit dem big money fella in dem hotel you got contack in."

"Mon," Reverend Peterson said, "I done got tree dem fella waitin f'me to make de call. I gone learn dat little tar-baby this mornin how she gone make dem ole mon cry to havin her juss give dem one more tousan dollar worth dat wild hairy lil ting."

D'Julliette sat his cup down and stared at the reverend. "Dat it f'dis ever day ting, mon; she know all bout usin dat ting now. After today you gone come one time ever week, an you bess be doin what I tole you mon." He leaned toward him and spoke quietly, which always frightened the reverend. "I gots to git rid dem two dogs cause dey gittin too old. Mon you better git me two more young ting like dat one in dere so we keep all dem rich fella hoppy."

"An we gits rich an go back to Kingston to open dat nightclub."

A rare smile crossed D'Julliette's face, "Yes mon, dat de dream I livin for."

There was no room between the nightmares for Pearl to dream. As the two men entered the room for her morning lesson she saw the hypodermic syringe in D'Julliette's hand. Another nightmare was about to begin.

14

OLD PAL—NEW INFO

By noon the following day, Yan spotted Great Issac marker on the tip of Hens & Chickens Reef, which lies twenty miles north of Bimini. The sea was calm and the old Huckins was up on top and running twenty-five miles an hour; pretty fast for a forty-footer. A little over an hour later he scanned the coast of Grand Bahama Island. LOA was pointed at a spot between the west tip, where the small settlement of West End lay, and the airplanes he saw landing at Freeport. It was six months since he came across in the Huckins, but he'd made many trips in previous years in his lightning-fast, twenty-four-foot Sea Craft. Even though her twin 200 HP Evinrude outboards drank gas like the twin Chryslers in the Huckins, he still missed her—especially the 65 MPH leaps from one wave to the next.

There it is, he thought when he finally located his landmark. Forty-five minutes later he was pulling up to the dock behind Harry's American Yankee Bar.

Harry Leskiewicz was an old buddy of Yan's. Harry retired from the Miami PD three years before Yan. He married a Bahamian lady five years before retiring and together they built the bar and restaurant on land she inherited from her parents. Her father's brother built the old hurricane house with wrap-around porches, in the early 1920's. He dug a channel from the small creek that ran through the middle of the property, right out across the shallows to the ocean.

"A lotta rum was carried out to those rumrunners by Sherylee's Uncle Moses," Harry told Yan when he first commented about the deep-water approach to the docks.

Yan entered the bar and was glad to see Harry standing there, behind it as usual. "Know where an old Gendarme can get a cold beer?"

"Saw ya comin' across the flats." The six-foot-tall, two-hundred-pound ex-cop spoke with a wide grin as he pointed to the bottle of Beck's on the bar.

"You wasted a lotta time chasin' crooks," Yan said as he lifted the bottle and drank. "You're a natural barkeep Harry."

"I'd still be chasin' the bastards if I hadn't met Sherylee."

Before Yan could comment, a voice blared through the pass-through opening between the bar and kitchen. "Luckiest day of that Polack's life." It was only a moment until Sherylee came through the kitchen door. She was only five-foot-tall and had never once made the scale go over the one hundred mark, but nobody gave her any trouble, whether Harry was nearby or not. She was tough and well liked. Even the black Bahamians loved the little fifty-four-year-old white Bahamian from Spanish Wells on Great Abaco Island, which lay on the edge of the banks east of where they sat.

"Hi Yan, what brings you over?" She grinned, "Been awhile; Polish fishing tournament?"

"Just checkin' to be sure your Carib Indian descendants hadn't eaten my old Gestapo buddy."

"No chance o' that," she said as she climbed up on the stool next to Yan. "Those cannibal cousins o' mine were damn choosy about what they ate. Why eat that greasy Polack when there was plenty of those spicy little Spanish folks around?"

"Y'got a point," Yan said, "I can't stand that damn Kielbasa m'self, I'd much rather have Paella."

"If you're gonna be around a few days I'll get the stuff and make a batch of it." She turned to her husband, "Whadaya think, darlin'?"

"Sounds great t'me."

"Super," Yan said, "been awhile since I've had it." He wobbled his black brush-like eyebrows, "Gonna put some curbs and whelks in it?"

She grinned, "Turtles eat crawfish? Conchs piss in their shell? Polacks have L n' R on the toes of their shoes?"

"Hey, c'mon now, that's gettin' personal." Yan grinned wide at the spunky little wife of his long time friend.

"Calls 'em like I sees 'em."

A few minutes of small talk later, she climbed from the stool, "Gotta get a buncha mango snappers cleaned for lunch. See ya later," Sherylee waved as she went back through the swinging kitchen doors.

"Working or vacationing?" Harry asked quietly when she was gone.

"Remember when that wealthy, black, Miami bank owner was found murdered in Freeport a few months ago?"

"Shitchess," Harry answered. "I got t'know Broadsword pretty good after that girl turned up dead. I was the lead investigator, y'know."

"Actually I'd forgotten all about that till I did a little micro-film work at the library. That was one of the reasons you retired wasn't it?"

"Yeah," Harry said. "I was ready to come over here and stay full time anyway, but that made my mind up. That little bagnigger walked away without a scratch, because he filled somebody's Christmas stocking with thousand dollar bills."

"Bagnigger?" Yan said with a question mark in his voice.

"Yeah, that's what these blacks call the light-skinned locals who have many of the local, rich, white Europeans convinced that the lighter color you are the more trustworthy you are." His teeth flashed as he mimicked the island lingo, "Mon, doan be hirin nobody what darker dan a grocery bag."

"And they go for it, huh?"

"Oh shitchess," Harry said, "most of the whites who have winter homes over here are scared shitless of 'em anyway. The blacker they are, the more scared they are. Really working out great for the local light-skinned folks."

"Well," Harry said, "his wife hired me to find out what the hell really happened over here."

"No shit. I met that little pile o' black dynamite a coupla times, and that was a couple too many."

"Yeah," Yan said, "she struck me that way too."

"Tough as she is black and they don't get any blacker. Mean as a Cuban crocodile too. She'll eat your ass when she's got a full belly just to show you she can." Harry looked hard at his friend and added, "Especially when there's money involved." Harry paused a moment before adding, "And Yan, I think there's some very big money involved, and also some very big—very heavy guys. She might wind up wishing she'd left all of that shit in her past n' went on with her life."

Yan drained the Beck's and asked, "Got som'n I can drive to Freeport?"

"Yeah," Harry answered, "just did a valve job on that red Mustang out front, and it oughta be driven a little to see if that's all it needed."

When Yan was standing, Harry added, "Som'n that the Bahamian Government doesn't want spread around is that there's been three men in Nassau murdered," he paused a moment, looking at Yan, "and all the same way." He held his friend's eyes a moment longer, while keeping his wide open and staring—eyebrows raised. "Keys're in it," he finally said, "we gonna see ya for dinner?"

"Sure's hell will unless I'm in jail again." When he reached the door he heard Harry say, "Or worse."

15

EMANCIPATION

Pearl had been enduring her torturous new life for almost two years when she finally decided to end it all. She was allowed to roam through the house, but was aware that D'Julliette might step out at any time to see what she was up to. She was taken to the fancy hotels in Miami and Miami Beach to spend time with the Big-Money-Johns that the reverend and D'Julliette arranged. Even though she was free for a while, she never knew when she was being watched.

On the day she decided to commit suicide she was standing in the bathroom wondering how she could hang herself. She thought about taking some of the pain pills that were always in the medicine cabinet, so she reached to open it when she suddenly stopped. She stared at the face staring back. Pearl reached up with a finger and touched her cheek then her lips and ran it down across her chin.

I'm still a very pretty girl. My God, I'm not even eighteen yet. She stood and looked hard at the young girl in the mirror. *Why should I kill myself? I still have my entire life ahead of me. If I can get away from these monsters I can get off of the heroin and still have a good life.* It was the first time since her capture that Pearl was thinking positively about herself. Something down inside of the spunky little girl had kicked in. *I'll kill that son-of-a-bitch instead.* She smiled broadly at the girl that was now smiling back at her. *Hell yes! It should be easy if I plan it all out. He says I'm the best he's ever had.*

He says I can do things to him that he never dreamed of. Her smiling eyes now had an evil gleam in them. *I'll show him just how right he is.*

A few nights later, Pearl's patience was rewarded. She stood in front of the huge mirror in the bathroom of the new Miami Beach Hotel and inspected her swollen nipples. *Why do these old white men try to chew the nipples off?* A few minutes earlier the old Judge said, "I'm gonna take a nap. D'Julliette said you can spend the night here in the hotel with me, so take this five hundred dollars and go down to the second floor shopping area and buy yourself something."

"D'Julliette would kill me if he found out I took money and didn't give it to him." She had been with the Judge before and knew exactly how to handle him. She gently took his limp manhood in her hand then looked up smiling, "But it's very nice of you to offer it to me."

He lifted her head, "Screw that goddamn Jamaican." He shoved the five bills into her free hand, "I gave him two thousand dollars for you to spend the night here with me, and beyond that he doesn't need to know another thing. You go enjoy yourself Ebony, and what he doesn't know won't hurt anyone." He smiled and lay back against the goose-down pillows and lifted his short, pudgy arms so he could put his fat hands behind his head. "I'll see you in a couple of hours, okay?"

"You're such a sweet, gentle man," she cooed, "I'll be back to wake you with a big kiss," she paused and gave the old Judge a sexy smile, "where you love it best."

They had walked through the outrageously expensive shopping area earlier, so Pearl knew just what she would buy. Ebony (One of the names she used with her Johns) went into the ladies room on the second floor and did what she did each time she was given shopping money by the men she entertained. She pulled out the little bag that she kept attached to her underpants and removed the cheap, but expensive looking watch, ring, and necklace. Before leaving, she looked into the mirror. *Uh huh, that looks like five hundred dollars worth of stuff.* She grinned, *Especially in this ridiculous place.*

Pearl walked slowly through the displays on the second floor, talking to the salesgirls. She was a regular, and all of them knew what she did for her living by the varied collection of men she always arrived with.

She was friendly with all of them, plus whenever she purchased anything she tipped them big. Pearl knew how to use men to enhance her precarious position, and they were always eager to please her—knowing that she always returned their favor later in the room.

A glance at the wall clock let her know that she still had an hour to roam around before returning to the disgusting old man in the room. She noticed a sign advertising the 24-hour lunch counter on the first floor, and decided to get a bite to eat.

When the elevator door closed she reached up and pulled her purchase from beneath the wig and looked at it a moment before returning it. *D'Julliette darling, you gone love my new toy.*

Awhile later, Pearl return to the penthouse apartment with what she bought concealed inside the expensive wig. D'Julliette bought it for her because he liked the way she looked in it. "Dem rich ole fella gone like you in dat ting too."

16

CARIBBEAN CONTACTS

Yan pulled the Mustang into the parking lot of the Island Princess Casino. He then went to the parking lot man directing half a dozen boys as they parked customer's cars. Yan handed the thin man a ten-dollar-bill and pointed to the Mustang. "Don't let anything happen to my buddy's car and there'll be another ten when I come out in awhile."

A wide white grin opened up on the man's face, "When Harry git dat ting runnin' again, mon?"

"Just yesterday," Yan answered. "Everyone knows Harry, huh?"

"Not really mon, but Sherylee my second cousin."

"My name's Yan, what's yours?"

"Elvis Pinder. What kinda name is Yan?"

"Polish, just like Harry."

"I like dem Polish folks," Elvis said, still smiling. "Dey make de bess sausages I ever eat."

"You know Danny Love?" Yan asked.

"All my tirty year mon, he my firse cousin."

"He still the bartender here?"

"Yes mon, but he now bar manager too."

"He working tonight?"

Another wide grin, "Dat little fella work ever night Yan, 'cause he got so much action goin' on all de time, ad he 'fraid he gone miss some ting."

"Good," Yan said as he turned to head toward the gaudy entrance. He stopped and turned back, "Hey Elvis."

"Yes mon."

"Who was your mama's favorite singer?"

"Smokey Robinson."

Yan just laughed and turned away again, but before he was ten steps closer to the casino, he heard Elvis say, "It were my doddy what name me. Who you tink he favorite singer was?"

Yan just waved over his head and laughed.

Before Yan was near the small bar, which was set up close to the entrance to get the customers drinking before they even got near the other ten bars spread throughout the huge new casino, he saw Danny Love. He slid onto a stool and watched the dynamic little five-foot-tall black man he met on his first trip, almost twenty years earlier. He was the bartender at the old Jack Tar Hotel, renamed The Grand Bahama Hotel, on the west tip of the island near West End. Appropriate name, since in a brisk ten minute walk you'd be standing in the Atlantic Ocean.

West End was a favorite spot a few years earlier for Yan and several other Miami cops. Those who owned boats capable of making the fifty mile trip from West Palm Beach to West End, came often to fish in some of the world's finest water.

Danny put a guide in Yan's boat that first trip, and he caught fish like never before. He tipped the small man generously, and used his many services ever since. "He knows everyone worth knowing," he once told Harry.

"You got that right," Harry said. "I saw a picture of him sitting with Prime Minister Linden Pindling on the flying bridge of the Royal Island Yacht. Y'wanna know som'n; go find Danny."

"Hi Yan," Danny said with a smile when he finally saw him, "when ya get in?"

"Docked at Harry's earlier. Got m'self a new boat."

"Hit the numbers big, huh?"

"Nope! She's just new t'me. It's an old Huckins, but I love it; live on it too."

Without asking, Danny sat a Beck's in front of Yan. "That's always what you said you were gonna do when you retired from the department."

"Yeah," Yan said, "took a lotta doin' but I finally made it. Don't even hafta pay dockage 'cause I got 'er on a mooring at Dinner Key."

"Nice place, I went there in a seaplane with Bebe Rebozo one time to navigate his houseboat, Coco Lobo back here to West End."

"You wouldn't recognize The Grove now."

"Yeah, I know whacha mean, look at this place. Freeport's getting so big that it'll be like a vacation in the boonies when I go to Nassau." He leaned forward and whispered, "This a pleasure trip or som'n else?"

"Som'n else."

Rick Magers

Danny turned and yelled at the young man standing on the customer side talking to a young white girl. "Hey Artnell, how bout watchin this bar while I show my friend around. Won't be gone long atol, mon."

When the man had his apron on, Danny said to Yan, "C'mon, we'll go to my office where we can talk."

"Damn Danny," Yan whistled after he was seated in one of the several padded chairs in the huge office, "you're damn sure movin' up aincha."

"Yeah, I've paid my dues though. Y'know how long I've been with these New Yorkers?"

"Not really."

"Half m'damn life, mon." He pointed to a picture on the wall of a much younger Danny Poindexter Love, standing amidst several older white men. "That picture of me is when I was hired as bartender at the Old Colonial Hotel in Nassau. I was just twenty-five and finally graduated from the University of Miami. Those Bay Street Boys were so happy to have an educated island black on the payroll that they paid me twice what they shoulda."

Yan accepted the beer Danny took from the small fridge next to his desk. "You mean to say you didn't insist they take half of it back?"

"My mama didn't raise no dumb pickaninny, mon." He grinned then continued, "I took their money till I saw that those English bastards were losing control. I called a friend in New York and told him I'd go to work at the hotel in West End if the job was still open." Another wide smile. "That was thirty years ago, and as they say, the rest is history."

"I'll be damned if I woulda believed you're almost sixty Danny."

"Almost my black little ass, I turned sixty in June."

"What day?" Yan asked.

"Twenty-fifth."

"I turned forty-five on the thirtieth. Two Cancers oughta be able to team up and take over this island."

"Not me," the little man said with a grin, "I'm retiring pretty soon and moving to Long Island."

"Jesus Christ," Yan exclaimed, "retiring in New York."

"You outa your gourd, mon? Shit no, the only Long Island worth living on is down south of Great Exuma Island."

"Never been down in that area of the Bahamas."

"I was born there and have fifty acres of good land that my folks left me. I'm gonna do a little farming and just take life easy. Hey!" He leaned forward, "Enough of this blah-blah about me, what can I help you with, Yan?"

After explaining everything to him Yan sat back and sipped his beer, waiting for Danny to digest what he'd heard.

"Yan," Danny said, "I think there's gonna be more to this than is apparent on the surface. That Judge had been coming here to Freeport a long time looking for young stuff," He paused and leaned toward Yan, "and other things."

"Well Danny," Yan said as he stood, "that's why I came to you." He pulled a roll of bills from his pocket and took ten one-hundred-dollar-bills from it. "Here's enough to get you sniffing around. I'm gonna take advantage of this nice weather and do a little fishing. I'll be at Harry's if ya wanna get together."

"That where you're heading now?" Danny said as he opened the door.

"Yep, ain't about to miss one of Sherylee's meals."

"Okay Yan, I know who to get in touch with that'll have all the details about what that rich black dude was up to." Danny grinned saying, "Other than trying to screw every damn young gal on this island. I can tell you all about that, because he always stopped by here to show off his latest teenage dream."

"Liked 'em young, huh?"

"Under twenty, mom, always under twenty. I doubt if I ever saw him with one older'n that."

Yan just shook his head before leaving, "I guess money lets 'em pick n' choose but I wonder what the hell they did after that fifteen minutes was over?"

"Probably spent the next few hours trying to get that worn out ole black snake to wake up again." Danny grinned and gave Yan a finger-to-the-eye salute, and closed the door before picking up his phone.

17

CONTRACT SEVERED

Pearl was kept so busy for the next few days that D'Julliette wasn't able to get with her. She knew the reverend was in bed with the flu and the two new girls were on a yacht out in Biscayne Bay. When she returned just after dark on Saturday night D'Julliette was waiting in the living room. Pearl could tell that he had just shot up his heroin by the way he spoke. *We're finally alone.*

Pearl was still shooting heroin into her veins, but because she wanted so badly to escape her nightmare, but she had been using the drug as little as possible. *I'll never get away from that monster. He's gotta die for me to have a chance, and tonight's the best chance I've ever had.* She took a few deep breaths then went to him.

"Hey darlin', let's go in n' get naked then come out n' shoot some shit together."

"Yes baby," he said as he rose from the couch, "I been needin' some o' dat good stuff you sittin' on."

He never entered the room with the mattresses without locking the door so she knew they wouldn't be disturbed, even if someone came home early. They both removed their clothes but Pearl kept the wig on, which D'Julliette thought she looked good in.

He lay back and stretched his skinny, needle-track arms above his head and moaned as she squat above him, and began the motions that drove men crazy for more. She glanced to be certain he wasn't watching her, but his eyes were closed as he moaned in ecstasy. She eased out the gift she bought herself in the hotel shopping area with the Judges money. She reached beneath her and held D'Julliette's balls tenderly as she opened her gift. When it was in her hand perfect she gave the straight razor a quick pull. D'Julliette gave only one scream as the straight razor flashed across his throat, but it instantly turned into a gargling noise. Pearl leaped to her feet, bent down and sliced off his penis, then threw it violently across the room.

As he gurgled and thrashed about on the mattress, Pearl turned him over so the blood would drain into the material. When he finally stopped moving she rolled the body into the closet then muscled the smaller mattress on top of him. She flipped the overhead light on and was glad no one had replaced the burned out bulb and only the one was left glowing. She used his clothes to quickly clean up the blood that didn't go into the mattress, then turned the bloody mattress over. After checking to be certain there wasn't any obvious blood to be seen on the floor, she tossed a rag on top of his shriveled penis, and then rearranged the remaining mattresses. She went into the bathroom and cleaned herself and dressed. When she returned, she looked around. *Nobody's gonna notice the little blood that splattered around.*

Pearl went to the single chair in the room that D'Julliette sat on to watched the reverend with new girls. He wanted to be certain they knew all the ways to please their customers. She pulled the chair beneath the light fixture and used the towel to turn it until it went dark in the room. She had months to adjust to the room as a dark place to live, because D'Julliette removed the bulbs when he left the room during the three months she was never allowed out of it. She easily found the door and pressed her ear and listened for sounds of someone in the house. Once satisfied that she was alone, she opened the door and slipped out. She used the key that she found in D'Julliette's pants to lock the door then went into the kitchen.

Under the light she took out the money she had found in his pocket and counted it. *Four-thousand-fifty-three-dollars. That's a start but I know he's got a lotta money in here somewhere.* She stood looking through the opening into the living room and thought about all the times he had went to get money for his drug deals. *He always went in that little bedroom he keeps locked then came out with the money.*

She took his keys and opened the door. Pearl had never even seen into the room, so had no idea what to expect. She stood in the middle and looked around. There was an old oak desk beneath a window with plywood over the drapes so it would appear natural to an outside observer—the entire house was that way. The only other two objects in the room were a wooden chair behind the desk, and another metal chair in a corner.

That money's gotta be in here. She sat in the chair and opened the top center drawer. *Nothing in there but junk. Maybe one of these?* After trying every drawer she thought, *He would have locked the one with money in it.* She went to the closet and turned the light on. *Empty! Nothing on the shelf either.*

She looked up to see if there was some kind of trap door leading into the area above the ceiling. Nothing! She carefully checked all of the walls for a special hiding place—Nothing!

Pearl sat at the desk again and let her eyes slowly cruise around the room. *This's as bare as a room gets.* For no particular reason, she reached under the desk and ran her hands around. She felt a shelf that didn't belong where it was, so she shoved the chair out of the way and got down on her knees. *Oh dear God thank you.* She pulled the string tied stacks of bills from the shelf.

In ten minutes, Pearl E. White was walking casually toward the bus stop with her big, straw, zipper-top shopping basket, which she had bought when D'Julliette took her to Nassau to entertain some Bahamian Government officials.

The bus took her to South First Street in downtown Miami where she blended in with the multi-racial group of people milling about. She flagged a taxi and told him to take her to the airport. She went into the ladies room and removed two thousand dollars and added it to her own money. After securing a locker for a week in the lobby, she went into the bar to have a drink to calm her nerves. She realized she would have to shoot up soon, so she went to the ladies room with the tape she had bought at the airport gift shop. Pearl quickly taped three packs of heroin to her right leg just below her crotch, then the syringe to her left. She only used half of the heroin in the remaining syringe then used the tape to secure it behind the toilet. I'll use this just before I get on the plane.

Pearl told the Nassau taxi driver to take her to the Old Colonial Hotel. She liked the old man's gentle voice, so when she got out she asked him if he had a card so she could call him when she needed a cab.

"Yes ma'am I sure do, an I preciates it if you calls me. Here you are."

Pearl took his card and studied it a moment, looking down at him when he spoke again.

"Big Joe's Island Taxi Service." He looked up at Pearl through his window and in a serious tone added, "All kine service ma'am. You need some ting, an I means any ting at all, you call Big Joe, firse."

Pearl leaned down and smiled, "I'll bet you're Big Joe."

A big smile now preceded another friendly line, "Yes ma'am, dat me f'sho, Big Joe in de flesh."

"Well Big Joe, I'll be needing you for a couple of hours tomorrow, okay?"

"I be here soon's you call, missy, or mebbe even sooner."

She handed him two twenties saying sweetly, "I'm gonna rely on you for everything I need Joe. Can you handle it?"

"Tomorrow missy, you juss tell Big Joe whachew needin' an you gone have it straight away."

"Great! Goodnight, Joe."

The young black at the desk said, "No luggage?"—with an obvious question mark in his voice.

"Everything was stolen at the airport in Miami. Big Joe is taking me to the best shops tomorrow, so I can get what I need for my stay in Nassau."

"Big Joe, the taxi man?"

"Are there two Big Joes on this island?" She wanted to scream, *you fucking moron*, but smiled at the young boy instead.

"Uh no, I don't think so. He's my cousin and I don't think there's another one."

You're right, Pearl thought, *you don't think; probably never have and never will*. "Well that's great," she said with a smile; "I'll keep all my business in the family." She took five, one-hundred-dollar-bills from her tiny purse and lay them in front of the boy. "This is just a deposit until I decide how long I'll be staying at your hotel."

The young clerk's attitude and demeanor changed dramatically as soon as his eyes fell on the five small, oval pictures of Ben Franklin. "We're delighted to have you stay with us Miss," he turned the revolving guest book toward him and read, "Ebony Elizabeth Albright."

Pearl accepted the key saying with a smile, "Just Ebony to you, since you're Big Joe's cousin."

The boy immediately had lusty thoughts running through his head as he answered, "Very well Ebony, if there is anything I can do to make your stay in Nassau more pleasant, you just let me know."

"I'll do that," she paused waiting for him to identify himself but soon realized that his mind and eyes were on her breasts, so she waved the key saying, "I'll see you later." In the elevator she thought, *That kid still hasn't figured out which one's the hole in the ground.*

As the elevator door closed, the clerk was thinking, *Even if I can't get dat one in de bed, I bet I still gone get a nice big tip from her.*

18

YAN'S RULES

Yan walked out of the casino and headed toward the rear of the parking area where Harry's Mustang sat. When he passed the little shack where he'd earlier talked to Elvis Pinder, he wondered where the tall, thin parking lot attendant was. Yan was looking around as he continued toward the Mustang. Voices alerted him to something going on in the direction of the car.

He knew better than to carry his gun in the Bahamas, even though he had a license to carry it in the States. He reached to be sure the leather strap attached to the slapjack hanging from his left pocket was where he could grab it. The large, round chunk of lead inside the molded leather was larger than an ordinary pocket watch, but unnoticeable to others.

"Stay way from dat car," he heard the distinct squeaky voice of Elvis. Yan heard a muffled noise like one of his punches landing on the body bag at his gym. "Umph." He knew someone had taken a punch and thought it was probably Elvis.

Yan stepped from between the cars and spoke to the three young white boys. "Teaching that nigger some manners huh?" He grinned as he approached. The closest one to Yan spoke first.

"What the fuck business is that of yours, old man?" The leather-bound lead landed on the boy's jaw, and that was the last understandable sentence he would say until the wires were removed from his shattered jaw several weeks later.

The chubby boy holding Elvis for the stout puncher, looked shocked as Yan landed after a short flight through the air, his right shoe striking the boy's knee directly on the side. The scream was somewhat muffled as Yan landed the slapjack on the holder's mouth. This boy would have trouble being understood for quite awhile too, but it would be considerably longer until he could walk again.

Before the last, heavily muscled boy knew what was happening, Yan had his arm high above the shaved head, and behind him as Yan squeezed his throat with his other hand. The boy was on his tiptoes crying blood as Yan removed his wallet. At the moment he let the boy's hand loose he smacked him on the back of the head and turned his lights out for awhile. Yan retrieved each boy's wallet, then stood back to look through them, while the two conscious ones writhed on the ground in pain.

"That's what I figured," Yan said to Elvis after checking to be certain he was okay.

"What dat, mon?"

"Miami trash. All three of 'em probably came over to make a drug deal and it didn't work out."

Elvis grinned, "Mon dat sho de trute. Whatever kinda deal dey was tryin ain workin out worf a shit."

Yan bent down and grabbed the boy with the shattered kneecap. "Shut up and listen to me," he said as the boy continued to cry. A short punch got the boy's attention. "I'm keeping all your driver's licenses, so I can find you if I wanna continue this discussion. When the ambulance comes in after while, you tell 'em a buncha white guys jumped you."

When the boy started crying again, another punch in the face shattered what was left of his nose. "You understand what I just said?"

"Yessir."

"That's good, I like that yessir; you're a fast learner. You tell Rocky Balboa there," Yan nodded toward the unconscious puncher, "and that other geek, that if anything at all happens to my cousin Elvis here," he motioned toward the attendant with a nod, "all of you assholes better go to Iraq or North Korea—somewhere safe."

"I understand," the boy said in a very shaky voice, "please don't hit me again."

"Make damn sure your buddies understand too, or you're all gonna be shark shit if I hafta come back.

"Oh, ow, oh, okay I will."

One last short punch then Yan said, "Another thing you better remember as long as I'm around." He got right next to the boy's bloody face before continuing, "You fuckers ever see me again you better get on the other side of the street because I can't stand the smell of chickenshit."

Yan let the head drop then turned to Elvis, "Can you call an ambulance after while to come and pick up these bad ass Miami hoodlums?"

"Yeah mon," he grinned, "I busy now but I call dem bye n' bye."

"Okay Elvis, I'm outa here then, 'cause I'm starved and our cousin," he winked, "has dinner's waiting."

"Tank you mon," Elvis said, "I tink dem fella goin hurt me bod if I doan let dem take Harry toy."

Yan spent the next day with Harry on his fast skiff, chasing bonefish on the flats between his place and West End. When they returned in the afternoon, Sherylee had a message for Yan. "Danny Love called and wants you to come to Freeport and see him when you can."

19

CAREFUL PLANNING

Pearl spent two days shopping for new clothes, luggage and a few things she thought she'd need to prepare for a quick trip back to Miami. She stopped at the Post Office in downtown Nassau and rented a box for a year. On the morning of the third day in the Bahamas she boarded an airplane bound for Palm Beach International Airport, using identification cards that D'Julliette had a forger make for her so he could take her to Nassau and 'entertain' a few of the big money men.

The Customs Agent in West Palm Beach looked at her Florida Driver's License, Voter's Registration and Birth Certificate, then as his assistant went through her one small suitcase he asked, "Do you have anything to declare that you bought in the Bahamas?"

Ebony Elizabeth Albright smiled sweetly, "No sir. I'm just back to visit my sister and see if she'd like to come back to Nassau with me for awhile." She gave the young assistant a big sexy smile as he smoothed her clothes and latched the suitcase.

Pearl told the taxi driver to take her to Miami, then leaned back and thought about the money in the airport locker. Two hours of heavy traffic later she paid the driver and entered the airport. She knew the heroin would soon be wearing off so she walked briskly to the locker and retrieved the basket.

After stepping into the Yellow Taxi in front of the terminal Pearl said, "Take me to West Palm Beach, please." The driver smiled broadly at getting a long run. Pearl opened the basket and removed a package of hundred-dollar-bills. When the driver pulled off of I-95 in West Palm Beach she asked him to stop at a mini-market so she could get a hot cup of coffee and a few things.

Pearl handed the counter girl in the Seven-Eleven a five-dollar-bill, after she paid for the coffee, roll of masking tape, and an assortment of snacks. "Would you please put two of those large brown bags in another big one for me?"

"Yes ma'am," the girl said eagerly as she pocketed the five-dollar-bill.

Once back in the cab, she told the driver to take her to a hotel near the airport. "Fancy and expensive," he said into the rear-view-mirror, "or regular and reasonable?"

"Regular and reasonable." She answered.

Thirty minutes later he stopped in front of the Alexander Hotel. After paying the fare, she handed him a ten dollar tip and headed toward the office.

"Just one night," Pearl said as she returned the driver's license to her purse. After shoving the change from the hundred-dollar-bill into her black leather purse, she went swiftly to the elevator. Before the door to room 305 was closed she went quickly through to be certain she was alone, then securely locked the door. The first thing she did was to remove the taped syringe from the inside of her upper right thigh. She opened the bible on the tabletop and put the small syringe just inside the pages so it wouldn't bulge too much and put the bible in the drawer all the way in the rear. She stood a moment thinking about her dwindling supply of heroin. *I hope my intuition's correct about Big Joe, and he's got me a supply when I get back.*

Before opening the basket she stripped and took a cool shower. Dry, but still naked she opened it and began counting. Two hours later she looked at the stacks of hundred-dollar-bills. "D'Julliette," she said quietly, "you sure made a lot of money from a few poor little girls." She smiled thinking, *Didn't do you one bit of good though, did it you lousy bastard?*

Pearl used the straight razor that she now carried in her wig at all times, to slice the bottoms of the brown bags off so she'd have a nice flat piece of paper once she slit them down the seam. After removing five thousand dollars she stacked half of the bundles of bills onto the paper. She stood thinking about the stacks of money. *Two-hundred-and-twenty-two-thousand-dollars.* After she had the first bundle wrapped with masking tape, she stood and rested her back. "What you put me through you bastard," she said quietly, "wouldn't be worth any amount of money," she smiled as she began on the second package, "but this's sure gonna help me start a new life and maybe pay back a few of those sick assholes you put me with."

Demons, known only to those few unfortunate souls like Pearl, were already planting their evil seeds into her still confused and very hostile mind—they would reap a bountiful harvest in days to come.

With the two brown packages in her island basket, she called the lobby and requested a taxi. Ten minutes later she told the driver to take her to the nearest Mail Boxes Etc., "Or a place like that where I can have something boxed and sent to a friend." When he stopped the taxi she said, "Wait for me so you can take me back to the hotel."

When the girl behind the counter had the two packages boxed and securely taped, she asked for the mailing address. Pearl read it from the piece of paper she'd written it on. Miss Ebony Elizabeth Albright. Post Office Box 1235. Nassau, New Providence Island. Bahamas. "Yes," she answered when the girl asked if she wanted insurance, "They're gifts for my friend."

"How much would you like to insure it for?"

"One hundred dollars."

When she was back in her hotel room, Pearl stripped and showered again, letting the cool water run over her body for a long time. *I gotta wait as long as I can before shooting up half that shit I have left. It's gotta last till I do the rest just before leaving to get on the plane back to Nassau tomorrow.*

20

ISLAND CLUES

Yan parked the Mustang and walked to the attendant's shack. He looked around for Elvis but didn't see him so thought, *Must not work during the daytime.* He stood inside the casino near the slots, which were lined up by the hundreds close to the entrance, and looked around to see if Danny was nearby. He didn't spot Danny but saw Elvis walking toward the coffee shop. "Hey Elvis," he moved through the crowd to catch up with him, "where ya heading?"

"Hi Yan," his pearl and gold smile gleaming, "coffee shop, how bout a cup, mon?"

"Sounds good t'me."

"I see you're walking like you're hurting," Yan said after they were seated at the counter. "From the other night?"

"Yeah mon, dat big fella crock m'rib, I tink."

"Ouch," Yan commented, "been there—damn painful."

"Mon," Elvis grinned, "ain nuttin like what mighta been if you ain dere t'hep me."

"Sure as hell glad I came out when I did. What happened after I left?"

"Ha!" Elvis laughed, "Police come wit dat amblance I callin bout an hour later, an dey say right away dat dem de guys what rob a taxi driver dat ver same day in de mornin time." He laughed again, "You gone loff you oss off if you dere lisnin at dem big boys cryin like babies when dem ambulance fella put em on dat stretcher." He forced his already large eyes open even larger as he mimicked. "Ow-ow-ow-oh-oooweee-ow, dat hurt me, ow-oh-mama."

Another grin, "What dem boy tink mon, dey mama gone come runnin cross dat wide ocean an rub dey baby head?"

The two men were on the second coffee when Danny walked in. "Hi Yan, hi Elvis." He struggled up onto a stool then looked at Yan. "You in a hurry this morning?"

"Nope, just rode in to talk with you about that fishing guide." Yan didn't trust anyone, not even a seemingly easy-going guy like Elvis, the parking lot attendant.

"Good," Danny said, "because I'm so hungry I could eat a horse-conch."

"Yech!" Elvis stood up, "I were gonna eat some ting, but mon," he looked at Danny, "you done spoil my taste talkin bout eatin dem nosty dom ting." He lay a dollar on the counter and turned to Yan, "Dat a tip. Doan let dat gal try make you pay for my coffee cause it free to me." He pulled his white yacht hat with the shiny black bill down and gave a small wave, "I invited today on dat foncy boat name Sea Lion what over here from Walker's Cay." He smiled wide, "De new captain my cousin."

Yan watched as the tall thin man left the coffee shop with liquid, dancer's movement. "He seems like a good man."

"He is," Danny answered, and he keeps his mouth shut." He looked at Yan, "He didn't say shit about what happened in the parking lot until I called him into my office, after I filled out the paperwork on those three assholes that," he grinned, "got beat up by a gang of white guys."

Yan sipped his coffee as Danny ordered, then asked quietly, "Find out anything about that Broadsword killing?"

Danny glanced around furtively before saying quietly, "I've got a coupla people digging in places, and they'll come up with whatever there is to find. One of the guys I talked to is a newsman who heard something while he was in Nassau." Another glance around to be certain that he wasn't going to be overheard, "There have been three more murders there in the last few months."

When Yan's eyebrows just lifted, Danny said, "Yeah, I know. A murder in Nassau ain't a big deal these days, but these were all done the same way as some others. He said the government's covering up the fact that they might have a serial killer on their little island." He pushed his cleaned plate away and finished the last of his coffee before standing. "Got a lotta work t'do, so I'll give you a call when I get some info from my guys."

Yan's mind was occupied with this latest information so he just nodded. "Thanks Danny, see ya later." Before he made it to the Mustang, Yan had made up his mind. *I'll catch a plane to Nassau and see what I can find.*

Rick Magers

21

RETIREMENT PACKAGE

Pearl waited until just before boarding time to shoot up the balance of the heroin that she left in the syringe. She wiped her fingerprints from it, and then rolled it inside a wad of paper towels before tossing it through the swinging door of the trashcan. She walked from the lady's room knowing she would soon feel better.

After arriving in Nassau she saw Big Joe leaning against his taxi smiling at her, so she knew she'd figured the beefy, fiftyish, smiling cab owner correctly. *Under that smile there's a very tough guy. The kinda guy I need to make a very good friend of.*

A few weeks later Pearl realized that even though she now had a large sum of money in the bank, it wouldn't last forever. She lay stretched out on her hotel bed talking softly to herself. "Big Joe's a good connection for my heroin but I gotta get a sugar daddy to cover all of these hotel bills." She jumped from the bed as a cat would jump from a windowsill, by pulling her legs to her chin and then releasing a spring somewhere inside that launched her out of the bed and onto the carpeted floor.

Pearl's movements were fluid and lithe as she strode to the full-length mirror in her bathroom. She stood a moment staring at the ebony-black young girl that had seen enough horror to last several lifetimes. She unbuttoned her designer cut-offs and let them fall to the floor. She slowly ran her eyes from the top of her head, past the tuft of kinky black hair between her legs, to the tips of her tiny, delicate, manicured toes. She turned, with the hand mirror held high so she could examine her rear end. Her eyes rested on a small scar on one buttock. "That's a damn good looking ass except for that scar. I hope I meet that black, big shot, Nassau government son-of-a-bitch that did that to me with his cigar, when D'Julliette brought me here that first time." She laughed as the heroin started flowing through her veins. "You ain't taking me to those bastards any more, you Jamaican pig." Pearl giggled quietly, "Or anyone else." She turned back to face her image thinking with a smile, *Dead Jamaican pig.* The heroin made her giggle repeatedly, then she said quietly to her other self, looking back at her, "Piggy got his fucking throat slit, didn't he."

She continued giggling softly as she removed her flimsy, flowered halter to study her firm, up tilted breasts, topped off with nipples like dark cherries. Again her eyes went to the small, almost unnoticeable scars on them. "Perfect boobs," she said to the image in the mirror, "except where that old, white millionaire burned them with his cigarette." Pearl leaned closer to the mirror to study her delicate, slightly oriental looking face. It shined as though water was running down across an ebony sculpture. She stood a full minute, motionless and unblinking. "D'Julliette always said that my face had been carefully sculptured by a beauty loving God. I know I'm beautiful but He sure abandoned me after He was finished."

Her Sugar Daddy was in Big Joe's taxi as she spoke to her mirror. "I can sure nuff do dat," the burly driver said to the distinguished white gentleman, who had a short time earlier arrived by private jet. Big Joe turned to the man before starting his engine. "But firse, tell me again who tell you to call for me to come pick you up?"

The elderly man held Joe's eyes in a stone stare for a moment before answering, "New York City Circuit Judge MacAmberett. He said you were the only person to trust in this entire city. He's about sixty, and…

Joe cut him off by saying, "Has red hair and a red mustache."

Joe grinned as the man commented, "I'm happy to see that Mister MacAmberett was correct about you." He sat silent as Joe pulled away from the airport. "Do you already have a young lady in mind, Joe?"

Joe glanced up at the man watching him in the mirror. "Sure do, prettiest young ting what come to Nassau in my lifetime."

"Head for Atlantis Joe," the passenger said, "I have a year round garden cottage there. After you drop me off perhaps you can bring her there to meet me?" The man leaned toward Joe and said, "My friend also said you keep your business dealings strictly between you and your clients."

"Dat zactly de way I always do all my business." Joe smiled at the image of the man in his rear view mirror, "I a catolick an I doan even includin my ver own personal business when I goin in dere wit dat priest to givin my confessions."

A brisk nod, "Excellent!" It accompanied the man's brief, shallow smile! "I believe we'll get along just fine, Joe."

Big Joe's passenger was actually German industrialist Hermann Handich. His factories were spread across the planet like an octopus—but with many more tentacles. His education prepared him for international dealings, and English was but one of the many languages that he was fluent in.

Big Joe delivered Pearl, who all knew as Ebony, to Mr. Handich's garden cottage on the grounds of the beautiful Caribbean resort paradise named Atlantis. With his business dealing being handled by capable employees, Mr. Hermann Handich was indulging himself with the many fantasies he had held in check for many years. He was ninety, and still able to enjoy most of his fantasies, but realized that his life was coming to an end.

After spending a year in Paris with a blind male stripper, he retired the young man with a lifetime pension in a home with servants on the French Riviera. His present fantasy was to spend a year with the most beautiful young black girl available in Nassau. He was momentarily paralyzed when he first looked at Pearl. He suspected that the silky black hair hanging to her shoulders was a wig, but it completed the picture in his mind so completely that he ignored it. Even after he convinced her to remove it occasionally during their sexual escapades he was still delighted with the short, natural Afro that lay beneath the many different wigs. "It makes you look like a Zulu Princess."

Even after a year with him, Pearl still liked the old man and even enjoyed his company. To her amazement she often enjoyed sex with him and even occasionally had a climax. "I'd like to believe that's true," he stated when she told him the first time it happened.

She quickly reversed her position and straddled his still rigid stomach to look him in the eyes. "Hermy, you can believe everything I tell you because I do not tell lies, they're too damn hard to remember."

Pearl was actually saddened when he finally told her that he was retiring her, and moving on to his next adventure while he was still capable. "As I explained in the beginning Ebony, I allow myself only one year with each new companion, then I move on to a new interlude. I've arranged for six thousand dollars a week to be sent to the First National Bank in Manhattan. There is a numbered account and code number, so you can live out your life wherever you choose. It will continue for fifty years or until the account has not been used for a thousand consecutive days."

"I'll miss you," Pearl said as she embraced the frail old man. "I thought all men were no good bastards until you came along." She was telling him the truth, because he was the first to treat her with dignity whether clothed or naked. Their sex was energetic and experimental, but was never allowed to impinge upon the other.

"My driver's here," he said as he nodded toward the front of the cottage. "I've left instructions that you may remain here as long as you like." He smiled at her then said, "If it's true that your life runs through your mind during the moments prior to death, this past year will occupy a large part of that time." He turned toward the door and grasped the handle, but paused and turned when Pearl spoke.

"Hermy, if you go broke just open a school to teach young men how to be real lovers, because you're the best at it there is, and you'll be rich again in no time atol."

After the door closed, she latched it and turned to get a fresh syringe from her locked valise, then went into the bathroom and locked the door from habit. Even though Mr. Handich knew she was using heroin, she never shot up in front of him. "Shit," Pearl said as she inserted the needle, "I don't hafta come in here and lock the door any more."

She floated on her inflated rubber seat to the whirlpool-spa at the end of the enclosed pool, which he had a crew build for her next to the cottage. She climbed up the steps, water dripping from her nude body, making it resemble a black marble statue. After getting a chilled glass of Nassau Royale she returned to lay in the warm water, and her mind began assessing her future. *You're a very rich girl Pearl E. White, so whatcha gonna do now?*

The heroin had relaxed her mind too much to ponder far into her future, so she stopped thinking about it. Money was no longer a priority, but as she lay relaxing in the whirlpool she thought about the amount of cash she had on hand. *Hermy has paid for everything since I met him, so I still have about a hundred grand of my—ha-ha-ha,* she giggled in her mind, *D'Julliette's money—plus about fifty grand of Hermy's that I stashed, and with the hundred grand cash he gave me just before leaving, I oughta be in damn good shape, for awhile.*

The following morning she sat sipping coffee and reading the morning paper. After her second cup she opened the drawer of the solid cherry wood hutch beside her, and removed a small calculator. After double-checking the figure she thought, *Over a quarter-million a year for the rest of my life.*

22

CLUES BEHIND A FOGSCREEN

The day Yan stepped from the plane in Nassau, the fourth victim of the killer, who was being called THE WIDOWMAKER, because investigators learned that each had a wife somewhere, had not yet been found. His body was spotted two days after Yan landed. It was found in a location near Sunset Bay, over five miles from Nassau. Yan's first stop was at Police headquarters. He asked the uniformed officer at the desk, "I'm looking for a Miami Police Academy friend of mine," Yan smiled at the light skinned man, "been awhile though so he mighta retired already."

The middle-aged officer was a third generation policeman and bonded immediately with men such as Yan. "You just gimme his name mon, an we see if he in dis computer." When Yan complied, the man turned away from the keyboard and smiled wide. "Ain gotta look too far f'dat nosty ole fella, c'mon." He rose and came around the end of the huge desk. A few strides of his long black legs hanging from khaki shorts, and he was at the open doorway of a nearby office. He nodded with his head toward the short, neckless, muscular black man hunched over papers. "Dat de onliest Polo McGuire in dis worl mon, or any other I spect, so dat muss be he." He returned to his desk as a drunk was being escorted in.

"Well I'll be damned," the man said through a wide, white, grinning mouth around a short fat cigar, "Yan Brodjevinski." He came from behind the desk to grab Yan's hand and begin pumping. "Man, it's been a long time, what brings you to Nassau?"

Yan matched his grin, "Just wanted to see if you'd remember m'name."

"We've both got the kinda names you don't forget," he smiled saying, "c'mon in n' have a seat Yan, and tell me all you've been up to. How long's it been anyway?"

"At least five years," Yan said as he pulled a chair from beneath a smaller desk. Fifteen minutes later Yan said, "And that's where I'm at now Polo, how boucherself?"

After a brief rundown about his personal life Polo added, "And about this time next year I'm retiring."

"How long you been with CID?"

"Almost ten years, and that's one of the reasons I'm finally retiring." He shook his head back and forth slowly, "So much crime these days that it's gonna put me in a grave if I don't get out." The lead Central Intelligence Division detective opened a drawer and removed a bottle. As he opened it to fill two small glasses of the golden colored contents, Yan spoke.

"Nassau Royale, mmm-mmm, been a long time."

"You need to get over here more often, Yan." He grinned as he handed his friend the glass, "Ain't as if we're on the other side of Europe."

Yan nodded as he sipped, "Been over to Grand Bahama Island several times but keep putting off coming here." He shrugged his shoulders and downed the last of the drink, as Polo held the bottle out to refill Yan's glass, "Dunno why—no excuse." He briefly explained about the rumors of murders in Nassau, and his client's desire to find the truth about her husband's death. "Are you high enough in the Investigation Division of CID to get me a little info?"

Yan's friend grinned around the stub of cigar. "I'm the end of the working line. The guy ahead of me just goes around shaking hands; hoping to get his big black ass in the Chief Inspector's chair." Polo removed the cigar and leaned forward, "Whatcha need, Yan?"

After laying out his needs, Yan said, "I'm gonna get a room over at the Colonial and enjoy that beach n' a few of those fancy rum drinks with umbrellas n' shit stickin' out."

"And some of that beautiful stuff on the beach," his friend said grinning as he stood and grabbed Yan's hand again. "I'll give you a ring as soon as I get what you need."

After checking in, Yan couldn't wait to get to the beach for a cold rum-voodoo, beneath one of the palm-frond-thatched bars, which sat on the beach close to the water. The barman was a professional tip gatherer who spoke quietly with any of his customers who indicated a need for conversation. Yan's eyes landed on the gorgeous young black woman as soon as she rose to walk to the water. He watched as she swam out a short distance, and then paralleled the beach for a short, brisk swim before returning to her seat beneath the huge umbrella. The black, skin-tight bathing suit glistened and made her appear naked. His eyes went to her crotch and expected to see pubic hair because of the illusion, which was broken when he spotted the small design on the stomach area of the suit. Yan's eyes were drinking in the mirage with sexual desires dominating his lust-filled mind, which didn't register what it was seeing until later. "That is one beautiful woman," Yan said to the bartender who turned to see who he was referring to.

"Yes mon, she sure is. She lived her for awhile a year or so ago, but she moved out and I've only seen her around here now n' then since."

"Is she friendly?" Yan inquired with subtlety.

"Not even a little bit mon," the man said as his head shook slowly, with his mouth pursed in mock sadness, "ain one fella I know but me what even get a hello from that one." He turned to look at her as she stood to adjust the umbrella, "Tssst," came the popping noise that Yan wished he could duplicate, "what a waste of woman that is, mon."

"Maybe not, Yan said, "she might have all she wants right at home. Is she a local girl?"

"No mon, she one o' your girls. Desk fella inside say she from Miami."

Yan grinned as he watched the gorgeous creature brush her hands across the short African style hair. After a long, slow sip of his run drink he said, "She might have a sugar-daddy over here."

"Yeah, mebbe." Tito the bartender's grin spread, "but I sho would like to shoot whoever that cowboy is outa the saddle for a short ride on that mare."

Yan sipped his drink, watching the women; especially the very pretty—very black one. His mind drifted back to the black Cuban woman that he'd spent fifteen years with. She was killed in an auto accident the same year he retired from the Miami PD—it almost killed him too. Alecia was the only woman Yan had ever allowed himself to get attached to.

Five months after they first dated they wound up in Yan's apartment for the breakfast he offered to cook. It had been a fun party but they were both a little drunk and a lot hungry. They devoured the bacon, scrambled eggs, fried potatoes and English muffins—then for two hours they devoured each other.

A month later Alecia moved in with Yan and a month later he asked her to marry him. She refused saying, "I'd love to Yan, but I don't think it's a good idea, because I'll lose my city pension plus all of the insurance and other percs I get."

Yan knew she was right. As the widow of a city policeman she'd lose everything if she remarried—she lost everything anyway when the teenager hit her head-on doing over a hundred miles an hour—Yan almost lost everything too, including his sanity.

Another woman was not a priority during the almost four years since losing Alecia. A few times, when the opportunity presented itself, he used the services of one of the prostitutes he knew and often used as informants. Their services were one of the percs of the job. It satisfied his body's lust but did nothing for the empty hole in his life.

Retiring was his salvation because opening his Private Investigator business kept him so busy just trying to survive that he had little time to dwell on his personal life.

Yan sipped rum for over an hour as he watched the women parade themselves back and forth. With each one he thought, *Not even close to Alecia.* Each time Pearl moved, he watched in anticipation, and was disappointed when she didn't stand up. When she finally did he thought, *Sorry Alecia darlin', but even though you were a ten, this gal's a ten-and-a-half.*

He was extremely close to THE BLACK WIDOWMAKER, but completely unaware. His natural detective mind knew something—but was temporarily short-circuited by lust and desire.

23

DEMONS ARRIVING

With the departure of Hermann Handich, Pearl began losing her last grasp on anything resembling a normal life. Demons from her tortured mind began appearing regularly to remind her of the nightmares of her past.

As the afternoon sun drifted lazily toward its western resting-place, Ebony walked along the dunes south of the Ocean Club of Atlantis, which followed the Atlantic Ocean. She carried flippers and mask in her hand and a spare syringe next to the razor beneath the new, luxurious, three-thousand-dollar wig. She was a mile beyond her garden cottage when she spotted the man in the shallow water ahead. It was one of several spots that she loved to snorkel and observe the tiny colorful fish as they scurried near her mask. As she approached, she saw the scooter parked beneath one of the many coconut palms.

Pearl stood and watched as the man floated along, breathing through the snorkel, totally unaware of her presence. When he finally stood and saw her watching, he smiled and began wading toward her. Her mind was playing many tricks on her lately. *That's the bastard who burned my titties in Miami, and laughed when I cried.*

"Hello," the gray haired, middle-aged man said as he approached.

"Hello to you too," she said with a smile. *The son-of-a-bitch doesn't remember me—good!* "See any big sharks?"

"Nope, nothing much worth watching in these shallow ponds." He stopped and leaned over to flip the water from his hair. When he straightened back up he transferred the flipper to his other hand and reached out to her, "My name's Bill Anderson, what's yours?"

"Pearl." The moment she used her real name she knew his fate was determined. "You live here on New Providence Island?"

"No, but I'd sure love to. I'm just enjoying a week of fun and sun that my company awarded me with after a very good year. How about you; live here?"

"No," she smiled, "but I come over as often as I can. I love to snorkel in the safe places along here and look at all of the pretty fish."

"I sure hope there's better places around, because there wasn't much here to see."

She pointed toward the tip of Paradise Island, another mile away saying, "There's a beautiful shallow lagoon on the end where there are more things to see than anywhere else I've been to."

"Hey," he said enthusiastically, "sounds great. Wanna ride on the scooter with me and show me where it is?"

She smiled coyly, "Got any beers or anything to drink in that cooler on it?"

"Sure do," the man answered—thinking, *My God what a gorgeous creature. Great time for Marilynn and the kids to stay home in Boston.* "Got a bottle of Sangria laying in ice, and some plastic glasses the guy gave me."

"Well let's get going then before it's too dark to see anything."

As they rode toward the tip of the dunes, Pearl was thinking sinister thoughts. *We see now if that Obeah Man's voodoo stuff was worth all the money I paid him?*

After he leaned the scooter against a palm tree Pearl said, "I'm just gonna swim around a little, but you go along that shallow reef right there and you'll see things you won't see anywhere else." She pointed to the gentle waves breaking across a reef just beneath the surface, about fifty feet away. She eased herself into the water and began walking across the shallow sand bottom. When he was snorkeling along the edge, she returned to the beach. When she saw him stand and lift his mask she yelled, "I'd like some of that Sangria, how about you?"

"Sure thing," he answered, "I'm gonna look along here a little more then I'll be right out."

Pearl opened the Styrofoam cooler strapped to the platform behind the seat. She placed two plastic glasses on the seat then reached beneath her wig for the tiny vial the Obeah Voodoo Priest had given her. As she unscrewed the top she recalled his words, *Dis gone make a mon like he dead, but he gone know ever ting what hoppen to him.*

She kept her eyes on him as she sprinkled half of the vial's contents into one of the glasses. After slipping the vial back beneath her wig she opened the bottle of wine and filled both glasses. Pearl then slipped easily from her bathing suit and walked to the water's edge with the two glasses and waited.

When the man stood and turned toward her, he remained motionless for several moments before heading her way. A smile spread across his face. "I never believed in mermaids until now."

"I'm not a mermaid Bill," she said and he was too absorbed to catch the subtle sarcasm when she said his name, "I'm just a horny girl that can recognize a real man when I see one." She handed him his glass of wine saying, "Put those flippers and mask on top of your bathing suit over there." She pointed to a spot at the edge of the water a few feet away, and then waded into the waist deep water. When he turned toward her his penis was sticking straight out, and she was pleased when she watched him drain the plastic glass and toss it on the sand. She walked slowly backward as he approached. Pearl recalled what the Voodoo man told her. *Half dis ting in he gloss an in ten minute he body be in de nex worl but he mind be right there witchew.*

She could tell by the man's eyes that something was happening to him. She stopped to let him walk closer to her. His motions were slow as he placed his arms around her slender body. When she reached down and grabbed his penis and slowly began jacking it back and forth, his expression barely changed. "Come with me," she said as she led him by the penis toward the beach. He followed like the Zombie he was becoming. She guided him down on his back and stood watching as his eyes slowly roamed her body. She looked both ways in the failing afternoon light, but could see no one. She straddled him and leaned forward so her nipple was near his mouth. She shoved it in but his lips were frozen as though they belonged to a dead man.

"What's the matter, BILL?" She said his name through clenched teeth, "Can't bite them like you did before. Here, maybe the other one will taste better. Still can't do it, huh? Well, maybe you've gotta have a cigarette to burn them with before biting them feels good to you." She sat up and looked into his eyes as she removed the razor from her wig. She was pleased to see that the old Voodoo man was right. *He gone know ever dom ting what hoppen to him, but ain nuttin he can do bout it.*

Pearl saw the terror in his eyes. The same terror, which the many sadistic men had seen in hers, as they indulged their sickness with her unwilling young body. She scooted down and grabbed his still erect penis. "I think you men get a hard-on even when you change your baby's diapers." She watched his eyes as the razor severed it. They didn't so much as flinch, but the panic and fear in them was enough to make her smile.

She carefully cleaned the blade and replaced it beneath her wig. The water at the edge of the beach was red as she dragged his still alive, but paralyzed body into the lagoon and turned it face down. After getting back into her bathing suit she carefully cleaned everything she had touched to remove her fingerprints. With her flippers and mask in her hands she looked at his body floating in an area of reddening water. "That's one bastard who won't bite and burn another little girl." She began the long walk back to her garden cottage as the palm tree shadows lengthened. She paused near one and removed the syringe from her wig.

Thirty minutes later, Pearl's blackness blended perfectly with the night as she moved silently across the dunes toward her garden cottage. Even if someone had been outside nearby, they would not have seen her. The heroin now running through her system had her mellowed, but she still retained a bitterness that was consuming her soul. *I'm going to pay back every one of those bastards I see for the misery that they gave me.* She smiled at the thought, and then said more with her breath than her vocal cords, "Ten times over."

24

DICKLESS DEADMEN

Yan picked up the phone in his room and listened as Polo said, "Stop by my office Yan, I've learned a few things." He dressed quickly and headed for the ROYAL BAHAMAS POLICE FORCE headquarters building.

Polo removed the stub of cigar, which he seldom did, and motioned toward the door, "Close it, Yan." He waited until Yan was seated then said, "I hate to admit this to another cop, but I really didn't know anything about this shit other than that there'd been a coupla murders with similarities." He shoved the stub back in his mouth and leaned back. "I ain't the only one around here that hasn't heard shit about this. The first guy turned up over on Paradise Island, floating in a red lagoon with his pecker whacked off, and those fuckin' mob guys who own that resort about had a shit-fit." He puffed till he realized it was out, then struck a match and lit the cigar.

"How about the newspaper?" Yan asked, "Seems like the Nassau Guardian woulda had everyone talking about som'n like that happening over here."

"Yeah, normally that's the way it would be, but someone musta either laid some heavy dough on 'em to keep it quiet," Polo grinned at Yan, "or whispered a deal in their ear that they couldn't refuse."

"Somebody you know raising expensive horses over here?"

When Polo just grinned Yan asked, "How about the other murders?"

"Number two was found floating in Lake Killarney with his love muscle a little shorter too." Polo held up his right thumb and forefinger a half inch apart, "it was down to about this much."

"Shit," Yan said, "two murders like that over here's a bit much, ain't it?"

"That ain't all. A third with his dick missing turned up over on East End Point about two months ago." He held up his hand when Yan started to speak, "Wait'll you hear about number four that the guys on patrol found awhile ago over in Sunset Bay."

Yan sat silent as Polo gave him the grisly details. He accepted the glass of Nassau Royale then after a sip said, "Still no mention about a serial killer in the local paper?"

"Not a word and ain't gonna be if I know those guys over at Atlantis. They're ten times worse than that shithead in the movie Jaws when it comes to keeping bad publicity away from their doorstep."

Yan nodded yes to a refill saying, "They might not be able to keep it covered up too long with so many Florida people, especially Miamians, coming over here regularly."

"Yeah, I figure in a week or less the Miami Herald will have a front page story about the dickless dipshits found floating near Atlantis." They both laughed, never dreaming how close the Nassau detective was to describing the story to hit the streets in Miami a week later.

Rick Magers

25

DEADLY SURPRISE

The demons that had only been visiting Pearl occasionally were now her constant companions. She would see a man walking along outside the casino, standing at a bus stop in downtown Nassau, driving by in his car, riding past on a scooter; anywhere—everywhere, and the demons would whisper. *That's the dirty bastard who shoved it so hard in your ass that you bled all over everything and couldn't walk for a week without hurting. Do you remember? You were just a little girl, and he ripped your ass open. Rotten men bastards.* Pearl would shake her head and walk away, feeling inside that the man was no one she had ever seen, but her demons were persistent. They seldom allowed her to go anywhere without them. Her time with D'Julliette had taught her how to survive anything. She strained to shut out the demons, but it was becoming harder and harder, because they were persistent.

When the slender young man stopped his rented Honda beside her, asking if she'd like to go for a ride—Pearl recognized him immediately. "Sure, you got something to drink in that box on the back?"

"No," the frail young man answered, "but it won't take a minute to stop n' get a bottle of whatever you like."

Pearl smiled alluringly as she said, "Get a bottle of Nassau Royale then pick me up here in ten minutes after I go to the phone company and make a call."

"You gonna be here?" His youthful smile revealed his lack of confidence in himself.

"Try me and find out," Pearl responded with only the flicker of a grin. As soon as he was driving away, her face turned to stone. *You thought I wouldn't recognize you if you cut off your beard huh? I still have scars on the back of my neck where you bit me as you rammed that thing in my ass, you son-of-a-bitch.* She simply stood back in the shadow of the giant rubber tree and listened to her demons. *That skinny little bastard is in for a helluva surprise.*

After Pearl was on the back of the long padded seat of the motorcycle, he said above the engine noise, "Where's a good place to go where we won't be bothered by other people?"

"Turn left on that road up ahead beside the grocery." Pearl used her slender black arm to point the way to Sunset Bay. "Don't go straight down the road," she directed, "turn right up ahead at that old burned out shack and go slow till you see a path on the left about a mile beyond, on down the road." Awhile later she pointed ahead, "There it is."

"Yeah," he said and turned onto the narrow grassy path running toward the ocean.

After positioning the motorcycle against the coconut palm, he walked to the edge of the water, then waded out to his knees. As he was involved with the scenery, Pearl was emptying the last half of the fresh vial she recently bought from the old voodoo Obeah Man. With the plastic glasses secured in the sandy soil of the path she poured each full of the sweet liqueur.

When Pearl was at the water's edge she saw her young man still standing with his back to her. She carefully inspected everything visible in both directions, even though she had seldom ever seen another person at this remote location on Sunset Bay.

"I just must take a short swim," he yelled as he removed his trousers and tossed them behind to the beach. He swam out a short distance then returned to the shallow water where he could touch bottom. He was grinning as he slowly walked toward Pearl, who was holding the two glasses of golden liqueur. One sweet and delicious—one sweet and deadly.

"I have a little surprise for you," he said as he slowly advanced toward Pearl. When he was finally in knee-deep water, with the crotch exposed, he smiled at the obvious shocked look on the young black girl's face. "Well sweetheart, what do you think? Can you handle it?"

26

EYE CONTACT

"**Jesus H. Christ,**" Yan blurted out, "any chance they're wrong?"

"They're cops ain't they," Polo said grinning, "but I'd say no because of who the cop is. He worked with me for a year as an investigator and he doesn't miss a thing; very thorough."

Yan squeezed his eyes shut as tight as he could and pressed his right thumb and pointing finger against them.

"I recognize that thinking technique of yours Yan, whacha got goin' on in that Polish head?"

"I dunno man, som'n just went flashing through but I'll be damned if I know what it was." He pressed his eyes again. "You said they started calling the killer The Widowmaker when they finally put a little article in the paper after that big story in the Miami Herald?"

"The Black Widowmaker; that's how it got put in the paper. All three of those first victims were married. One was a rich dude and his wife came here wanting to know what the hell we were doing about his murder. She hired a private detective while she was here to see what he could find. He located two people who saw the first two victims with a young black girl, not too long before they disappeared. Someone musta jumped on the newspaper's shit again because there's not been another mention about the murders or The Black Widowmaker since." He dumped the dead stogie in his trashcan and bit off the end of a new one. Before lighting it he said, "You know how that kinda shit travels; everyone who knows anything about the case is calling the killer The Black Widowmaker, but for all I know the killer might be a white crack-head."

"Black Widow," Yan mumbled. "Hmmmmm! I'm gonna go see if I can put this damn weird feeling to anything Polo, thanks. I'll stop by your boat before I leave." He turned at the door before opening it, "You do still live on that houseboat next to the bridge goin' to Paradise Island doncha?"

"Till it sinks or I die." His smile was wide, white, and sincere. "I'll be looking for ya, and so will Elaine."

Yan waved over his shoulder as he headed toward the front of the station. Polo watched him and thought, *That Polack's got the best damn intuition I've ever seen. I'll bet he's onto som'n.*

The same bartender was working the beach bar when Yan arrived a short time later. He ordered a Mt. Gay over ice and scanned the crowd as the bartender tried to fill the many orders of his crowd. A short time later his diligence was rewarded when he recognized the beautiful, young ebony-black girl in the same black bathing suit she wore the previous day when he'd seen her for the first time.

Yan sipped his rum for almost an hour, hoping she would come to the bar for something. The bartender remained so busy that Yan hadn't had time to say anything but a casual greeting. When he saw her rise and begin walking toward the bar, Yan's senses were working overtime as he scanned down to the tiny emblem on the front of her suit. *Dammit! I was right; that dark orange little thing's an hourglass.* His eyes were shielded behind the Polaroid's, so he was able to look directly at her as she ordered. Yan made a mental note that she ordered Nassau Royale Liqueur then handed the bartender a ten-dollar-bill and told him to keep the change. The hair stood straight out on the back of his neck when she picked up the glass and paused as she looked directly at Yan. Pearl wore nothing on her eyes, so he was able to see that she was staring straight into his eyes, to somewhere beyond—deep into his mind. During the fifteen seconds that she stared, he was thinking, *My God, she's reading my thoughts and knows that I know.* Pearl smiled slightly and returned to her beach chair. Yan drank another two glasses of Mt. Gay as he waited for her to leave. When she finally got up to leave he noticed that her glass was still sitting on the sand beside the chair. After watching her go around the end of the building he went to the chair. He already had one of the Ziploc Baggies open that he carried with him, so all he had to do was reach down with it and scoop it up.

Back in his room Yan sat the bagged glass on the dresser and picked up the phone. When the voice on the other end said, "Miami Police Department," Yan asked to speak to Detective Leskiewicz. When the gravel voice answered, Yan said, "Stan, this's Yan and I need a favor." Ten minutes of conversation later he said, "Yeah Stan, if that Jamaican pimp that got his throat cut open with a straight razor was using this little gal, then there's gotta be some DNA or fingerprints on her there somewhere. I'll go to the airport here n' ask the pilot to carry this glass she was drinking from with him, if you can get someone to meet the plane n' bring it to you."

"I been owing you one for a long time Yan, so I'll pick it up myself and hand carry it to the lab."

Yan lay back and locked his fingers behind his head as he thought about the confrontation with her at the bar outside. *I wonder if I'm imagining this?* He closed his eyes tight and concentrated on her dark eyes. The same chill ran along his neck. He opened his eyes, *Nope! There's damn sure some connection here.*

27

NEW HUNTING GROUNDS

Pearl stood motionless and looked at the glistening young body coming slowly out of the water toward her. "Surprised?" Their bodies were only a couple of feet apart when Pearl answered.

"Yes!" She turned away and set the drinks in the sand, "And I have a very big surprise for you too." Pearl removed the wig then turned around with it in her left hand as her right one positioned the hidden razor.

"Oh," Pearl's companion said, "your hair is so very… Her words fell from the six-inch wide gap in her neck that lay open just below the chin.

Pearl stood looking down at the thrashing young girl in water that was rapidly turning red around her. Both eyes were bulging almost out of their sockets as they stared at the sky. The thrashing stopped and the body they were in began shaking, as the water surrounding it became a darker shade of red. Pearl looked in both directions; seeing and no one. After cleaning the straight razor, her bathing suit, and body, of the blood that had splashed on her, she replaced her wig and then shoved the razor back into its hiding place. Pearl sat astride the Honda and turned the key. The motor started and sat there humming as she looked over all of the gauges and gadgets. *This big one shouldn't be any harder to drive than the small ones I rent.* She was soon heading back toward Nassau. Pearl leaned the motorcycle against a tree in the rear of a grocery store parking lot, and then after walking two blocks called a taxi. As soon as she was in her cottage in Atlantis on Paradise Island, she used a full syringe of heroin to settle her shattered nerves. She lay on the bed thinking about the recent strange event, which had her mind racing. *That couldn't have been the guy who hurt me so bad.* Pearl pressed her eyes with trembling fingers so hard they hurt. *I thought it was him with his beard shaved off, but that was a girl.* "A girl," she said aloud. "I've never been in bed with a girl." *What's happening to me?* She lay with her eyes closed thinking about the day. *That man at the beach bar knows.* She opened her eyes, and then narrowed them to thin slits as she thought about Yan. "He knows," she said quietly. Her young body was melting into the mattress as the heroin began taking control. *I gotta get out of here*, she thought as she began drifting away to another world. *I better get away from this small island and go to a big city.* She closed her eyes and began drifting faster and faster away; not to a world of her choice or one that she even liked, but a world that D'Julliette had taken her to. One that she was forced to revisit often—much too often.

The morning following the day Pearl killed the young lesbian, she was standing naked in the bathroom of her cottage. She taped six syringes to the inside of her thighs by wrapping clear medical tape around twice over three on each side, and then began dressing. An hour later she leaned in the taxicab's window and spoke to Big Joe, "After we go the Post Office and mail this I want you to take me to the airport."

During the ride, she had dumped all but two of the cigars onto the front seat for Joe to do with as he wished, then placed the heroin, which she had carefully wrapped before leaving her cottage, in the wooden box and crumpled the two cigars over it. After covering the box with two layers of the brown paper, which she brought with her for the wrapping, Pearl put the address on the front.

Ms. Ebony Elizabeth Albright
General Delivery
Main Post Office
Manhattan
New York, NY. 10012.

She sealed the package with the clear packing tape then exited the taxi. Pearl appeared relaxed and poised as she carried the package of heroin that Big Joe recently brought her, and another package, into the Post Office. A few minutes later she was back in the cab. "Okay Joe, take me to the airport."

Pearl leaned into the window and spoke quietly to Joe. "I'll be back in a few weeks, but I gotta get off this island for awhile." She leaned farther in and kissed him on the cheek.

"You know what, lil gal?"

"What?"

"I still ain got me none dat good stuff you sittin on." His huge face lit with a wide white smile.

Pearl grinned, "I never mix business with pleasure Joe and besides that," she reached in and pulled his ear, "you got more pussy chasing you than a fish truck." She loved his loud laugh, and chuckled as she walked toward the terminal carrying only one small carry-on bag. She never planned to return and wanted no delays looking for suitcases, plus with only one bag she knew that the Custom Agents in West Palm Beach would process her through quickly.

She was correct, and by afternoon she was boarding a flight for JFK International Airport in New York City.

A new phase of Pearl's nightmare was about to begin. New demons would soon arrive to assist her, as had the others, but these demons had ulterior motives. They planned to take total control of The Black Widowmaker.

28

HI TECH—TOO LATE

Yan picked up the phone the next day and listened a moment before saying, "Yeah Stan, what's up?" He listened silently for a few minutes. "Man, that's fast work, buddy. So now we know that she killed that Jamaican plus some guys and a girl here on New Providence Island." He listened a moment then answered, "I think these Bahamians will be happy to let Miami prosecute her on that killing, and hope all the publicity about the killings here will not reach enough tourists to matter." He listened to his friend again before saying, "I'll hang around the beach bar here at the hotel till I see her, then call you n' keep an eye on her till one o' your guys gets over here to arrest her."

He hung up the phone and headed for the beach. Yan climbed onto a free stool and ordered a Mt. Gay on ice from the new bartender, which he hadn't noticed until he sat down. "Tito off today?" Yan inquired as he scanned the group of people on the beach and in the chairs; hoping to spot the beautiful Black Widowmaker.

"No mon," the small, grocery-bag-colored man said with a smile, "he be comin bye n' bye to workin de evenintime shiff." Yan sipped as he continued his search for the girl.

29

CHECKING OUT—CHECKING IN

Pearl checked into a hotel in downtown Manhattan, then went immediately to the bank where her numbered account had been opened. After giving her account number and password, she signed the change-of-address card so her weekly allowance from German industrialist Hermann Handich would be forwarded to the hotel, until she decided where she would live. Her signature went through the identity process with no problem and she left feeling good.

The following day Pearl went to the post Office to retrieve her package of heroin and the one-hundred-and-twenty-thousand dollars she had also mailed to herself from Nassau. She mailed them both without Big Joe or anyone knowing what was in the packages inside her shopping bag the day she went to the Nassau Post Office. She felt good when she returned to the hotel and heard the clerk say, "Good afternoon Mrs. Craig."

Pearl wanted to use a name she would easily remember without thinking about it, so she checked in as Mrs. Tito Craig. She had spoken a few times to the beach bartender at the Old Colonial Hotel in Nassau, so his name would be an easy one to memorize until she moved.

Men would soon begin showing up in the New York City area with their throat cut, and their penis protruding from between pale swollen lips. The large package of powder she paid the Obeah Voodoo man five thousand dollars for would last through a list of many bodies.

30

TOUGHEST GAME IN TOWN

Yan arrived at the hotel an hour before Tito was due to begin his evening shift in the beachside bar. He took a quick shower then had dinner in the hotel dining room. Tito was just relieving the other bartender when Yan arrived.

"Whacha drinking tonight, mon?" Tito had his standard tip-harvesting smile spread across his face. Before Yan could ask about the beautiful black girl, Tito spoke while pouring Yan's Mt. Gay over the ice. "Mon, I hope you ain come special juss to see dat gorgeous little chunk of Yankee coal, cause she gone."

"Gone?" Yan almost shouted.

"Yes mon, I at the airport waiting on my frien, an she fly away."

"Son-of-a-bitch," Yan said slowly, "that gal's got some kinda survival ESP or something." He sipped his rum a moment, before asking Tito, "Did you ever get her name?"

"No mon, she ver, ver shy bout tellin any ting bout she ownself. I juss call her Missy." He turned to the calls from other customers, leaving Yan to think about her leaving so suddenly.

Shit, maybe she's been planning to leave for a long time. No! Too goddamn much coincidence. She slices that lesbo's throat then bores a hole in my brain with those beautiful cobra eyes, and suddenly she's on a plane outa here. He sipped the rum and thought about what Polo told him earlier. *That gal looked just like a man except there wasn't a dick. Short hair, almost like a crew cut and absolutely no tits at all.* Yan kept seeing that small, dark, orange hourglass on the girl's bathing suit. *She musta read the paper and liked the*

Black Widowmaker bit. Gives a Jamaican pimp a tonsillectomy from the outside, then a sex change operation on some married guys cheating on their wives, and winds up half decapitating a lesbian before hauling her cute little black ass outa here. He downed the rum and pointed at his glass for another as he pursed his lips in deep concentration. *She thought that gal was a dude. That's gotta be it. The gal had on a tanktop but her bottom half was naked. She musta dropped her drawers then turned toward this vicious little weenie whacker who flipped out when there wasn't a Kielbasa hangin' there for her to slice off. Bingo! One swipe and the lesbo's on her way to the beaver pie palace in the sky.*

He sipped on the rum as he rolled everything over in his head. Yan tossed off the last of his drink and lay a twenty on the bar in front of Tito. "Gonna catch an early plane outa here, so I'll stop in n' say hi next trip." He went through the lobby and was pleased to see a cab sitting empty in front of the hotel. "You know where that old barge that burned a few years ago used to sit? The one that sold the best damn fried chicken in the world?"

"Yes mon, sure do."

"How about Inspector McGuire's houseboat?"

"I knows right where dat boat sittin, mon."

"Okay, good," Yan said, "that's exactly where I'm heading."

Twenty minutes later Yan was walking down the gangplank toward Polo's huge houseboat. Two minutes after Big Joe dropped Yan off at Polo's he was on his cell-phone.

"Very good Joe." The man on the other end of the phone was a swarthy, middle-aged man in an office on Paradise Island. "I'll have a couple of my men take a ride over there and have a talk with that nosy bastard." Before hanging up, the man said, "Joe."

"Yessir, Mister D'Angelo."

"Next time you're here, stop at the cashier's cage and tell 'em there's an envelope with your name on it that you wanna pick up."

"Yessir," Joe said, "tank you ver much, sir."

"My pleasure Joe. I appreciate you keeping me informed about everything going on out there in your side of the world."

"Hey man," Yan said as he looked around inside Polo's boat, "You really made a lotta changes since I was here last."

"He hell," boomed a voice from the second floor. The tall, slender, middle-aged Chinese woman came walking down the wide spiral staircase smiling. "Well, Polo did carry some of the supplies in here for me to re-decorate this place with."

Yan turned and looked up as Elaine McGuire came down the stairs. "Damn Elaine, why is it we keep getting older," he motioned toward his squat, black friend with a nod of his head, "and you just keep getting more gorgeous?"

"You want the truth or you want me to bullshit you?"

"You wouldn't even have a clue where to start bullshitting someone, gal." Yan grinned as she approached.

"You learned too damned much about me during that year me n' Polo spent in Miami." She put her slender arms around Yan's six-foot-tall mass of muscle and hugged him hard. "Always great to see you, Yan."

"So what's the secret of your perennial, youthful appearance?"

She moved to Polo and wrapped her arm around his ample waist, nodding toward him. "He spoils me."

Two Heinekens later Polo said, "So you don't think this gal that they're calling The Black Widowmaker had anything to do with killing that rich black guy over in Freeport huh?"

"Nope!" Yan said, "His wife gave me all the info she had, and he never came to Nassau. I checked with the airport and they confirmed it."

"Wonder where she's heading?" Polo commented more to himself than to Yan.

Yan finished his can of beer then stood. "Hard telling, since none of us even knows her real name, but I hope there are some on-the-ball cops wherever it is, because I got a hunch she's a very sick puppy and there's gonna be a buncha dickless dead guys poppin' up where ever it is."

"You said she was probably abused," Elaine said.

Yan shook his head, "Yeah, probably got snatched or som'n and forced into this bad ass Jamaican's ring of hookers."

"At least," Elaine said, "she evened the score with that one."

"That's probably when it all started," Yan said, "and she might keep getting even till she thinks she's evened the score or gets killed."

"Or dies of old age," Elaine offered, "because she sounds like a pretty cool little gal."

Polo stood when he realized his friend was leaving. "Maybe she'll figure out a way t'keep 'em alive and start a Eunuch Work Force somewhere." They all chuckled and Yan headed up the gangplank. He stopped at the top and waved.

"Don't stay away so long next time," Polo said.

"I'll run over in my boat next time," Yan said and waved over his shoulder, then headed toward a small bar he stopped in the last time he visited Polo and Elaine. *Four or five blocks walking'll perk me up,* he thought. It was two long Nassau blocks through a section of businesses that had closed two hours earlier. He'd eventually come out on the busy street where bars and a couple of restaurants would be going till the wee hours. His senses came alert the moment the car passed him and parked a half block ahead. The odd belt buckle slipped out from beneath the leather belt as soon as Yan pressed the small latch button releasing it. His fingers were in the four holes and it was now a set of custom built brass knuckles, designed by Yan to perfectly fit his hand. The brass butt-piece rested snugly against his palm as he slowed his pace.

A young black man exited the driver's side, then a short, thick, white boy got out of the passenger's side. *Good! Only two of 'em*, Yan thought as he approached. Before they were within range, the black boy said, "Why the fuck you talkin all dis shit bout a buncha murders, mon? You some kinda goddom Dragnet, or som'n?" Yan could tell by the white boy's body language that he was reluctant to even be where he was. The moment the distance gauge in his head signaled NOW, Yan hit the white boy right on the left temple the moment he turned slightly to look at his black friend. He fell like a bag of sand. Before the black boy's mind processed the information, and sent a warning signal to his brain, he felt the brass knuckled shattering his jaw. Another blow broke his jaw and a few bones in his face, and he too he fell like a bag of sand.

Yan glanced at the white boy and saw no movement so he bent over the black boy and grabbed his shirt. Two more blows in the face completed the need for three-hours of surgery before beginning the six months of recuperation prior to resuming his career in crime. He was crying so loud, that Yan thought sure someone would come running, or worse yet call the cops. He had to get to Freeport the next day and get back on his case. "Shut the fuck up," he sneered. When the boy continued crying he hit him again in the face. "Hey shithead, I keep doing this until you shut up and listen."

A bloody mumbling indicated he would stop, so Yan said very clearly, "Your boss cost you both surgery for nothing. That little bitch had nothing to do with the case I'm on, and I could care less how many guys she whacks." Yan hit him one good blow on the forehead, to put him out until they were found awhile later. "That's only a little of what you two bastards woulda done to me." He turned when he heard the white boy moaning. *I'll be damned, I thought sure I'd killed that one.* He shook his head as he continued toward the bar, *Getting old I guess.*

The following day, Inspector Polo McGuire read the report of the beating near his boat. He recognized the names as two young men working for the people on Paradise Island. The black was a local punk who had been in trouble all of his eighteen years. The other was a white Bahamian from Grand Bahama Island who was also eighteen and already had an arrest record. He kept going back over the photographs of their condition when admitted to the hospital. He smiled when he read the descriptions of the possible weapon used. *Yan ole buddy, those brass knucks still leave your signature on a body.*

Rick Magers

Polo picked up the ringing phone from his desk. "Yessir, I asked them to have you call me because I've got good news. I now have evidence that our little Black Widowmaker was from Miami. She left our island and probably won't be back." He listened to the Chief Inspector for five minutes then answered, "Thank you very much sir. I'm happy it came now to help with your election campaign, and I'll have everything you need in your office before I leave."

Now that's my kinda bonus, he thought, *Elaine's gonna love two free weeks in Jamaica at the Captain's mountain cottage.* Polo took a few moments and leaned back with his fingers folded behind his head as he thought about Montego Bay. *Thanks Yan,* he sat back up to begin organizing the necessary papers for his commander. *And thank you captain,* he thought, and then got busy so he could get home to tell Elaine.

Back on Grand Bahama Island, Yan climbed into the Mustang and headed for the Island Princess Hotel and Casino to see if Danny was around. He glanced at his watch and was surprised to see both hands sticking straight up. "Damn! Noon already," he said aloud, "time flies when you're havin' fun." He was also surprised to see the parking lot packed with so many cars, as early as it was. He pulled to the rear of the lot and parked beneath the big rubber tree, and before he was even out of the driver's seat he saw Elvis coming toward him.

"Hey mon, you juss gittin bock from de big city island?"

"Airplane motors're still warm," Yan said, "everything going okay with you?"

"Yes mon, but ain been so good for Danny. Some big fella bout broken he dom neck."

"No shit man, what the hell was that about, he been slippin' through the guy's window for a little romp with his wife'r som'n?"

"I dunno mon, he ain say shit bout dat deal."

"He workin' today?"

"Oh yes mon, he a funny lookin little fella wit dat ting on he neck, but dey too dom many touriss peoples here dis week-end, f'him to be layin roun on de beach."

"Week-end," Yan said, "what day is it?"

"Dis Saturday, mon." A big grin spread across the tall, thin man's face. "Whachew do mon, git all hung up in one dem foncy Nassau gal an nobody spray water on you?"

"Not hardly," Yan replied, "the only one that interested me was a cut above all the others, but her price was more'n I figured I could handle, so I let her get away."

Yan started walking toward the casino when Elvis's squeaky voice stopped him. "Dem two young fella what you smack up pretty good ain been bock round here atol, mon."

"Good, I hope it stays that way." Yan waved over his shoulder and continued toward the entrance. He spotted Danny at the small bar near the entrance to the dining room the minute he entered. Danny saw him coming and had a cold Beck's on the bar when he sat down. "You wrestling for a little extra dough these days?" Yan's grin was met with a scowl.

"I wish. This was a little message sent by DeMarco over at the big casino where that rich dude's body was found." He glanced around then said quietly, "That red headed goon of his coulda broke my neck if he wanted to, but he said he was just warning me to stop sticking my nose where it wasn't wanted."

Yan felt the blood that was running through his body, begin to heat up. "This's because of the info you were trying to get for me?"

"Yeah mon," the diminutive bartender said quietly after another furtive glance around, "there's som'n fishy about this deal you're working on, and it ain't yesterday's snapper."

Yan was almost speaking through clenched teeth when he said, "I'm really sorry I got you involved in this shit, Danny."

"Mon," Danny said, "I'm always involved in whatever the hell's going on around here, but I got a hunch that this's a little bigger'n either of us know." He casually looked over Yan's shoulders and in both directions before picking up the bar towel to begin wiping near Yan. "I got a buddy at the morgue so I ask him to stop by for a few free ones. When nobody was here at the bar I asked him about that rich stiff he worked on awhile back." He continued wiping as he kept an eye out for any strange ears listening. "The guy had a hole behind his right ear, and when my guy's boss went in there he found a twenty-two hollowpoint slug." He just kept wiping but stared at Yan intently, "Or what was left of it."

Yan sipped the beer as his brain digested this recent and unexpected news. He had let himself accept the thought that the guy was with some girl and had a heart attack or stroke. *Bet that rich black fucker was fronting the dough for these casino guys, then came over here n' got outa line with 'em.* He drained the bottle and stood up. "I'm gonna run back to Harry's and hope Sherylee's got som'n good cooking for tonight. He opened his wallet and pulled five one-hundred-dollar-bills from it and gathered them together. "Thanks Danny," Yan said, "watch your back, pal."

Danny slipped the bills into his pocket and continued wiping the bar as he watched Yan walk toward the door.

As soon as Yan left Freeport he noticed the black Cutlass behind him about a half-mile back. He shot ahead of the guy then turned left at a bar he was familiar with and pulled into the parking area behind. He quickly returned to the front then stepped inside, and watched the car go on past toward the west. *I'm getting spooky I guess. Probably just someone going to West End.* He bought a six-pack of Heineken and returned to the Mustang. After he was inside the car Yan slipped the brass knuckles on and snapped the belt in place where they were removed. He reached beneath the seat and brought out the heavy slapjack. Yan lifted his buttock up enough to slip the deadly, round chunk of leather-bound lead into his left rear pocket with the knob-end handle sticking out. *Better safe that sore*, he thought then pulled back out on the road, heading west toward Harry's American Bar.

Two miles later he saw the black Cutlass pull from a side road and get behind him again. He was familiar with the highway between West End and Freeport, because of the many trips he and his Miami PD fishing buddies made a few years earlier.

He studied the car and determined that there was only one person in it, so he made a turn onto a dirt road that ended at a bay, too shallow for anyone to be fishing on from shore. *Might as well get this shit settled, so I don't hafta be sitting around wondering about it.* He stopped the car, quickly got out, and was leaning on the door with his arms folded against his chest, when a redheaded man got out of the black Cutlass and approached.

When he was only a couple of feet away from Yan he snarled, "You're a smart mother-fucker aincha." It was to be the last words he would ever say, with the exception of a few moans. Yan's right fist full of brass hit the man on the left jaw and the sound of shattering bones could probably have been heard a good distance away if anyone had been nearby. The two men were alone on the small road, so no one saw the left hand with the slapjack move from the rear of Yan's body and end against the other man's head with a sickening thud. A grunt came from his mouth as he began falling to the ground—a journey that was hastened by another two blows. The first was the brass knuckles coming up as the man's head was going down. The second was another thud as the slapjack landed against the back of his head. The redhead was still moving as Yan removed the brass from his hand, and then replaced the slapjack. He glanced around to be certain he was not being watched, then lowered himself far enough to grasp the man's head and give it a quick snapping twist. The breaking neck sounded like a dry stick being broken over a knee. He dragged the dead man's bulky body to the rear of the Cutlass then got the keys from the ignition. Even in the great shape he was in, it was still a struggle to get the guy's body in the trunk. He slammed the lid, then wiped his prints from everything, and tossed the keys on the seat before getting back in the Mustang.

Yan drove the short distance back to the same bar and went in. He ordered a Mt. Gay and ice then handed the bartender a twenty-dollar-bill. "Will this be enough to use your phone to call my buddy back in Freeport?"

"Yes mon, dat be zackly de correck amount. He pointed to the end of the bar, "I bringin dat ting to you dere."

Yan took his glass and climbed up on the end barstool. "Thanks," he said when the old man placed the ancient black dial phone on the bar in front of him, then returned to his television game show. "Operator can you connect me to that big casino across from the Bahama Princess?"

"Juss a minute an I do dat."

When a voice was on the other end Yan said, "I got an important message for Mister DeMarco."

"One moment please and I'll connect you."

The voice said, "This's DeMarco, who's this?"

"A guy you better quit fuckin' with pal. You also better send another goon right away to get that damn Cutlass off of Chiggerdunes Road. It's a coupla miles outa town toward West End and if you don't get someone out there soon, that red headed pussy you sent's gonna start stinking. And pal, if you fuck with Danny or anyone else tied t'me you'll wind up in a goddamn trunk too." He hung up and drained the rum. "Thanks a lot pop," he smiled at the old man, "I'll see you next trip over." The old man was trying desperately to decipher the words on the board as Vanna White put a T in one of the spaces, so he just gave Yan a little wave.

That night after dinner, Yan brought Harry up to date on everything; except the redheaded guy in the trunk. "I wanna get back to Miami and see what I can find out about this Broadsword murder here in Freeport, before I get in touch with his wife."

"Leavin' early?" Harry asked.

"Yeah, I'm always up before the sun, so might as well get moving. Am I all paid up or do I still owe you for anything?"

"Nope, fuel was all there was. The drinks're on us this time."

"But," Sherylee said, "everything's gonna be double if you wait so damn long to get back over here."

"Going back through Bimini?" Harry asked.

"Nope, I wanna stop in Riviera Beach to haul the boat out and get her bottom painted. I don't want anything to do with those thieves in Miami. I also wanna go out n' talk to Ryco Marine; Rybovich's old place, to see how much it'll cost me to get the bottom covered with epoxy fiberglass."

"You'll just take a leisure cruise on the Intercoastal all the way to Miami then, huh?"

"Yeah," Yan grinned, "plus I know a coupla pretty nice joints along the way where a guy might pick up som'n worth spending a little time with."

Rick Magers

"Yeah," Sherylee smiled, "and a few months of penicillin shots to get rid of it."

"Jesus Sherylee," Yan said, "you'd make a guys wet dreams turn to thunderstorms."

Yan sat on the flying bridge and adjusted the engines until the boat was effortlessly remaining on top of the slight chop, at twenty miles an hour. *Man-oh-man, this's as good as it gets.* The twin 440 Chryslers ran perfect all the way across the Gulfstream's sixty-mile span between West End and the Palm Beach Inlet. Long before noon he was entering the inlet and circling Peanut Island, the Coast Guard Station in Riviera Beach. He tied the Huckins to the end of the main pier and walked toward the office of Florida Marine.

"I'd rather do my own work," Yan told the counter man filling out the work form. "I'll give you five-hundred-dollars now and we'll settle up when I leave, okay?"

"Great," the young man replied and turned the form around for Yan to sign. "Just show the guy in parts this when you get supplies," he motioned toward the building next to where they were standing, "right over there." He picked up the ringing phone as Yan headed next door.

"Can you have that stuff brought to the boat when they get around to taking her outa the water?"

"That's her coming out now, isn't it?" The old man pointed toward the yard.

"Sure's hell is," Yan said, "wonder what took 'em so damn long to get to it?"

"We've got a new yard boss that knows what he's doing, and if those bozo's don't shit n' git it, they're lookin' for a job the next day." He showed Yan his Halloween pumpkin grin as he shoved the material order to him for his signature. "This stuff'll be there when you're ready t'go to work on her." He tore Yan's copy off and handed it to him then returned to the back room to continue putting up stock.

"Helluva nice Huckins y'got here," the yard foreman said, "the bottom looks in good shape. Is painting it all you plan to do?"

"I don't think she'll need any hull work," Yan answered, "but how about taking those props off and have 'em checked."

"No problem, she vibrating?"

"Just a little at twenty-two-hundred, but when I run her on up to three thousand she smoothes right out so I don't think it's much."

"Okay, I'll get 'em off m'self as soon as we get her blocked up. All they oughta need is balancing and we've got a damn good man doing it now. I'll check your cutlass bearings and stuffing box too while I'm at it."

"Great," Yan said, "while you're getting her set up I'm gonna get som'n to eat. I'm starved, is that Dunkin' Donuts still up the road?"

"Damn sure is and better'n ever, 'cause my old lady's the manager now. See that old Ford pickup right there?" The man pointed at an old truck parked nearby. "The keys're in it. Run on up there n' tell Margie I want her t'send me some lunch back, cause we've got a big one coming in soon and I can't get away."

"Thanks! Yan Brodjevinski, what's yours?"

"Pete Brannigan."

"Okay Pete, see you in awhile." Yan was impressed by the way the man issued orders to his crew in the same manner that Yan would want to be treated if he worked there.

31

THE BIG APPLE

Pearl was very satisfied with the hotel that the airline steward recommended. "The Hambreckt Hotel in Manhattan is new and very nice," he said, "and it's much cheaper that most of the others; especially if you plan to be there awhile."

She used the same story on the desk clerk. "My bags were stolen as I was using the ladies room in the West Palm Beach airport, so I'll be shopping tomorrow for an all new wardrobe." She smiled as she handed him ten, five-hundred-dollar-bills. "I've worn most of them at least once anyway, so it's time to go shopping. This will take care of the moment and I'll decide soon how long I'll be staying."

"I hope you will be staying here with us for a long time Mrs. Craig." The balding robot behind the counter spoke like HAL from: 2001 A Space Odyssey."

Pearl's smile was the one practiced many times before the mirror, and it seldom failed to work it's magic on men—even male robots. "I hope so too; I've been looking so forward to seeing New York."

Before Yan made it to Miami on his Intercostal Waterway trip from Riviera Beach, Pearl had already emptied her net and found a French millionaire inside. It was a very good catch, because the aging man was on the final laps of a long race, and was thrilled to have the beautiful young black girl for a companion. Mrs. Craig, the young widow, was content allowing him to indulge the few fantasies he still enjoyed; in exchange for the private cottage that he set her up in on the hotel grounds, and the new wardrobe that he insisted she have, which complimented the fortune in jeweled paraphernalia he would shower her with during the seven months he had left to live—in delirious sexual splendor.

A short time after Yan had the Huckins moored again to his buoy at Dinner Key, the New York Police Department had already found a man propped up in an alley with very little blood left inside. It was spread out beneath him as his sightless eyes stared with milky horror. His severed penis hung from his mouth like a stubby swollen tongue.

Because of a newspaper account of this first of many identical murders, and a retired Miami cop reading it and then calling them, many NYPD cops would soon be referring to the 'perp' as THE BLACK WIDOWMAKER; even though many of the victims had never been married. Pearl was paying back the men who had used her one-by-one as she located them—she thought. Her demons helped by pointing out the men who had abused her so horribly as a young girl. *There's another one. Remember the time he bit your thighs inside so bad you could hardly walk. He's the one who ripped mouthfuls of hair from between your legs then laughed as you cried. He shoved his lit cigarette inside you when he was finished and laughed harder as you ran to the bathroom. He was the worst of them all Pearl, so let's make him wish he had never been born.* "Yes," she quietly answered her demon. "He's also the man who shoved the neck of a champagne bottle in my ass so hard, that I had to go to a doctor."

A short time after settling into her cottage, Pearl and her demon followed a man into the alley. She removed the pint of MD 20/20 from her purse. It was laced with the powder the old Obeah Voodoo man had made for her before she departed Nassau. He was only too happy to share the cute little black girl's wine. He soon began wilting to the alley floor as his eyes focused on what his failing mind was sure was a demon standing above him with a straight razor in its hand. He couldn't even blink when the demon shoved something into his mouth. Pearl's first New York City victim sat like a discarded statue as his life drained from the stub where his severed penis once hung.

Pearl's second, third, fourth, fifth, sixth, seventh, and eighth victims all met similar fates. She had mastered the art of combining deserted areas—dark alleys—desperate men. It was a deadly tri-fecta with only one winner.

After the old Frenchman fell into an exhausted sleep each night, following Pearl's sexual therapy, she slipped into her all black outfit with the orange emblem, and moved across vast areas of the Big Apple. She was always careful—always cautious—always deadly. She was driving several Police

Department Chiefs crazy as her deadly escapades moved freely from one end of the city to the other. Pearl reveled each morning over coffee while reading accounts of the killer, which all news reporters were now calling THE BLACK WIDOWMAKER. She felt like a movie star; she felt good—invincible.

Her days were occupied with the French Sugar Daddy, lounging poolside, with occasional trips to the cottage for sex. When the urge to prowl the dark streets became an overwhelming series of flashbacks into her nightmare past, Pearl used the same technique each time. She applied subtle innuendoes and coy teasing to stimulate her aging companion. By nightfall, she had drained all sexual power from him, and sent the old man into a peaceful sleep, resplendent with dreams such as few men ever enjoy. He was out for the night. She was out for the night also, but with vastly different results.

A short time later she met the Reverend Jedediah Simon Peterson again—she thought.

32

SURPRISE DEVELOPMENT

Yan enjoyed a leisure cruise on the Intercostal Waterway, stopping several times for drinks and a bite to eat. Rather than press on through to Miami, which was only seventy miles away, he spent three nights at the docks of waterside restaurants. The last one was the Miami Marina, where he knew an old police buddy lived aboard a sailboat with his rottweiler. He checked in and paid for one night, then headed for the area where his friend docked. As soon as he turned onto the finger-pier, Yan spotted the dog lying stretched out like a Haitian laborer after lunch, and knew Turbo was on board the boat.

"Hey Mad Max," Yan yelled at the hundred and twenty pounds of muscle in a black fur coat. "Hey you lazy turd," he said as the dog's head lifted to see who was calling his name, "everyone's gonna know you're a pussy if ya don't jump up n' bark."

"Hell," the voice came from below deck, "everyone around here already knows he'd help 'em carry my shit to their car." The gray crew cut came up out of the passageway first, followed by a wrinkled brown face on a head bigger that his rottweiler. "Hi Yan, what brings ya here, business or pleasure?"

"Little o' both Turbo, how ya been?"

"Y'really wanna know?"

"Nah!" Yan never thought his friend; Captain Mike Turboni would survive the shooting when he first heard about it. He was glad he did, for two reasons. One: he liked the stout Italian better than any other cop he had ever worked with. Two: he knew that Turbo still had good connections in the city.

"Good! 'Cause I hate to hear an old man cryin' about all his fuckin' problems, especially when it's me doin' the crying. Wanna beer?"

"Does a Polack shit with his shorts on?"

"I just sprayed some shit down below to kill a few million roaches, so lemme get a six and we'll sit on deck." He returned coughing with a six-pack of Budweiser. Yan knew what the tin plate in his hand was for so he reached for it.

"I'll take care of Max," he said as he stepped off with the tin pie pan, and Turbo handed him one of the beers. "Slurp time ol' buddy," Yan said as he poured the beer into the pan he'd put before the dog's snout. He climbed back on the sailboat and took the beer his friend offered.

"Whacha need, Yan?"

"I'm workin' a case for a black millionaire's widow, and ain't getting anywhere with it. I figured the guy was humping something too wild for an old guy t'be riding in the first place, but looks like I was wrong about him. He got himself whacked by a pro, over in Freeport." He took a long drink before adding; "Think you can find out if the department has anything on it?"

"Broadsword?" Yan's friend said with a question mark in his voice.

Yan just looked at him a few moments then said, "That bullet in the head make you psychic?"

"No, but it sure made the Goody's Powder people happy." He tilted his can and drank as he looked at Yan. When he lowered the can he said, "Been outa the country awhile, aincha?"

"Yeah, the Bahamas."

"You don't have a client now. She was whacked about a week ago." He took another short sip then asked Yan, "Did you meet her pet gorilla?"

"The one that could have AK-47's in shoulder holsters without 'em being seen?"

"Yeah, big monster. He was with her when she got hit. Happened right at their estate after they entered and were getting outa the limo. That guy musta been som'n to see in action. He killed two of 'em and took seventeen bullets before going down. They said he was found with a full clip in his hand and one of his guns had an empty clip beside it, so he musta been trying to reload when one of 'em put one right between his eyes, point blank."

"Damn," Yan said, "sounds t'me like they were in deep with a buncha real badasses."

"The two stiffs were illegals. Downtown's pretty sure they're Cubans, but it'll be hard to authenticate that unless someone comes forward and claims the bodies. Cuban, Colombian, who can tell the difference when they're cadavers?"

"Well shit; I was just gettin' interested in this case." Yan tilted the can and drained it. "Got another one o' these for an unemployed PI?"

"Get any bread up front?" Turbo asked as he handed Yan another beer.

"Just a few bucks for expenses. I think I'm gonna start demanding more up front before I start digging."

The next morning's sun shined on Yan's back as he headed across Biscayne Bay toward Dinner Key. *Lady, you sure didn't get your money's worth, and there ain't a damn thing I can do about it, but hope that wherever you are it's not a bad place.* He began easing the throttles forward to see if the propellers were still causing the boat to vibrate. After running the matched set of 440's at different RPM's, he said aloud, "Mrs. Tamerlane, I'm putting that fifty grand to good use. Thanks!"

33

NIGHTMARE REVISITED

Pearl was trying to cut down on the amount of heroin that she was using. Unsuccessfully, but she was trying. The faces of some of her victims were occasionally compromising the vengeful feelings that she held against all men. Victim's faces would suddenly flash in her mind but they didn't match the face of those people who had hurt her during her time with D'Julliette. She was becoming confused.

The many demons that were now her constant companions came to her aid when she had doubts about her mission. *What difference does it make which men you kill? They're all alike. They'll all hurt you if you give them a chance.* So many demons had moved into her head that she found it difficult to think about anything else at times.

Her efforts to cut down on the heroin began paying off. Pearl felt better than she had in a long time and hadn't been out at night prowling the ghettos; searching for the men who had hurt her so terribly. Or any man who happened to be alone and near her.

<u>Then it happened.</u>

"Can I help you, Miss?"

Pearl was thunderstruck—glued to the floor of the Manhattan apparel shop.

The honey colored Jamaican clerk looked at the beautiful young black woman a moment. Her intense stare made him uncomfortable so he politely said, "I'll be right over there arranging shoes, if you need any help." He smiled and quickly moved to another section of the store.

Pearl's mind was locked on one thought. *Reverend Jedediah Simon Peterson. I've waited a long time for you. Thought I'd never find you again, huh?* She left the shop but only went to the café across the street, and sat outside sipping Cappuccino, while intently watching the apparel shop's door. She was waiting for The Reverend to exit.

Her patience was rewarded at noon when he came out and began walking toward the busy intersection. She placed a twenty-dollar-bill beneath her cup and began walking in the same direction along the sidewalk on her side of the street. When she saw that he was crossing to her side, she picked up her pace so she wouldn't lose sight of him.

Pearl wasn't worried about being recognized as the woman who was staring at him an hour earlier. She always carried a different colored wig and blouse in her huge shopping bag. After ordering her Cappuccino she went inside to the lady's room as a dark haired lady wearing a red silk blouse. She returned to her small curbside table as a blonde in a pale blue satin blouse.

Pearl was only a short distance behind Jedediah when he entered a small Greek restaurant. Knowing that after his lunch break he would return to the apparel shop where he worked, she swiftly headed toward it.

Her brief time in the shop earlier didn't allow her to observe the inside very thoroughly, or how many other clerks worked with The Reverend. When the young oriental girl asked if she needed help, Pearl replied, "No thank you, I'm just browsing for a gift." She smiled her very best friendly smile asking casually, "My, this is certainly a big shop to be working all alone."

"Oh no," the girl replied, "I'm only alone when the manager is having his lunch," she smiled sweetly, "then when he returns it's my turn."

Pearl smiled saying, "Bon appetite, and enjoy your hour."

"Oh! Don't I wish; no we each only take a half-hour."

"Oh dear," Pearl replied, "that's hardly enough time to dine properly."

"I know, plus we hardly ever have customers from eleven till two because everyone else is having a casual lunch, so we really could take an hour." She smiled saying, "But you know how the bosses are." The young girl shrugged her shoulders as she cocked her head slightly and screwed her mouth into a sarcastic leer.

"Well dear, I must run along." Pearl exited the shop and looked for a taxi to take her home to her apartment.

She had plans to make. *Tomorrow will be a day that I have dreamed for a long time.*

34

BOATING TO YACHTING

Yan sat silently listening as the man spoke. "Mister Leskiewicz, I own the largest and best collection of classic old Huckins Yachts in the world, and that's the only reason I'm willing to go so far to get yours. It's not only in top condition but it's also one of a very few of that model built." He leaned back in one of Yan's two new chairs and looked around the undecorated, sparsely furnished office.

Yan had been thinking about the deal that the man mentioned only briefly during his call from Jacksonville a week earlier. *This guy wants my boat bad so I might as well see how far he'll go.* "Well Mister Holbrook, here's a problem I have with the idea of trading for a sailboat. You can tell by looking around my office that I'm not living the high life like Sam Spade or Mike Hammer." He took a moment to collect his thoughts, and then looked around himself. "Sometimes I think I shoulda stayed on the force and went for thirty. Oh well, too late now so here's how I see it. There's no reason to have a sailboat without Radar, Satellite Navigation, top notch radios, autopilot and all the rest of the equipment needed to safely cruise." He paused to let his words sink in, but wisely began talking again before the man could speak. "And I ain't about to swap a comfortable boat like the one I have for a sailboat that I can't cruise on." He paused briefly before adding, "And I damn sure can't afford to install that kind of expensive equipment."

The man sat silently looking at Yan for a full minute before speaking. "Yan, I recently lost a deal for one like yours in pretty fair shape because I tried to get a better deal from the old widow who inherited it, so tell you what

I'll do." He leaned forward, resting both hands with manicured nails on the edge of the old steel desk. "My son owns Blue Water Brokerage in Jacksonville, and has plenty of good but not brand new equipment in his warehouse. Many wealthy yachtsmen replace their electronic equipment as soon as something new hits the shelves, so how about if I have that forty-four-foot fiberglass and teakwood Sea Voyager outfitted completely with good equipment?" He sat motionless and stared across the cluttered desk.

Yan's mind was racing as he weighed what he'd just heard. He'd been thinking for a long time about getting a sailboat and learning to sail, so he could cruise the Caribbean. *Better not get too damn greedy.*

Yan pursed his lips in thought as he considered his options. He knew what kind of boat a Sea Voyager was, and the photos the man brought with him looked good. Finally he leaned forward and spoke, "Tell you what Mister Holbrook, It's a deal on one condition, and that's simply that everything be working when your men deliver the sailboat. If you want the Huckins hauled just give me a call and it'll be on the ways when you get here, as long as you're willing to pay the bill. Since the sailboat's made of fiberglass I'll just use my scuba gear and inspect the hull and fittings myself."

"No need to have your boat hauled, Mister Leskiewicz because I know how well a Huckins is built. Plus," he grinned at Yan, "I inquired around Dinner Key when I arrived and learned that you recently returned from a cruise to the Bahamas. A hull in poor condition would not make that trip and still be sitting on a mooring line as your Huckins is." He stood and offered the manicured hand, which had probably never done one day's work. "Deal! I'll call the office from my mobile phone the minute I'm in my car, and the Sea Voyager will be ready to leave tomorrow."

Yan shook his hand asking, "You heading back north to Jacksonville right now?"

"Not on you life Yan, I'll visit friends I went to school with here at Miami Beach High, then accompany my crew back home aboard the Huckins."

Yan smiled, "You really do like 'em huh? Not just another investment."

As he gathered the photographs and contract he smiled, "Yes indeed, I love them. My father owned three during my young years on Key Biscayne and I learned then the difference between a fine yacht and a wooden hole in the water. I'll fax my lawyer this contract and have him fax it back to me pronto Yan, so we can wrap this deal up as soon as they arrive with the Sea Voyager." He turned with the open door in his grasp and smiled at Yan. "Congratulations on wringing that electronic equipment out of me. If you ever want a job as a yacht salesman you know where to find me." He walked to his Cadillac as Yan watched through the sign on his door.

Rick Magers

Five days after Simon Holbrook shook Yan's hand to seal the deal, the phone on Yan's desk rang. He punched the button that allowed him to listen to the incoming call, and when he heard Simon's voice he punched the button that he painted red, so he would stop accidentally pushing the one that disconnected the call. "Yan here, hi Simon."

35

FLAWED REVENGE

The following day, Pearl sat at the same small table in front of the tiny café across from the apparel shop in Manhattan. The same waitress served her, and recognize the young African American girl, who was built like a small model; dressed in the very latest fashion and wearing an expensive blonde wig. She was the one who gave her the generous tip the previous day. The dumpy waitress remembered details like clothing.

The following day an older lady was now seated at the same table, sipping plain coffee like a peasant. She was wearing clothes that hung on her like something a stingy aunt would send as a gift rather than throw away. She wore cheap plastic frame glasses beneath a head of kinky black hair, which wasn't done in cornrows or anything. It was simply there, nothing to look at—or remember.

Pearl's eyes narrowed when she spotted Reverend Jedediah Simon Peterson returning from his lunch break. Pearl's patience was being rewarded. She had paid for the coffee when the waitress delivered it, so she put a dime beside her saucer and watched the door across the street—and waited.

No customer's had entered since she arrived at the café, and as soon as the young female clerk opened the door to leave for lunch, Pearl was up and heading across the street. When she entered the store it was with a plan; one similar to those used to deal with men who had hurt her. She went directly toward the rear of the store, because she knew that The Reverend would follow.

He arrived at the revolving display of jackets a split second behind Pearl. He began to speak, "Can I help y…

The razor flashed across his throat so fast that he stood looking at Pearl for a moment before blood gushed from the wound. Pearl had learned from past mistakes, so she leaped back as soon as her razor went across his throat, avoiding the splatter of his blood.

As the clerk lay dying, she quickly changed blouses and stuffed the one she'd been wearing into her huge shopping bag. She adjusted the dark red, three-thousand-dollar, human-hair wig, pulled on the satin jacket that matched the slacks that were beneath the removed skirt, pulled down the slack's legs, put on the expensive sunglasses and departed the store. Pearl was out in less than five minutes after entering.

She casually walked two blocks before flagging a taxi, and then directed him to take her to Coney Island—miles from where she lived. She paid and tipped him generously, then headed toward the shops. Pearl took the cup of coffee from the McDonald's clerk and went to the ladies room. She was alone, so she dumped the coffee down the sink and tossed the cup in the trash bin. Inside the stall she swiftly changed wigs, slacks, blouse, and pulled on a light windbreaker from her bag. She opened the black garbage bag she brought and stuffed the wig and clothes inside and rolled the air out before tying a knot tightly to discourage someone from peering into it. After checking herself thoroughly, she exited the stall and shoved the bag into the trash bin. Pearl then washed her hands and removed several paper towels to place on top of the garbage bag so it wouldn't be noticed.

The black lady departing by the side door of the McDonald's didn't resemble the one that had just entered by the front door. This young girl was wearing a very stylish; silver streaked wig, expensive designer jeans and matching blouse. On her feet were designer deck shoes made from soft Llama hide. The diamond engagement ring, and gold wedding band on her finger would prevent any curious police officer from considering her as a possible prostitute.

Pearl walked casually for three blocks then flagged a taxi to take her back to Manhattan and drop her a few blocks from a movie theater. She had been hearing about a movie titled Chicago so she bought a ticket and watched the film, as any possibility of the killer's identity sunk to the bottom of New York City's bowl of human gumbo.

The following morning Pearl sat at her table, sipping coffee and reading the paper. When she located the story about The Black Widowmaker striking again, she was perplexed. Her eyes went from the picture of the victim to the text below. Her eyes went back and forth while reading the text and studying the photo. *That wasn't the Reverend.*

She read it again.

Lesley Dillman, the manager at Delonge's Fine Apparel was found dead by his clerk when she returned from a brief lunch. She stated that she was never gone more than a half-hour. The young girl became hysterical and had to be sedated before being transported to the hospital. Police hope to learn more after she feels better. Police Captain DeCapotto stated there is evidence that this is a killing by the notorious Black Widowmaker, because a witness saw a black lady leaving the store. Mr. Dillman was born in Yonkers and leaves a wife and three children. Mrs. Dillman will become the latest widow to be created by The Black Widowmaker, if Captain DeCapotto is correct.

Pearl's eyes went back to the photograph of the man whose throat she had cut. *He doesn't even look like the Reverend. Simon was tall and thin and this man is short. Simon was the color of honey and this man is almost as black as I am.* She threw the paper to the floor and let her head fall back against the seat's backrest. *My God, will I never escape this nightmare?* She sat up and opened her eyes. "I've gotta get the hell outa this city before I'm caught, and spend the rest of my life being handled by prison guards worst than D'Julliette.

Later that same day she called the Tudor Hotel on Miami Beach and inquired about a suite. When she was satisfied that the price was reasonable, she said that she would have her bank wire a draft for three months. Pearl then called her bank and recited the code number and password so that they could transact the payment. She also had them forward her weekly six-thousand-dollars to their branch in downtown Miami Florida.

A call to the airport assured her that a ticket to Miami would be waiting at the United Airline desk at JFK Airport. Pearl called the desk and informed them that her mother was dying, and that she was leaving immediately for Los Angeles and requested a bellboy to please come to her apartment and assist her.

By the time he arrived, she already had everything that she intended to take with her packed. She handed him a one-hundred-dollar-bill saying, "I do not ever leave an apartment cluttered like this. There are many things here that I no longer use, so you may have everything in here if you will see to it that nothing of mine is left behind, then straighten up this place a bit." She smiled at the young man, knowing that he would take everything, "Deal?"

He smiled, eagerly saying, "Yes ma'am."

Four hours later, Pearl E. White was at thirty-thousand-feet and heading due south toward Miami—and Yan Brodjevinski. Her life was about to start getting better—for a while.

Rick Magers

36

GAS TO SAILS

Yan and Simon Holbrook went to the Courthouse and completed the transfer with no problems, since each was the owner of their yacht, and had clear titles to each. Yan stood with Murphy O'Brien and watched as the Huckins weaved its way slowly through the moored yachts. He smiled when they were finally beyond the boats and was able to start giving the twin 440's a little more throttle. As Simon's captain increased the throttles, she raised in the water to begin running on its speedboat style, hard chine hull. Yan said to his friend, without taking his eyes from his beloved Huckins, "Ain't another boat on earth that big that runs as majestically as a Huckins."

"Yer right Yan, but I do believe you just took one helluva leap up the yachting ladder." He took the few steps to the dock and walked slowly along the length of the Sea Voyager. "This is one damn fine sailboat, Yan."

The Huckins was only a spot in the distance with white spray flying as it cut through the light chop on the water of South Biscayne Bay. Yan turned and walked to his new yacht. "I've been thinking a long time about trading for a sailboat but I never thought I could get an even trade for one like this." He turned a grin to Murphy, "I was leery as hell till the guy at the courthouse looked the paperwork over and said that everything was on the up n' up."

"Know whacha mean; almost too damn good t'be true." Murphy walked to the stern and looked at the name. "Y'ain't gonna leave a name like Sweet Suzie on the damn thing, are ya?"

"Ha, y'know where that name came from?"

"Some rich shit's little bimbo I reckon."

"Nope, Simon said that he got it from a guy that sued the Jacksonville Port Authority for running over him and his boat with one of their tugboats."

"Ha! Hot damn, I love a story with a happy ending. If one of these Yankee hemorrhoids so much's bumps me with one o' their goddamn Cadillac's I'll be changin' the name o' me houseboat to Sweet Sue's Gone Fishin'."

"I hope it happens Murph, and I'll turn 'em down if they try to hire me to do a background check on you."

"Oh! Shit no Yan, take the job so you can doctor the son-of-a-bitch up. If they get a real background check on me I'll be lucky if I don't hafta give 'em my houseboat."

"Okay, deal. I gotta get to work now so I can get the hell away from this millionaire's dock and back out on my mooring buoy."

"Got much t'do?"

"Nah, just a few minor changes. Oughta be able to get back out there by the weekend."

"Okay, I gotta get ready to go to work. You have the key to the shop, doncha?"

"Yeah and I'll be using the band saw and table saw later on today. I'm sure glad they let me use 'em, even if they are yours. That fat little turd in the office can be a prick when he wants to, and he usually wants to."

"Don't I know. He's gonna be a sorry little mole if I find a better deal up at the Miami Marina, 'cause I'm gonna show him a few things that the streets of New York City taught me before I leave."

Yan laughed and stepped aboard his new yacht as Murphy lumbered toward his houseboat.

Three days later, Yan had the drawer beneath the forward starboard bunk modified with a false bottom, with the Uzi and clips strapped securely in place. The teakwood steering cockpit had the perfect place to hide his spare Sphinx and clips, so by Friday he was clamping the long-shaft Seagull outboard motor to the bracket on the stern. Murphy was standing with his long boathook to prevent the dingy from bumping the sailboat as Yan maneuvered away from the dock. He stood watching as his friend headed toward his mooring buoy.

37

FIRST CONFRONTATION

Pearl sat watching the coastline of Florida as the airliner cut through the clear air of Florida, descending toward Miami. A short time earlier she had gone into the toilet and shot up a small fix of heroin to calm her jittery nerves. She was now relaxed but was having a mixed variety of thoughts. *How could I have thought that dark man was the Reverend? Could I be going insane? Were some of those other men not who I thought they were? What will the rest of my life be like if the police catch me? Could a doctor help me get off of this damn heroin? Would he turn me in to the police? Is there anyone who can help me? Does anyone on this earth care about me?* Her mind remained blank as she stared out of her window. Small tears formed in her eyes as she thought, *No! I'm all alone in this terrible world.*

Pearl had enough heroin taped to her thighs to last until the package she had mailed to the Tudor Hotel arrived. She was mentally and physically exhausted, so she asked the taxicab driver to take her directly to the hotel. *I'll shop for clothes and the things I'll need tomorrow. All I want right now is a hot bath to sit in for an hour.*

At the desk, she pulled her most charming and alluring mask down over her still perplexed face, as she spoke to the middle aged Cuban clerk. "This is the third time that my luggage has been lost by that same airline." She shook her head from side-to-side slowly and smiled,

"I don't believe in lawsuits for trivial matters but I certainly would like to give some big shot in their office a piece of my mind." She signed the form and took the key from the man who found it impossible to keep his eyes from her ample breasts. "I'm expecting a package soon, would you please let me know when it arrives?"

In a heavy Hispanic accent he answered, "Certainly Mrs. Craig." The beautiful young woman in the most expensive looking wig he'd ever seen, smiled and followed the bellboy to her suite. His eyes were locked to her ass, moving with the rhythm of her legs. The Cuban's thoughts were filled with lust, *I would give a week's salary to spend a night with that.* He was very fortunate that it would never happen, and had it; he would have paid far more than a week's pay.

A week later, Pearl was relaxed. Her heroin had arrived on time and she was happy with her new wardrobe. She was bored with the aging clientele of the hotel that she'd been having brief conversations with. She decided to take a taxi to Miami and see if Flagler Street had changed much since she was last there.

She was about to meet someone who she had been close enough to touch several times during her stay in the Bahamas, but had never spoken a word to him. She would know exactly who he was the minute she saw him—and she also knew that he was aware of exactly who she was.

Pearl E. White's life would soon change dramatically.

38

ENCOUNTER—DE JA VU

Yan only had three small investigative jobs during the first month after trading his Huckins cruiser for the Sea Voyager sailboat. He occupied his time by going over every inch of the boat to familiarize himself with it, prior to going out under sail for the first time. After the first divorce job was completed and he was paid, he was hanging his new sign in the window of his office when Murphy stopped the Jeep. "Mornin' Yan, didja catch that guy dippin' his noodle in some new sauce for that cute little client?"

Yan finished locking the door and walked over. "Sure's hell did, and also paid for the camera lens I had t'get to snap the pictures for her, to convince him not to let it go to court." He grinned as he rested his hand on the roll bar behind Murphy's seat, "I could sell those pictures to Hustler Magazine."

"Whaja do, break in on 'em and just start clicking?"

"Shit no! The dumb asshole took her down in the Keys to what he thought was a deserted beach way down in Lower Matecumbe."

"Did they see you?"

"Nope! That new two-thousand-dollar lens pulled 'em in so close I could almost smell the roses." He grinned again.

Murphy laughed saying, "That's his name ain't it?"

"Yep! Merrill Theodor Buchett." Yan chuckled, "little gal's got a great sense of humor. She refers to his as M T Bucket."

Murphy grinned, "Dunno 'bout before, but I betcha the goddamn bucket's more MT now that when he first jumped her." He leaned to the side to read the sign Yan had just hung on the inside of his door. "On a case for the

Governor—please leave a message at 305-367-6579." He turned back to Yan, "Lemme see that nose." He leaned close to look at Yan's nose, then said with a grin, "Nothin' yet but you're gonna be the new Polack Pinocchio if you don't watch that lying."

Yan knocked Murphy's hat forward over his eyes and laughed. "A little bullshit grows good tomatoes so maybe it'll perk up my limp detective agency."

"Change your name, 'cause nobody wants a damn Polack Private Eye stumbling around in the bushes."

"How about Yan O'Brien?"

"Now your're cookin'. Everyone knows that the Irish are a sneaky bunch o' fukkers."

"Might just try it. You still planning to go sailing with me this week end?"

"Sure am. I need a little break away from this place. That new kid they hired seems to know where everything is now and the places to keep an eye on."

"That the kid who wears snakeskin boots n' has a belt buckle bigger'n a dinner plate?"

"Yeah, and can you believe he asked if he could wear his pearl handled 44 magnum?"

"You gotta be shittin' me."

"Nope, I was in the office when he asked peckerhead."

"Boy, that's exactly what we need. Some scared shitless kid driving around at night with a goddamn cannon on his hip."

"Ain't gonna happen, but I betcha he's got a little pistol in his jacket pocket."

"I'm heading out to hook up that new Rule bilge pump, so I'll see you later."

"Have fun." Murphy drove off as Yan headed toward his dingy. "I'll see ya Saturday morning," he yelled.

Murphy steered as the small Seagull motor shoved the sailboat through the water at a couple of miles an hour. When they were clear of the other moored boats, Yan began turning the winch that raised the jib. The light breeze filled it, so Murphy shut off the Seagull and raised it out of the water. Yan was turning the crank on the mainsail winch and the two men were soon sipping a beer as Yan steered toward Stiltsville, to run through the channel that would carry them past Fowey Rock Light and into the Atlantic Ocean.

The sailboat handled perfectly as it sliced through the moderately choppy seas, and Yan was more pleased than ever with his swap. Murphy was impressed with Yan's handling of the sails. "Those courses that you took sure did the trick ol' pal, you're handling this thing like you been sailin' all your bloody life."

"That was the easy part, but now I've gotta learn navigation, and I know just enough about it to realize how hard it's gonna be; especially for an old fart like me."

"I thought you had all of that new electronic navigational stuff on here?"

"I do, but I still wanna know how to do it with a sextant in case I'm off sailing somewhere and lose power or som'n, and can't use it."

Murphy opened them each another beer saying, "Makes sense."

The two men sailed north to Baker's Haulover and entered the bay to anchor for the night. The return trip the following day was uneventful, and long before dark they were back on Yan's mooring buoy. "Well captain," Murphy said through a beery grin, "I reckon you're ready to head off into the Caribbean for some wild adventures."

"After that navigational course Murph, I plan to do just that."

Yan completed the course with ease and took the boat on a cruise to Bimini. During the next month he went out sailing every chance he could, and was becoming a competent sailor. He finished a case for a business that was suspicious of a claim of injury on the job by an employee. He banked his fee and decided to celebrate at his favorite Cuban street café on Little Havana's Southwest Eighth Street, on the south side of the Miami River.

With the plate of picadillo and rice wiped clean with the last of his freshly baked Cuban bread, Yan was sipping a tiny porcelain cup of Cuban coffee when he looked up and almost dropped it. He hadn't noticed the young black girl enter and sit at a table on the other side of the café, but he couldn't help but notice her now. She was staring directly at him.

39

EYE—TO—EYE

~ again ~

Pearl took a taxi to the Miami Library and spent two hours each day for three straight days on their computers. D'Julliette had insisted that she get a Miami Library card as ID to go along with all of the other identification he demanded she get. It was all phony but the name was the same on each piece, so she used it when necessary.

The library aide who went to the table full of free-to-use computers was impressed at how fast Pearl learned the basics, and told her so. "It usually takes someone who has never used a computer longer to learn how to use the mouse than it has you to be able to search the Internet." She smiled and replaced the vacated chair to the table behind, and glared at the young girl who left it in the aisle. She smiled at Pearl and said pleasantly, "If you need any help just come and get me."

Pearl began searching for any information on heroin and how to get off of it. Her first day of searching was very disappointing but the second and third provided her with enough encouraging data and notes that she felt better than she had in a long time when she left. She smiled at the freckled young girl who had helped her, "Thanks a lot Melissa, I'll be back when my head cools down."

Pearl always felt comfortable in the Cuban section on the south side of the river, so she went there often to browse through the shops and have lunch. She was in a crowd of pedestrians walking past a small street café when she spotted the man who had looked at her so intently, a long time previously when she was living in Nassau. She never forgot how he looked at her.

She crossed the street and stood facing the window of a shop, so she could watch him. She casually walked from window to window and kept an eye on Yan. When he finally stood and left, Pearl watched as he went to an older van and got in. She memorized what it looked like and went back across the street to the café to have lunch. She purposely spoke to the young Cuban girl who she had watched serve Van his lunch and coffee. "Is that big handsome hunk who was sitting here, your boyfriend?"

The girl smiled, "Don't I wish. No! He's a private detective that loves only the sailboat that he lives on." She leaned down and said quietly, "I know, because I really gave it my all to get him interested."

"Does he come in here often? Maybe I'll give it a try myself." Pearl smiled at the girl and gave her a sly wink.

"He loves Cuban food and coffee so he's in here at least four days a week about this time of day."

Pearl had her lunch and coffee then handed the girl a twenty saying, "You're gonna see a lot of me, Coralline but don't tell him I asked about him, okay?"

"No baby," she replied as she slipped the twenty into her pocket, "I don't wanna crimp your style." She smiled and said, "I am gonna watch though, because if you get him then I'm gonna change my moves to yours." She grinned, and Pearl grinned back as she left the café.

The next day, Pearl had the taxi drop her off two blocks from the café and she walked casually toward it but on the opposite side of the street. She alternated between window-shopping and sitting at the fresh fruit bar; sipping delicious, chilled concoctions and eating sliced papaya drenched with key limejuice. Yan didn't show up on the first day but on the second day, before Pearl had finished her first coconut and mango drink, she saw the same old van pull in and park.

She sipped and watched as he sat at the same table where she'd eaten her lunch two days earlier. She waited until he ordered, and then she slid from the stool, paid the elderly Cuban fruit-mixologist, crossed the street and went directly to Yan's table.

"Hello," she said, "can I sit with you?"

Yan was a little shocked to see her suddenly standing there in front of him, but in a strange way he had known all along that they would one day meet. He kept his voice calm as he stood, "Certainly, I've been expecting you."

"Really," she said as she pulled the chair out and sat, "since when?"

"Since the day in Nassau when our eyes locked." He smiled very slightly and asked, "Have you had lunch yet?"

"No, is the food here good?"

"What did you think of it yesterday?"

It was Pearl's turn to be surprised, but she remained cool and even smiled saying, "So you've been watching me."

"Yes!" He leaned forward, "How many people would you think spend an hour looking in the windows of stores in one block?"

"Well," she leaned back in the chair and smiled genuinely, "you are a detective, aren't you."

"Sounds good, but I'm actually just a working guy who takes dirty pictures of husbands and wives cheating on each other."

"You do know who I am then, don't you?" Pearl was now leaning on her arms, crossed on the table in front of her.

"I knew who you were while I was still in Nassau, but with some good investigative work I now know a lot about you." Yan smiled when he said, "I'm probably the only man who knows the why and how of The Black Widowmaker's life." The smile was gone as he stared intently into her eyes.

Pearl's eyes narrowed as she said, "There's one other man who knows all about the WHY of my life." She bitterly emphasized the word why.

Yan held her gaze as he slowly shook his head from side-to-side. "The good Reverend is no longer with us."

Pearl sat staring at Yan for a very long time, as he neither blinked nor took his eyes from hers. When she finally spoke it was a whisper. "He's dead?"

Yan remained silent a moment then leaned forward to say quietly, "Of the many things on this earth that I hate and will not tolerate, abusing a child is at the very top. By talking to the officers who first found you, then to those who investigated that Jamaican's death, I began putting the picture together. I located The Reverend only last week and asked an old police friend who owed me a favor to cancel his contract."

After a lengthy pause Pearl finally spoke. "Why did you do that?"

"I knew that you would come for him eventually and I didn't want to take the chance that he might somehow get you back under his control."

She just sat shaking her head until the waitress finally made a stop at their table. "Hi, I see that you two finally met." She smiled wide at Pearl, "Would you like to eat or just having coffee?"

Pearl looked up at the same young girl that had spoken to her on the first day, "Do you still have the curried goat with yellow rice?"

"It says daily special on the menu's flyer but it's really our specialty and we have it every day."

"That's what I'll have then with hot Cuban bread and a Cuban coffee now, please."

"How about you?" The waitress looked down at Yan.

Rick Magers

"I haven't had goat since friends in the Bahamas made it for me a long time ago so yes, I'll have the same and coffee too, please."

After she left, Pearl asked Yan, "Why did you do that for me? The only person who ever did one single kind thing for me was my grandmother." Tears flowed from her eyes as she added, "And I got her killed."

"How do you figure that?" Before Pearl could answer, the coffee arrived. After a brief explanation by Pearl about talking about the money her grandmother had saved for her education, Yan said, "I have something in the van that I think you'd like to see." He stood saying, "I'll get it and be right back."

Pearl watched as he walked out and down the street to his van. Her curiosity was at its highest peak when he returned carrying a brown grocery bag. He handed the bag to her saying, "You can have that if you want it, because I believe it was your grandmothers."

Pearl removed the small steel box, which had once held her grandmother's hard-earned dollars. They were the same dollars that were to carry her granddaughter to college and a brighter future. The very same box, that because of a careless word from Pearl, had cost her grandmother her life, and Pearl her entire future. She sat silently holding the box while running her hands across every side. Tears began running down her cheeks, making them shine. She looked up at Yan several times and tried to speak, but couldn't.

Yan sat silently watching the young black woman that he knew was a deadly killer. Some inner urging began the day that he locked eyes with her at the beach bar in Nassau. He had relentlessly dug deeper and deeper into the case of the Jamaican found with his throat cut in his old stomping ground of downtown Miami. A favor here and a lucky probe there began to paint the picture of a young girl's nightmare; one that she hadn't deserved——one that she never should have been forced to endure.

Pearl wiped her eyes and cheeks after a long silent period of staring at the small box. She replaced it in the paper bag and looked at Yan. Her eyes now had a completely different intensity and were searching deep into the white eyes of the man sitting across from her. "Yes, that was the box that gramma kept putting every spare dollar she could earn into." She looked again at the bag sitting on the table beside her then asked, "How did you get it?"

With a very serious face, Yan said in a professional, moderated voice, "I was a damn good cop and I'm a good detective. I finally located an old guy who had been seeing two young punks that he hated, hanging around your grandmother's house just before it burned. I got an ID on 'em and asked some guys on the street who owed me a few favors, to begin searching." He took a sip of the fresh coffee that the waitress brought, before continuing. "When my street troops started asking questions about these two creeps I guess it brought some unwanted heat on the people that they dealt drugs for, and they were both found hanging in an old deserted freighter on the river."

Pearl had remained silent the entire time that Yan spoke, but now said, "I hope they both suffered terribly."

"I do too and apparently they did, because their boss musta wanted to know why someone was trying to find them. There were several body parts missing."

Pearl looked intently at Yan when she asked, "Why do you hope they suffered?"

"That old shack that you and your grandma lived in burned so fast that it didn't burn her body very much. I got a hold of the report and autopsy records, so I know what those two bastards did to her."

Pearl's cry when she saw the small steel box put it all behind her, and there were no more tears. She looked at Yan a long time before speaking. "You really do care about people, don't you? Uh, I don't even know your name."

"Yan and yes, I care a lot about people like you and your grandma. That's what America's made of; hard working people that only want to be able to get ahead." She noticed that his eyes became almost fierce when he said, "I want every animal like that damn Jamaican and his preacher pal flushed down the toilet along with punks like those two who killed your grandma."

"I was never bitter about anything when I was a young girl," Pearl said quietly, "but I've become a very hard, bitter woman."

Yan leaned forward, carefully and gently taking her tiny hand in his huge paw. "Pearl, I can help you turn all of the past around if you'll let me."

She liked the way that he held her hand but not possessively. "You even know my real name."

"Like I said," he grinned slightly, "I'm a damn good detective."

Pearl grinned back, "Damn sure must be."

40

A NEW LIFE BEGINS

Pearl and Yan's love affair began slowly. They met every day for lunch at the same small Cuban café, and afterward walked along the sidewalks looking into the windows as they talked—getting to know each other.

He realized that she was very serious about getting help to kick her heroin habit. He used underground contacts, made during twenty years on the Miami Police Department, to get her more and better identification. She soon had a passport as authentic as Yan's.

They first made love during a day cruise on his sailboat, and she moved aboard shortly after.

"Yan," his pal Murphy said after meeting Pearl, "you really hit the jackpot there ole buddy, she's not only gorgeous but nice too." He removed his hat and wiped the sweat from his brow, "That barbecue sauce she made for those ribs I cooked for us the other night puts all of that store stuff to shame."

"Murph," Yan said smiling, "I think I started falling in love with Cheryl Craig the first time I laid eyes on her." He didn't tell his friend where and how they really met, but he was certain that it was true. He felt something strange that day in Nassau when she first stood and stared directly at him for a long time.

"Changin' her old name to the new Mrs. Cheryl Brodjevinski wouldn't have as pretty a ring to it, but it might be a helluva good deal for you."

Yan smiled broadly saying, "Y'never know."

Yan worked tirelessly to get Pearl undocumented help with her addiction, and after a few months she was winning the battle. During very difficult times for her he would sit for hours, holding her in his arms; asking for nothing; just being there for her—a first for Pearl.

Yan temporally closed his office to be with Pearl every minute during her withdrawals, so they went sailing as often as weather would permit. She immediately loved sailing and was soon able to handle the boat and use all of the electronic equipment. Yan began teaching her how to use the sextant, and was amazed at how fast she learned to use it competently.

One bright winter afternoon Yan asked, "Would you like to spend Christmas in the most beautiful place that I've ever been?"

Pearl came to his open arms and lay her head against his chest as she asked, "And where, Captain Ahab would that be?"

"Montego Bay, Jamaica."

41

WOUNDS THAT NEVER HEAL

After making gentle tender love to Pearl for an hour, Yan held her in his arms. She laid her head against his chest and whispered, "Do you really love me, Yan?"

He had thought about it many times since she moved in with him on his sailboat, and after much soul-searching, decided that he truly did love her. What had begun as lust and curiosity was slowly replaced by love and understanding.

"Yes Pearl, I love you deeply and will never let anyone abuse or hurt you again." He gently pulled her closer and held her until he drifted off to sleep.

Several times during the past several days, since they had departed Miami on the Sea Voyager, which they renamed LOA, after the Sea-God, he looked from Pearl's glistening, naked, ebony-black body stretched out on the top of the cabin, to the beautiful, sleek lines of the sailboat. *Damn I'm lucky. Most men never have one beautiful woman and here I am with two.*

Pearl slid easily from his embrace and walked into the forward salon. Before reaching into the recessed area where books were kept she glanced at his long muscular frame on the bunk of the small guest compartment. He was certain that she had been able to get completely off of the heroin, and she was going to let him keep thinking that way until she finally did.

She never understood why, but there were times when she absolutely had to have a fix. She smuggled in a package sufficiently large enough to take care of her occasional needs during the month they planned to be in Jamaica. She wasn't thrilled to be going to the homeland of the monsters that had ruined her life, but since she had killed one and Yan had the other one killed, the word Jamaican didn't bother her like it always had.

She knew that Yan's natural detective's mind would spot needle tracks on her arms or legs so the few times she felt the pressing need to shoot up she was careful. The image in the mirror was more pleasant than at any time in her past several years. She smiled at her face thinking, *You're a very lucky girl to meet someone like Yan, who truly cares about you.*

She raised her tongue and carefully inserted the small needle. When she was finished, Pearl looked hard at the young girl again. *We're gonna get off of this shit little Black Pearl so there's no chance of ever being the Black Widowmaker again.*

She flushed the syringe and needle with alcohol and returned it to its hiding place, then went up on deck. She sat watching the beautiful blue water as it gently rolled along the sides of the boat as it made its way slowly past Florida toward the tip of Cuba. She knew that Yan would then take the wheel and navigate the sailboat around Cuba and on toward Jamaica. She thought it was Yan when she heard a voice behind her. She turned smiling but was shocked to see one of her old demons standing at the wheel, grinning at her.

Pearl watched the grotesque little creature for a moment, and then when a cold chill ran the length of her body, she went below and pulled the heroin out again. *I thought they were gone for good,* she thought as she shot up a syringe that had three times as much as the last. After replacing the package she returned to the deck, hoping to be alone.

~ She wasn't ~

She sat on the cockpit's fiberglass bench behind the captain's chair and pressed her fingers tightly against her eyes. When she looked up there were two demons; twins—staring at her. As one spoke, the other pointed at the cabin's passageway leading to the area where Yan lay sleeping.

He fooled you little girl; that's D'Julliette down there in the bunk. That wasn't him that you killed, it was his twin brother, just like we are. The demons turned and looked at each other then laughed. *He fooled you because he knows you are an April fool and will believe anything that he tells you. He's taking you to his island to make a slave of you forever.*

"No," she said quietly and shook her head. *That monster is gone because I killed him. No! It can't be.* Again she pressed her fingers against her eyes.

Look! April fool.

She opened her eyes and saw one of the demons standing next to the passageway, pointing. The demon behind her leaned down and whispered into her ear. *Don't believe us; go look for yourself.*

Pearl cautiously leaned far enough forward to see the bunk where she had recently made love to Yan. *Oh dear God, no!* She jerked back, sweat running from her as though she had stepped from a shower. *It is D'Julliette.* She was trembling all over as she sat staring at the opening.

The hideous demon leaned down once again to whisper; *His brother is dead, so if you kill him you can be free. Act now—do it now—be free or be a slave forever.*

Pearl looked at the sheath tied to the guy wire. Yan kept a razor sharp knife in it to be used for emergencies. She leaned forward again and saw D'Julliette lying on his back. *I can't go through that again. Oh dear Jesus what must I do? I'm afraid, and I would rather be dead that live like that again.*

The voice she next heard was gentle and kind, not the voice of the demon. She turned to see Jesus standing on the deck, holding the guy wire and shaking his head slowly up and down. *It is the only way to be free, my child.*

She turned back to the sheath then slowly stood and removed the knife. She held it behind her as she silently went down the steps and moved to the side of the bed. She looked at the sleeping Jamaican who had made most of her life a nightmare, and as swiftly as a striking cobra the blade went across his throat.

Yan's eyes came suddenly open as he thrashed about, trying to understand what had happened. They opened wider than Pearl had ever seen a person's eyes. His gaze locked on her briefly but soon his movement slowed and his eyes began clouding. In only seconds he lay still, as Pearl looked down at the only man who had loved her and treated her with kindness and respect.

As she stood there looking, the Jamaican turned into Yan.

Oh my God—oh sweet Jesus, what have I done? He loved me and I killed him. Ohhhhhhhh, ohhhhhhhh, she wailed like a wounded animal as she stumbled up the steps. She stood holding the bloody knife as the voice came again.

What difference does it make which man it is? They all want to use you then watch you cry as they burn you with cigarettes, bite you, shove things in you, cut their initials on your body, and put those horrible drugs into your veins.

Another, deeper, more sinister voice spoke, and pearl looked around. Satan was now standing where Jesus stood only moments earlier. *Man is your enemy and mine, my child. You have done well to rid the world of them and shall stand with me as we cast many more into my fires. Ha-ha-ha-ha-ha-ha-ha.*

Satan's laughter rang like a huge bell inside her head. She squeezed her eyes tight and shook her head, but it only got louder. Tears were running freely down her face as she climbed from the cockpit and sat on the raised teakwood railing across the stern. She looked up at the beautiful, clear blue Caribbean Sky, and spoke to a God that she had never really known—one that had never come to her rescue—had never punished those men who had hurt her so bad—never stepped in to help her dear old grandmother—never even acknowledged that she was one of His children.

When she spoke it was not with bitterness. It was only the sad defeated voice of a young girl lost in man's cesspool of desire and greed. "Lord God in heaven, wherever I'm going it won't be as bad as where you dumped me." She closed her eyes tightly and pulled the knife deeply across her wrist. She opened her eyes and looked around the empty deck thinking, *Even the devil has deserted me.*

She dropped the knife and shoved a little with her feet. Her tiny body hardly made a splash.

The beautiful sailboat moved swiftly beyond the reddening area, and before it was its own length away, even the stain was gone. It had blended with the vast ocean—as though the young girl had never really existed.

In a way, she hadn't.

THE END

Rick Magers

ABOUT

Satan's Dark Angels

This book is eight short stories with a beginning and end. During a lifetime of traveling the world, I have met every type of person that walks, crawls, slithers, or otherwise makes his or her way along the perilous path of life.

All of the characters in this book were taken from these people I have met.

After reading this book you will forever find yourself looking at the people you meet, and those that you already know, or thought you knew, and wonder; *what unseen emotions are lurking just beneath that veneer of smiles—and what festering wounds have never healed.*

They'll stick to the walls of your mind so vividly, that chances are you will take one or all of these characters to the grave with you.

Once these characters are uploaded into your subconscious database, it is also a distinct possibility that simply by being aware of their hidden traits—that knowledge might save your life.

Satan's dark angels really are out there—everywhere.

Rick Magers

SATAN'S DARK ANGELS

<u>A BEGINNING</u>

8
very dark
short stories.

<u>AN ENDING</u>

PERHAPS
THE
END
?

Rick Magers

TABLE OF CONTENTS

CHAPTER	PAGE
PREFACE	139
First Angels	141
1. YOUNG WARRIORS	143
Black Angel	159
2. GIANT SOLDIER	161
Island Goddess	174
3. DREAM LOVER	177
Determined Angel	191
4. GAY RECRUIT	193
Amazon Angel	207
5. VENGEFUL LADY	210
Soaring Dark Angel	226
6. TRAINED WARRIOR	228
Demon Twin	243
7. DARK PROGENY	245
Satan's Baby	262
8. DARK CHILD ANGEL	263
9. The Beginning of the End	280

PREFACE

Are demons really among us?

How else can we explain a young mother sending her two young children, while strapped in the back seat of her car, down a boat ramp to a terrifying death?—A star athlete cutting the throat of his ex-wife and her friend—Surely demons will visit his children later in life—A seemingly normal young man blowing up a building in Oklahoma, killing innocent people—Foreign demons directing their slaves to commit the kind of destruction and death as happened twice at the World Trade Center—Ted Bundy's rampage of terror and death—John Wayne Gacy masquerading as a smiling clown, while all the time committing acts of unimaginable horror—The Zodiac Killer—The Boston Strangler—Son-of-Sam—Jeffrey Dahmer—The list climbs into the thousands—Millions?

Without the assistance of demons, would a young man shoot a harmless singer of songs such as John Lennon?

Could Jim Jones have dreamed up his sick scheme without some help from demons…which we now know were with him all of his life?

Were there demons present to blow up airplanes full of innocent travelers—When Idi Amin decided to take hostages—Did demons hold the Ayatollah's cruel hand—Did they laugh as Papa Doc slaughtered thousands in Haiti—Saddam Hussein's demons have been his only companions all of his life.

Where does it end?

We try with modern techniques to explain the behavior of these imposters posing as human beings. We often give them better treatment than we can afford ourselves, in an attempt to cure them. Can we possibly be the same species as these ghastly creatures? We constantly seek answers. Bad childhood—Poverty—A few too many of these chromosomes—Not enough

Rick Magers

of those—Lack of education—Suppressed because of race—Job stress—Financial stress—Sexual stress—His dog loved his sister better——Blah, blah, blah.

. . .

We do not tolerate this type behavior in other animals. So why do we allow those creatures to run rampant with their deeds of horror? Because they're MADE IN GOD'S IMAGE? I think not. THEY ARE NOT HUMAN? They're impostors conducting a cruel campaign of terror, carnage, death and destruction. They work for a higher power than we can realistically conceive.

SATAN

They obey only SATAN. He issues orders and they slip silently into our homes—walk brazenly into our lives to begin killing, torturing and devouring us.

We have long known that these DARK ANGELS are humankind's enemies. As soon as we locate these imposters they must be removed from our beautiful blue planet if we are to guard our human way of life. Unless we wake up soon: I fear that a similar ending to the one in this book of fiction will soon be upon us.

Many just like them are out there plying their skills of death and destruction—Perhaps sitting next to you—At the next desk—Playing with your child—knocking on your mother's door?

I hope you enjoy this collection of stories. Each is based on actual people that I met, or read about in newspapers, or watched on the television news. Be careful who you associate with, and think about the demons—that really are out there.

For Satan finds some mischief still for idle hands to do.

Isac Watts: 1674-1748

Rick Magers

First Angels

Alain Catrich was a very thin, gawky kid. He also had terrible zits all over his face, and even though he did everything his mother said would help, they were getting worse. On top of all this he also had a slight lisp. None of these physical characteristics had a lot to do with why the other kids at school and in his neighborhood, wanted nothing to do with him. His official nickname was Alleycat, but most just referred to Alain as, 'That freak.'

He was by every definition of the word a weird kid. Two weeks earlier he had finally arrived at a place he had dreamed of. Finally! "I'm a teenager. Now I'll hang out with the older guys 'n do some really neat shit."

It hadn't yet happened and he was extremely disappointed. When he showed two teens his brand new, razor sharp bootknife; snugly fit into his black leather boot, two fifteen-year-old boys just laughed at him and walked away. Alain took the small notepad from his rear pocket then got the pen from the neck of his T-shirt. As he was writing the two boys names in his book he said quietly aloud, "You'll both regret not teaming up with Lucifer and me."

His mother talked his father into allowing Alain to have his head shaved. All of his hair except the very top was cut off, and what remained was dyed bright red. "All the kids do stuff like that," she said.

"Okay," the father replied, "but he's not getting his ears pierced, or any of that other shit." He stared at his wife a moment, "Don't give me one of those looks. Dammit Mary, have you looked at that freak's room lately?"

"Oh Joseph, he's just experimenting with his new teen world, and a lot of kids think the Devil is a cool thing to be into." She flashed a sexy smile and put her arm around him. "Nothing'll come of it dear, and he'll grow out of it as soon as he discovers the world of girls and sex."

Alain had only one true friend. Bradley Morrison was still only twelve, with another six months to wait before he too would be a teenager. He was allowed to spend the night at Alaine's house whenever he wanted. His single mother was glad he had a friend, because other kids didn't seem to like her son. "Brad," she told her latest boyfriend, "is simply too bright for most of these kids around here." She was also glad to be rid of him for a weekend, so she and her boyfriend could have the house all to themselves.

She was right though, about Bradley being bright. That was the primary reason he and Alain became friends while they were still small children. Had they lived awhile longer both boys would have undoubtedly been tested and found to be in the genius category. It was not to be; they would both be dead within the coming week, along with many others—Most of which had their names written in Alleycat's little book.

1

YOUNG WARRIORS

You are one of those that will not serve God if the Devil bid you.

William Shakespeare

Joseph Catrich was a marine: to the bone. After his four-year stint of active duty he promptly joined the active reserves. Within five years he was Sergeant Catrich, and in charge of the armory in Prenton, Iowa. Prenton wasn't a big city, but it was big enough to allow Joseph to stock his own small arsenal at home without taking a great risk. He maintained a large list of weaponry and constantly sent in requisitions for more.

Joseph proudly displayed the weapons he had added to the inventory since taking over the job. "Take a look at this baby," he said to his brother, visiting from Atlanta, when he accompanied him to the armory. Joseph handed him the WW II bazooka. "Put'r up on your shoulder and you'll see what you missed."

His brother thought all of this was just so much 'boys-n-toys,' but he complied. "Not as heavy as I thought one of them would be," he said as he handed it back.

"Got five missiles for it too," Joseph smiled, "but we can't fire any on 'em till I get more in stock." He took a long pull from the can of beer then grinned. "When I do, watch yer ass; whoosh." He made the loud noise as he rested the weapon on his own shoulder. When it was back where it belonged he said, "Look at these," and slid a wooden box marked LIVE GRENADES on the top out so he could open it.

"Damn Joe, you could start a war with what you have right here."

"Or end one somebody else started little brother." When he closed the box and began sliding it back beneath the bench, his brother whistled softly.

"Are all six of those full of grenades?"

"Goddamn straight bro, and I got a box of 'em home that's full and ready to go if I ever need 'em."

"Jesus H. Christ, Joe, they'll put your ass in Leavenworth if they find out your stealing shit from the government."

"Not a chance. I'm the only guy that keeps track of what's used on maneuvers, plus I do all of the ordering of weapons, ammunition and supplies to keep this place running." He finished his beer and stood, "C'mon let's go up 'n get another one." On the way up the stairs he added, "Best of all, this place was so screwed up when I took over that they didn't have a clue what the hell was in here, so I had to inventory everything." He turned and grinned, "I did too, right after I stocked my house with everything I needed. Wait'll you see my shit." He grinned at his brother, "Ole Sodomy Hoosain didn't have better."

His younger brother just shook his head, "Joe, I hope I'm the only guy you've told this to."

"Better believe it bro, ain't another guy on this earth knows squat about my stash."

"Keep it that way Joe."

Alaine and Bradley had the house all to themselves on Saturday. His parents had gone to nearby Hobart to visit friends for the day. Bradley watched as Alaine worked with the large padlock his dad had on the steel door to the little room in the basement. He held one small, thin, steel pick in the key receptacle as he manipulated the other slightly larger steel probe. When the lock snapped open after only a minute or so, Bradley gasped slightly, and let his breath out.

"Wow man, that's just like Richard Widmark did it in that war movie we watched the other night. He slit that Nazi's throat then went in and picked the lock on . . . He was interrupted by Alaine.

"Yeah, yeah, for Christ's sake man, I was with ya, remember?"

"Oh yeah. Sure man, but . . . He was stopped by a cold, emotionless stare from his friend.

Richard Widmark…World War Two movies…ancient jargon. With all of the new, special effects movies, coming out almost weekly, these two kids only watched re-runs of old war movies. Their schoolmates and neighbors were correct: much more so than they could possibly have imagined when they commented, 'Those are two very weird kids.'

"Holy tornados," Bradley yelled when Alaine opened the lid on the wooden crate.

Alaine stopped in mid-motion and looked hard at Bradley, "Goddammit Brad, it's torpedoes not tornados; holy torpedoes."

"Oh," the young boy said, sheepishly. He considered Alaine his leader, mentor and spiritual counselor. He tried very hard to do what Alaine expected of him, especially now that his friend was a teenager. After all it was Alaine that introduced him to the wonders of Satan.

When the wooden lid was resting against the wall behind the box, Bradley leaned closer. "Holy torpedoes, are those real hand grenades?"

"Shit no, they're Flintstones Grenades made by TOYS 'R' US, see right here." He held one of his father's hidden grenades close to his friend's eyes.

Bradley leaned close to find the writing then yelped like a hit dog when the steel grenade hit him between the eyes. Not enough to really hurt, but enough to startle the 'boy. "Ouch! Why'd you do that?"

"Because you're a fuckin' dumbass. Of course they're real, whadaya think dummy? That my dad'd have a goddamn box of toy hand grenades."

An embarrassed and hurt Bradley whimpered.

"Quit whimpering like a baby or you don't go on the mission with me." Alaine replaced the grenade carefully then closed the lid. His friend was admiring all of the rifles in the rack on the wall. "That's an Uzi. It's my pop's favorite Submachine Gun."

"Can I take it down and hold it?"

"Sure, just be careful; don't drop it." He watched as his friend held the small weapon up to his shoulder. "Real piece o' shit. Fires a 9mm bullet that ain't much bigger'n a damn 22. Jews made 'em to hunt rabbits with during the war, 'cause food was so scarce." He pointed to the next rifle, "Now there's a man killing piece of machinery. That baby's number one in my book; an all American killing machine."

Bradley carefully replaced the Uzi then moved to the one Alaine was referring to. "Wow! Just like the one Broderick Crawford used on those Japs when they came up outa the sub." He waited as Alaine lifted the weapon from the gun rack. When he handed it to him, Bradley could hardly believe how heavy it was. "Man oh man, you'd hafta be a helluva man just to carry this baby around all day."

"You're right," Alain said, his voice crisp with authority, "she weighs 8.8 pounds empty, then when you snap that 50 round ammo drum into place it's a man sized weapon."

"They call these choppers, don't they?"

"Yeah, but only in the movies. It's really a Thompson Sub Machinegun."

"Is this round thing where the bullets are?"

"Yeah and it's loaded n' ready to go, so keep your finger off the trigger. That sweetheart fires 800, 45 caliber bullets a minute at 920 feet a second. Gimme one o' those and I'll take on any four fuckin' Jews with their little rabbit rifles, and I'll send 'em all up to a matzo ball picnic in Jew heaven." He smiled somewhat crookedly.

Bradley had no idea what a matzo ball was, but he joined his friend in laughter.

Alaine took the weapon from Bradley, and as he was putting it back in its place the boy asked, "What the heck is this humongous thing?"

"That's a B.A.R., and it stands for Browning Automatic Rifle. Dad says that's the gun we won World War Two with."

"Holy torna . . . uh torpedoes, musta took two men to handle that baby; it's almost as tall as I am."

"Little over four feet long, and if you thought that Thompson was heavy, here try this." He handed it to his small friend. "Over twenty pounds with that twenty round clip of 30 caliber bullets. Keep your finger off the trigger, 'cause all o' these babies are loaded and ready."

Alain laughed when his friend couldn't keep the barrel up without shaking. He took it from Bradley and pointed it at the far wall and held it there for a full minute.

"Wow! I don't know how you hold that sucker up that long."

"Practice. I've shot this sweetheart a lotta times. (Truth was that his father wouldn't consider letting his freak son fire any of his precious weapons. As far as he knew his son didn't even know they existed.) Wide open this baby'll fire 600 rounds a minute at 2800 feet a second." He returned it to the gun rack, then turned a grin toward Bradley, "That's cookin', huh?"

"Sure's shit is, dude."

Alain by-passed several rifles and shotguns, and moved to the end of the rack. "Here's what we'll use on the mission." He handed one of the short rifles to Bradley then took one for himself. "Watch how I remove the bullet magazine, so I can swing the folding stock back into place." His friend watched as he removed the clip then folded the steel stock into position. Replacing the clip he said, "Now let's see you do it."

Bradley seldom had to be told anything twice, if he was interested, and never needed a second lesson if the person showing him took time to explain. Alaine praised his quick prowess with the weapon. "These are Kalashnikovs but most people call 'em an AK-47. They're as wicked as a hand held weapon gets. Fires a NATO 7.62 round." He opened the drawer beneath the bench, holding a bullet up for Bradley to see.

"Now that's a bullet, dude." Young Bradley didn't even know for sure how a bullet worked. He thought the whole thing went out the barrel until Alaine explained it to him. Again, he explained to Bradley that they were going on a mission for Satan soon, and that he would train him in everything he would need to know. It sounded like a great adventure, so Bradley was excited and ready to follow Alaine.

"Damn straight, this weapon'll empty that thirty round clip at 600 rounds a minute on full automatic, and they're heading at the target at 2,350 feet a second." He grinned and wobbled his eyebrows, "What it hits it kills." He replaced the weapon saying, "Remove that live clip so I can show you how to dump an empty then re-clip with a full one in a hurry." They moved to the open area in the basement so Bradley could practice. Alaine had spent many hours in this room practicing until he could do everything with his eyes closed. "First, swing that steel stock back under and forward, 'cause we won't be using them." Ten minutes later he was satisfied that Bradley had mastered the art of quickly changing from an empty to a full clip.

Alaine instructed his friend to take his button shirt off, but to leave his T-shirt on. He carried the assault rifle back into his father's special room (that no one had ever been in) and returned the full clip before replacing it on the rack. He returned with a pistol in a leather holster. Bradley just stood as Alaine slipped the shoulder holster over his left shoulder then pulled the elastic strap behind his back and brought it around so he could put his right arm through it. He pulled the strap from the bottom of the holster down to fasten it under the boy's belt, then snugged it up with the adjustment buckle. The weapon now rested snugly beneath the child's armpit, with the butt facing forward. He stepped back and smiled, "You're ready for combat, soldier."

"Man, this's so cool." He stepped around the corner so he could see himself in the large mirror, which he'd noticed as they entered the basement. "Wow! Is this cool or what?"

"There's nothing in the chamber so be careful not to drop it but take it out and see how it feels in your hand."

Bradley faced his own image and removed the pistol. He pointed it at the face, which no longer belonged to a boy. The face he saw in the mirror was much older, and belonged to a man ready to go on a mission that his commander was preparing him for. The diminutive little redheaded child, who limped from an accident while riding his bicycle, no longer lacked confidence. He could take on the world with the skills he had learned tonight from his leader and friend Alaine Catrich. In a few days he would have a chance to prove it.

After straightening up everything that they had disturbed, Alaine took a moment to double-check all of his father's weaponry before re-locking his father's secret little room. He turned to Bradley, "C'mon soldier, let's go up to my room 'n smoke some dope, then call up the Devil."

"Shitchess," the kid said as he followed him up the stairs, "that last time was a blast."

After entering his bedroom, Alaine locked the door. His young friend asked, "They allow you to lock your door?"

He took a long pull on the marijuana joint, and held his breath so his lungs could extract the THC content of the weed, then passed it to Bradley, who clumsily tried to imitate his leader. When he finished coughing, Alaine looked at him through thin slits; "No one comes through that door unless I tell 'em to."

"Shit man, I can't even close the fuckin' door to my room when I'm in there."

Alaine pulled the joint down to a nub then passed it to Bradley. When he was forced to exhale he spoke like a wise old man. "When you get a little older Brad, you'll understand that you gotta make these assholes respect your space." He let a sneer spread across his face, "Or else."

Alaine began placing black candles around a small statue of the Devil. He ordered it from the Internet, using his mother's credit card number, knowing she never checked her list of many purchases before paying the bill, so he occasionally ordered things he wanted, but was careful not to spend too much. Alaine had a good deal and knew it, and didn't want to blow it.

Bradley was spending the night, so while Alaine prepared everything for their trip into the dark underworld of Satan, he dumped his bag onto the bed he always used. He held up the new, black, artificial leather trench coat that he had talked his mother into buying him, "Hey Alaine, will this do?"

He turned to his young friend and scrutinized the long coat, then stood up. "Looks okay for now, but later on, when I have a lot of members, everyone's gonna have to have real leather like mine." He returned to lighting the many black candles he had carefully placed around the altar, arranged in the middle of the room. Over his shoulder he said, "Hang your stuff in the closet and let's get ready to welcome Satan."

During the next hour, Alaine chanted in a language Bradley couldn't understand. He just lay back into the huge pillows piled against the wall and smoked dope.

Alaine had been seeing the demons for quite awhile. At various times they would pop up in the middle of a classroom, and at other times they would be sitting on the shoulders of someone he hated. Today they were all over the room. He repeatedly asked, "Brad did you see that big red demon that just walked through the wall into the living room?"

He knew his little friend was stoned to the gills, so when he replied, "Yeah man that's cool." He ignored him thinking, *Don't worry, you'll be seeing them soon enough.*

It was still light outside, but with the curtains closed it was dark and eerie when Alaine turned off the lights. He let all but a few of the candles burn out, which made it very spooky to Bradley: he loved it. He watched through thin slits as his friend went to the closet. When Alain returned moments later, he was wearing the long, pure leather trench coat that had blood red letters on the back: SATAN'S DARK ANGELS. He shoved the toothpick into the joint, like Alaine had showed him, and pulled it down to the wood before plucking it from the pick like a hors d'oeuvre. He swallowed it and watched his leader wave incense sticks around his head as he chanted: now in English.

"Oh mighty Satan, Divine Lucifer, King of Babylon, Prince of Tyre, please bless this humble servant with your presence." He reached beneath the bed and pulled out a brown paper bag. When he dumped the contents on the small coffee table near the altar, its head lay beyond one end and its tail trailed over the other edge. Bradley sat up.

"Oh mighty Satan, ruler of the dark world beyond, I have brought an offering for you." He picked the black cat up by its tail and began chanting again in that language Bradley couldn't understand. He soon returned to English, "Soon my Lord I will send you many offerings far better than this." He laid the cat back on the altar and began swinging the incense sticks again. "Please hear your devoted servant, mighty Beelzebub and come forth." As Alaine chanted in that strange language again, Bradley lay back into the pillows. He was too stoned to light another joint so he just lay and watched his friend. A moment before dozing off he saw a glowing red light begin to get bigger and brighter in the far corner of the room.

Be sober, be vigilant; because your adversary the devil, as a roaring lion, walketh about, seeking whom he may devour.
The New Testament.

✲ At the very moment that the two young boys were smoking dope and toying with Satan, another two boys a little older were walking into a restaurant a thousand miles away. Without a word they pulled two pistols from beneath their shirts and opened fire. The police later counted thirty, 9mm shell casings scattered among the four dead bodies and eleven seriously wounded. Two of the dead were children. The two young men were never apprehended.

✲ An hour earlier several men opened fire into a crowd watching an outdoor soccer game. Many later stated that it sounded like a war zone with thousands of shots being fired. The police said it wasn't thousands, but the shooters were using automatic weapons to be able to have fired the two hundred and thirty-one shell casings they recovered. Four persons were killed and seven seriously wounded. One of the dead was a child. None of the shooters were ever caught.

*As Bradley was sleeping like the baby he really was, and Alaine was talking to Satan, a car with four white-hooded men stopped in front of a small, white, wooden church in a little rural town. Joyous, high-pitched singing was accompanied by a slightly out of key old piano. Three of the men got out and lit the wicks protruding from the gallon jugs of liquid. They ran to the open windows and threw them into the room. In twenty seconds they were gone as if they had never been there. The following day would find them at their jobs; going about their business. The church was a total loss. Three of the singers died in flames, nine others were burned badly, but would eventually heal, three were burned so bad that they would forever feel the pain of that night, a young girl would spend the rest of her life blind; sitting in a wheelchair. No one was ever caught.

The perpetrators in all of these incidents no doubt shared one common obsession. They worshipped the Devil and most had been seeing Demons for a long time.

For where God built a church, there the Devil would also build a chapel— Thus is the Devil ever God's ape.

Martin Luther.

The following morning Alaine didn't argue with his mother when she insisted that he and his little friend attend church with them. As the two boys dressed for breakfast, Alaine turned to Bradley, "Ever been to a Catholic Church?"

"Nope, mom don't go to church," he replied, "says it's all a bunch o' bullshit."

"How old's your mom?"

"Mmmm, thirty I think, or maybe thirty-one."

Alaine bent down and pulled the trouser leg up above the top of his left boot, so he could snap the sheathed knife inside, then zipped the boot back up to the top. After pulling it back down over the highly polished, black leather boot, he turned to his friend, "She's pretty cool then for an old broad." He watched as the young boy applied the thick gel to his green hair, and then coaxed it into spikes protruding at all angles from his oddly elongated head. "Pretty cool man, when mine grows out I'm gonna have it shaved down the middle then make spikes like yours on the sides."

"Sounds cool dude, I'll do mine the same way when you do."

"I think I'll have all my members do their hair that way."

When they arrived at the breakfast table, Joseph Catrich said, "You guys skipping church and going straight to work at the circus?" He grinned at them as they sat down.

"Nothir," Alaine answered his father in a subdued, lisping voice, "we pwan to go to church with you and mother."

Bradley noticed that his friend never spoke with the lisp around him when they were alone, but always did around his parents and the kids at school.

The family arrived at the church early, so the boys were allowed to wander around until it was time to go in. "Wait'll you see the shit that goes on in there Brad. Remember that movie we watched about the middle ages where the High Priest was doin' all that weird shit before they sacrificed all those people."

"Yeah man, I loved that movie. That was so cool when all the blood started running down the altar."

"Same shit in here without the blood and sacrifices."

"No shit!" Bradley's eyes were wide as he looked at the monstrous, ornate temple.

"Yeah man, tall goofy hats, all kindsa different colored robes, smoking cauldrons, totems everywhere, chanting in some strange language," Alain turned a severe stare at Bradley, "voodoo and evil in its highest form."

Alaine was watching something else: Demons. They were perched on all of the ledges. Some were huge, with long tails hanging down. Others were so small they could barely be seen. A few were on fire with flames shooting out from their eyes, while still others were beginning to melt and run down the face of the building. Suddenly he saw him. Forty feet up, standing on the edge between several of the Demons—Satan: his arms folded across his chest. He was dressed in black, with blazing eyes glowing deep within his red face, while his tail kept swinging in the air like an agitated cat. He looked down at Alaine and grinned.

"He's here."

"Who?" The little boy next to him asked.

"Lucifer." He nodded with his head toward the top of the church. "Can you see him?"

"Oh yeah man, cool." All he saw when he looked in the direction his friend motioned was a bunch of pigeons standing on the edges of the huge old church.

Rick Magers

The next morning, as the two friends waited outside their school, Bradley said, "Man, I can't believe the shit that went on in there yesterday."

Alaine grinned at the boy, "So now you wanna be a Catholic, huh?"

"Shit no, I'm gonna stick with you and Satan, that other shit's too weird for me." As the two boys stood alone next to the fence, a group of boys a couple of years older came along the sidewalk toward the gate. They were all wearing football jackets with insignias; designating them as players. When they were beside the two boys, but separated by the fence, the older of the group stopped and turned to them. "Hey Alleycat what's with the black trenchcoat, you with the Secret Service'r som'n these days?" He laughed and turned to his friends for approval. They gave it by mimicking his laughter. Another of the boys said, "Tha'cher shadow, Alleycat or are you babysitting today?" All of his friends laughed.

"Thith's my fwiend and you can kith my ath you gook motherfucker."

The oriental boy screamed and took off toward the gate with the other five boys right on his heels. By the time they reached the gate, Alaine and Bradley had disappeared inside the school. They slipped into the janitor's room where they usually hid to smoke a joint, bending down to catch their breath. When he was finally able to talk Bradley said, "Man, they're gonna kill us when they find us."

Alaine waited until he had control of his breath, so he would sound cool and tough. He reached into the pocket of his trenchcoat and pulled a revolver out. With a wide grin he said, "I just might be a pretty hard guy to kill."

Bradley leaned way over to get a better look at the pistol. "Holy smokes, what kinda gun's that?"

He held it for his friend to admire, "Nine millimeter Sphinx. Latest Swiss made job with double action and a sixteen shot magazine." He replaced it then said as casually as he could, "This baby sends death out at eleven hundred and fifty-five feet a second." He pulled a marijuana joint from his pack of Camels. After a long toke he handed it to his friend then grinned again, "Yeah! I sure as hell might be hard son-of-a-bitch to kill."

After releasing the smoke from his lungs Bradley asked, "How do you know about all of these guns and stuff?"

"My dad's got a shelf fulla books on every kinda weapon there is. He doesn't read 'em but I sure as hell do." The two boys very carefully eluded the other boys all day, then met at the gymnasium when school was out. They knew the older boys would be at the football field, so they walked carefree through the gym. "This's where the mission's gonna take place, Brad."

Still high from the last joint they had smoked a short time earlier he replied, "Hey man, that's cool."

"Yeah it is, and the whole damn football team's gonna be here with their prissy ass girlfriends."

Rick Magers

"How do you know they'll be here?"

He looked at his small friend with the green spiked hair, "Just leave that to me, dude." He accepted the joint and pulled it to his lips then swallowed the tiny remaining nub. As he exhaled the smoke he said, "Got it covered."

As they stood in the gym, two younger boys came through the door with basketballs and a pass to use the facility. They walked up smiling as they dribbled their balls. The smaller of the two said, "Hiya Alleycat, what's happ'nin' dude?"

The other waved with his free hand, "Hi Alleycat, hi Brad."

Alaine reached out and grabbed the boy by the front of his shirt and pulled him in, lifting him until his basketball shoes were barely touching the floor, and his face an inch away. The boy gripped his basketball with both hands as Alaine screamed in his face. "What the fuck is this Alleycat, bullshit?" He emphasized the last word, "don't you know my name, athhole?"

"Uh, uh, uh," the boy stammered, "no, I don't. All I ever heard anyone call you is Alleycat."

Alaine attempted to imitate his tough movie idols and throw the kid across the floor a good distance, but all he accomplished was a throw that made the young boy stumble backwards until he regained his footing. "Ith Alaine you little athhole, so don't lemme hear any of that Alleycat cwap again." He stepped menacingly toward the boy, "Now, whath my name again thithead?"

From three feet the ball struck Alaine dead center in the face as the boy yelled, "Weirdo; you stuttering freak." Before Alaine could recover enough to give chase, the boys were through the gym door and running.

Alaine rubbed his face and saw blood on his hand from the bleeding nose. "Oh shit," he said as he leaned against the wall. He pulled the black handkerchief from his pocket, and dabbed at his sore nose. Bradley hadn't moved since the two little boys had approached. Alaine looked hard at him, "You were sure a lotta fuckin' help, man."

"Uh, well, uh, man those guys were fast's lightning." He looked quizzically at his friend, "Why'd you jump his shit anyway, man?"

"Why did I jump his shit?" The second time he was almost screaming, "Why'd I jump his shit? He dissed me man. You can't let anyone disrespect you man, never! No! not anyone, anywhere." He stormed toward the same door the two young boys had just escaped through. "C'mon, I'll walk with you to your house before I go home."

Bradley followed his friend from the gym, thinking, *he sure didn't yell at those football players this morning, and he ran like hell when that Japanese guy took off after him.* At his house he said, "I'll walk over to your house in the morning and walk to school with you."

Rick Magers

"That's cool man," Alaine responded and headed for his own house. "I have important mission plans to work on." As he walked along the sidewalk he thought, *No football practice on Thursday after school, so that's when the mission will be.*

Tuesday and Wednesday went along smoothly at school with no major incidents. Thursday began with a bang, figuratively, but Thursday was the day of The Mission.

~ A bigger bang was coming—literally ~

What Lucifer lost by pride, Mary won by humility. What Eve ruined and lost by disobedience, Mary saved by obedience. By obeying the serpent, Eve ruined her children as well as herself and delivered them up to him. Mary by her perfect fidelity to God saved her children with herself and consecrated them to his divine majesty." Satan has been conquered by Mary's "Yes," and therefore she is the enemy of the devil:

The Holy Bible

Alaine had never fired the Heckler & Koch .45 caliber pistol. Actually he had never fired a pistol or rifle of any kind. His father just said "No" when he asked to go with him target practicing. Alaine heard him tell his mother Mary, "That kid's just not the gun shootin' kind." Even though he knew his parents both slept like dead people he was still as quiet as a cat burglar as he assembled his gear for today's mission. When everything was on the table and floor nearby, he picked up the Heckler & Koch. He had read and re-read everything about every weapon he planned to use this day, so he expertly screwed the silencer to the end of the barrel. He had already activated the slide to place a bullet in the chamber, so he now put the safety on fire and headed upstairs. It was an hour before dawn as he inserted his lock picks into his parent's bedroom door. When he heard the lock open he picked the pistol up from the floor and silently entered.

He stood a moment looking at the back of his mother's head. *Mary, you are the enemy of my true master. You have desecrated all mankind with your obedience to his enemy, the evil God in Heaven.* With that he sent a half inch wide piece of lead and copper into his mother's head. He instantly moved the silenced weapon toward his father's face. He held it perfectly steady as he waited and hoped he would wake up. He badly wanted to ask, "Think I'm ready to shoot a gun?" When he didn't move, Alaine put a bullet between his father's eyes. He was pleased that he was as good a shot as he knew he would be. He aimed and fired two more into his father's brain. "You are as guilty as this Gods whore, Joseph." He then shot his mother two more times in the brain. He turned and saw the demons standing in the doorway.

One was short, and glowing red with yellow eyes; penetrating the darkness like a searchlight seeking a disaster-struck vessel. It stood in a crouch between a taller demon's legs, which had two identical heads: one atop the other. When it spoke, both mouths moved together but with two voices, which echoed when it growled, 'Master says you are doing very good. Today you will stand among the very highest of our Lord Satan's Disciples.' They disappeared when he walked to the door and closed it without looking back.

A few minutes after dawn he heard the doorbell ring. *Right on time*, he thought when he saw Bradley standing on the porch. "Ready for some breakfast," he asked after the boy had entered and removed the long black coat. He had painted SATAN'S DARK ANGELS on the back, and turned so Alain could see his handiwork.

"Yeah, if your mom don't mind."

"Hey man," Alain said, "That looks cool; I'll fix us some bacon and eggs. They're both still dead to the world." He grinned and added, "Both of 'em got wasted and probably won't be getting up this morning." *Or any other morning*, he thought with a smiled as he began placing a pound of bacon in the electric skillet.

After breakfast they went to the basement to get the gear for their mission. Bradley was hesitant but followed Alaine's orders. He held his arm out so the shoulder holster could be put on.

"I'm giving you this Smith & Wesson 9 mm automatic. Now remember it's got one in the chamber and the clip's got twelve more in it, ready to go. Remember how we practiced putting the safety on fire?"

"Yep, sure do."

"Good, now let's sling this Thompson on you shoulder."

"I'm getting to carry the Thompson instead of that other gun?" He asked as excited as a boy that was just told he was going to Disney World.

"Yeah man, but the ammo drum'll stick out too much, so I put a thirty round clip in it with another one taped on it upside down. Remember how to switch 'em?"

"Damned straight, bro."

"How do you get her to start firing?"

Bradley grinned, "Pull the slide on the side back and let go then pull the trigger 'n let 'er rip."

Rick Magers

"Good soldier, Brad." He slapped him on the back, "Damn good man. Leave your coat off till I get my gear on, or you'll be swimming in sweat 'fore we get outa here." When he came from the little gunroom, he had his shoulder holster on and the AK-47 hanging from a strap over his shoulder, same as he'd rigged for Bradley. "I'm using the Sphinx, 'cause it's got a fifteen round clip 'n one in the chamber, and I'm a lot more experienced than you."

Once Bradley had his trenchcoat on, Alaine picked up two hand grenades and placed them in the boy's right pocket. He then took two more around and put them in the left pocket. "Heavy ain't they?"

"Damned straight dude, I'd hate to hafta carry all this shit a long ways."

Alaine laughed, "Living close to school's got its up side."

"You got that right, man."

Alaine placed three grenades in each of his own trenchcoat pockets then said, "Let's go 'fore mom 'n pop get their heads back together." Bradley noticed the sinister grin but said nothing.

There was almost no one on the sidewalk as they covered the three blocks to the school. "Practice holding the Machinegun next to you with your hand in your pocket."

"Yeah, I been doin' it just like you taught me."

They slipped into the school through a basement door just like they usually did, and went to the rear of the janitors supply area to remove their weapons. They quickly stashed them in an unused locker, then Alaine placed a lock on it. They left the room unobserved and casually stood aside from the other students.

Before classes were finished for the day Alaine waited in the hall near the bulletin board until there was no one nearby. He quickly removed the sheet of school stationary, which he stole to type his message on, then tacked it to the board and returned to class.

<u>It read</u>

ALL FOOTBALL TEAM MEMBERS MEET AT THE GYMNASIUM
AFTER SCHOOL TO RECEIVE AWARDS AND COLLEGE OFFERS.
BRING FRIENDS.
FREE COKES AND COOKIES.

State Awards Commission

When the bell rang, Alaine and Bradley went quickly to the basement, where each smoked a joint before heading toward the gym. Alaine said, "Remember now, watch for my signal then pull the pins one-by-one and throw all four grenades into the crowd, then bring out the Thompson and spray 'em with lead." Alain's wicked grin frightened Bradley and caused a chill to run along his spine.

"Got it." Bradley's voice had a slight squeak in it, so Alaine looked at him.

"You all right man?"

"Damned straight, dude." The child spoke with confidence, but felt as though he would vomit.

When they arrived, there were more people inside than Alain had hoped for. He didn't have to take out his little book to see who was in it. He mentally checked off all of the people who had ever made fun of him. "Okay Brad, take up your position over near the girls bathroom where you'll be pretty much alone. Don't forget to watch for my signal." He watched as the green spikes wobbled toward the corner of the gymnasium. He casually moved to the other corner where he was not far from Bradley and could signal him. When he realized that most of the football players were huddled together only fifteen yards from him he looked hard at Bradley, then nodded his head.

Alain's first hand grenade went off with a thunderous roar that momentarily confused him. He hadn't expected such an explosion. He threw one as far over the center of the pandemonium as he could, then pulled the pin on his third grenade. When it exploded he looked at Bradley; staring at the carnage, and standing motionless like he'd been flash frozen. He had pulled the pins, as he was told, but still held both grenades in his hands. Alaine turned in time to see the football player who had laughed at him earlier in the week, running at him screaming. He pulled the pistol from the holster beneath his armpit as though he was a seasoned war veteran. As deftly as he had practiced, he flipped the safety off and at three yards hit the boy three times in the chest. He looked down at the damage the 9mm slugs had done and was amazed.

The grenade explosions tossed body parts everywhere, and everyone wanted out. Alaine replaced the pistol and got another grenade. It exploded near the door and tossed more bodies into the air to fall in pieces around the room. He looked again at Bradley; still frozen in the same place with blood and body parts on his small frame.

Alaine removed another grenade and rushed at his friend screaming, "You fucking wimp." He threw the grenade then flattened himself against the concrete wall next to the coke machine. After the huge explosions he looked where his friend had been standing. Nothing! *Musta had the pins out like I told him.*

Two more senior football players saw that he had nothing in his hands, so they rushed toward him. They barely had time to be shocked when the AK-47 started barking slugs into them. They died heroes and would be remembered as such. Kids and teachers were running around screaming as

Rick Magers

Alaine continued spraying the gym with bullets. When it quit firing he switched to the clip taped to the empty one and began firing at anyone who moved. It too finally emptied, so he let it hang down beneath the trenchcoat as he picked off people with the deadly accurate 9mm Sphinx. When it finally clicked on an empty chamber he tossed it down and reached in his pocket for another grenade. He pulled the pin and surveyed his work. He looked up and saw the demons all clapping and cheering. They were everywhere. Several were hanging from the basketball hoops. He watched as others ran across the dead bodies laughing and screeching like nothing he had ever heard. Screeching louder and louder and louder until he could stand it no more. He clutched the grenade close to his chest and released the pressure holding the lever.

THE END

Alain was born Oct. 4th----------LIBRA.
Bradley was born Feb. 11th-----AQUARIUS.

Demoniac frenzy, moping melancholy and moon-struck madness—Death on a pale horse.

John Milton

Rick Magers

Black Angel

Preston Childers didn't even live in the same state as Alain Catrich, but he moved along life's perilous path to the same toe-tapping beat of a similar demon. He loved a little cocaine every now and then but he sure as hell wasn't a genius. He also didn't need drugs to see the demons that had been sent to guide him along the path to immortality. Since a child he regularly saw and heard them speak.

He and his gang buddies were drinking wine on the roof of a twenty-story building. All eleven were naked, including the two young girls they had enticed to the roof with drugs and wine. They had all had sex with the girls at least once, and one was enjoying the oral sex, that a young pre-teen girl was giving him, as he performed oral sex on the fatter girl as she stood spread legged over his face.

The demon spoke now to Preston. 'See what the evil women do to our soldiers? Man is weak and they shall destroy his strength and will to do Lucifer's work. Cast them out, so you can take your rightful place as commander of these strong, young, soldiers of Satan.' Preston rubbed his eyes with his balled fists and looked out over New York City at the millions of flashing, blinking, colored lights. The demon spoke to him again, 'A spawning ground of God's evil work. There are women down there that are at this very moment enticing strong young soldiers away from Lucifer's work, just as these two did.'

He looked toward the edge where the voice came from. Standing on the parapet was a demon he had not seen before. It was less than two-feet-tall but had a barbed tail five-feet-long. Its ears protruded only a couple of inches above its blood red head, with silver horns protruding a foot high. The demon's eyes were a blazing fire in its head, and drool ran from its swollen, pus filled lips. In gnarled talons it held a penis as long as its tail. The demon wrapped the tail around it to begin massaging, then thrust the penis violently into its mouth and began sucking.

Preston watched silently as yellow liquid ran from the demon's mouth. It removed the penis and grinned malevolently at him. 'See! See? Even I succumb to these evil women's wicked ways. Cast them out and begin your war against Christ and his evil disciples.' The demon pointed a long talon at the naked woman moaning over his friend. Cast them back to their God before it is too late.

Preston was six-foot-four-inches-tall, and weighed almost three-hundred-pounds, so it was easy for him to lift the girl from his friend. Before she could scream or even think about what was happening, she was falling toward the pavement far below; her best friend not far behind.

His friend jumped up with his penis still pulsing. "What the fuck you doin', man?"

"They're God's evil worshipers and must be cast out."

"That was goddamn good head man." He followed his friends to the edge of the roof to look down, but couldn't see a thing in the blackness far below. He turned to Preston, "Man, I wish you coulda waited a minute 'fore you launched that missile-bitch; that was some good lip I was getting', dude."

One of the men spoke in a whiskey-slurred voice, "Hey m'man, that's pretty cool. That fat bitch fell like a rock but the skinny one looked like she was gonna fly, for a second." He laughed loud as he began putting on his pants.

"Yeah man," another said, "juss for a second there," he made a motion with his open hand going down toward his feet, "zzzwoosh, bitch flew like a fuckin' boulder." He laughed so hard he had to stop and bend over.

Another of Preston's friends said, "You're too fuckin' much m'man." He held up his open hand and the two men smacked them together. "That was just too damn cool, man."

Another said, "Yeah bro, you the boss."

On the way down the stairs one of the men said, "Them stinky pussy got flies, but they sure don't fly." They were all still laughing when they reached the street. No one else had seen the demon on the roof and no one saw it; now sitting on Preston's shoulder with its tail lying across the other shoulder, resting on his chest.

2

GIANT SOLDIER

One more Devil's-triumph and sorrow for our angels, one more wrong to man, one more insult to God.

Robert Browning

Preston Childers had four strikes against him in a five-strikes-and-your-out game. (1) He was black. (2) He was poor. (3) He was uneducated. (4) He was born—one strike to go.

Preston was proud that he was black, unhappy that he was poor; embarrassed that he was uneducated, and very aware that he was much smarter than the young men he hung around with.

Brutus Childers looked across the bare wooden table at his wife Anndrisha. "We's gone be livin' like dis de ress our lifes less I moves us up to where Sam living." He sat quietly looking into the dark blue lagoon of cheap wine in the bean can he held.

The petite, twenty-year-old girl, the color of honey, reached for the bottle of MD 20/20 and filled her plastic Seven-Eleven cup. After slowly draining half of it she spoke to her husband, "Preston gone be six 'n startin' school soon, so if we's goin', less go fore den."

An ever-curious boy, the unusually tall Preston had his secretly hidden glass against the wall of his bedroom, with his ear pressed to the bottom of it. His parent's conversation came through the thin wall as though it was being broadcast through their small radio. When he heard his father's response he grinned and put his secret spy device away.

The huge, illiterate shrimp boat deck hand, looked hard at his wife for a brief moment, then let the grin that she loved spread across his face, "We's goin' to New York City come August." When she jumped up and ran around the table to hug his neck he scooted back so she could sit on his lap.

"I's been wantin' to leave this cracker town for a long time darlin'." She sat on his lap sideways and hugged his thick neck.

"Fo da nex tree month I's goin' out on ever baitshrimp boat what need a man, an You work ever shiff at Burger Baby what dey let you, an we's outa here, darlin'." He held her in his muscular arm as he stood to drop his pants to the floor. He never wore under shorts, so his penis was erect and throbbing as he helped her pivot around so she could be lowered down on it. He sat back in the chair and eased her down while entering her. She always had a climax in this position, so she was soon in a slow, galloping rhythm.

Preston had cut a small hole in his wall two years earlier. He now removed the picture of Malcolm X and pulled the small wad of cotton from the hole. He stood on the chair and pressed his eye close. He had watched shows for two years that men would have paid more than his mother earned, to be allowed to watch.

Brutus had his tiny mother's large breasts out and was sucking first one then the other, as they each people moaned and mumbled. The young black boy didn't understand a thing about sex, but was sure it was something they shouldn't be doing, because they were always so secret about it. For a long time he had been seeing strange things. Things that scared him, but when he told his mother that he had been seeing crazy little people in his room, she said, "Juss you imagination stretchin' its legs chile."

His imagination was working overtime tonight.

May I meet him with one tooth and it aching, and one eye to be seeing seven and seventy devils in the twists of the road, and one old timber leg on him to limp into the scalding grave. There he is now crossing the strands, and that the Lord God would send a high wave to wash him from the world.
John Millington Synge

As the old Buick pulled out of Chester's Hammock, Alabama three months later, six-year-old Preston sat with his knees toward the back of the seat looking out the cracked rear window. Several of his friends were running along the dirt road waving at him. He smiled when he saw his strange little friends running among them. Some had several legs and some had two or three heads, but they all had one thing in common: they were on fire—he sat quietly and watched. He had long ago tired of hearing his mother tell him about his imagination. As his father made the car go faster, the kids fell into the background, but the demons continued coming. Soon they were merging into one, and by the time they caught up with the Buick, the remaining one leaped to the back bumper and stood grinning at Preston. He was blacker than the youth, but alternately glowed red, yellow and orange beneath the long silver horns protruding through the short kinky hair. Molten red saliva ran from its mouth; the demon saying, "I am with you." The flowing red cape, which had been billowing behind, suddenly swirled forward and enveloped the demon. The cape went flying in the rushing wind, and Preston was startled to see a goat standing on the trunk lid. As quickly as it had appeared the goat jumped from the moving car and ran into the nearby swamp.

Preston closed his eyes as hard as he could squeeze them. After a minute or so he opened them and saw the little town and all of the area around it blazing. "Good," he said quietly as he turned around and opened his new Devils & Demons comic book.

By the time Preston was ten-years-old he was an accepted member of the New York City street culture. His few short years in Alabama had not infected his mannerisms or his speech, so anyone listening in on a conversation by young Preston Childers would never have guessed his origins.

"Man you better come up with that five," the unusually large Preston was speaking to a boy he had cornered in the alley, "or your mama ain't gonna recognize that pretty face of yours when you go home tomorrow."

"Man," the scared boy that had borrowed three dollars from Preston said with a shaky voice, "I thought I could steal it from mama's purse, but she ain't bring no goddomm guys home dis week, so she ain't got any money."

"Tough shit," Preston slammed him against the wall, "ain't my problem asshole; I want my money."

After regaining his breath the boy asked in a frightened voice, "I can rip off my uncle for a pistol." He looked pleadingly at the big boy who demanded respect from all the kids on his block: even some in their teens. "Will that square us?"

Preston turned the front of the boy's shirt in his huge hand and leaned so close the boy closed his eyes, "With bullets, and it better shoot okay."

Rick Magers

Who will remember, passing through this gate, the unheroic dead who fed the guns? Who shall absolve the foulness of their fate—those doomed, conscripted, unvictorius ones?

Siegfried Sassoon

*On the very day young Preston Childers made the deal for the pistol, another young boy was making a deal with a pistol. This boy was twelve years old and was less than half Preston's weight, but already six-feet-tall and looked much older. He had none of Preston's street sense. He was a white boy from a good, middle class family that had been turned on to the wonders of crack cocaine by one of the older boys from his school. After trying everything he could think of to get enough money for another fix, he took his fathers small pistol and walked into the nearby liquor store. Without a smile or any other emotion showing on his face he walked straight to the old man standing behind the counter and shot him in the chest. With his heart punctured, the old man lay dying on the floor as the young gunman worked frantically to open the cash register. The sound of the pistol shot brought an off duty policeman running. When he entered the store he was facing the barrel of the pistol held by a skinny man behind the counter. His aim was much better than the bandit's, and his bullet hit just above the nose. Several bottles of twelve-year-old scotch had twelve-year-old brains scattered across them.

The demons he had been living with departed in search of a new host.

For want of a nail the shoe is lost, for want of a shoe the horse is lost, for want of a horse the rider is lost.

George Herbert

The following day Preston met the boy with the pistol. After removing the six bullets from the revolving chamber he pulled the trigger several times. Satisfied that it was a good gun he replaced all of the bullets, wiping his fingerprints from each shell carefully. With it in his pocket he smiled at the boy, "That's cool m'man, now any time you need some scratch, just lemme know." When the boy smiled back, and started to leave Preston grabbed his shoulder. "Don't be borrowing no bread from nobody but me."

The boy shook his head emphatically and disappeared down the alley. Preston watched the frightened boy run then turned to exit the alley by the rear. Standing among the garbage cans along the walls were several of his demon friends. Each congratulated him as he passed by. 'Hey m'man, you're doin' great—You're the main man—Keep 'em scared of ya, dude.'

Ten-year-old Preston swaggered along the dark alley with complete confidence. *As long as I'm with Satan,* he thought, *I can do, or have anything I want.*

When Preston was twelve-years-old disaster hit the Childers family. His mother was crying when he returned from school one afternoon. He cautiously approached her asking, "Whazapnin' mama?"

Through sobs she shakily replied, "You daddy dead, son."

The six-foot-tall boy had no understanding at all about the emotion everyone referred to as love, so he simply stood and waited for his mother to explain.

She dabbed at her eyes then continued, "He carrying some business for your Uncle Sammy, when someone shot him."

The youth had the savvy of a twenty-year combat veteran of the streets; the only thought running through his head, *daddy got careless.*

He turned toward the door, and then said over his shoulder, "Got som'n to do mama, I'll be back later."

Preston helped his father deliver some of the cocaine on several occasions, so he had a good idea where he would locate his Uncle Sammy. An hour after beginning his search, he saw Samuel Preston Childers leave a bar. He approached the tall, skeletal thin, cadaverous black man that he admired since meeting him. "Hey Uncle Sammy, got a minute?"

The skeleton turned then displayed a wide, white grin in its sunken, fleshless face. "Hey little dude' whacha up to?"

Preston stopped in front of him and spread his thick arms, "You call this, a little dude?"

Sam shook his head approvingly up and down, "Yeah man, you damn sho is growin' up. Whachoo now, 'bout fifteen?"

"That's right," he responded, (no one would believe this hulk could only be twelve years old) "and I'm ready to go to work, so how 'bout you giving me my dad's business?"

Sam looked at the boy through skeptical eyes, "You heard about your old man, huh?"

"Yeah, mama juss tole me, but that ain't important now; shit, he gone anyway." He looked hard at his uncle, "I wanna make some real money and ain't nobody know these streets better'n me, so whadaya say?"

Rick Magers

Sam grinned, "Man, I bet you is tough 'nough t'handle it; shitchess, you in little bro."

It was a good business decision, because by the time Preston really was fifteen he had made a lot of money for his uncle. He was also making good money himself plus a reputation that he was not someone to cross. The demons, which were constantly with him now, encouraged his ruthless dealings with adversaries. 'That's right; you the man, so don't let 'em take advantage of you just because you're not schoolhouse educated.'

One that did (or tried to) was a short little Jamaican man who thought the young boy would be an easy target. He watched Preston as he worked his drug route and soon had the spot where he would rob him planned. It went without a hitch. The Jamaican stepped from the dark doorway and placed the barrel of his revolver against Preston's head. As he leaned against the alley wall to be frisked he looked down and saw a tattoo on the man's hand. It might as well have been a judge handing out a death sentence; instead of the word DEATH beneath a skull.

It took Preston less than two weeks to locate the man with the tattoo. His turf was only a couple of miles away so it was easy for Preston to have a couple of his friends keep an eye on the Jamaican and find out if he ever followed a routine.

His men soon reported back with what he had hoped for. "He goes to this one whore every night after he leave the bar where he works."

Preston's blackness was indistinguishable from the blackness of the doorway in the alley, close to where the Jamaican would exit from the whore's pad. When he passed the doorway later that night he felt the blow on the rear of his head and fell to the asphalt. Preston held the Colt 38, which he had taken for the five dollars owed him years earlier, in his hand. He knew it would make a loud noise so he used the best silencer he had at the moment. He shoved the barrel as far into the panic stricken Jamaican's mouth as possible before pulling the trigger. There was blood and brains all over the asphalt but very little noise.

The Demons jumped with glee. 'Good! Good job, you da man.'

For God created man to be immortal, and made him to be an image of his own eternity. Nevertheless through envy of the Devil came death into the world.

The Apocrypha

Rick Magers

By the time Preston was eighteen he was becoming very prominent in the dark catacombs of New York City's underworld of drugs. The money he was making was substantial, and at times he enjoyed all that it could buy. At other times he would pass it out to street people telling them, "Walk away from this madness before it is too late. My master is coming soon to gather his forces to begin the cleansing war." Usually these hopeless, homeless people would look at the huge black man, and then nod their heads in agreement. Most knew the man by reputation and others sensed that he was not a man to disagree with. They were right.

Preston saw his demon friends all the time now. He was aware that he had been chosen to lead the war against God and his White Angels, because no one else ever saw the demons. He no longer told others about them and as time passed, his gang of thieves, rapists, thugs and murderers soon forgot how crazy he seemed, during the period when he talked constantly to someone they thought he had been referring to as De Mon. Many thought, *Dat boy crazy as a bedbug,* and avoided him like the plague.

One full moon night, Preston moved through his asphalt jungle as silently as a tiger and twice as deadly, when he heard a noise ahead in the alley. His eyes had long ago adjusted to night travel, since he rarely moved outside in daylight—he was at home in darkness. On feet designed to be clumsy, he nevertheless moved stealthily ahead as silent as a cobra. To Preston's eyes, the white man's face stood out like a beacon as he leaned against the wall, while a young black whore squat on her knees and worked feverishly on his penis to earn her drug money for the next fix.

Preston's demons had merged into one, and now it stood beside him with it's long black arm lying on his shoulder. It was pointing a six-inch, razor sharp talon at the man a few feet ahead. 'There is the true evil that God has turned loose on this earth.' It whispered in his ear, 'they must be wiped out.'

In one swift, silent move, Preston had the man's neck in his right hand. The man was jammed against the wall with his shoes just above the filthy floor of the alley. He pulled a wad of bills from his pocket and handed them to the terrified girl. "Take this and go." As he spoke, there were red, yellow, and green lights flashing on and off all around him, and his head felt like it was going to explode.

This was happening more often lately, and he never knew when it would be upon him. Through the flashing lights he saw the white face with its tongue sticking out. The man was clawing at Preston's arm with both hands and with one last effort he used all of his fingers to attempt to make the crazy giant stop squeezing his throat. Both of his arms suddenly felt like they were made of lead. As Preston's flashing lights began to fade, the white arms dropped to the man's side. His last sight was of two men looking at him. One was red and had two enormous horns sticking up from its head. The other was black with red eyes that glowed like two chunks of molten glass in a patch of tar. Two demons.

'She's the cause of all of this evil,' the demon whispered in Preston's ear, as the long talon pointed at the young whore limping toward the street. He held the limp body against the wall for a couple of moments as he watched her move to the sidewalk then turn the corner and disappear. He dropped the dead man and walked swiftly after her. When he reached the street he looked in the direction she had gone. Nothing—vanished!

The young whore had been on the streets since she was ten-years-old. The moment she turned the corner out of the alley, she ran as fast as she was capable; with the frozen knee a pimp had destroyed years earlier. She had smelled danger many times, but had never heard so many alarms going off inside her head at one time. She knew the door was not capable of being locked, in the old rundown apartment building ahead, so she ran up the concrete steps as swiftly as her game leg would allow. She quietly closed the door behind her and scurried beneath the stairs, and lay among the urine soaked papers, empty bottles and rats that were now scurrying away from the intruder. They would soon return.

Preston turned the corner as the door closed. He looked hard ahead to catch a glimpse of the fleeing whore. Nothing! His eyes and brain began to scan the area as efficiently as radar could scour the skies for enemy aircraft. The street was deserted this late at night, and the few lights that had not been broken out cast an eerie glow on the walls of the buildings. He knew that the alley he had just left was the only break in the solid concrete ahead. His uneducated mind efficiently calculated how far a crippled person could go in the time allowed. He moved slowly ahead until he was at the bottom of the concrete steps, leading to the door of the old apartment building where he once lived. The only changes in this part of town were birth and death, so he knew it would be unlocked.

There were no flashing lights now, and the demon was no longer with him. Preston was now one of SATAN'S DARK ANGELS on a mission. He stepped into the room and closed the door, remaining motionless and listening. All of his senses were highly tuned. He was like a cat searching for its prey; huge flat nose twitching—smelling the air in the tiny enclosure. He heard a soft noise, barely distinguishable. *Rats*, he thought, *they always be rustling around in them papers under the stairs, but das not them now.* He listened as his nose finally picked up her scent. He stepped forward and bent down, "C'mon outa there, girl."

The fourteen-year-old whore was trembling. She still held the wad of bills the giant had given her. She tried to be quiet but she was trembling so, that the papers she was lying on were rattling.

"C'mon outa there girl," he repeated.

She consoled herself with a thought, *He juss wantin' some head f'dat money.* She spoke in a whisper, "Yessir, I comin' out now."

When she was standing beside the stairwell, and resting one hand against the wall to keep her trembling legs from letting her fall, the cobra struck. It hit her in the tiny neck just as it had the white man in the alley. There wasn't much fight left in her after the last few years, so she quickly went limp. The flashing lights began going off again and several of the demons were in the hall with him now. 'You got the bitch, good. She's the reason we don't have enough soldiers like you.'

He released his grip and let her dead body fall to the floor. The money he had given her was spread around nearby. There would be a celebration in the morning as the building dregs began coming back into the day world. The money would provide a celebration for a short time. There would be another celebration and feasting tonight also—Rats! They had run from their spot, but soon returned. Others would hear the gnawing and rush to join their fellow ghouls. The smell of blood and fresh flesh soon permeated the entire building, as rats began arriving in large numbers.

The first man down the stairs in the morning turned to his companion as he began picking up the money, "Sure glad those damn rats don't like the taste o' money." He turned a toothless grin toward the old woman with him.

"Looks like a child."

After all the bills were in his pocket he stood and looked down, "Can't really tell what it was."

"Don't really matter none," his thirty-year-old companion responded through rotten teeth, "let's go get some wine and crank."

*About noon on this same day twelve young boys were taking turns raping a nine-year-old retarded girl they had lured into a secluded area of the park. When they finished their sport each took pleasure in urinating on the sobbing, bleeding young child. As they all swaggered from the bushes in search of new prey, a band of hideous demons danced around the girl a moment then ran to catch up with their own prey.

Life imitates death and is often but a movable feast.

An observation

Rick Magers

It was shortly after Preston tossed the two whores from the top of the building, that he decided the only way to serve Satan was to become celibate. He was convinced that he had been chosen to lead the war in the overthrow of God and his White Angels. He spoke often to the men in his drug running gang about giving up their ways with women. "They's the means by which God can make you do things you shouldn't, and wouldn't even be thinkin' 'bout if they wasn't rubbing their nasty body all over you all the time." He was a very forceful man and all knew he didn't take well to being ignored, so they all agreed with him and didn't say anything about their desires to have a woman when they were near him. When they decided to get a woman for the night, they did it in an area far from their turf. There were from ten to twenty men working for Preston at different times and they all feared him: for good reason.

One thing his new fanaticism about keeping away from women did was make his business bring much more money in; his men were spending more time moving drugs, and less time setting up rendezvous with whores. They weren't happy about it, because all of the whores in their area knew better than to charge for their services, or they wouldn't get the drugs they needed to survive. Preston's gang now controlled all drugs in his considerably large area.

"Man, I hates this shit," one of his men was saying to another of Preston's runners, "all dis free pussy an we's gotta go way to de udder side o' town 'n pay some bitch for it."

"Let dat word get back to de boss," the man replied, "an you ain gonna have nuttin' to get dat pussy wit." He grinned wide adding, "Sides dat you makin' mo money dan de damn president of motor-fucking-ola." Both men laughed but realized that both points were true.

Preston's drug delivery business had reached the point where all he had to do was pick it up from his uncle and pass it to his main man, Bromo. This man was almost as big as Preston, but lacked the cunning and viciousness required to handle a bunch of men like these. He got his name due to a Bromo Seltzer addiction, which he had suffered from until a ten-year stint in Attica helped him shake it. The Bromo was making him shaky and mean when he couldn't get it, so his convict friends introduced him to cocaine. He was only fifteen at the time he entered Attica, and already well over six-feet-tall, weighing close to three-hundred-pounds. Most thought he was about twenty years old, so when asked about his age, that's what he told them. It was the first time he had ever been arrested, so his official record listed him as twenty-years-old, and got him five years closer to the grave—which wasn't far away.

Bromo wasn't illiterate. He learned to read and write in prison and even earned his GED certificate. He had a natural grasp of mathematics, which was why he never wrote anything down. If Bromo gave a man five kilos of cocaine to deliver, he'd better have five kilos money when it was time to collect. Preston liked the man from the moment they met, and never doubted his word regarding amounts of product or money. He advanced him to the head position below him within a year.

A jealous runner thought he should have the job. He couldn't believe anyone could remember so many different figures without writing them down, so he shorted him five thousand dollars, thinking it would turn Preston against Bromo. Preston asked the man to come and tell him what had happened.

Bromo leaned against the warehouse wall, behind a seated Preston, when the man came to explain, and hopefully secure the job from the newcomer. "Dis de deal mon," he began, as he looked at his huge young boss, leaning on arms the size of the smoked hams he often dreamed of one day having to eat all alone. It had always upset him to see the huge hands with fingers the size of bananas spread out on the desk in front of him. He was aware what those powerful hands could do, when the man was irritated. He also knew that nothing made his boss madder than to be cheated. He moved ahead cautiously. "Dis new man got a good head f'numbers 'n stuff like that boss, but he mess up on the amount he givin' me lass week." A wide smile crossed his black face, "He ain't mean to do dat I sho, but he oughta be writing them number on paper."

He was certain that he had presented his case well enough to at least get to enjoy the five thousand dollars, and maybe even get Bromo's job. He felt confident when Preston returned his smile as he stood. He watched as the giant black man pulled a wad of bills from his pocket and came around the table.

"You reckon you pretty good with bills?" He began spreading the bills in his hand out to form a fan. "How much you think I got right here in my hand?"

The man was nervous now, so he stuttered a little. "Uh, uh, uh, about a thousand dollars I reckon."

"Nope!" Preston grinned, "Five." He had the man by the neck so fast that even Bromo didn't see his hand move. When the man's mouth popped open from the pressure, Preston began shoving the bills into it. "This gonna be the most expensive dinner you ever had, motherfucker."

As the bills were shoved into his throat, the man's eyes bulged out like a grouper snatched from the ocean depths. Preston removed a short stick he had in his rear pocket and began shoving the bills far into the man's throat—all five thousand dollars. The man clawed frantically at Preston's arms, but before he could do any damage, Bromo had them pinned to the floor beneath size sixteen shoes. Bromo thought for sure the man's eyes were going to pop from his head as Preston continued shoving the bills down his throat. Before the last few were shoved in, the man quit twitching and lay still.

Rick Magers

"Leave this thievin' son-of-a-bitch right where he be; we movin to a new place." He casually headed for the gated elevator, which was the only entrance to his place of business. Bromo followed, and on the way down Preston turned to him, "When I trust a man I trust him all the way—when I don't, he dead."

Now, a few years later, Bromo was thinking, *This man gone crazy 'bout dis shit. Devil, demons, evil womens.* He shook his head from side to side, *He gone get ever one of us killed.*

After a few weeks of thought, Bromo knew what he had to do, and approached Preston. "Boss, less go up on the roof where we won't be bothered. Ise gone explain my new ideas to you."

"Sure man, I love to go up there 'n look at dem city lights on a dark night like this."

"I got us a couple bottles of Mad Dog. About time we taking a little ress from dis business."

Preston had an elevator installed in the fifteen-story building he now owned. It ran from his offices on the fourteenth floor to the fifteenth, which was his warehouse for the drugs he got from his uncle. It then continued to the roof. There was no other way to get to the roof—he thought.

When they arrived on the roof, Preston stepped out and looked up at the sky. "This gonna be a more better world after me and Satan finish with that God up there."

"Here you go man," Bromo said as he handed a bottle of wine to Preston and removed the other one from the bag. He knew his boss's paranoid ways, so wasn't surprised when he handed the bottle of MD 20/20 back.

"You take dis one, 'n I gone drink yours."

Exactly what I knew dat crazy motherfucker gonna do. "Sure boss, here you go." He had learned in prison how to remove a twist-off cap and replace it without disturbing the seal. He could tell even in the dark that Preston was listening for the telltale crackle of the aluminum seal breaking free of the cap when he twisted it. Bromo had opened his bottle by this time and said, "Man, that is the most beautiful city in the world, huh?"

Bromo was amazed that Preston was able to drink the entire bottle of wine before he finally collapsed. He called to the two runners that had been waiting in the darkness on the far side. He paid the two ex-marines five thousand dollars each to climb from the thirteenth floor up the outside and be waiting on the roof just in case. "I'm glad all went the way it did, 'cause there'd be a lot to explain if you had to shoot him." He looked at the huge black hulk a moment then said, "C'mon, let's get this crazy April Fool off of here."

With considerable difficulty the three men finally got the three-hundred-and-fifty-pound man up on the edge and on his way to the alley far below.

THE END

Preston was born April 1st----------ARIES

An April Fool.

Rick Magers

Island Goddess

A belief in a supernatural source of evil is not necessary; men alone are quite capable of every wickedness.

Joseph Conrad

    Yorda Poleski was a model student all the way through grammar school; making the honor roll in his senior year at Brahdam High School. He had several colleges to choose from, because of his wealthy father's connections, and could have gone to Harvard, but enrolled in Central College instead. His father was visibly upset with his son's choice of school, but kept silent.

    Lundren and Gromma Poleski gave their son everything he had ever wanted his entire life, so it was expected that they would not interfere with his school plans. They didn't, but wondered why he would choose such a small, unimpressive school for the most important part of his education. They discussed it between themselves but after months of futile words, were no closer to his reasons than the day he dropped his bombshell on them. Part of the reason was the unending string of social gatherings they attended; parties out—and at the Poleski Estate. There never seemed to be any one-on-one time for the shy, introverted son of the successful immigrant Poleski family.

    The other reason was that the two doting parents never questioned their son's actions. If he didn't come home from a social event, all he had to do was tell them he would be home the following day.

    The real reason that he decided to go to Central College was the pretty, young, black girl from Jamaica, who had started school at Brahdam High in the eleventh grade. He had never so much as spent time alone with a girl, mainly because his shyness, but Baileen Darden recognized something she had been searching for in the handsome young boy. She reached inside him, and lit a flame. Before the eleventh grade reached the Christmas holidays the young boy had his first sexual encounter—he was hooked.

    Baileen was soon sharing something else with Yorda. Her grandparents had passed it to her parents, who in turn passed it on to their young daughter. It would change the young man's life drastically, and send him spinning down a dark tunnel of despair. It would also send his loving, if somewhat distracted, parents into a dark tunnel of another kind. Yorda had found Voodoo.

If Mr. and Mrs. Poleski had been asked about their opinion of Voodoo, she would have answered, "Oh, it's just some weird goings on that the blacks do at their parties." Mr. Poleski would have replied, "It's just an excuse the blacks use to drink their dope and have orgies. A religion? Ha! There is only one true Christian religion, and that is the one dictated by His Holiness from the Vatican in Rome." He always shoved his chin out after his rehearsed, senseless, verbal masturbation on religion. "All others will burn in hell when the day of reckoning arrives."

Yorda's parents compared equally, in their lack of knowledge, of all matters beyond the maintaining of their financial empire and the way of life they enjoyed.

The first time Baileen invited Yorda to stay overnight, while her parents were away; she introduced him to her religion. He sat quietly and watched as she lit one hundred candles. He had learned to maintain an iron will over his inner emotions, so when she returned with a freshly killed chicken he sat stoically rigid against the seawall next to her parents yacht and watched.

As incense permeated the area, she began to dance slowly with the dead chicken. The quiet music in the background had a primeval rhythm that Yorda had never heard, and it turned his senses on. He watched mesmerized as she slowly undressed then began rubbing the dead chicken all over her body. While holding its limp head in one hand, she flipped it between her legs, grabbing its feet with the other. As she slowly ran it back and forth between her legs she said, "Take your clothes off." She continued to dance as he removed his shirt first, then his trousers after kicking off his shoes. She saw the bulge in his shorts and commanded, "All of your clothes."

Yorda was self-conscious as he stood before his first girlfriend with his erect penis protruding. He swallowed hard when she began caressing it with the dead chicken, but he remained like a statue as she went to the small altar in the center of the candles. His eyes were riveted to her beautiful black body, roaming slowly up her perfect legs to her plump buttocks. He caught glimpses of the black silky hair between her legs, but moved quickly to her large firm breasts, which caused his insides to boil. His eyes went back and forth between the two dark red cherries that protruded at the tips of her breasts. His attention was diverted when he saw her pick up the knife. He drank in the scene like a man saved from the desert by a water bearer.

She picked up the chicken's freshly severed head and began speaking to it in a language he knew wasn't her native tongue, then tossed it violently out into the water. "Here my lover, take this pill and it will help you converse with the demons." He obeyed and promptly swallowed it. She picked up the chicken's headless body and began swinging it to splash blood over Yorda.

Rick Magers

Baileen then laid the chicken down, to pour blood from the plate the chicken had been draining into over her glistening body. Once again she picked the chicken up and was speaking the same guttural words into its headless neck. She began spinning around with the chicken held at arms length, and then threw it as far out into the darkness above the water as she could.

Yorda remained standing. Unnoticing—uncaring; blood running slowly down his naked body, completely mesmerized by this lovely apparition who seemed to care about no one but him. She came to him and held his erect penis in one hand and the cheek of his ass in the other. "Bring yourself into me before they arrive."

As he guided his penis into her tight, velvet smooth, moist opening, he wondered who they were and when they would arrive? At this very moment it could have been the Brahdam High School Band and he could not have prevented himself from continuing. He was not yet aware of the power of her drugs, but the pill was taking effect—Voodoo demons would soon arrive.

1

DREAM LOVER

Give me the daggers. The sleeping and the dead are but as pictures: 'tis the eye of childhood that fears a painted Devil.

Shakespeare

Yorda Poleski lay beside the naked, beautiful young Jamaican and looked into her smiling eyes. The glowing light of the fire, in the early evening darkness, made the seventeen-year-old girl look much older—wiser—exotic. This was the first time in his life that he didn't feel self conscious, inferior, or embarrassed. He felt in total control of his life. In fact he felt as though he could handle anything—anywhere—any time. He looked from her dark eyes up into the sky and could see far into the next galaxy and beyond. The stars were crashing into each other, causing great explosions of every color imaginable. "Oh wow," he said as he looked back at Baileen Darden, "I feel, uh, uh," he sat up and looked into the fire that had eyes looking back at him. He stared into the face in the fire. It had yellow and green flames shooting from its eyes. He repeated quietly, "I feel uh, uh. . .

"In control," she whispered suggestively as she sat up and put her arm around his narrow shoulders.

Yorda turned to look into her eyes; now also sparkling with many different colors. Her face was still beautiful, even with the blood drying black against its honey color. Her body was changing shape as he watched. Her voice now came to him as though from a deep tunnel, "IN CONTROL," she repeated.

"Yes," he answered as he turned to look at the face in the fire. It was now rising from the glowing embers, flames still shooting from its eyes. The eyes stared intently into Yorda's. "Yes, I'm in total control of my destiny." He turned to her as she reached her arms around him from behind, grabbing his throbbing penis.

She lay back onto the grass with her arms spread open toward him, "Come into me again."

He rolled over on top of her to look into her eyes. They began to glow deep inside the now changing face. It was an older, more beautiful, mystical—much more desirable face. As he entered her, the mouth that now had fangs instead of teeth whispered, "Now you are mine forever."

Their desires exploded simultaneously as he felt claws enter his buttocks and hold him close to her as she shuddered with spasms. When their slow, rhythmic gyrations subsided, he lay spent on top of her. After a few moments she released her hold on his buttocks and he rolled over on his back with his eyes closed. "Incredible," he said with them still tightly closed. "Absolutely incredible."

Yes! It was. The voice was deep and more like a whisper of the wind. Yorda turned toward the voice and saw the old man standing in the middle of the fire; now blazing, even though there were no big logs in it.

"They are here," Baileen said in her calm, lilting, singsong, Caribbean voice.

Be sober, be vigilant; because your adversary the devil, as a roaring lion, walketh about, seeking whom he may devour.

The Holy Bible

When Yorda was finally able to pull his eyes away from the apparition in the fire, he turned back to Baileen. She too was now ablaze, with several hideous little demons gathered around her. They were touching her naked body as they danced around. One jumped up and locked his legs around her waist, and began suckling her breasts. Another had his face buried between her legs. The others were pawing and licking her beautiful slender legs.

'Desire.' He turned back to the old man standing in the fire when he heard him speak.

'Desire fuels mankind's destruction.'

Yorda awoke the following morning with the early sun washing his naked body as he lay in the grass. "You hungry, sleepyhead?" He raised his head to look at Baileen, walking naked toward him. The chicken blood from last night's ritual was washed away, and her body had sheen to it as though she had been rubbed with oil. His penis automatically began rising. "You go take a shower, we'll take care of that later." He stood, surprised that he was not in the slightest embarrassed to be standing in front of her with a throbbing erection. "C'mon, I'll show you where the shower is."

He stepped from the shower and toweled off as he walked toward the kitchen. He could hear Baileen rattling pans. "You are so beautiful, Baileen," he said as he watched her naked body moving through the kitchen.

She turned a radiant white smile to him, "Tank you, an you a hondsome young hunk o' mon, you ownself," she said in her quaint Caribbean singsong voice.

"That was fabulous last night." He felt an uncontrollable urge to talk about it.

"It was for me too," she said over her shoulder as she prepared bacon and scrambled eggs, "it was you first time wasn't it?"

Yorda was quite amazed that he felt no embarrassment at all around his pretty Jamaican girlfriend. "Yes," he paused a moment then added, "how about you?"

She laughed gaily then answered, "No mon, I have lovers before, but never one like you." She moved the skillet over onto a cold burner and walked to him. With her slender, almond colored arms around his neck she said, "I feel so close to you Yorda; like I've know you all my life." She kissed him long and deep as he lifted her up so she could wrap her legs around his waist.

He pulled a chair from the table with his foot and sat gently down. He kept his hands on her slender waist, holding her up as she guided him into her. He sat motionless as she gripped the dowels on the chair with her toes and began slow, rhythmic motions. After their passion was spent he rushed back to the shower as she laughed and continued fixing breakfast.

As Yorda ate he asked, "Did you see the same things I did last night?"

"Dunno? When de Obeah come dey come in all kine of ting. I all de time see different one; sides you was out a long time, mon."

"Out?"

"Yes mon," she replied laughingly in her native voice.

"How long?"

"Mmmmmm, bout two hour."

His mouth hung open. "Jeez, I don't even remember falling asleep."

"You wasn't asleep, boy." The same singsong voice with laughter built into it, "You was in trance."

He just sat and stared out at the back yard through the open French doors. "Yeah, I kinda remember feeling really weird as I was watching the fire. Was it that pill you gave me?"

"Dat pill help you lose you modern, city-boy self and let the jungle animal inside you come out, but ise de one that put you in a trance." She smiled at him coyly, "You my slave forever now."

He matched her smile with a pearl white one of his own, "Sounds like a good deal to me." After he finished his breakfast he looked at the clock on the wall, "Wow! It's later'n I thought. My folks're coming home early today, so I'm gonna have to get dressed and head on outa here." He moved close and pulled her to him, "Older people always say we're too young at our age to know what love is, but Baileen there isn't a doubt in my mind that I'll love you forever." He gently kissed her forehead as he hugged her.

Self-reverence, self-knowledge, self-control. These three alone lead life to a sovereign power.

Alfred, Lord Tennyson

* As love was bursting from Yorda's young soul, for the beautiful Caribbean Goddess that fate had blessed him with, a bomb was bursting from its container aboard an airliner high above the earth. As almost three hundred people screamed in terror while falling from the sky, a band of demons floated among them screaming in pleasure before departing to re-join their earthly hosts.

...

A short time later, she smiled as he kissed her again then headed for his home, a short walk away. The young Caribbean girl was now dressed in one of her favorite casual dresses. It was hand painted by a Jamaican artist, and its many colors hung loosely over her frame. When she returned to the kitchen she opened a small piece of brown grocery bag paper and dumped its contents onto the table. She ran her finger through the several strands of hair and toenail clippings she had taken from Yorda while he was in a trance. Baileen carefully returned them to the paper and secured it with several rubber bands.

When she looked up, it was into the molten green eyes of the same demon that had been her companion for a very long time. His black skin smoldered as he opened his mouth to reveal festering pustules that oozed a thick yellow substance between long, gray, slime-covered fangs. The voice was the same whispering one that Yorda had heard last night, coming from the old man in the fire. 'You have done well, little Mermaid.'

The smile he saw was not the same sweet one that Yorda saw. It was a sinister smile followed by a wicked laugh. "Yes mighty Obeah Mon, Prince of all mon, Master of Darkness. Yes, he now mine forever." She smiled and spoke in a sinister voice, "And yours too."

The Devil showed unto him all the kingdoms of the world in a moment of time.

The Holy Bible

Prior to her father relocating his business and family to Miami Florida, Baileen Darden's last two years in her hometown of Montego Bay, Jamaica in the West Indies was the beginning of a downward spiral into the black world of demons that would forever alter her young life.

Prior to the arrival of her mother's brother Randall, from Miami, everything in the young island girl's life was as good as it gets.

When her tall, bronze-skinned uncle arrived, she stood beside her mother at the airport. She had never met him, and was anticipating meeting the adventurous man her mother talked so much about over the years. When her mother began waving to the smiling man in line, Baileen said to her, "He as handsome as you said he would be mama."

Ayeelah Darden smiled at her daughter. "Yes chile, dem girl always be chasin dat handsome brother of mine."

After hugging his sister, then swinging her around, he turned his attention to the young girl standing nearby. "Doan tell me dis dat little girl you been writing me about?" He looked at his sister with a huge, white smile full of gold teeth.

"Dat de very same one," she responded.

At six-and-a-half-feet-tall the two-hundred-and-fifty-pound man had no trouble at all picking little Baileen up by her tiny waist and laughing as he held her high. "You lookin like a complete woman stead o' dat little baby girl you mama been talkin bout." He turned completely around then gently set her on her feet.

When her father arrived home that night, she could tell that there was not a warm feeling between the two men. The cool reception Boone Darden gave his brother-in-law confirmed the feelings. Baileen had felt something at the airport. *Som'n not right bout dis slick fella.*

Four days after Randall Madsmith Pope arrived, he waited until his brother-in-law left to go to his dry cleaning/laundry business. He spoke to his sister, who he knew would have to be at the plant soon to assist her husband, "I gone ride up dat mountain to see some dem fella I growin up wit. You tink you can take de day way from dat sweathouse you sorry husband makin you slave you pretty self away in, an come ridin wit me?"

"No mon," She smiled, then said more sternly, "an Boone doan makin me do dat work. I work wit him cause we gone move to Florida soon."

Randall Pope turned to his pretty young niece, "How bouchew little butterfly, you gone ridin up in dem mountain witchew Uncle Randall, an show him where all dem folk livin now?"

"I uh, uhm, uh," she stammered.

"Sure she go witchew," her mother said, "she doan git away from dat laundry in de summertime near nuff."

"Well den," he smiled at Baileen, "dat settle. Get you tings an less git goin."

In her young girl's mind she knew something was wrong, but Baileen had been raised to trust her parents' judgment, so she gathered together a straw basket of items and followed her Uncle Randall to his rental car.

An hour up into the mountains he pulled the car onto a small dirt road and stopped moments later under a grown over canopy of tree limbs. He reached beneath the seat and produced a bottle of rum, "Less have our ownselves a little drink," he grinned.

She was frozen with fright, and just shook her head no. She watched as he drank several times from the bottle, and kept looking silently at her.

"Girl, what de matter witchew?"

Still she couldn't speak because of the fright. She shook her head from side to side as he reached out to hand her the bottle.

"Shit," he said loudly as he placed the bottle on the dash and reached out and grabbed her around her waist. "What de matter girl, you tryin to play dat hard to get deal?" When she didn't answer he pulled her so quickly toward him that she wasn't able to prevent him from reaching down and ripping her panties off. Before she could think of some way to keep him away he had entered her. Her eyes bulged out of their sockets as he plunged and plunged until he finally broke through her virginity. She screamed once sharply from the pain then began sobbing as he pumped away until his lust was satisfied.

"Well I be goddomm," he said as he held his limp penis and looked at the blood on it. "Who ever gone believe you still a virgin girl?" He laughed and grabbed the bottle of rum. After a long drink he reached behind the seat and grabbed an old T-shirt he had thrown there the day before. "Here, clean you pussy up wit dis." He sat watching as she turned away from him and cleaned herself as good as she could. "Clean dat shit off de seat too, bitch."

After she cleaned everything, Randall leaned close and said menacingly, "Girl, keep you mout shut bout dis less you want you daddy dead." He took another long drink then added with a nasty chuckle, "An I won't bat one eye bout killin dat sorry ass niggah."

For the next week Baileen went about her days normally for fear that her uncle would carry out his threat against her father. She felt that it was all her fault anyway, because she had known she shouldn't have gone anywhere alone with him.

She breathed a sigh of relief when his plane finally lifted from the runway, bound for Miami. Her mother looked at her and smiled, "So whachew tink bout Randall? He quite a mon, huh?"

She just shook her head then looked away. Her father spoke up loudly, "Quite a mon dat feller is, oh yeah, he a drug mon sellin dat nosty shit to all dem kids what gotta go steal money so dey can make dat fella rich." He turned after his speech and walked to their car. On the way home his wife remained silent for quite awhile.

"You don't know he do dat f'sure, Boone."

Her father made that snapping sound with his tongue against the roof of his mouth and the back of his upper teeth, that Baileen loved so much, then glanced from the road ahead to his wife. "Ayeelah, ever body roun dis place know what he do." He returned his eyes to the road but continued, "Woman, he git dat shit from here."

Ayeelah Darden had also heard the talk and knew it was probably true, but she felt compelled to defend the little brother she had raised after a home fire killed their parents and left them orphans. "How come he doan visit when he comin to get dem drugs?"

The snapping sound again, and now Baileen was grinning, "Woman he doan come an git dem dom drugs he ownself, he got mans here what send him what he ax for."

The balance of the ride home was silent. Baileen sat in the rear, thinking. *Uncle, one dese day you gone wish to God you ain do dat to me.*

From all the deceits of the world—the flesh—and the Devil.

The Book of Common Prayer.

✻As Randall Madsmith Pope was speeding through the sky toward home, and Baileen Darden was dreaming of the time when she and her demons would exact their revenge, a distraught young man was entering the Mr. Burger Basket in his small hometown. He was talking loudly to himself. Many around him thought it weird that he was wearing a long raincoat on a clear day.

Rick Magers

The sixteen-year-old boy opened the raincoat and brought up a 12-gauge shotgun that had been hanging from his shoulder on a strap. When it finally clicked on empty, three children and one old lady lay dead among several wounded customers. He let the empty shotgun swing down then raised the military assault rifle hanging from the other shoulder and began firing. When the thirty round clip was empty he calmly walked through the wounded and dying bodies looking at the tables. When he located one that had an uneaten tripleburger, supersize fries and gallon 'o' gulp, the short three-hundred-and-fifty-pound youth sat down and frantically began eating as though he was near starvation.

Later, at police headquarters he told the investigator, "Those skinny people are all evil and my demons have been telling me for a long time that they should all die."

All that we see or seem is but a dream within a dream.

Edgar Allan Poe

Ayeelah Darden had introduced the dark world of the occult to her daughter Baileen on her thirteenth birthday. "We gone up in dem Mountain tonight," she told her daughter, "an you gone learn bout de oldest religion on dis eart, darlin. De Obeah mon gone show you how Voodoo make you life better when you needs it."

The young girl was only mildly interested at the time, but after being raped by her uncle she developed an obsession with the magic of Voodoo and all of the demons the old Obeah man could call forth when she visited him.

The ancient old man was always pleased to see the young girl. In the new, modern time he seldom met a young person that showed any real interest in Voodoo. "You learnin de voodoo good little one." His voice always intrigued Baileen because of the way it came as a whisper; sounding as though it was coming from some dark corner far away, and just passing through for her to hear. He held a piece of brown paper in his hand and carefully placed the buds of sticky marijuana on it, then sprinkled the white powder along the length of it before rolling it into a tight cone.

This was the time that Baileen loved. As soon as her lungs were full of the potent smoke, she began seeing the demons. Some of them would be smiling at her, and others would be glaring at her frightfully, but she never felt afraid. She knew that these hideous little creatures would be the soldiers that would win the war raging inside of her.

Rick Magers

Her mother was concerned about her daughter spending so much time with the Obeah man, but since her teachers said she was doing well in school, she figured it was just a young girl's curiosity about the world of the occult. *After all, I was bout de same way when my mama firse tole me bout de Voodoo.*

But Ayeelah hadn't been the same as her daughter. Baileen was obsessed with her newfound religion and planned to learn all she could about its mysterious ways. The Obeah man told her about all of the various ways she could call on the dark spirits to attend her sessions. He also instructed her in the uses of various drugs that would, if used correctly, place another person under her complete control. "And," he said in his whispering voice as he leaned so close, with his nose touched hers, "wimmins got de mose potent drug of all; she ver own body, an if she use it corekly, a mon gone do whatever she say."

After a year of his teachings she decided to try what she had learned on a young boy from her class at school. "Mama," she said looking at the young boy, "doan like me to go near dat water when daddy not wit me, so doan tell nobody we goin dere tomorrow." She smiled alluringly at him then added, "You like swimming naked?"

The young boy could hardly wait for Friday's classes to let out, and barely slept that night. He slipped quietly away from his house and headed toward the beach, a few miles away, where Baileen said she would meet him. When he arrived she was already in the small cave that they both knew about. When Baileen saw him she jumped up and ran to the smiling young boy, giving him a deep kiss with her tongue actively probing his mouth. "Come, let's light the candles," she said as she grabbed his hand.

Moments later the candles were casting shadows on the walls of the little cave, as they smoked the potent ganja spliff. He failed to notice her sprinkling the powder into the end of the huge paper cone before saying, "Finish dis while I take dese clothes off."

So absorbed in watching the beautiful girl slowly removing her clothes, that he puffed away the remaining marijuana—laced with her potent voodoo powder. "Now you take dem ting you wearin off too," she said: dark mischief dancing in her dark eyes.

The fifteen-year-old youth stood naked before Baileen as she stepped forward and gently grabbed his erect penis to begin slowly running her hand back and forth along it. He shivered uncontrollably when she gently pulled his lips to her breast. She allowed him to suck one for a moment then moved his mouth to the other nipple. "Come," she commanded, "we must call de Obeah to be here wit us when we makin dis love for de ver firse time." She looked at him with her eyes opened wide, "Dis be de firse time witchew too, yes?"

"Oh yes," the boy stammered, with the lie obvious on his black face. "I

Rick Magers

ain ever been wit a girl like dis before."

Lying niggah, she thought, *you been stickin dat black snake in plenty dese girl roun town.*

He sat across from the candles, which were shoved in the sand, and watched her breasts as she chanted in a tongue he had never heard. When the green-eyed demon with black smoldering skin slowly appeared, the young Jamaican boy didn't see him. When he spoke to Baileen, the words came as a snarl through its long, gray, slime-covered fangs. The boy didn't hear or see the demon as it leaned toward the naked girl, and growled. 'You are doing well my dark angel; he is under your control now.'

"Come," she commanded as she abruptly stood, "less go for a swim firse." She darted toward the nearby water. Before she was through the shallows and into deep water he was on his feet and after her. *Dat some potent shit,* he thought as he struggled with his already wobbly legs, *I gots to fine out where she gittin dat shit. I gits dem white girls in Ocho Rios to smoke some dis weed, an nex time I goin roun dere I git m'self some dat fine white cootin.*

He beat the water with his arms as he tried to catch his beautiful naked prey, but soon felt the cramps begin in his stomach. He saw that she was returning to him, so he yelled. "I havin trouble, I gots to go back to de lan." He attempted to turn and swim toward shore, but couldn't make his body obey his commands. He heard a splash and turned to see a green eyed demon with black skin staring at him. He screamed once before slipping beneath the surface, never to return.

"Yes," she said aloud as she put her clothes back on, "I finds de right mon an I gone be able to have him do ever ting I want." She gathered up the candles and anything else that would make it appear that someone had been in the cave, then began the long walk home through the trees, so she wouldn't be observed.

Baileen cried with the rest when told of the tragic swimming accident that took the life of her classmate. Later that same week her father told her they were moving to Miami as soon as her school year was over. She cried again, and her mother said, "It gone be alright darlin, you sure gone fine plenty young people in dat big city."

Neither parent could see that it was tears of joy falling down her brown cheeks. Later that night she sat amid the candles and looked her smoldering black demon in the eyes. "My darling Lucifer, you have answered dis poor girls prayers. Soon I gone be nex to my new mon. I closing my eyes an can see him already. With your help Oh Mighty Lord of Darkness he gone help us do our work." She tossed the crystals, which the old Obeah man had showed her how to make, into the candle flames. Instantly a cloud of sparks flew toward the ceiling, then the room was cast into total darkness. The only thing left to be seen, were two glowing green eyes. The whispering voice came through the blackness. 'The Master will be with you every step you take and He will protect you from all harm.'

In the darkness she answered, "I now His slave forever."

> *Wherever God erects a house of prayer*
> *The Devil always builds a chapel there.*
> *And 'twill be found, upon examination,*
> *The latter has the largest congregation.*
>
> Daniel Defoe

Throughout her senior year of high school, Baileen cultivated her new young lover, Yorda Poleski. He became so dependent on her that if she couldn't work it out to be with him for a while each night, he would fall into a deep depression, and only her presence could relieve it. His parents had already been considering a move back to their permanent home in South Florida, so it required little discussion by Yorda to allow him to move to Miami and continue his education.

Baileen brought him farther and farther into the dark world of Voodoo. He claimed to see the demons she spoke of, but she knew he was too good a person to ever see them. She didn't care if he saw them or not. *He will now do as I say until he is no more.*

As they began their first semester at Central College he continually asked her to get an apartment with him so they could be together more often. *You mean get dis pussy more often, boy.* Baileen was not easily fooled.

She smiled at him one afternoon as they lay naked in Yorda's room, while his parents were away on business, "I tell you why I not able to come live witchew." She lowered her dark eyes and compelled tears to fall freely. "My uncle take me when I were a young virgin an now I scared to be away from my mama and daddy, cause I all time tink he gone come do dat ting to me again one night." She lifted her face so he could see the tears then added, "You help me take care dat bod fella, Yorda, an we gone get us our own place where we can love ever morning before we gone to class, den come home an love all night too." She watched as he absorbed her pleading words.

"Your uncle? My God what kind of uncle would do that to a little girl? How old were you? Is he your real uncle or..."

Baileen pressed two fingers over his lips as she brought her naked body on top of him. After they finished making love she said quietly, "I can fix it so dat uncle tink I want him. He gone pick me up tinkin we gone spend de night in he apartment, but you gone be waiting to shoot him when we come driving in dat big convertible car."

"I don't have a gun, do you?"

She liked the way he didn't hesitate about killing her uncle.

"Yes, I steal one from dat silly ole janitor at dat high school." Actually she had offered him sex for the 38 revolver knowing he would never admit later that it was his.

"Good," the once-shy, introverted young man said, "when can we do it?" All the boy could envision was he and Baileen coupling in their apartment morning and night—foolishness of youth.

"I fix dat up while you be lookin roun for a nice apartment." She smiled coyly at him, then slowly moved her head down between his legs to seal the death-pact.

Over the next few days Baileen suggested to her mother that she invite Randall over for dinner. "Daddy doan like Randall, darlin," her mother replied.

"I knows dat, but he you only brother, mama."

Randall Pope was finally invited to the Darden home for dinner. He arrived alone in his white Cadillac convertible carrying gifts for all three on his kin. His sister Ayeelah smiled as she thanked him for the beautiful wristwatch then went to him for a hug.

Boone Darden set his gift unwrapped on the end table thinking, *he probably trade drugs for all dis junk.*

Baileen held the necklace up for her parents to see, then went to her uncle and hugged him. "Tank you so ver much, Uncle Randall." She handed it to him and turned around so he could place it on her slender brown neck.

Boone had been sworn an oath to be civil to Randall. "Doan you start makin no stuff wit my brother or I gone call all my Obeah out to pay you back." Ayeelah looked sternly at Boone, who had seen what her Voodoo could do when she was mad. He relented and swore he would not start trouble.

Ayeelah was pleased with the meal and after a couple of drinks in the huge living room, Randall stood. "I muss be goin now to look after business." He embraced his sister then shook Boone's hand. "Very nice evening Boone, tank you mon."

Boone reluctantly shook his hand. *I muss go straightaway an wash dis hand after touching dat snake.*

Baileen spoke coyly, "I'll walk out to de car witchew, uncle." She smiled sweetly as she locked her arm in his.

Boone watched thinking, *dat dom woman done put Voodoo on she own daughter to be nice to dat rotten bostard brother of hers.*

Rick Magers

"Oh my, dis de nicest car I ever see," Baileen crooned as she watched him get behind the wheel. "I love to go ridin witchew one dese days."

Before starting the engine he looked up into her smiling eyes. "Little girl, lookin to me like you done growed up since I lass see you."

"Dat what hoppen when a girl come to de big city." She smiled as she opened her eyes wide, "She muss learn to swim or sink, an uncle, I ain no sinker."

"Well girl, why doan you come roun my apartment one dese evenin an we talk bout what kinda swimming you can do if you come work with me."

She leaned on the edge of his chrome windshield trim and leaned toward him to accentuate her extra large breasts. "You know where dat Lazy Jane Health Studio is?"

He was interested, "Dat one juss down from dat college you goin to?"

"Dat de one. Pick me up dere after I finish tomorrow night at seven."

He turned the key and brought the huge engine to life, then looked up into her beautiful dark eyes, "I be dere darlin. I lookin forward to an evening witchew."

If he had looked closely at her eyes he might have seen something there that would have warned him, but his eyes were on her breasts as she said, "I lookin forward to being witchew too."

As the Cadillac pulled from the waterfront estate of his successful brother-in-law, a smoldering arm draped over Baileen's shoulder. As the pungent odor of sulfur penetrated her nostrils a whispering voice said, 'it's been a long wait but you have him in you web now, little spider.'

As Randall Pope rolled along the highway toward town he thought, *dat little jewel done had some dese little boy peckers, an she ready for a real dick again.*

After school she met Yorda at one of the concrete tables in the yard behind the college. "Here de gun," she said as she handed him a brown paper bag, "it loaded an ready to go. All you do is walk up to the car an stick it nex to he head den pull dat trigger. Den when he go down you keep pulling till ain no more bullet den drop de ting an run away. Ain no body gone know who dat fella wit de mask on he face was. When you roun de corner pull dat ting off you face an trow it down an walk slowly cross de street an into dat big overgrown park." She looked at him and watched for any signs of fear or reluctance to follow her orders. *Good, I got dis foolish boy wrap completely roun my finger.*

"He's picking you up at seven, so I'll be near his place by seven to start easing over when I see that Cadillac."

"Good," she said then stood. "I goin home now to get ready to meet my dear Uncle Randall."

"I think I found us an apartment you'll like."

Rick Magers

"Good," Baileen said with a smile, "we go 'n look at it tomorrow." She turned and walked away as Yorda sat silently and watched her ass swaying, and thought of all the wonderful things he would do with her body when they had their own apartment. He picked up the brown paper bag and headed toward his home.

The white Cadillac pulled up in front of the health studio at exactly seven o'clock. Baileen slipped into the passenger's seat as he pulled onto the road. Thirty minutes later he pulled up in front of a row of new apartment houses in south Miami and parked in front of one. He was so absorbed with his young niece in her plunging neckline micro-mini. which barely contained her nipples, that he never heard the jogger approaching the car until the gun went off. He slumped forward as the gunman emptied the pistol into his already dead body. Baileen waited until Yorda was around the corner before she began screaming.

Randall Pope was well known to several police departments in the Greater Miami area, so the investigation was less than aggressive. Within two weeks it was classified as an unsolved drug related crime.

Yorda and Baileen enjoyed their new apartment for a little over a month before he was found dead in the water near a secluded section of Key Biscayne. His death was listed as accidental drowning.

At the funeral Baileen stood with tears falling down her golden cheeks. She had sobbed quietly the entire time the service was conducted. Everyone knew they had been friends and lovers since he had arrived from Jamaica, and ached deeply for her loss at such an early moment in her life.

There was one though that didn't feel sorry for the young girl. He laughed as he draped his long smoldering black arm over her shoulder. 'There will be many men for you to teach that you are not a warm hairy hole for them to camp in when they are heated.'

THE END

Yorda was born March 9th------PISCES.
Baileen was born July 4th-----CANCER.

Rick Magers

Determined Angel

And thus I clothe my naked villainy with odd old ends stol'n forth of holy writ, and seem a saint when most I play the devil.

Shakespeare

Charles Holden was as mild mannered as a man could possible be. No one could recall him ever raising his voice in anger, and when confronted with disappointment or adversarial situations, he simply went about his business. His business was running the City of Hanslip. He had patiently worked his way from a clerk typist job for the city, twenty-nine years earlier, to his present position. Charles had been the City Manager for three years and loved his job. He was good at it, but knew that the new Mayor didn't like him. It wasn't that he didn't like Charles Holden personally. Mayor Ruben Ostermyer didn't want any homosexuals working in key positions within his fast growing city.

"For Christ's sake James," he said to his Police Chief, "the freeway's coming almost right through here, and we're gonna have growth like no one but me seems to foresee." He looked hard at his friend of many years for a moment before motioned at the cocktail hostess to bring them another drink. "James, I don't give a rat's ass what kinda kinky shit those kind wanna do, but I don't want any of 'em working at City Hall or anywhere else where they'll be representing this city." He took a sip of his martini then looked at the Chief again. "I know it not legal to discriminate, but dammit I worked hard to get this job and I plan to make a success of it because my next stop's the State Capital."

James Pruitt had known Ruben for thirty years and had no reason to think he wouldn't make it to the State Capitol. For his help in cleaning up the city, Ruben had promised him a job in the Capitol Building. He planned to do whatever was required of him to see to it that Ruben's plans worked out. *I could double my retirement with a cushy job up there.*

Almost nightly, since Ruben was made Mayor of Hanslip, Charles complained to his live-in friend and lover, Morrison Hemp. "That beast is hell

Rick Magers

bent on ruining my life." He sipped white wine from cut crystal as he quietly contemplated the situation. "Thirty years I've worked in this city to establish myself, and that hick's gonna try to take it all away." He burst into tears, "I just know he is."

Morrison put his soft hand on his lover's shoulder. "In the two years I've been with you dear, I've noticed that everyone likes you, so I don't think one man can possibly cause you to lose you job."

Charles touched his friend's offered hand, "Oh Morris, I do hope you're right."

The first avenue of attack that Chief Pruitt took paid off in blue chips. He tossed the read-out from his home computer on Mayor Ostermyer's desk, when they were alone and having noon cocktails. "Great start," the mayor said, "this oughta get the little faggot rattled." He laughed, "Once we get a couple of wounds open we'll start rubbing salt in 'em, and before long he'll be glad to get the hell outa here." He poured them each another drink from the martini shaker. After handing one to the chief he said, "James, you're gonna make a damn good Lieutenant Governor."

4

GAY RECRUIT

There comes a time in a man's life when to get where he has to go—if there are no doors or windows—he walks through a wall.

Bernard Malamud

Charles Holden had always been very discreet about his homosexual affairs. He had been even more so since being appointed City Manager by his very best friend, Jennifer Saxton, three years earlier. Two years after she appointed Charley, as she referred to him during her twenty years as Mayor, to be the new City Manager of Hanslip, she was diagnosed with liver cancer. Six months later she was dead. That's when Ruben Ostermyer entered the picture. That's also when Charles Holden's life began a fatal spiral downward. It was also the beginning of regular visits by the demons that had been dropping in on Charles occasionally for most of his life.

Ruben Ostermyer had been in some form of local politics for his entire thirty years in Hanslip. He was twenty years old when he came from nearby Brokenoak to apply for one of the two jobs being offered on the Hanslip Police Department. After a strenuous week of academic tests and a complete physical examination, there were four applicants left from a list of fifty. Ruben was one, along with a man his own age named James Pruitt. The two men hit it off the minute they met.

On Friday the four men were notified that they had all passed their tests and physical exams, but that the jobs would go to the two men qualifying highest on the athletic ability tests, beginning Monday. The other two applicants were from a town named Copper Hill about fifty miles away. Those two men gathered up their things after being told to be back at eight AM on Monday to begin the rigorous physical testing, and headed for Copper Hill. Two burly men followed them from a safe distance.

Ruben and James remained unseen as they followed the two men from one bar to the next in Copper Hill, until around midnight when the opportunity they had waited for presented itself. They stopped their car and watched as the two men parked their pickup in a secluded spot, away from the group of customer's cars. They stood patiently in the shadows of the trees next to the pickup and waited. They had already pulled leather gloves on their hands, before slipping on brass knuckles. As soon as they heard the distinct voices of their two job competitors, they pulled the black ski masks down and adjusted the eyeholes.

It was almost a silent attack, and over in less than a minute. Ruben and James were both tough young men, but Ruben had suggested earlier, "Let's use these to be damn sure they're down for the count." He grinned as he handed James one of the two sets of brass, which was part of a growing collection of weapons he had started collecting a few years earlier. With almost no sound leaving the small area of the brief battle, the two other job applicants were ready to be picked up by an ambulance when someone later found them lying unconscious next to their truck.

The two remaining Police Department applicants stopped at the Candlelight Bar as soon as they got back to Hanslip. The locals referred it to unofficially as The Cop Shop, because it was where Hanslip's thirty policemen did their drinking. Both men were regulars at the bar, and when they entered the greeting was warm and familiar. "How's it going with your testing?"

"Real good," Ruben answered.

"Yeah," James added, "it's down to four of us and I think we got a damned good chance of getting the jobs."

"We're pulling for you two, 'cause you're local boys." The fiftyish, gray-haired police officer, patted Ruben on the back. "Hell ole son, Brokenoak's just a suburb of Hanslip, and I went to school with your daddy James."

The two young men from Copper Hill were stitched up and out of the hospital by the middle of the week, but their Hanslip police careers went down the drain with their blood. As they attempted to sort it out over the next few months one said, "I guess we musta really pissed someone off that night we were bar hopping?"

"Yeah," his friend replied, "we were both pretty shit-faced."

While the two men's heads were still aching from the concussions, two new names were being added to the Hanslip Police Department's roster. Patrolman Ruben Ostermyer and Patrolman James Pruitt. Ruben knew from the beginning that it was simply a stepping-stone toward the top, and James said right from the beginning, "I'll be chief of this department one day." They were both correct.

So spake the fiend, and with necessity, the tyrant's plea, excus'd his devilish deeds.

Milton.

Charles Holden sat sobbing at the tiny table in the French breakfast-nook. He had closed the porte-cochere in earlier in the year himself, and put a window where the door had been, because Morrison Hemp, his live-in love of two years had commented about a friend's. "I simply adore that quaint little extension he has for his morning tea."

When Morrison came walking into the room with his silk bathrobe hanging open, he heard Charles sobs and went quickly to him. "Oh poor darling, what's the matter?"

"That goddamn Nazi bastard Mayor, that's what's wrong."

Morrison moved in behind Charles and began massaging his shoulders. "Don't let that big turd upset you sweetheart, you were here when he showed up and you'll be here when he goes after bigger fish." He began gently hacking at Charles's shoulders with the sides of his hands. "Does this help?" He asked in a shaky voice as the karate-like blows picked up momentum.

"Mmmmmmm, yes, but then everything you do to me with those lovely hands makes me feel better instantly."

"Don't let that big goof get to you. Tension and upset will put you in a grave quicker than those biscuits and gravy you love will."

Charles knew it was true. The demons, which had plagued him since he was a small child, had been showing up nightly since Ruben Ostermyer had been appointed Mayor by the City Council. When Ruben was a police officer, he was well-known as an equal opportunity bigot. He hated everyone except a WASP. "Niggers, Spicks, Homo's, Catholics, Hippies, ... The list went on and on.

Charles' demons woke with him and went to bed with him since Ruben took over. They constantly whispered in his ears, 'poison the bastard—hire a hit man—get a gun and wait in the dark.' "No! No-no-no," he'd often blurt out, "I'm not that kind of person." He'd even done it a couple times at work, and that was really bothering him.

Everything was fine until that night a couple months earlier, when he and

Morrison went to a birthday party at The Daisychain Bar, a short distance outside of New Orleans. It was a known gay bar, but far enough away that they felt sure there wouldn't be problems. And it wouldn't have—until a fight broke out with some street toughs and a couple of gay men leaving the bar. The gay men just happened to be karate experts and put five of the toughs in the hospital. It was bad enough that the police had to be called, but the news media had a field day with the story. Charles about had a heart attack when he was shown a copy of a newspaper with his face there among all the gay men; watching the ambulances carry the Rocky Balboa wanna-be's to the hospital.

Soon after, the new mayor came into his office and closed the door behind him. He tossed a copy of the same paper on the desk in front of Charles. "What were you doing in that bar with a bunch o' goddamn faggots?" He stretched to his entire six-foot-six-inch, perfectly sculptured frame that easily supported the 250 pounds he maintained within two pounds: year round. His feet were spread apart and his fists were at his side, clinched so tight the fingers looked as though there was no separations between them. He glared at his City Manager and waited for an answer.

In the type of weak, meek voice that Ruben hated, Charles said, "It was a birthday party."

"A birthday party," Ruben said it in mocking tone. "What's that? You guys all get naked and take turns buttfuckin' each other while you sing happy birthday?"

Charles was so upset he couldn't even answer the mayor. He simply sat there turning redder by the second, until Ruben turned and stormed from the room. The second the door slammed, a group of his demon friends floated down from the ceiling; where they had been hanging, and took up positions around his desk.

'You don't have to put up with that kind of bullshit. That type of abuse is against the law and you could get him fired. He probably fucked his own mother when he was a kid. Kill the son-of-a-bitch. Yeah, we'll help you.'

Charles heard a sound behind him and turned. There was the Devil himself, standing half in and half out of the huge glass window. His face was a mass of molten, black pustules, teeming with worms slithering in and out. His eyes were a color he had never seen before—blood, dried black with a red sheen. The only word that came into his mind after seeing The Beast was *hate*. As Charles watched he thought, *His eyes are the color of hate.* When the Devil leaned forward, Charles was surprised at the amount of horns on his head: several, protruding in all directions. When the Devil spoke, the words came out in a gnarled whisper.

'Come unto me and I will rid you of these evil people who are trying to destroy you.'

Another noise behind him and Charles turned.

"Are you all right, Mr. Holden?" It was his secretary.

He looked at her with a blank expression for several moments, then turned quickly around. Nothing! The Devil was gone—the demons were gone. He turned back. "Yes! Yes," he was finally able to mumble, "just the mayor and I working out some of the city's problems." He smiled at the woman he had known for almost thirty years.

She returned the smile, "Charles, I know there's no problem you can't work out when it comes to this city." She returned to her desk in the outer office, and went back to reading the article that went with the picture of Charles Holden.

Inside the office Charles held his head in his hands with his elbows resting on the picture of him at what was suppose to be a fun evening with friends.

As men are to men so shall they be to themselves—and all others.
An observation.

As Charles Holden was dealing with his newfound infamy, two events were about to make a much bigger festival for the news media.

*Young Billy Bradwork stood silently and watched his fifth grade playmates walking up the ladder to slide down the sliding board. He held in his right hand a plain brown paper bag; much like the ones the other kids had their snacks in. His eyes were glazed over as he thought about the words that his father stung him with at the breakfast table for the last time. "Ease off on the bacon there fatso, there's two more of us gotta eat too." He thought about all the other insults he had suffered through at the whims of people every day. He smiled when his favorite demon whispered in his ear. He had been seeing demons for a long time, but the one whispering now was his favorite.

'C'mon Billy, you can do it. Remember when that red headed one standing there said you couldn't go on the sliding board because you're too fat? How about the cross-eyed girl that had to tell you in front of everyone, how much she liked you. All of the pretty ones and she had to tell you that. There, there, the one with the buckteeth, he's the one that keeps squealing like a pig every time he sees you. All of them Billy; they're all out to get you. They don't think you're tough enough to do anything. Well ole son, let's show them today.'

The demon was jumping up and down on Billy's shoulder as he removed the gun. He had taken it from his father's hiding place, and then casually returned to the breakfast table and shot his parents repeatedly. He then calmly replaced the spent shells with fresh bullets and headed toward the school, a short walk from his home.

He let the brown bag fall to the ground as he walked toward the children on the sliding board. Now there were several demons dancing all around him. The first bullet hit the red head in the side of the head—point blank. The second one went into the bucktooth boy's stomach. The little cross-eyed girl was as frozen as a deer in a spotlight. He walked slowly to her and shot her in the good eye. He walked into the school and shot three more children and was sitting on the floor putting the other bullets he had in his pocket into the gun when a teacher grabbed the gun and took him into the principal's office.

He later told his psychiatrist, "Demons and the Devil have been talking to me for a long time."

. . .

*A thousand miles away, a respected Cub Scout leader and deacon of his church, was deep in the woods with his small troop of scouts. They had hiked into the woods to a location near a lake, for an overnight campout. After hot dogs were cooked on the fire, he fixed them all fresh lemonade. Within fifteen minutes of drinking the refreshing concoction each boy drifted off into a deep sleep. One by one the scout leader pulled the unconscious children's pants down and used them for his sick perverted sexual satisfactions.

In court a year later, lawyers for the state argued that he must have planned to kill all of the boys, and would have, if the two hunters hadn't been suspicious of him and investigated.

He had amassed a fortune in real estate, so was able to engage the best defense attorney to handle his case. His defense was temporary insanity due to hallucinations about demons talking to him—telling him to do these terrible things. He was found guilty of simple child abuse, and given a four-year sentence. After serving twenty-two months he was released.

The man's wife divorced him as soon as the incident happened. Upon his release he moved to San Francisco. Three years later he was caught after killing a twelve-year-old street urchin that had been living with him. Three more child murders were attributed to him—as many as twenty others suspected as being his handiwork.

After two years in jail he was finally brought to trial and found insane. He still talks with the demons that started telling him what they wanted him to do, while still a young boy. He had often told many people about the voices, but not one person believed him.

> *From his brimstone bed, at break of day,*
> *A'walking the Devil is gone,*
> *To look at his little snug farm of the world,*
> *And see how his stock went on.*

Robert Southey.

As Charles grieved about his problems with the new mayor, the mayor was talking with his long time friend, Police Chief James Pruitt. "This is just what I was hoping you'd find." He closed the manila folder and handed it back to James. "I wish to hell you'd found some real sick shit on that fairy running this city, but apparently he's been careful not to get caught with his dick in some little kid's ass."

"Don't worry Ruben, when I shove a night stick up his sweetie-pie's ass, who he's living with, and break it off, he'll be so upset he'll start fuckin' up big time, 'cause he's in love with that little daisy." The Chief gave his friend a leer then turned to leave.

"James."

The Chief turned at the sound of his name. "Yeah Ruben."

"I ain't gonna forget this when it's time to move to the state capitol building."

"I know you ain't, Ruben. We've been a pretty good team; why break it up?" He flashed a grin through his black mustache, then wheeled around and swaggered his two-hundred-fifty-pounds toward the door. At six-foot-four-inches tall, he was a couple of inches shorter than Ruben, but still made an impressive looking figure in his uniform.

Ruben smiled as he watched his friend walk away. *He's sure got that John Wayne, two-by-four shoved up his ass, walk down pat.* He shook his head slightly and smiled before going back to his paperwork.

Chief Pruitt waited until Saturday, then he and another patrol car drove up to Charles's house, a few minutes after dawn. He wanted to be sure the City Manager was home. The two cars arrived with sirens blaring and lights flashing. "Police, open up." The two burly officers waited only a few seconds as they were told, before bashing in the front door. Seconds later, the two officers and Chief Pruitt were shining a light into the eyes of the two naked men as they attempted to awake.

"Oh my God, sweet Jesus" Charles screamed, "what's happening?"

The older officer with the continuously red, booze-nose held a pistol aimed at Morrison Hemp who sat up in bed. "Are you Morrison Hemp?"

"Uh, why yessir, I'm Morrison Hemp." The diminutive twenty-five year old replied.

"On your feet Tinker Bell, you're under arrest."

"Arrest?"

"Arrest?" Charles echoed his lover, his voice and face a mask of shock, aghast at the events taking place in his own home.

The second officer's pistol was now pointing at Charles. "You too Mr. Holden, on your feet."

"Oh dear Lord," Charles said as he looked around, "I'm naked. I'll get my pajamas from under the bed." He started to reach beneath the bed, but the officer's pistol came to within a foot of his face.

"Reach under that bed and you'll be wearing this copper jacket." The policeman was wearing a look that warned Charles that he was deadly serious about shooting him. "On the floor, NOW," the officer yelled.

The two men were handcuffed and led to the patrol cars as naked as they had been in each other's arms only a few hours earlier. When Ruben heard about it he actually wailed. "Oh sweet Jesus, I just love it." To himself he thought, *James, you're a goddamn piece o' work, ole son.*

As the Chief and the Mayor reveled in the aftermath of the morning's events, Charles Holden sat on a cold steel bunk. He was in a jail cell with a smelly blanket wrapped around him; weeping like an old Negro woman at a funeral. "Oh Lord, Lord, Lord, what's happening. Oh dear God, what's happening to me?" It wasn't God that answered his prayers though. It was a whispering voice that he recognized, causing him to look up. There was the Devil standing in the cell in front of him with several little demons dancing around at His feet. Again the voice came to him as though it was echoing off the walls of his mind.

'I say unto you again my child, come unto me and I will save you. Release yourself from this false God who commands these heathens to cause you this pain, and I will help you deal with them. Bow your head to me, Satan, the only true ruler of all who seek release from the white angels who inflict pain to all who do not bow to the whims of their Heavenly master.'

"Yes! yes," Charles cried, "please help me: I am yours."

There is in every man, at every hour, two simultaneous postulations—one towards God—the other towards Satan.

Charles Baudelaire.

Morrison Hemp was charged on an out-of-state morals charge and handed over to the California Federal Marshall, to be returned to California to stand trial for the charge, plus leaving the state and jumping bail.

Charles Holden was charged with aiding and abetting a fugitive. His lawyer explained the seriousness of the charge and the possible outcome of the trial. Charles sat on the bunk and cried like a child. The lawyer disguised his disgust and waited. He silently looked at the small, round, fifty-five-year-old man with red hair, hanging down on both sides, just below a shiny bald head with red sideburns hanging below jowls; wobbling as he cried. As the lawyer waited, he looked at the much too bushy mustache and wondered, *probably uses that to dust his buddy's nuts while he's ridin' the rod.* He was hired personally by the Mayor of Hanslip.

"I, I'm okay now I guess," Charles said shakily, "what should I do?"

The lawyer paused as though he had to ponder an answer. Charles couldn't possibly have known that he was Ruben's brother-in-law. He was brought in and temporarily put on the City of Hanslip's payroll to represent the hapless City Manager. "Tell you what Mr. Holden, lemme talk to this uh, Mr." He paused again and appeared to be looking for the mayors name, "Uh, yes here it is, Ostermyer and see what can be worked out."

As Charles waited he prayed again, but this time he was praying to the only thing that had offered him any hope. "Satan," he said softly out loud, "if you can hear me please tell me what to do."

The day's light illuminated most of the tiny cell. A growling whisper came from the only darkened corner.

'Can you give your soul to Me; releasing all allegiance to the heavenly God and his vengeful white angels?'

"Yes! Oh yes, just please help me."

The voice now came in a much lower growl and had a new tone of hate in it.

'When you speak to Me you will forever refer to me as Master.'

"Yes Master." Charles' voice registered complete surrender.

'Do as they say and when they have dealt with you, then I will deal with them, and they will wish they had never heard your name.'

Rick Magers

"Yes Master."

Charles lay on the cold hard bed and slept better than he had in a long time. His dreams were filled with demons torturing the mayor and the police chief.

The following day the lawyer returned. "That mayor's a pretty hard fella," he said as he sat his briefcase on the bunk, beside Charles. "He says he doesn't want to see you have to spend a few years in prison." He paused to look directly at Charles, who now felt like a turtle crossing the freeway, not knowing from which direction danger would come. "Knowing what they do to fellas like you in there." The kangaroo court lawyer knew they had the little man by the short hairs.

Oh Master, please help me. He placed his face in his outstretched hands then ran his fingers through the long red hair hanging down from the area between his bald head and his large, sausage gravy swollen ears. He looked up at the distinguished gray-haired lawyer, "What did Ruben say?"

The crooked lawyer opened the briefcase, then removed several papers stapled together. "He asked me to draw up an agreement between you and the City of Hanslip." He handed the papers to Charles before continuing, "If you will resign from your job and release the city from any pension agreements you have with it, then you are free to leave this jail immediately."

Charles was silent until the man's words sunk in, then he gasped, "I, I, uh, I've devoted my entire working life to this city." He buried his face in his hands again; "I'm ready to retire with thirty years service in a couple of months." He looked up with tears flowing down his puffy cheeks. "He's telling me to just walk away?" He was now openly sobbing.

"No Mr. Holden, he's not really telling you anything. He merely wants to help you avoid going to prison. What you do is entirely your decision." He took the papers back and put them in the briefcase before snapping it shut and preparing to call the jailer. After yelling once to be let out, he turned back to Charles. "I'll return here at five this afternoon, then you can either sign these papers or prepare to go to trial." After stepping through the open jailhouse door he turned when Charles spoke his name.

"Could I beat this thing?"

"No." The lawyer turned and followed the jailer from the cellblock.

Charles felt as though the blood had been drained from his body. Too tired to speak, he thought, *Master please help me, before I go insane.*

A burst of flame startled him until he saw Satan standing in the middle of it, smiling like his grandfather did when he was a small boy. Suddenly he felt warm and peaceful throughout his entire body. He smiled back when the apparition spoke; now in a kindly voice.

'I will deal harshly with this servant of your enemy soon, but now you must search for inner strength, then we will work together my son, and deal these two evil men a blow that will make them beg for your forgiveness.'

"Oh yes, yes, yes, Master. I'll make them beg on their knees before I forgive them."

Satan chuckled. *Of course you will my son, of course you will.*

The flame shot out between the bars on the one small window, and was gone. Left behind though were demons of every size and description to keep their Master's miserable new dark angel company.

Charles was dozing peacefully when the lawyer returned. He quickly signed the papers and was released. When he inquired about the personal things in his office the lawyer said, "You are never to go in the City Hall building again, Mr. Holden. As a matter of fact, I can tell you from what I've heard that you will be much better off if you sell your house and move away from here."

When Charles heard about Morrison being sent back to California, he went into a deep depression. Instead of having his front door repaired, he secured it permanently shut and used the side door. For two full days he didn't even notice that his good neighbors had looted his house of everything of value. He simply drank until he slept, repeating the destructive cycle until he was nearly a zombie. When he finally became so sick that he thought he was going to be forced to go to the hospital, he took a shower and forced himself to eat. By the following morning he ate again, and felt much better as he searched for the TV clicker. Suddenly he realized there was no longer a TV, stereo, fish tank, Wal-Mart imitation Ming Vase: nothing. *Stupid assholes*, he thought as he looked through the house to see what else was missing, *probably trying to hock that priceless nine dollar, collector's vase for enough to buy a bunch of beer and booze for their redneck party this weekend.*

He returned to the living room and slumped down into the huge imported French couch, which was too heavy to easily steal, folding his arms across his knees, "Oh God, what's hap... He was startled upright by the crack of lightning and the roar of flames. Standing in front of him was Satan. The worms crawled in and out of his festering skin—his eyes a color Charles had never seen—sparks of electricity jumping across his fangs when he spoke.

'If you insist on begging God to help you, then I will abandon you to his loving care.' His laughter made a knot form in Charles's stomach.

"Oh Master, no!" He fell on his knees and begged, "Please, Master, please don't abandon me like all the rest. It was just a slip of my tongue, God has never answered my prayers: never."

When Satan leaned down out of the fire to speak to Charles, he was no longer the same devil that Charles was used to seeing. He had seen this head on the ancient buildings of Europe, and many times in his nightmares as a child. It was swollen and grotesque, with eyes that bulged from their sockets. Snakes slithered from its nose, and when it opened its mouth it was half the size of its head. When it whispered, the voice however was the same. Charles was beginning to understand; *Satan can be anything he wants to be.*

'Then listen carefully as I tell you what to do.

Strangely, Charles was unafraid of the hideous creature confronting him so close; actually feeling comfort in its presence. He listened intently as Satan detailed the course of action Charles must take to settle the score with these people who had abused him.

'Begin today.'

"Yes, Master."

The creature returned to the fire. The original Satan smiled at him the same way his father did when he had done something right, then disappeared through the ceiling. Charles looked at the undamaged carpeted floor where the fire had blazed then at the undisturbed ceiling, "Yes, Master."

That same day, he contacted a Realtor to sell his house. He moved to nearby New Orleans, and began following the steps Satan had laid out for him. He bought a newspaper and slipped into a sidewalk café. As he sipped cappuccino, he casually read through the paper. Suddenly he leaned forward and looked hard at the picture of the man looking back at him. "Heh, heh, heh," he chuckled quietly as he read the few lines below the picture. "Prominent attorney Landis Holt died Wednesday night in a car crash between Gulfport and Biloxi. His brother-in-law, Mayor Ruben Ostermyer of nearby Hanslip, contacted our office with details of Mr. Holt's life. He was…

Charles folded the paper and smiled as he finished his coffee. "You said you'd take care of that lousy bastard and you did. Thank you, Master." Everyone in the tiny café was startled when the ground shook slightly, actually knocking over several glasses. Charles tossed five dollars on the table and headed for his tiny apartment. He was smiling broadly.

Charles sold his car and bought a new one, then with the help of a gay friend he knew he could trust, the two men created a new woman to replace the ex-city manager of Hanslip. For several weeks he drove the short distance to Hanslip at about the hour he felt the mayor and chief would be finishing their workday. It paid off, because not every workday, but almost, the two old friends, Mayor Ruben and Chief James Pruitt would meet behind City Hall at five o'clock. The two used Chief Pruitt's unmarked city car for the short ride to the Royal Lion Lounge for cocktails.

As Charles Holden sat alone in his tiny apartment, his depression had been replaced with a lust for revenge. The life he had planned with Morrison was destroyed, as was any hope of a decent future for him. Instead of dwelling on it, he thought about pain. Not any pain, but horrible, lasting pain that would make Ruben Ostermyer and James Pruitt scream to their pitiful God for help. He dreamed of bones protruding from their arms and legs as they writhed in agony.

After answering his phone, he replaced the receiver and smiled. "I knew Jacquellyn would come through," he said aloud as he adjusted his new wig and put his purse over his shoulder, before heading to his car.

He parked in front of his friend's house. Jacquellyn Dubouise had at one time been Ralph Crant: Ex-marine, and Sergeant at Arms of the local armory. His career as a female dancer had taken off, but he kept in contact with many of his old pals, who thought he was still good ole Ralph; just making a good living as a female impersonator. He finally connected with the items that Charles had offered a thousand dollars for. Charles left his friend's house and returned home as excited as he had been as a young boy at Christmas time.

Once inside his apartment he removed the object his friend had given him from the small, cheap rug it was wrapped in. He lay it out on the floor and opened the instructions Jacquellyn had written down for him to study. He opened his purse and removed the two other pieces of equipment he had requested, and laid them on the coffee table. As he smiled he thought, *Ralph, you're a one-in-a-million.* He began to intently study the instructions for the operation of the two different types of equipment. Demons danced in his dreams that night.

From a safe distance he studied the area behind the City Hall building, and waited for the two men to enter the unmarked police car. *Right on time*, he thought as he watched the two men enter, then slowly drive toward the highway. In two minutes he was positioned exactly where he knew he would be able to enter the highway when they drove past. When they did, Charles pulled out onto the highway and followed them toward The Royal Lion.

Charles was ecstatic with joy as he watched the light ahead turn to red and saw no one in his rear view mirror. Master, this is going even better than you said it would. He pulled up beside their car and tapped the horn, then lowered his window. "Excuse me sir," He said in his best middle aged lady voice, as he looked helplessly pleading at the mayor, sitting only a few feet from him in the passenger seat. When he saw the window coming down he removed the pin on the hand grenade and waited.

When Ruben turned to ask what the lady wanted, he saw something come through the window and land near his feet. His brain had not yet sorted out what was happening when the grenade went off.

Charles was already around the corner by then and heading toward City Hall again. The police cars were tearing out of the police parking area behind the building when Charles pulled into his old parking place. He got out and went to the rear passenger side and opened the door. After removing the long box from the rear seat he walked briskly into the building. Stopping at the collapsible table displaying brochures, a large coffeepot, Styrofoam cups, sugar, and artificial creamer—he laid the box down and removed the lid. After taking the light weight military AR-15 from the box, he checked the thirty round clip to be sure it was still secure. Before heading into the new City Manager's office he checked to be sure the safety was off. The door was open and the man that he knew must be a friend of Ruben's was sitting behind his old desk. Without a word he fired one round into the man's head. His membership at the indoor firing range was paying off. When he returned to the hall there were several people in it, curious about the noise. *Curiosity killed the cat*, he thought as he opened fire. When his thirty round clip was empty, nine people lay dead, four were dying, and three were seriously wounded. A moment before his gun clicked on empty, two policemen entered from the side door. Before they began firing their twelve-gauge shotguns, loaded with double ought buckshot, into the ex-City Manager of Hanslip, they noticed him toss something toward them. They had a brief moment of realizing what it was when the grenade went off. No one saw them, but around the horribly mangled body of Charles Holden a large group of demons danced and squealed.

THE END

Charles was born Jan. 12th-----CAPRICORN.

Nor one feeling of vengeance presume to defile, the cause, or the men, of the Emerald Isle.
William Drennan.

Rick Magers

Amazon angel

Nineteen-year-old Shirleen Davidson worked harder than even she thought possible, to become foreman on the new forty-story building construction site. When she first applied for the job of laborer, twenty years earlier, the men at Hammond and Hammond Construction laughed and told her to go home and have a baby.

She did go home, but not to have a baby. Mrs. Davidson looked at her daughter and said, "Why don't you apply at the cafeteria dear? They're looking for a waitress."

The nearly six-foot-tall, attractive blonde teenager with size eleven feet, looked at her mother the same way she looked at the slightly retarded bag boy at Grossman's Market. "I don't wanna be a waitress mother, I want to learn how to build houses and buildings."

Mr. Davidson sat quietly in his easy chair and listened to his daughter's complaint. "C'mere Shirleen." He leaned forward and rested his arms on his huge knees. He was a large man by nature, and a fat man by choice; he loved to eat and was seldom without something in his mouth.

She came into the living room and waited patiently until he had finished chewing the long, black, twisted licorice hanging from his thick lips. "Honey, if you really want to get into that kind of work, then you'll have to show 'em you're serious." He put another piece of licorice in his mouth. Again his daughter waited until he spoke again. "Keep going back to that outfit every day and tell 'em you want another application. Sometimes girls just get a notion in their heads, then before you know it they're off on another course. You show 'em you're serious and I'll bet you get that job."

That was the kind of encouragement she needed at this pivotal moment in her life, so she leaned down to put her arms around his neck. "Thanks pop, that's exactly what I'm gonna do." She straightened up and smiled, "They'll get so sick of me they'll give me a job just to get me outa their office."

That's just what she did, but they didn't make it easy on the determined teenager. Finally on the sixth visit to Hammond and Hammond, the personnel manager realized he had a very stubborn young woman seeking a job in construction, so he decided to get rid of her once and for all: he hired her. Much to his and everyone else's surprise, she took everything the foreman

Rick Magers

and crewmembers on the various jobs they put her on, could dish out. Even the hard-core male chauvinist workers soon admired her spunk.

Shirleen enrolled at the Jr. College in structural engineering; going to classes two and three nights a week. She bought every book on carpentry, plumbing, electrical wiring, and ironwork that she could locate. All of the books were soon limber, well worn from obvious use, and full of notations. Each had gummed post-a-note flags on many pages with reference notes. Within a year there were very few pages that didn't have either a red line under a sentence or entire paragraphs covered by yellow highlight. She loved the work and was determined to succeed.

After two years of pushing wheelbarrows full of site trash to keep the construction areas clean, she was promoted to carpenter's helper. Five years with the company and she was a union carpenter. Another five and she was lead carpenter capable of anything the job required.

Shirleen had no desires at all to get married and have babies. She had dated several men and had enjoyed sex with some of them, but decided that it wasn't, as she told her best friend, "Worth the horseshit you have to put up with to get it." She gave up dating completely and devoted her time to learning her trade. It took her over ten years to get her masters degree in structural engineering, which paved the way for her to get the job of head foreman on the current building site.

She left the male jibes behind long ago as a construction worker, but now that she was telling men what to do, it began again; with far greater intensity. Male egos could not handle a woman telling them anything, least of all how to do the jobs that they had been doing the same way for many years. "Things change," she told them, "and you have to stay up with the changing technology if you plan to remain in construction." The resentment continued to build.

Months passed, but the men made it obvious that they wanted their woman boss to be replaced by a 'real foreman.'

Shirleen began having severe headaches. There were days that they were so intense she could barely do her job. One day during the lunch break, about ten men came to her. The burly one in front, who had been one of her best friends when she was just another carpenter, spoke up. "Shirleen, you're the head foreman, right?"

She looked up from the blueprint she'd been studying, "That's right Leon, whacha need."

"Some head, foreman," He said the last word with mocking emphasis as he pulled his penis from his trousers. All of his followers filed suit.

She was not the kind of woman that was easily rattled, so she calmly looked at each mans protruding penis then replied, "Ain't this a bitch, about a dozen pricks standing here and not one decent dick in the bunch." She returned to her blueprint as if nothing had happened.

In her apartment that night, it was a different story. Actually it was similar to every other night for the past month or so—tears. She rested her head on the table where she sat with a half-empty bottle of scotch, and sobbed, as she pressed hard on the sides of her throbbing head. When she looked up, she saw the demon sitting on her sink counter. He was dangling his long legs over the edge as he held the counter with his sharp claws. His skin was red and his eyes burned deep within sunken sockets. Yellow fangs showed when he spoke.

'Time we paid them back for all the hurt, isn't it?'

Rick Magers

5

VENGEFUL LADY

He that troubleth his own house shall inherit the wind.

The Holy Bible: Proverbs

Shirleen Davidson spent her thirtieth birthday alone in her apartment, drinking scotch. It should have been a great time in her life.

The forty-story building she had been given by her bosses, at Hammond and Hammond Construction, as her first head foreman job, was not only coming in on time, but considerably under budget. It had taken twelve hard years to prove to them that she could do the job as good or better than any man on their payroll. They appreciated her steady, skilled hand, which shoved their profits much higher on the projected scale than they had hoped, and they showed it with a bonus check for $10,000.00.

Her mostly male co-workers showed their feeling for their female boss in a completely different way. They came to the site as a large group one night, and trudged drunkenly up the stairs then left a large sign on her desk. It read in large letters: Happy Bitchday Bitch. Every man then shit on top of her desk, before returning to the dingy little bar in nearby Beer Can Alley, to laugh the evening away at her expense.

As the bottle of birthday scotch she had bought herself went down, her misery went up. Her verbal mumbling began. "Why in the hell can't those guys see that I'm just trying to get us all off this job 'n onto the next one with no injuries or problems?" Several straight scotches later it became, "Stupid bastards can't see beyond the ends of their pitiful little pricks." She tossed her head back and howled with laughter. Gasping for breath, she poured another three ounces then smiled. "Bet there ain't a decent one hour stiff dick among that buncha pricks.

'Need a little help lady?'

At the sound of a voice in her securely locked apartment, she whirled around and almost fell from the barstool. Standing in front of her was a molten black mass of pulsating flesh. From its head protruded several two-foot-long horns that were more like tentacles as they moved around sniffing the air. The creature's eyes burned like a fire viewed through the isinglass on the front of her grandma's old coal stove. Shirleen smelled sulfur when it leaned toward her.

'I can help you pay those God loving fools back.'

She sensed movement to her right, so she turned her head slightly, keeping her eyes on the apparition in front of her. It took a lot of will power to tear her eyes away and look. There on the sink counter top, was the same demon she had first seen many months earlier. The red skin glowed as did it's eyes, and the claws were still terrifyingly long. Through the same yellow fangs it spoke in the same echoing whisper, as if coming from within a long deep tunnel.

'We can help if you will give yourself to the Master.'

Shirleen Davidson wasn't used to asking anyone for help. She filled the glass in front of her with the last of the scotch then threw the empty bottle at the pulsating black creature as she screamed, "I don't need any goddamn help from anybody." She drank the scotch and lay her tortured head on the bar top and was soon asleep.

The demon merged into Satan as he stood smiling. 'I'll soon have another Dark Angel to fight them with.' He went out the open window as a puff of smoke.

When she awoke the following morning, Shirleen smelled sulfur. Looking around she saw nothing out of place but the shattered bottle in the corner. That brought back the dream she had during the night. She wrinkled her brow and grasped her temples with the first three fingers of each hand. *Or was it a dream?*

While flushing out the previous night's scotch with coffee, Shirleen thought about all of the hard work she had endured to get where she was. *Ten goddamn years of going to school nights and doing without everything, including a good lay now 'n then, just so I can listen to a bunch o' testosterone-driven wimps, that can't handle working for a woman.* She poured herself another cup and walked out onto her fourth floor balcony, overlooking the sprawling city that was quickly turning into a real metropolis: *With my help this little burgh has become a thriving city.*

As she looked at her nearly completed, forty-story building in the far distance, her mind wandered back to a couple of encounters with males that helped her make the decision to put them in her rear view mirror: permanently.

Anderson Amerson was a date she had over a year earlier. She was already fed up with the ridiculous male ego, which seemed to be a designed part of the male of her species, and when combined with the macho image of themselves, along with enough testosterone to keep a bull elephant mounting several females daily, it was fast becoming more than she could bear. Andy, as he preferred to be called, seemed like a different breed of man though. They met quite accidentally at a downtown art exposition; leaving a few hours later for dinner and a drink together. The dinner was lousy, she recalled, and the drinks watered down. *That conversation was such a refreshing change,* She thought, *from the hammer swinging, dick wagging, hooting bunch of near-apes I'm forced to work with.* She soon found herself searching for time to be able to spend a lunch or a coffee break with Andy.

Anderson Amerson was a professional sculptor. Not a famous one, but one that made an adequate living with his work, which he enjoyed and loved talking about. Various projects he had completed in his thirty-nine years, were often the topic of conversation. When Shirleen stated casually that she was in construction he nodded, then continued with his description of the bronze plaza statue of the governor, which he hoped to land as his next job. "I'll go to the state capitol to take measurements of the governor, then... He looked deeply into her soft, summer sky, blue eyes, "I'm sorry Shirleen, there I go again, loading you up again with the details of my boring life."

She found his coal black eyes mesmerizing and sexy the first time she met him. His six-and-a-half-foot frame made her feel slightly daintier in his presence. She smiled and said, "You haven't said one boring word since I met you Andy."

He finished detailing his plans for the biggest sculpture of his career, and outlined several more over the following week as they met nightly for dinner. Soon the dinners were at her apartment and the wine was followed by his suggestion for her to buy a new waterbed. The waterbed survived but their relationship didn't.

It had been so long since she was in bed with a man, that her orgasms were brief and unfulfilling. On their third trip to the waterbed, she waited until he had his orgasm, and then began coaxing his penis erect again. When she could see that it was going to remain hard, she climbed on top so she could manipulate it into the position where she could ride it into a long, satisfying climax. When she was satisfied, her attempts to satisfy him again were brought to an abrupt stop when he spoke. "Let's have another glass of wine." She could tell that his mood had changed, so she dismounted and agreed, following him into the living room.

"What was that all about?" he asked; his black eyes penetrating her mind.

She truly didn't understand, and told him so.

"That taking the male lead thing, by climbing on top."

She began to steam up, sensing that her last orgasm might just be exactly that—her last. "There's nothing male about being on top Andy." She kept her voice calm as she tried to explain it from a woman's point of view, "On top, a woman can control everything better so she can be completely satisfied."

He just stared at her a moment then began putting his clothes on. "I've been satisfying women, by being on top for twenty years, so I'm not gonna start getting into that kinky shit now."

She was stunned into silence, by a nearly forty-year-old-man's stupidity. She watched as he finished dressing then headed for the door. He turned and looked at her with dark eyes that now didn't seem sexy at all: just empty like all the others.

"Thanks for the dinner, sorry I was such a lousy lay." He closed the door behind him quietly.

She was not the type of person to let something like this slip by without a final word, so she went to the door. He was standing with several others at the elevator waiting. She called to him and when he turned said, "You're right Andy, you are a lousy lay." She closed the door and replaced the wine with a bottle of scotch. Before the night was over she was talking with the demons again.

Her last male encounter was a couple of months after the memorable evening with Andy. She was watching the Super Bowl in a sports bar in nearby Jasper City. She often went there for a few drinks, because she knew none of her male workers would be there. As the afternoon progressed into evening, she found herself attracted to a burly man a little younger than herself. They talked football until the game was over, and then decided to go have a late dinner together.

"What kinda work do you do, Bobby?"

"I'm in construction." The reply came with a warm smile.

"Well now, ain't that something, I am too."

"Hey Shirleen, that's cool."

She sent him another warm smile. He and the drinks were warming her up nicely.

"No kidding, construction huh? What kinda work do you do?" His reply sounded so sincere that she felt a little warmer and replied confidently.

"I'm the general foreman on a new building going up." The man's mouth actually dropped open.

"General foreman?" He looked incredulous. "You're a general foreman?" he repeated, "with a bunch 'o guys like me runnin' around doin' whatever you tell 'em to do?" More looks of disbelief.

"Yeah," Shirleen answered cautiously, aware now that he was sounding hostile. "I've been in it since I got out of high school." She was a little shocked when he shoved his chair back from the table and reached into his rear pocket for his wallet. Tossing a twenty on the table he said, "Cunts like you is why guys like me'll never be foreman." He turned and walked out so fast that she couldn't even get in a reply. She just sat there and watched him disappear. When the waiter brought the steaks he said, "I saw the gentleman leave very abruptly, is he coming back?"

"No, he's gotta go home and soak his tiny little balls in salt water to toughen 'em up, and you're wrong; he's sure as hell no gentleman. Put his steak on my plate and take the rest of his shit with ya." She ate both steaks and never tried another man for anything except doing what she wanted at the job site.

Satan hadn't been by for a visit in a long time, but his demons were constant companions lately as she struggled desperately to cope with the hostility she received from many of her once-friendly male working companions. The empty scotch bottles were now so numerous that she carried all away in the case she bought them in and discarded them in a nearby dumpster, so the garbage men wouldn't see how many there were. The headaches were getting so bad that it required more, and stronger medication to get through the day, then seek relief from a bottle of scotch in the sanctity of her demon filled cell.

A woman in a foreign land,
of which, though there he settle young
a man will ne'er quite understand
the customs, politics, and tongue.

Coventry Patmore.

On the Monday after the lonely birthday celebration, spent with her demon friends, Shirleen arrived early as usual to begin planning out her work schedule for the day's projected construction. When she saw the piles of dried Friday night feces all over her desk, she stood silent for several moments looking at it. Her fighting spirit had never let her lose control in front of any of her men, but as she stood looking at the very personal insult, she came very close on this Monday morning. As always she shook her head briskly and walked to the temporary elevator to which she had one of three keys: the other two being in the possession of the Hammond brothers. She unlocked the gate and descended past the first floor and into the basement. She walked with a deliberate stride to the temporary guard shack located only a few feet from the elevator. She found exactly what she thought she would, so she raised the tiny camcorder she always carried with her to record progress and problems as they happened. As the low-light sensitive film recorded the fat, uniformed young man, his tongue hanging out like an old outboard motor starter rope, broken from too many pulls. It also placed the time and date on the film. She left without saying a word thinking, *Useless fucking males. If I had twenty good women that knew construction, I'd send every one of these limp-dick-wagging assholes down the road; but even the good women're too busy riding their pussy into early retirement.*

She locked the elevator behind her, and immediately called the security firm that handled all of the Hammond Brother's building sites. In as short a time as an ambulance could have been there, the head supervisor was pulling into the site. The man knew that she could back up what she told him on the phone minutes earlier. "Get a goddamn guard over here right now that weighs less than a fucking water buffalo." She was screaming into the phone, so a deep breath was required to settle her down. She spoke again calmly, but in a tone that left no doubt in the man's mind that she was dead serious. "Don't let me see that piece of shit on a site of ours ever again," she paused a moment before continuing, "and Charles, if I ever find another one of your guards asleep on my site you'll be looking for another place to stack your useless deadwood. When you get rid of that shithead, come to the elevator and ring me."

She spoke into the intercom later telling him, "C'mon on up." She unlocked the gate and waited as the short, baldheaded, red-faced, perspiring, nervous little man stepped off.

"C'mere Charles and look at this shit. She waited a moment as he stared at her crew's artistic handiwork. "You're goddamn lucky Charles, do you realize what kinda damage could have occurred while your baby elephant was off in lala-land?"

"Shirleen, uh Missus, uh Miss Davidson this has never hap…

She cut him off in mid-word. "Knock off the line of bullshit Charles, I just wanna be sure you get the message." She used the kind of body English she learned in self-assertion courses in college. She took a step toward him to lean down until her face was almost touching his. Her tone was a combination of warning and aggression, "Do not let this ever happen again." She clipped off the last word as though she had used bolt cutters, "Now get the fuck outa here, I have work to do." She closed the gate behind him without another word and locked it.

She waited until her entire crew was on the floor and getting ready to remove their gear from the steel boxes, temporarily welded to the floor. She walked toward the dozen men in the same manner she had with the security guard. "Hold on a minute boys." She accentuated the last word then paused to let it settle in. "There's a little mess on my desk, and even though I can't prove who was involved, it really doesn't mean shit, because I don't hafta prove a fucking thing to you buncha jerk-offs. All I have to do is say go and you're all lookin' for a job, while I'm talking to the union hall. I'm going to the main office and register this, then show 'em the video I took so they'll see what a bunch of real winners they have on their payroll. When I come back either have my desk as clean as the day it came out of the box, or don't be on this jobsite." She turned and entered the elevator then watched the men turning from one to the other for support. As she passed the crane she looked at her watch and spoke to the operator, "You're suppose to be up in that son-of-a-bitch with it running at eight o'clock not eight-o-five."

God created woman. And boredom did indeed cease from that moment—but many other things ceased as well! Woman was God's second mistake.

Friedrich Wilhelm Nietzsche.

* At the very moment Shirleen opened her second bottle of scotch, and was laughing at the antics of her demon friends, who were now her only constant companions, another young woman was having to confront demons. They, however weren't demons of her own making. The demons belonged to her ex-husband. They had been sitting on his shoulders for a long time, even in his younger days on the playing fields where his athletic abilities were making him a world celebrity. They had been whispering in his attentive ears for a long time, about the abuse the young woman cowering in front of him now, had been directing toward him. A razor sharp knife flashed in front of her young eyes and it was the last thing she or her new boyfriend ever saw unless it was one of his demons, grinning maliciously at them as their life drained into the dirt.

* Not far from the spot where she died, another band of demons were screeching with glee, as a group of young boys beat an old man to death. They used sticks picked up only moments earlier from the park, where the homeless old man had been forced to make his home. 'Yes, yes,' the Demons screamed, 'beat him until the other eye falls out.'

* Over a thousand miles away, a young man from a very wealthy family beat a young girl to death with a golf club. She wouldn't perform the type of sex act on him that he wanted. He screamed, "I always get what I want you little bitch," he continued screaming at her, as the demons he had talked to as a young child, screamed even louder. 'Beat the bitch—stick it in her eye—stick it in her pussy.' Several Demons screamed, as he continued sticking and probing until his uncontrollable rage was satiated, and the demons had crawled back into the diseased cavities of his mind; as they always did after his rage abated. He looked down at his handiwork and grinned, "Now you know who you were dealing with don't you." Many years later he was still walking among us with the same demons calling his name. He did until a tough detective decided to see him punished.

* Many miles to the south, a young man was waiting in the bushes with his demons. When they said the time was right, he detonated the bomb he had planted at the abortion clinic. As the building disintegrated and a policeman lay dying along with a severely wounded nurse, the demons began screeching and jumping up and down. The scared young man ran to his nearby truck and vomited, before climbing in to drive away. He turned to his right and saw Satan sitting beside him grinning. 'You are going to become one of my best Dark Angels in the war against God and his pitiful little band of white angels.' Satan laughed so hard that the frightened young man almost ran off the road. So busy was he getting the truck back under control, that he didn't see Satan drift through the closed window as a puff of smoke.

. . .

Shirleen was still capable of forcing herself to get to the jobsite early. She always tried to set the pace for the day's scheduled tasks, but it was getting harder and harder for her to function without the pills she now relied on to get her up for the day—others helped her back down at night.

Her old friend, when they had worked together as carpenters on the job, and occasionally as frenzied lovers in the night, was now becoming her worst tormentor.

Lane Grover was a small man with black hair and beard. Until Shirleen became his boss, he was one of her closest friends. His change in attitude confused her until she thought about some of the things he had said to her, when she had no real reason to contemplate their meanings.

She had been reflecting on them lately and had a better picture of the man that was making her life a living hell. "Baby I'm gonna be the superintendent of everything Hammond and Hammond has going, one of these days. You just concentrate on keeping me happy baby, and I'll see to it you go right up with me." She did, but at the same time she continued going to school as Lane kept spending his time in the joints on Beer Can Alley.

"Fuckin' little loser," she said as she refilled her glass, "right from the git-go; a two bit, fulla shit loser. I was simply too stupid to see it."

'We kept telling you.'

She looked over at the kitchen counter, where one of her demons was sitting with his long green legs hanging almost to the floor. He was grinning through a mouth full of sharp, pointed teeth as he continuously flexed his foot long fingers; three-inch claws shining at the ends.

'We kept telling you that he was no good, and was only using you.'

She looked up at the little demon sitting on the wagon wheel light fixture, above the table. As he grinned at her, a blue, vile, thick liquid flowed from his mouth, disappearing before it hit the table. His voice came as a rasping, rumbling echo, bouncing off of the walls inside her head.

'I told you many things you ignored, as you prayed to your God for help in understanding these things that will never change, until you change them, with My help.

As she watched, the little demon oozed down through the spokes of the wheel, suddenly reforming as Satan. He was now the smoldering, black-skinned apparition she had come to expect whenever he spoke to her. His eyes glowed red at times; black and yellow smoldering embers…far back in the hideous head at other times. Worms were the one constant thing; always crawling in and out of the skin on his face. He no longer frightened her as He had in the beginning: in her mind He was becoming her savior.

'Are you ready to deal with this fool that has hurt you so bad, and will continue until you are no longer in charge of anything?'

"Oh yes! Yes, yes, please help me before I go mad."

'Then come and lay down with me, and I will enter you as you have never been entered before. You will feel pleasure as you have long dreamed of and then you will be mine forever.'

"Oh yes, yes, I need some pleasure so much," she was on her feet and removing her clothes as she headed for the bedroom, "oh yes, I can't wait."

'Stop and lay down right where you are, and we will travel together to a distant place you have never even dreamed existed. NOW!

His command came in a raspy voice—she could go no farther. She dropped to the floor and lay naked as He brought his smoldering body to her. Her flesh trembled with pleasure as He spread her legs and inserted a penis so hot that Shirleen thought she would melt from the inside out. As he began to move as no man had ever moved on top of her before, she began to see visions of a place she could never have imagined. It was full of maidens that were lolling around clear pools, splashing each other—laughing and smiling. There were no men in sight, and as Satan moved around inside of her she watched the naked young girls touching each other. Each time one kissed another's nipples, she felt a rushing orgasm like she wouldn't have believed possible. Over and over, each time one of the poolside maidens lay her head in the lap of another, Shirleen's orgasms increased until she felt as though she would faint. Another girl being touched by a young girl—another orgasm; on into the night. She finally felt Satan leaving her body—standing, looking down. His voice came as a rushing wind.

'You are now mine forever, and I will help you deal with this fool. Listen carefully and I will tell you what to do.'

The following morning, Shirleen was still asleep on the rug naked, when she heard the alarm going off in the bedroom. She surprised herself by jumping up feeling rested for the first time in months. After stopping the alarm she returned to the living room and reflected on the evening. *Wow! What a dream*, she thought then noticed something on the carpet where she had been sleeping. "Oh for crying out loud, I had an orgasm while I was dreaming." She smelled something odd and leaned down to smell the big stain on the rug. When she straightened up she was puzzled. *Sulfur?*

For the next couple of weeks everything went great for Shirleen. She felt rested for the first time in many months and her evenings were relaxing and pleasant. After a couple drinks of Scotch she was able to sleep until morning. She realized after a few days that she hadn't been seeing the demons that always came with the Scotch—which was where she thought they came from.

Standing on her balcony, the first Sunday of her newfound rest, she thought, *Thank God that those illusions of Satan are gone too. My God what a strange dream that was.*

A wind came whistling across the balcony out of a cloudless sky. She had to grab the edge of the wrought iron rail and hang on tightly to keep from being blown over the side to the pavement far below. Gusting, gray-black clouds were rushing in and out of her apartment, and each time they passed her they almost ripped her grip from the rail. The final black gust swirled around her like a tornado and as it departed she heard a familiar voice booming inside of her head, getting fainter as it left with the wind.

GodGodGodGodGodGodGodGodGodGodGodGodGodGodGodGodGodGodGod

It all happened so fast that she hadn't screamed or yelled. The sky was clear again, without a breath of air, as she stood dumbfounded listening to the voice echo across the city. Her mind was spinning as she watched the dark little cloud zooming across the clear, blue, afternoon sky. Suddenly the air was filled with the overpowering scent of sulfur, but before she could turn around to see where it was coming from a pair of smoldering arms encircled her waist. A thought came rushing through her mind as swiftly as the gusts of wind had swept across her balcony. It wasn't a dream—I was never dreaming—it was real.

'No!' The voice thundered in her head, 'It wasn't a dream. You are now one of my dark angels—listen carefully.'

The smoldering black arms began to tighten, as the worm filled face came forward on a long tentacle neck. It moved about in the air like a cobra, its eyes glowing deep within the hideous face. When it's mouth opened, two tongues leaped out and grabbed her on each side of her face. As a rumbling began deep within the head, strangely she didn't feel frightened; more like a child being scolded. She could not remove her eyes from the eyes of Satan.

'Never,' the voice thundered, 'say the word God again, or I will tear your body and mind into a meal for my errant dark angels who are never satisfied, then throw you into the eternal pit to feed them.'

The tentacle tongues pulled her face to his, and as another tongue slipped inside her mouth and began tenderly caressing, she could feel the worms pulsating on the black skin against her tender white cheeks. As she stood in Satan's embrace on the balcony, she felt something easing up under the housecoat that was all she had on. Soon he was once more inside her, and she loved it.

'I will make you a queen in my denizen of dark angels, if you obey my every command from this day forth.' The tongue was still exploring her mouth as he lay her on the balcony floor. The voice was not coming from his mouth, but was entering her mind from some internal force.

She sensed that she could answer him without using her own mouth, and knew he had heard her when she replied. 'Yes my Lord, I will be yours forever.'

The orgasms began again as the visions of lovely maidens lounging near the azure pool filled her tortured mind. Their carefree laughter and nymph-like actions were very soothing, as Satan took her up a long winding staircase of emotions she had never experienced. Combined with the explosions of lust, were feelings she had almost forgotten. After so very long she was once again feeling secure, loved, and needed. It was all she had ever wanted. From her father, her employers, the men she worked with, those who worked for her, those she tried to love—all of them. They all however wanted a Shirleen that didn't exist, except in their own selfish minds. Without a word said she knew that Satan was the first to accept her for exactly what she was, so she used her body in every way she knew how, in an attempt to make him understand. She closed her eyes, letting her mind close with his. 'I will be your slave until the end of time.'

'There is no end of time in my world—there is no time.'

The voice somehow seemed different, so she slowly opened her eyes. She found herself looking into eyes that were identical to her own. Above her was her father as a much younger man. She was seven-years-old, and he was smiling as he humped frantically, naked on top of her. "Don't ever tell mommy or she'll leave us and go far away. This'll be our little secret, okay sweetheart?"

Shirleen closed her eyes tight, as she always had when her daddy came to her room. When she opened them it was almost dark as she lay on the concrete floor with her nightgown up around her waist.

She lay there and looked up at the stars as she cried silently to herself. *Oh daddy, I loved you so much, why did you have to make me feel so bad?*

Which of us has looked into his father's heart? Which of us has not remained forever prison-pent? Which of us is not forever a stranger and alone?

Thomas Wolfe.

A long time later, Shirleen rose from the floor. Looking out over the blinking city she felt wonderful and wished Satan was still with her. A voice suddenly came to her—she knew not to turn and look because it was inside her head.

'I am still with you. I will always be with you. Soon we will rid you of these vermin who torment you, and then you will lead my dark angels to greater retributions across this land.'

Shirleen was once again invigorated, and tackled her work with a vengeance that her crew of men hadn't seen in awhile. Her ex-friend and lover, Lane Grover watched her with a leery eye. "What the fuck's got into ole tub o' tits lately?" He and the small group of men, that considered him their mentor, were standing around the coffeepot during the morning break. Their main topic of discussion the past few days had been the dramatic change in their superintendent, Shirleen. "She's gettin' laid somewhere I think," the stout young carpenter commented with a leer.

"Bullshit," Lane Grover said with a cynical snort, "that fucking Leo-the-Lion bitch's been bush trimming one of her friend's cunt with her teeth." He got such a good round of laughs that he continued, "Ain't no guy gonna put his dick in that cow." He grinned at each of his followers as he awaited praise for his wit. After their guffawing ceased he added, "Even ol' Slick Willy wouldn't rent that bitch an apartment under his Oval Office desk." As the men he bought beers, for every day after work, laughed and wiped tears from their eyes, Lane turned and walked away toward the wall he was constructing on the far side of the building. He pulled himself up to his entire five-foot-five-inch height and did his best imitation of the John Wayne Walk. He knew they were watching.

When he was back on his wall across the room, the older man who had only recently joined his crowd said quietly, "That little runt can sure strut his stuff, can't he?"

"Yeah man," a young worker said, "struts all the way to the bar to buy us another round." He chuckled as he headed for his own project.

A large, slow-witted blonde carpenter commented before following him, "Little turd can strut all he wants, just so he keeps buyin' the beer." He grinned at his work-mate and pulled the hammer from his tool belt.

During the following weeks, Shirleen ignored their snide remarks and continued giving them their orders for the day's projects. On a Friday night after all of her crew had departed the job-site, she was going over her blueprints when the deep rumbling voice that she was now very familiar with echoed inside her head.

'Tonight's the night my dark angel. Tonight they pay. Listen carefully.'

Any woman who chooses to behave like a full human being should be warned that the armies of the status quo will treat her as something of a dirty joke; that's their natural and first weapon.

Gloria Steinem.

* At the exact moment that Shirleen was listening intently to Satan's voice in her head, four young high school boys were listening to the demons who had taunted each of them their entire lives. They had formed their own gang the previous year, naming it THE SCORPIONS. Each boy had been born between October 24th and November 21st. They had agreed to only allow members to join if the were under the Scorpio sign in the Zodiac. They had slipped into the school to lead the football team's mascot away to their waiting van. Now, many miles from the school, they were at a small river they knew few people visited. The billygoat was hanging from a tree limb by his hind legs.

The four boys passed the marijuana joints around as they danced and wailed around their bonfire. The demons that had danced around in their heads were now dancing with them. Periodically one of the boys would pick up the sharp knife and slice a little more from the screaming, terrified goat. When there was only whimpers coming from the hapless animal, the tall, skinny, stuttering boy said, "Llllets kkkkill it now and go gggget something elelelelse to tttttorttture."

The short, fat boy with eyes so close together that they sometimes appeared to be one big Cyclops eye screamed, "YES! Let's go get a little girl this time."

"Get the pan," their self ordained leader commanded.

The huge, lumbering boy with buckteeth protruding so far out of his mouth he had difficulty eating, came running with the small pan they brought for the ceremony. He held it as instructed by his leader, who slit the goat's throat. When it was full of warm blood he stepped back and thrust his head back to howl at the full moon overhead. When his breath left him, he began drinking from the pan. It was passed around until it was empty.

When they left a short time later, the only thing they took with them was the knife. The goat remained hanging from the tree, above many beer bottles. "That's enough for one night," King Scorpion, as he preferred to be addressed by his peers, said. "But," he looked from one of his followers to the next until he had stared hard at each, "next time we get us a young girl."

They did!

. . .

Shirleen sat in her car and waited. She was parked only a short distance from the bar where Lane Grover and his cronies drank every day after work. She watched as they came from the bar a short time later and piled into Lane's new dual-cab pick-up truck. Before he could pull away from the curb she pulled up along side and blew her horn. When her old friend lowered the window she said, "You still sitting on a box jerking off, you fucking little runt?" She grinned and gave them the finger then took off in a cloud of dusty

Rick Magers

gravel—with the men not far behind.

'Good! Lead them to the slaughter, my lovely dark angel.'

She followed the route out of the city as Satan had previously directed, and was soon traveling along the winding coastal highway that skirted notoriously close to the edge of the cliffs, which ended on the oceanside rocks far below. She looked at her speedometer and was surprised to see it registering over a hundred miles an hour at times. She had never driven at this speed before in her entire life, but felt as comfortable as if she was on a casual Sunday afternoon drive.

The winding road prevented her from seeing their truck, but the headlights showed them to still be in pursuit. She slowed until they were right behind her, then when Satan said, 'NOW' she gave them the finger out her window, and pressed the gas pedal to the floor. At one hundred and twenty miles an hour she was on the one straight stretch of highway on the route. Shirleen had driven this same stretch of highway many times because of its beauty, so she was aware that the straight stretch ended into a deadly hard curve not far ahead.

'Pull over now,' Satan's voice rumbled in her head with a deadly tone.

As she slowed and pulled into one of the many picnic spots, Lane and his group of friends roared by so fast that it startled her.

'Let's go watch them try to fly.' Satan's voice was now filled with humor as his laughter echoed all the way to the spot that the truck left the highway.

She pulled to a stop and watched as the truck full of drunken men crashed down the cliff, flipping end over end, and finally landing on the rocks—bursting into flames.

Satan laughed one more time then growled deeply. 'More dark angels for my army.'

Suddenly he was sitting beside her on the seat, grinning through a face that was now glowing like a hot charcoal fire.

'Drive ahead to the motel just beyond the next curve, so we can make love before I must leave you for a while, my darling dark angel.'

As Shirleen headed toward the area he spoke of, she attempted to place a motel, but in her memory there wasn't a motel for about a hundred miles. She was surprised when she rounded the curve ahead and there it was—ABADDON MOTEL.

She had come to trust Satan entirely, so she pulled in and stopped. The clerk was a kindly old man that smiled warmly as he gave her the change for the one-hundred-dollar-bill she handed him. With the key in her hand she followed his instructions to find the room, and was soon inside a warm, cozy bungalow. Satan was lying naked on the bed.

She had never seen his naked body until this moment, and it intrigued her. Every inch of his flesh was alive with worms, crawling in and out as they did on his face. They seemed such a natural part of him that she found them appealing. Without a word she removed her clothes as he watched intently. When she was naked he spoke.

'Take me into you and receive my burning seed.'

Shirleen placed her mouth on his as the writhing worms began caressing her lips. She felt his tongue going deep into her throat as his rhythm sent her to the world of ecstasy she had come to long for. She closed her eyes and breathed deeply as her mind filled with visions of lusty maidens caressing one another. When she opened her eyes awhile later she was laying on the bed alone. Her eyes were fluttering and before she could move—she was asleep.

The pain hit her so hard that it literally jolted her from sleep, sometime in the wee hours of the night. Certain that she was being gripped by spasms of diarrhea; she stumbled to the bathroom and straddled the toilet. Within moments she realized it was not diarrhea. Something was coming out of her. She lifted herself with her powerful legs until she could look. As the smoldering black creature was hanging half out of her, the floor began breaking open to reveal a glowing cauldron of flaming beasts, creatures, demons, and apparitions of every description. They were all reaching up to her as the creature slipped out and began falling toward them. It turned and looked at her, then smiled a sinister smile she had seen many times as a young child. It was her father's face as a young man, but quickly changed to the fat, perspiring face he wore when she saw him as a child—humping atop her. Saliva dripped from the creature's mouth as it fell screaming toward the bubbling, smoking cauldron of sulfur below. She felt her legs leaving the ever-widening chasm, and was soon falling toward their howls and laughter.

Moments later, a young man and his family were passing the exact spot. "I'm so tired Smokey, ain't there a motel along here we can stop at?"

He placed his arm over her shoulder as he steered the station wagon full of kids and dogs on down the highway, "Not for about a hundred miles darlin'."

THE END

Shirleen was born August 9th-----LEO.

For god created man to be immortal, and made him to be an image of his own eternity—nevertheless through envy of the devil came death into the world.

The Apocrypha.

Rick Magers

Soaring Dark Angel

Sheldon Hamilton III was a Viet Nam fighter pilot with a distinguished war record, and had medals to prove it. He still served his country as a Naval Reserve pilot—often flying simulated missions with live ammunition. He was accepted by the servicemen he worked with, but most kept distance between him and them. "He's a little weird," was a common comment by his peers.

Since returning from Viet Nam, Sheldon established himself as a good stockbroker and financial advisor. He spent three years going to school nights to get his master's degree in business management and international finance. At the firm he went to work for, Sheldon worked tirelessly and was soon considered by his employers to be one of their best men. His fellow employees felt the same way his fellow navy men did. "There's just something weird about that guy."

Sheldon was approaching fifty, unmarried and unattached to anything except his job. For that reason his employers could care less that he was a little odd. Hours at the office meant nothing to him. He was often still there working on a client's portfolio when Mr. Brohmeir opened in the morning. A shower and a coffee later, he would be back at the office as fresh as if he had just returned from vacation.

Stanley Brohmeir commented often to his partner Rod Strait, "Give me a few more weirdo's like Sheldon, and I'll alter the New York Stock Exchange."

Sheldon's house was on two acres in a secluded section of Pensacola, Florida. A ten-foot stone wall topped with razor wire surrounded it.

Sheldon was paranoid, certain that the many Viet Cong he had killed in Viet Nam were going to come for him. He already had the home on the two acres when his wealthy parents died, making him sole heir to millions of dollars. He immediately had construction on the wall started. He said nothing about his inheritance at the Air Base or the office downtown.

No one had ever been to his house and few even knew where he lived. After initial interest about the newcomer died down, no one paid any attention to the strange man at 666 Bayou Blvd.

For over a month, the demons that had returned from Viet Nam with Sheldon were constantly popping up inside the house. At first he was startled to see them sitting on the wall or swinging from the razor wire, when he came from the office or the base. After a few days he expected to see them and was disappointed when they were not there to welcome him home. He would always feel relief when he entered the house and saw them sitting on top of a lamp or hanging from the ceiling by their sharp claws.

Tonight the pounding in his head was almost unbearable. The red flashes with blazing yellow borders were coming every few minutes. The tall, thin, chocolate colored demon with skin as smooth as the body of a new car, stepped forward and held out the container of pills. Sheldon took two this time instead of one, and threw them into his mouthful of bourbon. The demon set the container down in front of Sheldon and smiled as his skin began changing—resembling an alligator. It was no longer thin, but now bulged in all directions, with white foamy breath when it laughed.

'Ha! I said you would need me again.'

Sheldon heard another voice and looked up at the ceiling.

'You need us all.' The shiny black demon hanging from the ceiling was melting down toward him. He couldn't move—didn't want to move. He was in a trance as he kept his eyes riveted to the blazing red eyes, as the demon oozed toward him. Suddenly it released its hold and disappeared. He looked around to see if he could re-locate it, but there were now dozens of demons, all exactly the same as the one that was hanging above him moments earlier. Their shiny black bodies were pulsing with lights inside. He turned when he heard the voice of the alligator demon sitting in front of him.

'What are you waiting for? Those gooks are the ones that caused all of your troubles. It is time Sheldon. The Master wants you to act now.'

He turned again when he heard the demons all chanting. 'The Master says it's time—The Master says it's time—The Master says it's time.'

Rick Magers

6

TRAINED WARRIOR

God and Satan use the same tailor. It's all in the eye of the beholder. Truth?—Deceit?

An observation.

Sheldon Hamilton III followed the bombers he was assigned to cover, across the Thailand and Laos borders, at target-run altitude. As the bombers approached their target and prepared to release their load, he and his fellow fighter pilots spread out slightly above to look for enemy fighters that might be lurking, ready to strike down on the bombers. He and the others watched with satisfaction as the bombs found their mark along the North Vietnam coast, and still no enemy fighters in sight. The bombers climbed into the clouds as they turned toward the border and relative safety. Sheldon and his group waited until the bombers were on course for Thailand only moments away, then descended to make their usual run along the North Vietnam coast to release their own small arsenal of death and destruction.

    They had made this same run so many times in the past few months that they had become complacent about the enemy defenses on the ground. "Buncha fuckin' gooks with muskets and shotguns," was a common, laughing attitude among these courageous, young aerial gladiators. In the area they were about to unleash their cannon and machinegun fire, it was for the most part true. Old men and young boys alike were actually firing shotguns and ancient muskets at the screaming jets, which were destroying their lives. It was a futile attempt on the part of these peasants, but the government of North

Vietnam encouraged it and kept them supplied with ammunition.

"Let these invaders know that we will never stop until we are all dead or have defeated them."

With the shotgun shells and musket powder, the government also brought an occasional load of more modern weapons to distribute to the young men along the borders of their country.

Linh Thuoc Vhow was lucky a few weeks before Sheldon began this last run in his multi-million dollar jet fighter. He was given an AK-47 and enough ammunition to practice with—and he did. To his friend's amazement, the thin, determined, fourteen-year-old, four-foot-seven-inch-tall, always too serious boy that didn't weigh eighty pounds, was a naturally good shot; as Sheldon Hamilton III was about to find out.

The moment Linh heard the approaching drone of the enemy bombers he ran from the waterside where he was repairing his father's fishing nets. He slipped two bandoleers of ammo-clips over his tiny, delicate shoulders and grabbed his beloved automatic assault rifle. As he ran to the spot he always fired from, he checked the selector switch to be sure it was on semi-automatic. His friends who had also been rewarded with AK-47's never took theirs off of automatic. They loved the feeling of power it gave them to feel the many bullets spraying from their barrels, at the silver messenger's of death zooming over their heads. They were so low at times that they could see the helmeted demons at the controls.

Not young Linh Thuoc Vhow. He was a serious, determined young warrior, who would go on to become a leader of his people in the fight for their own freedom. His mission in his present moment of time was simple. "I'm going to shoot down one of those silver devils."

As Sheldon's group ran low along the coast, emptying their guns on fishermen, women, children, oxen, anything that had the ill fortune to be in their sights on that balmy day, the air was filled with the pop-pop-pop-pop-pop-pop-pop of automatic fire coming from below them.

It couldn't be heard amid the noise of the jets overhead, and the machine guns on the ground, but there was a completely different sound pattern coming from the bunker that Linh had prepared as soon as he was presented with his AK-47.

Pop-pause—pop-pause—pop-pause. The child was carefully taking aim, as he slowly squeezed the trigger like he was taught. As he stood stoically defiant to face the screaming jet coming straight at him, bullets were hitting the ground all around. As the first of the jets roared by he lay back against the dirt wall of his bunker so he could steady the machine gun that looked out of proportion in his tiny, bird-like arms. In his sight now was Sheldon's jet fighter.

Sheldon never heard the determined, rhythmic, pop-pause—pop-pause of the little boy's rifle, but he felt the results. He had never been hit but had been told by many that had and made it back, "It's probably like getting hit by one of those small water moccasins in the rivers around your Pensacola, Florida home. You don't know where'n the hell the little bastard gotcha, but you damn sure know he did."

They're right, Sheldon thought as his jet reacted to something he couldn't quite put his finger on, *I've been hit by one of their popguns.* He continued along the coast toward the two towns of Vinh and Ha Tinh where he always emptied his cannons before turning for the Mekong River to cross Cambodia and head for the Thailand border. Moments after notifying his support group that he'd been hit, his plane started acting strange. "I've shot m'wad," he said into his helmet microphone, "and I'm climbing outa here." He suddenly realized he wasn't climbing back to safe altitude as he always had. The aircraft was not responding to his commands. When the warning light flashed on to alert him that he had mere seconds to evacuate the cockpit if he wanted to live, he screamed into the helmet, "Shit! I'm outa here." He was still yelling, "Gone to silk—gone to silk," as he activated the eject device.

Within a few brief moments a young child was elevated to the type of hero-status that would carry him into national politics for the remainder of his long, successful life. In those same moments Sheldon's life began a journey into a hell from which he would never emerge.

Victorious warriors win first and then go to war, while defeated warriors go to war first and then seek to win.

Sun-Tzu.

Sheldon floated gracefully into the waiting hands of the same people he had just been spraying with bullets. It wasn't going to be a good day for the six-foot-seven-inch-tall—two-hundred-and-sixty-pound, blonde, blue eyed, American Naval Pilot. As he drifted down, he glanced in the direction of where he knew the Mekong River would be. Before hitting the ground he calculated the route to it. He was first and foremost a backwoodsman; enlistment and subsequent pilot training came from his father. With Admiral Sheldon Hamilton II RET you didn't have many options once he decided what course you should be set upon. A man either went with his plan, or got away from him. Sheldon Hamilton III couldn't get away, so he became what his father had always wanted him to be—a naval pilot.

"The mental strain was really a bitch," he once confided to one of his few friends, "because I don't give a shit about all this silly crap a million miles from home. All I really wanna do is take charters out in the swamps around Pensacola to fish 'n hunt." He smiled self-consciously at his buddy, "But I guess I ain't alone?"

"Yeah," his pal commented, "seems like many of our parents miss their flight then want to control their children's lives to make up for it."

His training in military survival, which he thoroughly enjoyed, plus his own natural wilderness cunning and savvy, would save his life in the next few weeks. What the huge, blonde American would endure at the hands of his temporary, little brown captors, would change him forever.

His ordeal began about forty miles south of Ha Tinh, near the Cambodian border. At this point he calculated he was only about fifty or sixty miles from the Mekong River, and if the opportunity presented itself he'd head for it and hope to meet up with a US Patrol Boat. More than any other man in his outfit, he devoured the maps available of the terrain he'd be flying missions over—just in case. *I know this area as well as those swamps around Pensacola*, he thought, and then had one last glance toward the Mekong River area before slamming into the ground.

Before his chute was even level on the ground, the local people were beating him with sticks. He was saved by the arrival of a North Vietnamese Officer on a motorcycle, who forced the peasants back until his men arrived on foot. Sheldon was taken to a small, temporary holding cell in the town of Dong Hoi, just South of Ha Tinh—one of his earlier targets.

"You will be held here until a truck comes next month to transport you to Hanoi." The child-size young officer glared at the tall American pilot then continued, "I will personally make your stay here a very pleasant one," he leaned forward and looked up at Sheldon, "for me, that is."

The reality of the situation he was in hadn't yet hit Sheldon, so he responded casually, "Where'd ya learn to speak such good English?"

The rifle butt hit him in the back of the head and he fell forward on his long arms, as stars danced around in front of him. "You do not ask questions, Yankee killer, my Major will do all the asking—you answer."

The young man in front of him waved whoever was behind him away, then smiled again. "You are very lucky I arrived when I did, or you would have been killed by those villagers." The little man leaned back against the adz-hewn table and looked down at Sheldon.

When the stars went back to where they had come from he began to get back on his feet. He didn't see the nod from his captor but the stars returned abruptly as the rifle butt struck again. This blow sent him all the way down and onto his side looking up at the young Major's smiling face. "I like you down there. You will soon learn that you do nothing until I tell you to." He clapped his little hands together several times and Sheldon couldn't help thinking, *looks like a kid playing patty-cake.*

You will certainly not be able to take the lead in all things yourself, for to one man a God has given deeds of war, and to another the dance, to another the lyre and song, and in another wide-sounding Zeus puts a good mind.

Homer.

Two of the young major's rag-tag soldiers came running at the sound of his clapping hands, and carried Sheldon from the tiny thatched hut he had been in since arriving in the village. The cell he was thrown into was little more than a pigsty. Mud covered sticks and river reeds for walls, a thatched roof that allowed him to see the stars at night—usually twinkling through the rain that kept him continuously soaked.

During his two weeks there, the tiny major's routine never varied. Before dawn he and one of his small goons would come in with a bright light and interrogate Sheldon. Within minutes the beatings began. Baby goon held the light as the major kicked Sheldon. Even though the kicking hurt, Sheldon couldn't help thinking, *At least he's got tiny feet and no boots.*

At noon, another beating, then as soon as he settled down after dark with his only meal of the day, the major would return for his evening entertainment. When he and baby goon left, there would often be so much mud and dirt in the bowl of rancid rice that more mud was eaten than thrown out. Two weeks later when his comrades resumed their strafing runs along the nearby coast, Sheldon's strong, organized, productive mind was undergoing destructive changes—demon's were arriving.

The major came at a run on the fourteenth morning, yelling orders. His tattered squad of tiny soldiers began assembling around, what looked to Sheldon as he peered from his cell, like a safari. Several of the inhabitants of the village were adjusting large packs on top of their heads, while others were tying bundles to their bicycles. Sheldon was grabbed by two of the major's soldiers, while another tied his hands securely in front of him. The rope was secured to the rear of a cart pulled by an old man, and off into the jungle the safari moved. He could see the major ahead, leading the way. *Toward the Mekong*, he thought as he mentally reviewed his position. *Good! At least it's a step toward home.*

As they progressed farther into the jungle, Sheldon demanded of himself that he recall the maps he had studied so exhaustively. Before long his mind was back at the table looking down at the maps of this area, as his feet mechanically carried him along behind the cart. When they entered the village he was fairly certain it was Ban Na Phao, a known Viet Cong Guerrilla bunker, which the Rangers had not been able to knock out, because it was so far inside the Cambodian border. *If I'm right, I'm only about thirty miles from the Mekong River.*

Sheldon found that his accommodations were no better in Ban Na Phao, but at least the major was now too busy to beat him regularly. He made only one trip to see Sheldon, and that was the second morning after arriving. After a round of kicking by the major's tiny feet, which left Sheldon with a bruised eye and a bloody nose, the major spoke in his squeaky shrill voice. "My General says you are an important captive and will provide him with much useful information when he arrives next month. I am to feed you well, and see to it that you are in good shape to begin the interrogations with my General." He leaned down to leer at Sheldon, "And you will need much strength to survive only one day. I have watched my General interrogate you Yankee Pigs." He turned and left the mud-hut-cell.

Ain't gonna happen, you little pissant.

He heard a voice and looked around, then realized that it was inside his head.

'We can help you if you'll let us.'

It was so realistic that he instinctually looked around again. seeing nothing, he never-the-less sensed that someone was with him—or something.

On his third day, he met the only friendly North Vietnamese he had ever talked to. His name was Tan Du Dhao, and he spoke perfect English. "I went to college in California but returned to fight for my country." He looked at Sheldon through black, penetrating eyes, "You understand?"

"Of course; we must all do what we think is the right thing. How else could we live with ourselves?"

"I do not agree with the treatment of our prisoners. I am but a lowly corporal, so must wait until I am in a more powerful position." He looked hard at Sheldon again then added, "And when I am, all like this arrogant peasant major will be removed from all military decisions."

Sheldon remained silent, but thought, *tomorrow'd be all right with me.*

During his weeks at Phao, as all referred to the tiny village, Sheldon made nightly trips to reconnoiter the area, and determine which course to take when his plans were set. Each trip was during a torrential downpour. None of the captors thought it possible that any American would even consider an escape attempt through their wild country, so security was just lax enough to allow him to move cautiously toward the small river he could hear in the distance.

He spotted the lone sentry on one trip. The man squatted near a large tree for protection from the rain, and moved his head back and forth as he surveyed the area. Sheldon spent an hour watching the man to see if he did anything unusual. Once satisfied the guard was just putting in his time, and not aggressively guarding his assigned territory, Sheldon continued moving through the mud on his stomach as he surveyed his escape route.

Tan Du Dhao brought extra food for Sheldon each night, and talked for an hour about all of the wonderful things he had seen and done in America. "When we are free of this burden I plan to return to finish my education, so I can enter politics in my country, to make it a better place for my people." He flashed a boy-like grin at Sheldon, "Or become a hot-shot LA Lawyer."

Sheldon sincerely liked the young man that was treating him humanely, and returned the smile. "Come home 'n be a politician, those LA Lawyers're all crooks." They enjoyed a laugh together, then the young man handed him something. Sheldon looked in his hand as the soldier explained.

"That is not as good as your American medicine, but rub it on those sores and it will help a little. I will try to get you a tube of some better salve that we occasionally receive from Hanoi."

Fifteen days after arriving, Sheldon knew the day had come to leave. *Die or be free tonight. This's the kinda rain I've been waiting for—it's now 'r never.* It was after midnight when he slid from his cell on his stomach. He had saved the extra food that his one friend, Tan Du Dhao had brought, so he could keep up his strength as he ran for the Mekong River, and hopefully an American Patrol Boat.

He spotted the guard at the river, as usual squatting beneath the same tree. He moved with all of his wilderness stealth and cunning, learned during a lifetime in the swamps of Florida. When he was close enough to hear the man's breathing he pounced on the little man like a Tiger. The small soldier was in the river with his head being held beneath the surface by the six-and-a-half-foot tall American, who still weighed almost two hundred pounds. The little man had no chance at all to avoid his death. Well! He had one—should have stayed in college in California. When Sheldon rolled the man over to relieve him of his equipment, he said quietly, "Shit!"

As he removed the gear and slung it around his own neck he thought, *of all the damn people to be out here on guard tonight, why did it hafta be you, Dhao?*

As Sheldon began his journey to the Mekong River, he had company following him. The demons, that would play such an important part in his coming years, were slithering through the dense forest with him. For years afterward, each time he saw a demon it would have the face of Tan Du Dhao.

The haft of the arrow has been feathered with one of the eagle's own plumes. We often give our enemies the means of our own destruction.

Aesop.

✱ As Sheldon was making his way toward the Mekong River, and the Patrol Boat that would rescue him, another man was making his way stealthily through a jungle-like environment. The little man sneaking through the park in Chowalla wasn't a woodsman like Sheldon, but he was good enough not to be heard by the ten-year-old girl he was following. The demons were yelling so loud that he was afraid she would hear them and run. 'Get the little bitch and let's have some fun.' Their screaming echoed inside his head.

This was his seventh town and she would be his ninth victim. A six-year-old boy lay dead not a mile from where he was at this very moment. *A double last week and, a double tonight; not bad.* His MO was working perfectly. Find a new town a long way from the last. Check it out good, and then park the car where it'll be okay. Start walking until it's dark, and a victim becomes available.

Law enforcement's MO should have worked as well as his: even better. He had been arrested twenty-two times for child molestation. His jail Psychiatrist had evaluated him as a probable repeat offender, incapable of ignoring his impulses.

"He's been a bed wetter all of his life; to this very day as a matter of fact," she reported. "He began torturing animals to death in horrible ways when he was only seven-years-old, and finds great joy in recalling the grisly details. His father left when he was four and his mother blamed him for it, often waiting until he was sound asleep to begin beating him with a broom handle. That's when he developed the severe stutter, and probably when he began thinking about abusing children." She looked pleadingly at the panel she knew would do nothing—once again, "I strongly recommend that he be permanently incarcerated, until he has been thoroughly checked out, because I believe he will soon begin killing children"

They didn't—he did.

. . .

Rick Magers

Sheldon Hamilton III finished his last few months of active military duty in the Naval Hospital only a short drive from his parent's mansion in Pensacola, Florida. After regaining the pounds he lost in the wilds of North Vietnam, he was given a clear bill of physical health. He was given a routine psychological assessment prior to his discharge from the hospital on his birthday. It was a warm day in May, and the dynamic young man felt like he could whip the world. The papers containing his pertinent information passed unread beneath the eyes of one Admiral and two Commanders.

They did not pass so easily beyond one energetic, determined young psychiatrist. She silently read Sheldon's psychological profile repeatedly, then packed the papers in her briefcase and took them home over the weekend, to further study this man she referred to as, "The strangest person I've encountered yet."

Doctor Marylynn Davis placed a call to her hospital boss, Admiral James Hopkinn at his home. "Admiral Hopkinn, can I help you?"

"Admiral, this's Doctor Davis, I wouldn't bother you at home, but I think I have a serious situation here in front of my eyes."

"Let's have it then," his manner was abrupt and indifferent.

"Admiral, we're set to discharge a man from our hospital tomorrow morning that I feel is not ready to cope with the outside world." The Admiral ignored his guests long enough to listen to the young doctor explain in detail her misgivings about Sheldon being turned loose.

"Doctor Davis, I'm glad you take such an interest in your patients. I'll be in there first thing in the morning to look his records over and further discuss this with you." He hung up the phone and returned to his guests.

"Problems James?"

Admiral James Amadeus Hopkinn smiled at the Congressman from the adjoining state, then answered. "Just one of our civilian head shrinks that thinks she's gotta baby-sit every guy that comes crawling outa the jungles over there." The following morning the Admiral had signed the papers releasing Sheldon from the hospital before Doctor Davis was even dressed for work.

Two months later, Sheldon signed himself into the Naval Reserve and was soon doing the one thing that he loved, other than roaring through the swamps in his airboat—flying.

He stayed so busy during the first few years, that he hardly ever had a visit from the demons; constantly lurking in the shadows, and biding their time with infinite patience.

Sheldon's initial degree in business management got him an interview with the most prominent firm in the Bay Area, BROHMEIR and STRAIT—Financial Consultants. Stanley Brohmeir was a member of the same country club as Admiral Sheldon Hamilton II RET. Rod Strait was a board member on one of the Admiral's many businesses. The two men were more than happy to accommodate the elder Hamilton. Their stability and wealth was firmly rooted in his wide reaching financial empire. When they realized the potential they had in the young Naval Officer, they were very pleased.

Sheldon attended college at night for three grueling years to attain his Masters' Degree in business management and international finance. In no time at all he was considered the top man in the office. It was soon made official as he ascended to the position of Senior Vice President, passing several that had been there many years. His employers knew they had a gold mine in Sheldon, but his co-workers felt the same way his fellow navy associates did—"Something's really weird about that guy."

Sheldon was fast approaching fifty—unmarried—unattached to anything except his job. For that reason his employers could care less that he was a little odd. Hours at the office meant nothing to Sheldon, and he was often there working on a clients portfolio when Mr. Brohmeir opened in the morning. A shower and a coffee later he was back at the office, as fresh as if he had just returned from a restful night's sleep. "Now let's get started and get some work done."

Stanley Brohmeir often commented to his partner, "Give me a few more like Sheldon and I'll alter the NEW YORK STOCK EXCHANGE."

Rod Strait always had the same answer for his partner, "I just wish he was a little more aggressive with the people working under him." Rod would shake his round, pudding face until the hanging jowls flapped, "He let's them do whatever they please."

"And you 'n I," Stanley always countered with a wry smile, "take the profits to the bank."

The first thing Sheldon did when he was released from the hospital, was to begin searching for a piece of land to build a house on. He located two wooded acres on the northwest side of Pensacola, Florida that was slowly being developed into a neighborhood of large homes on acreage rather than lots. He bought the property ten minutes after the Realtor showed it to him, and then immediately contracted a land development firm to bulldoze it perfectly flat. The few residents that had already built in the area were certain this newcomer was going to have a landscape company come in to plant special trees, shrubs, ornamentals and such—they were wrong.

Two years later, the six thousand square foot home was finished and Sheldon began moving in. Other than the one-hundred-yard-long, paved drive to the house, there was nothing but grass. He contracted a lawn maintenance company to mow it regularly and give it whatever was needed for it to remain healthy.

On a bright Sunday morning, the week before his wealthy father died,

Sheldon answered the doorbell. Standing on his verandah were four dour, heavily perfumed, bluehaired old women. Each stood beside a large potted plant they had carried to the porch with them. He simply stared silently at them as their chosen leader spoke. "Good morning," she said through a ghastly plastic smile, "I'm Mrs. Overstone, Doctor Overstone's wife. This is," she turned to introduce one of her subordinates—Sheldon simply slammed the door closed.

When the four old ladies accepted the fact that there wasn't even a slight wind capable of accidentally slamming the door, they picked up their plants and left. The main comment shared among them was, "Strange, strange man." They soon found out just how strange their new neighbor was.

Sheldon's mother had preceded his father to the grave by two years, so when Sheldon Hamilton II was laid to rest, their son Sheldon Hamilton III became the sole heir to a vast fortune. As always he went about re-structuring his life with military precision. The first thing he did was quit his job. The second and only other significant thing was to contract with a construction company to build a wall around his home. Not just a wall—THE WALL. It would soon become known as The Prison Wall at 666 Bayou Blvd.

The house of everyone is to him as his castle and fortress, as well for his defense against injury and violence as for his repose.
Sir Edward Coke.

Sheldon personally inspected each day's results, and when not satisfied he had changes made before they went too far. When it was completed, he had exactly what he wanted—a poured concrete wall three-feet-thick, ten-feet-tall, finished inside and out with imported Tennessee stone, on top were four-foot-tall steel posts placed six-feet-apart, and strung with the same razor wire used by prisons. The entrance was a masterpiece that he created by use of his own personal engineering. A steel door twenty-feet-long moved in and out of the wall, much like a pocket door inside a house. It was hung from a steel beam spanning from one side to the other, which was also topped with posts and razor wire. The heavy door rolled on small inflatable aircraft tires, barely making a sound as it opened and closed.

The electronic opening and closing device was his idea, which he had a security firm perfect. The only way in or out was with knowledge of the security code, which changed every thirty seconds. Even then the two master codes, and an often-changed password had to be entered into the hand held unit before the steel door opened to allow his car to pass. All current info to gain access was automatically uploaded into Sheldon's hand-held device.

As soon as the rear bumper moved past the electronic eye the door quickly closed. During this time four Rottweilers sat patiently and watched the entering automobile. They were trained to silence, and should anyone but Sheldon Hamilton III step from the vehicle, or attempt to enter through the gate, they would not live five minutes. No barking, no warning, nothing. Attack—kill.

The young female doctor had hit Sheldon's nail right on the head a few years earlier. He was paranoid to a very high degree—P^{10}. Demons of many descriptions were now part of his daily entourage. Men working on the grounds often commented, "That weirdo's always talking to things that're not there."

Nights were the worst for Sheldon. Even with the entire grounds flooded with lights, Rottweiler patrol loose, motion sensors scanning, bulletproof Lexan panels ready to fall into place over all doors and windows; and yet he still detected the enemy sneaking about, just beyond his wall. "Oughta have dogs on the outside too."

'Why don't you take care of those damn gooks like we did in Nam?'

Sheldon looked hard at the gnarled little demon sitting in the potted palm near the door. As he stared at the demon its face began to change until it was once again Tan Du Dhao shaking his head back and forth.

'Why did you kill me? I was your friend.'

Sheldon had long since quit explaining, "Goddammit, I had to escape and I'm sorry Dhao." He spoke harshly and then simply turned and walked away. Through it all though he continued flying simulated missions for the Naval Reserve. His iron will could still cast off the demons long enough for him to function as a top-notch pilot. His missions often took him over the target range, using live bombs and ammunition in his on-board arsenal.

With the completion of THE WALL, Sheldon seldom left the premises except for his military duties. A special steel vault was added in the wall for deliveries, so he could order everything he needed. The outer door would be electronically opened when he heard the buzzer, and then secured before opening the inner door to remove supplies. His four Rottweilers would dutifully accompany Sheldon as he drove his golf cart to remove the various supplies he ordered; his paranoia was growing, and the army of demons outside his compound, were also growing in number. Even in the daytime now the demons would often sit atop the razor wire and stare down with their contemptuous Tan Du Dhao faces. The dogs would look up at the top of the wall and growl menacingly whenever Sheldon pointed at the demons, "Kill those bastards if they come in here."

It was a cold, near-dawn day in November when Sheldon climbed into the cockpit of his Navy jet. Even the ground crew noticed how lackluster and sagging Sheldon appeared. They were so used to his energetic approach to every mission that they wondered aloud, "He must be comin' down with this flu that's goin' around?"

"Yeah," another groundman commented, "gotta be, 'cause he's always gung-ho when it's a live ammo day, like today."

Once strapped in, Sheldon felt a little better. Tired! I'm so damn tired I could sleep right here. The radio brought him from his temporary stupor and he mechanically followed the tower's instructions. Moments later he was airborne. "I'm not gonna be able to go on unless I get those gooks that're trying to break in," he commented aloud to himself—he thought.

He had flown this same mission so many times that he controlled the plane without even thinking about what he has doing. *All I do is doze anymore. I never sleep; sleep! Oh man what I'd do for just one night's sleep—so long, been so damn long since I slept.* His exhausted mind was wandering aimlessly.

As he passed north of the city he came around to his heading then looked up from his control panels. Plastered to the windshield of the aircraft were two small yellow demons. The bodies were as hideous, and the faces were the same as all the rest—Tan Du Dhao. "Oh God, leave me alone."

The mouth of each demon opened and screamed, 'No! You killed us. Why did you kill us? We were your only friend.'

Abruptly Sheldon pulled back on the stick, sending the plane shooting almost straight up. His wingman watched in surprise as he radioed the tower for instructions. At thirty thousand feet, two more joined the two demons. Now Sheldon had four Tan Du Dhao's looking mournfully at him. He brought the Jet over on its right side and began a spiral toward the city below. At ten thousand feet he leveled off and began looking between the four demons on his windshield. He spotted the landmark he'd been searching and headed for it.

The morning air still had a brisk nip to it as the four pungent, bluehaired old ladies parked and approached the steel gate to The Prison, as even they referred to Sheldon's home.

Mrs. Overstone led them to the opened trunk of her Towncar, so each could get one of the potted palms she had ordered special for the occasion. They sat them in front of the steel gate on purpose, so Sheldon would have to take them in with him. "Or drive right over them," her friend Mrs. Lundt snickered.

"Oh don't be silly Madeline, these palms were imported from Madagascar and cost three hundred and thirty dollars each. I'm certain Mr. Hamilton will recognize the value and take them in to plant." As she turned toward the car to leave, Mrs. Overstone heard the plane. It sounded very low, so she began searching the sky. "Look," she pointed, "I'll bet that's Mr. Hamilton."

"My goodness," Mrs. Maldonnif commented, "I've never seen one flying so low before." She couldn't keep her eyes from the jet as it approached at less than five hundred feet, with full flaps down.

'Bring her in nice 'n slow Captain, and we'll show you how to take care of these bastards.' The four demons left the windshield and were now crowded into the cockpit with Sheldon. They no longer wore the face of Tan Du Dhao. They were demonic in every sense of the word. Their eyes burned fiercely and their skin smoldered with the scent of sulfur. These were Sheldon's demons—his favorites. They had helped him escape the jungles of North Vietnam, and since through many a long night of no sleep as they all watched for the Viet Cong to attack his home; to carry him back to the jungle to be tortured for the killing of so many of their people.

'Look, look,' one of the demons pointed a long, stiletto finger toward the house inside the stone wall below. 'See them standing there? They're inside now. See?—they're everywhere.

Sheldon could see the enemy crawling over the stone wall as he flew by for an inspection pass. *Made it out just in time*, he thought, *they musta sent the whole battalion from Vinh.* He was satisfied with what he saw, and knew exactly what must be done. He began bringing the flaps back up as he increased power. He banked the jet around for the first pass then reached forward and armed all weapon systems.

The demon sitting on his shoulder pointed. 'See that tank at the gate?' "Roger that," Sheldon replied into the helmet's microphone. At this moment, many people listening were finding it impossible to decipher what the fighter pilot was doing. "Gonna take the tank out first."

Mrs. Overstone and her ladies stood like large perfumed sheep and watched as the jet went around, and then began coming straight toward them at a much faster speed. They all saw the napalm canister drop from below the jet, but it was the last thing they ever saw.

The hideous little green demon standing in Sheldon's lap began screaming and jumping up and down.

'We cooked 'em—whatta hit—toasted those gook bastards.'

Sheldon gained altitude as he brought the plane around to line up for another pass. When he began his run he looked ahead and saw hundreds of the enemy rushing toward his house. Even at his altitude he could see that it was an army of just one man—Tan Du Dhao. His bomb made a direct hit on the house as he pulled into a steep climb.

He came around and began a strafing run. His cannon and machinegun bullets plowed the lawn, as the Viet Cong danced and waved their weapons at him as he passed by. On the last pass that he would ever make, he looked ahead to see one lone little boy leaning back against his bunker. The rifle looked ridiculously large in the fourteen-year-old child's hands. He looked intently into Linh Thuoc Vhow's eyes but he didn't recognize him. He continued looking into the intense eyes as he drove the nose of the jet into them.

THE END

Sheldon was born May 3rd-----TAURUS.

But how shall we expect charity towards others, when we are uncharitable to ourselves? Charity begins at home, is the voice of the world; yet is every man his greatest enemy, and, as it were, his own executioner.
Sir Thomas Browne.

Rick Magers

Demon Twin

Brandisha Omahasha Candide wasn't the slightly overweight young woman's real name. She was born Betty Ann Brown and the name suited her just fine for the first twenty years of her life. When she began her junior year at Hamiltonville College of the Arts, she became intensely interested in the world of the occult. Before long she was spending less and less time with the people she started college with. As the summer sun and warmth gave way to the cool days of fall and the changing color of the leaves, she was spending all of her free time with her new circle of friends. They all shared a passion for the dark world of the occult. Each had his or her own special devotion, but warmly greeted each other as brothers and sisters of THE DARKNESS.

When Betty Ann attended her first séance she knew immediately that she'd found her calling. "This is what I want to do." Her spiritualistic tutor was a professor of social sciences. He was only a little older than Betty Ann, but had an air of depth and understanding about the dark side of life that she had always wondered about. He conducted séances on a regular basis for her select group of friends. At his suggestion she began searching for her new spiritual name.

"If you are going to become a professional spiritualist you must choose a name that will reflect upon your inner self," he said to her after one of his séances. "It should be a name that will also cast a shadow of mystery and intrigue on you." After several séances she handed him a slip of paper with her present name written across it. He read it slowly to himself, then aloud for the others to hear. "Brandisha Omahasha Candide." He turned to her and spoke softly. "Yes, you've chosen a good name. It will be your name from this day forth."

The professor was impressed with Brandisha's intense devotion to the art of calling forth the spirits from THE DARKNESS. She was soon receiving one-on-one tutoring from him, and before the end of her junior year they were lovers. During the summer months, prior to beginning her senior year, they spent a great deal of time in each other's arms: naked. He didn't teach the summer classes he ordinarily did, so they could spend more time together. He had a great passion for all things that interested him, especially sex. Each had enjoyed sexual pleasures with many partners, but from the moment they coupled, each intuitively knew that a special fire had been lit inside. Brandisha moved into his apartment at his urging, so he could devote more time to teaching her about the fragile world of the séance. It also allowed them to devote more time to exploring the flaming depths of their passion.

The summer weeks passed into months, and soon she was well into her last year at Hamilton. Their passion for each other's body remained intense as they explored new and exciting ways to give each other physical pleasure. Her passion for what she knew was to be her life-long career was more intense now than ever. "I want to conduct the next séance," she told the professor one evening, as they lay naked in front of the fireplace.

He looked deeply into her coal black eyes; unaware that special Contac lenses altered their color. They were extremely unusual on such a fair skinned woman, and they mesmerized him. Finally he answered, "Yes, it's time." She smiled and leaned down between his legs. He sat rigidly as he watched her brown hair being flung back and forth. He gasped repeatedly then lay slowly back onto the plush rug. Three fires lit the room—one behind the grate in the fireplace—one inside the professor—one inside Brandisha. *Yes*, she thought as she pulled the remaining passion from his throbbing penis, *my own séance.*

7

DARK PROGENY

First there's the children's house of make believe, some shattered dishes underneath a pine, the playthings in the playhouse of the children. Weep for what little things could make them glad.

Robert Frost.

Three-year-old Betty Ann Brown was more excited than she had ever been. "I'm going to the Cherokee Indian Camp to meet my father," she told her friend at the Atlanta apartment house she shared with her mother and her mother's boyfriend.

"Is he a real Indian?"

"Yes," the exuberantly happy, smiling, hazel-eyed little girl replied triumphantly, "he's the Chief."

"Whachew wanna go see dat damn Indian for anyway?" Chester said. Alma Jessica Brown gave her boyfriend Chester, a look of utter despair.

"How many times do I hafta tell ya? That son-of-a-bitch oughta be payin' me some money for draggin' his kid every goddamned place I go." She continued packing the things she felt she would need to spend the weekend in the tiny North Carolina resort town.

The tall, thin, black man came to her and put his arms around her from the back. "Hey."

Alma straightened and turned to him, "What?"

"I been supporting you 'n that little girl since she born, so why you gotta go pushin' that useless sucker for money?"

"Cause he owes it to me."

"Baby, you was wigglin' 'n jigglin' juss like he was at the time, so why you think he's gonna give you money?" It was a losing argument and Chester knew it. He had talked to her about the trip for two days straight, with no progress at all to talk her out of going. He lightened up and turned her around, then smiled at the young woman he truly cared for. "You juss wanna play in that big bingo game, doncha?"

Alma looked up into the smiling black face, which she had actually begun to like, "How in the hell am I gonna get in a two hundred dollar game, Chester?"

He had planned to give her enough to play all along and had the two, one-hundred-dollar-bills in his hand. "With these," he said as he brought them in front of her eyes.

Alma had thought all along that Chester would give her enough to play with, because she was aware that he cared for her. *Probably cares more for me than anyone ever has in my whole life.* For this reason she used his emotions to get the things she wanted—right now she wanted out. *I'm gonna wind up stuck with this black bastard the rest o' my life if I don't get the hell outa here.*

"Thanks darlin'," she said coyly as she took the two bills. "If I hit that two-hundred grand we'll go to Vegas for a little vacation." She continued packing her two suitcases, then shoved a few things into a brown grocery bag for her daughter. "Gonna run us over to catch the bus?"

"Sure," her boyfriend answered as he picked up both of her bags, "get Betty Ann in the car, 'cause that bus's gonna be here in about fifteen minutes." Ten minutes later they were parked in the VFW parking lot waiting for BENNY'S BINGO BUS to pull in.

Thirty minutes later the bus was heading east on 285. In a little over an hour they had picked up a load of bingo-biddies in Gainesville and were heading toward Cleveland, Georgia about an hour away. Six more ladies boarded the bus, carrying huge bingo bags filled with a wide assortment of bingo paraphernalia. Daubers, battery operated fans, snacks, cardholders, good luck charms, plus plenty of sandwiches, and drinks; making each bag bulge like a foot hassock. The driver turned toward Alpine Helen when he left Cleveland, on the off chance he'd get a few more paying riders when he stopped in front of Flossie's Funnel Cakes to stretch his legs and get a cup of coffee.

Alma always sat in the front, so she ask the driver, "Why didn't you go straight on to Clarksville then take the highway right into Franklin?"

"Woulda if we'd been full," the driver responded, "but I gotta try to fill this thing up, and a lotta folks know my schedule, so we might get a bunch in Helen, Hiawassee, or Haysville." He turned his fleshy red face toward her and grinned, "I've filled her up by goin' this way before." He returned his gaze to the road ahead, then looked up at the rear view mirror before adding, "Takes as long one way as the other, just a little more driving for me is all."

Alma told Chester that she was going to stay with her girlfriend in Cherokee, North Carolina for a few days, so she could try to get Betty Ann's father, Louis John Sequoia to pay her the money he owed her.

"What you gonna do if he says he ain't gonna pay you?"

"I'm gonna have the son-of-a-bitch arrested, that's what I'm gonna do."

"Baby, why don't you just forget about that stupid goddamn Moeheeheegan and stay here with me, so I can look out for you?"

"He's a fuckin' Cherokee, not a **Moeheeheegan**," she emphasized the word he had used, "and the bastard said he'd send me a hundred dollars every month to take care of his kid."

"You stayin' at the same girlfriend's house where you stayed the last time you played bingo up there?"

"Yeah," Alma answered, "Linda; the one that works at Big Boy Burgers."

The first thing Alma learned when she got to Cherokee, was that Linda no longer worked at the burger joint. The second thing was that she'd left the tourist town a month before Alma arrived. "Shit," she said aloud when the waitress at Big Boy's informed her about her friend.

"Sit," said the black-haired little girl with smiling hazel eyes, sitting beside her.

Alma turned an angry face toward Betty Ann, "Just shut up and sip your coke."

There was a third, and wonderful thing Alma found out later that night at the Cherokee Bingo Hall. Her luck was finally changing. *Oh dear God,* she prayed silently to herself as she stared at the one remaining number, which in moments would change her life, *please make oh-sixty-seven come up in that bowl of ping pong balls.*

The age-old epithet: God works in mysterious ways, was certainly true this night. The stocky young Cherokee Indian sitting high in the chair, plucking numbered ping-pong balls from a clear dome as they came shooting into the tube, reached out and grabbed the next ball. "Oh-sixty-seven." His voice rang clear and distinct through the speakers.

Only a nano-second was required, for the number being called and displayed on one of the many monitors throughout the huge packed bingo hall, to register inside Alma's head. The bolt of lightning that pierced her brain caused a screaming eruption from her lips: "BINGO."

The hungry, sleeping little girl on the floor beside her, opened tired eyes for a brief moment to look up at her mother, who was standing and waving at someone. They fluttered momentarily, and then closed as she returned to her dream world.

A kinder God would have let her remain there—forever.

Alma was ecstatic when she was informed that the blackout prize had been increased to three hundred thousand dollars. "Are you sure you want cash?" The old Indian at the pay-off window looked concerned at the young woman standing on the other side of the bars.

"You're goddamn right I want cash, Geronimo, and God help the motherfucker who tries to take it from me." Alma planned to leave no trail that could be followed. She put the packet of bills in her purse alongside the loaded Colt .38, and shook the sleeping little girl on the wooden bench beside the pay window. "C'mon girl, let's go get a hamburger."

That brought tired Betty Ann back to the world of hunger. She hadn't eaten a bite since the bologna sandwich that her mother had given her on the bus, many hours earlier. "Oh boy," she said with a huge grin, "and some fresh fries too?"

In front of Big Boy Burgers Alma got out of the taxi and walked around to the driver's window. "Here," she said as she handed the young Indian a hundred dollar bill, "keep this Goddamn thing running till I get back in about one minute, then I want you to take me to Cincinnati." She stared hard at the driver, "That okay with you?"

The dark brown face lit up, "Damn right, I got a girlfriend in Cincinnati." As Betty Ann waited patiently for her burger and 'fresh fries' to arrive, Alma wrote on a napkin. She folded it with a ten-dollar-bill inside, and then placed it in the little girl's jacket pocket.

"Show this to anyone who asks who you are," Alma said. She placed another ten-dollar-bill on the table then said, "I gotta go to the bathroom; I'll be right back."

Betty Ann never saw her mother again. The little girl wasn't getting off to a very good start in the Game of Life. Alma Jessica Brown climbed into the running taxi and leaned forward to tell the driver, "Okay chief, let's go to Cincinnati."

And I will put enmity between thee and the woman, and between thy seed and her seed; it shall bruise thy head, and thou shalt bruise his heel.

The Holy Bible.

Rick Magers

By the time Betty Ann Brown was thirteen she was finally placed in a loving foster home, but the damage had already been done. All of the tender care and loving that the middle aged, childless couple showed her couldn't overcome ten years of neglect and horror. Betty Ann had been thrown into the disgusting, black abyss of humankind. She had experienced things that a child should never even see at such a young age. Betty Ann Brown met the monsters that walk among us every day. The kindly old man next door—the sweet little old lady down the street—the saintly preacher—the helpful bus driver—the teenage boy with candy; each using the innocent little girl for their own sick perversions. Yes! The innocent little girl had seen too much; especially during her time with the many foster parents that took her in: for three reasons only. Money—Sex—Work.

A few days before her fourth birthday, the first foster parents the welfare worker placed her with, asked for permission to take her to Asheville. The foster father was a used car salesman accepting a new job. It was in her new home in Asheville that Betty Ann met her first monster. As the afternoon sun flooded her room she turned to see her new mother entering the room with a glass of whiskey in her hand and an evil gleam in her eyes.

A short time later she began having visitors: demons.

Children begin by loving their parents—as they grow older they judge them—sometimes they forgive them—sometimes not.

Oscar Fingal O'Flahertie Wills Wilde.

*As bad as it was for Betty Ann Brown, it was about to be a lot worse for two children not far from where she was being molested by her new 'mother.' Another young, sick, demented mother was adjusting the seat straps of her two young children seated in the rear of her car. She smiled as it rolled quietly down the boat ramp into the water. As the cries of her two children echoed across the glassy, nighttime lake, several demons that had been the young woman's constant companions for a long, long time began dancing. She looked at each hideous little troll-like gargoyle as they danced around, and her smile grew wider. Their screeching was drowning out the cries coming from the sinking car as her children were drowning and screaming, "Please help us, mama."

Rick Magers

• • •

When she was nineteen years old, the smiling one-hundred-and-forty-pound, five-foot-four-inches tall, black-haired girl, blessed with her father's high cheekbones, was ready to head off to college. She was now Betty Ann Coolidge, and after loading her car with baggage, she turned to her adopted parents and hugged each. The six years of love they had given her was the only love she had ever known, and she held them tightly. She was apprehensive about leaving the only secure home she had ever known, but there was so much Betty Ann wanted to see out in the world. She kissed them tenderly, with tears flowing down the faces of all three, and slowly drove away as she watched them in the rear view mirror.

Her first two years at Hamiltonville College would make boring stories, told to boring people around the Sunday dining room table. Which is exactly what she did, as often as she could get back home to the only two people on earth who loved her.

Demons that visited her dreams, and dropped in occasionally to be with her on lonely nights were easily shooed away like annoying flies at a picnic. Her tortured young mind was healing itself—but then she met the BROTHERS and SISTERS of the DARKNESS.

Her new circles of friends were enjoying their freedom away from home, and blissfully entered the world of the occult to relieve the boredom they complained about constantly. "It's just something to do."

Not with Betty Ann: she was mesmerized. After her first meeting with the group, she could hardly wait for their next gathering. "Betty Ann," her classmate said, "this is Professor John Poston." She was thrilled to be meeting the professor of social sciences they had told her about. He was only a little older than she, but was their mentor and spiritual guide as he led them into the dark world of the occult.

The professor conducted regular séances for a select group of students. Betty Ann begged her friends to talk the professor into allowing her to attend, and soon she was one of the few who never missed a session. It soon became obvious that she had found her calling; passionate flames burned within Betty Ann. It also became obvious that a flame of passion, but another kind, burned inside the professor. He spent more and more of his free time tutoring the girl that looked more Indian at times than Geronimo. Looking at her profile he thought, *My God, she looks like she oughta be sitting in front of a teepee.*

Betty Ann knew her friends were jealous and making cracks about her, but she had found her calling in life and didn't care what they had to say.

"Please teach me all about the world beyond, John." She and the professor had become lovers soon after meeting, and he found the exuberant, slightly overweight young woman captivating. At twenty-six-years-old, John Poston had seduced most of the students that had caught his eye, but there was something about Betty Ann that made her stand out from all the others.

"Those dark, hazel eyes have a fire in them like I have never seen before," he told a friend one evening. "I swear I can see a demon in there at times," he laughed.

Mounted atop her lover, Betty Ann was a sexual demon herself—driving on to a crescendo that fettered John Poston as he gritted his teeth, while she gradually developed a motion that excited him several times as he lay prostrate beneath his wild young lover. It was after these exciting moments for her lover, when she would exercise her considerable willpower to gain one more toehold in her climb to the top of the occult world on campus—always succeeding.

By November, she and John had moved into an apartment together off-campus, so she could spend more time learning about the dark, mysterious, world of the occult. And also so he could enjoy more of his wild young lover. One week after moving in, they had a few friends over for her birthday on the June eighth. The twenty-year-old Gemini had an announcement to make. As the guests gathered around her cake full of candles she said, "This is a birthday and a deathday party." She looked solemnly at each before continuing. "Betty Ann Coolidge died tonight." Again she stared at each a moment before continuing. "A new person will now occupy her body and mind. Please welcome," she spread her arms wide, "Brandisha Omahasha Candide."

John Poston stepped forward smiling, "I suggested she search her soul for a new name that better suits her, since she plans to become a professional spiritualist." He turned and looked into her eyes for several moments then added, "I think it's the perfect name." The young professor was so high on a variety of drugs, that he wouldn't even remember being at the party in an hour. John Poston's birthday came around on the seventh of March, which placed him almost directly in the middle of his sign. Being a Pisces did not make him more susceptible to the use of drugs and alcohol, but being a true primitive Pisces did. More than any other sign in the Zodiac, a primitive Pisces will use more drugs, alcohol and other vices than any sign. Only a Scorpio equals their lust for sex. John and Brandisha Omahasha Candide matched up perfectly—almost.

When your demon is in charge, do not try to think consciously—wait—obey.

Rudyard Kipling.

Rick Magers

Brandisha had her first flashback a few weeks after her twentieth birthday. She was resting with her cheek on the bearskin rug in front of the fire, knees buried in the lush fur, toes gripping the rug, as John mounted her from the rear. It was her favorite position, so it wasn't the first time, but something he did, said, touched—something? She never figured out which, but it set her afire inside like never before.

At first she fought it, but soon the images of her first foster father fondling her naked young body became so intense that she screamed, "Off! Off. Get the hell off of me, you filthy bastard."

John was so stoned on cocaine that he didn't respond to her cries, so she twisted around, ejecting his penis then rolled over and kicked him in the chest. He fell back, but then scrambled to his feet and stood looking down at her. "Goddamn babe, what the fuck's happ'nin?"

She looked up at her foster father standing there, and kicked at him as she lay on her back screaming, "Keep away from me, keep away, keep away, no, no, no, no, stop. Please stop." She was now lying on her side with her legs pulled tight against her body, and her arms wrapped around her knees, sobbing. "Don't! Please daddy, you're hurting me. Please stop, oh no, no, no, no, no...oh, ohhhhhh."

She was weeping so hysterically that John backed away and stood against the wall beside the fireplace. He stood silently and watched as she rolled over to her other side; all the time holding tightly to her knees, keeping her legs pulled to her chest. He listened in awe to her sob as she begged someone to stop hurting her. This was the first time he had ever seen anything like this. It was especially disturbing because it was so out of character for Brandisha. He retrieved his pants from the couch and continued watching as he put them on. *She's in some sort of a trance. I better keep an eye on her.*

John sat on the couch for an hour and watched as Brandisha sobbed. He had placed the couch cover over her earlier, and it settled her down, but she continued sobbing quietly. The effects of the cocaine wore off and his mind cleared up enough for him to begin wondering what she was experiencing. He was a little alarmed when she abruptly sat up and looked around until she located him.

"Hey! Whacha doing sittin' over there?" She stood and let the cover fall from her naked body, "This pudgy bod doesn't turn you on any more?" Her grin was playful and sincere as she walked toward him. "Hmmm, must not, I see y'gotcher britches back on."

He reached out and pulled her to him, "You turn me on too much babe that's the problem, you wear this old man out." He didn't know what had come over her but he didn't want to do anything to bring it back. All of

Professor John Poston's past sexual conquests had been purely physical, but with Brandisha it was different. "I think love is a pile of shit," he had said many times to his drinking, drug taking friends. "Stab 'em between the legs 'n move on to a new warm hairy hole." He had no idea what the word love even meant, but he was feeling something for Brandisha that he'd never experienced before. "That fire's not putting out enough heat babe, lemme get that cover and how about curling up here on the couch with me?" He returned and wrapped it around the two of them as they settled into the giant old parlor couch.

Brandisha turned her eyes up to him, "Do you love me, John?"

"Damned right I do babe, damned right." He wasn't aware of any feelings he could call love, and was also aware that he was lying to her.

It was enough for her to hear the words though, so she purred and snuggled into his arms as she drifted off to sleep.

The next few weeks passed so quietly, in the same routine pattern as the previous few months, that John had almost forgotten about her strange behavior in front of the fireplace. He knew something was wrong the moment he opened the door. The grocery bag had been thrown into the corner of the foyer; cans, packages, cheese and meat strewn across the floor. He stood quietly listening for sounds, of what he didn't know. He heard a conversation going on in the bedroom, so he walked quietly toward it.

"Why did you treat me so bad? I thought you were going to be my new daddy, and I loved you."

As John stood silently beside the open door, he realized it was not a conversation, just Brandisha alone and rambling on about something he knew nothing of. He would soon learn that the young woman was never really alone any longer. He moved away from the doorway and went to the kitchen to begin picking up the broken dishes and other items she had apparently thrown in anger. *What the hell's she mad at? Me? Something strange is going on inside that squirrelly head of hers.* After sweeping the broken glass into a pile on the linoleum, he went to the foyer and began picking up the groceries. He noticed the meat and cheese was still cold. *She must have just come home a short time ago.* He turned when he heard her footsteps and was relieved to see her smiling.

"Hi darling, I was gonna get those but thanks for pickin' 'em up." She turned and headed for the kitchen so casually, that he thought, *something serious is wrong with her.*

"Oh sweetheart, you're too much really." She turned to him with her arms open. After depositing the food on the counter he stepped into her open embrace. "You're so sweet to clean up that mess for me."

He hugged her close for a moment, and then asked quietly, "What's wrong, babe?"

Rick Magers

Brandisha remained silent as she hugged him tightly for several moments then said in a whisper, "I'm having flashes of things that happened to me as a child. Frightening things that I don't know what to do about." She looked into his eyes, "John have you ever seen demons?"

He took her by the hand and led her toward the sofa by the fireplace, "What kinda demons, babe?"

"All kinds! Have you ever seen any?"

"No! Not that I recall; when have you seen demons?"

"Usually when I'm alone, and these flashes of things that were done to me, start coming back."

"Do they try to harm you?" He didn't really understand what was going on inside her head. *Something is bad wrong here*, he thought.

"No," she answered quietly, "they just suddenly show up and sit and watch me. Lately they've started talking to me."

"What do they say?"

Her brow furrowed in thought as she tried to explain. "They say things like, we can help you if you'll let us, or, the master can pay them all back if you ask him." She turned to John, "I don't know what to do darling, they don't threaten me or anything like that, but it's scary when they show up."

He held her close as he tried to imagine what it was she was experiencing. *She only uses the coke I give her, so it ain't that or I'd be feeling the same shit.*

"Hon," she said, "I've been thinking about this, and have an idea."

"What's that?" he turned to look into her dark hazel eyes.

"Conduct a séance; just you and me. Maybe you can call the demons to appear, then ask them what they want and why it's only me they come to?"

John was feeling something for another person for the first time in his life, so he looked deeply into Brandisha's eyes. "Think it'll make you feel better?"

"Yes!" She answered. "These flashbacks are really messing my head up, and maybe a séance will give me some answers." Brandisha wanted someone to love so badly that she had attached herself to the professor like a barnacle to a ship. She had been through several séances with him and had complete confidence that he could call the spirits—good, bad, or otherwise, from her past. She needed answers. As she held him close she was looking directly into the eyes of a frightening demon sitting on the Japanese drum in the corner. She was neither frightened nor concerned. They don't scare me any more. It's kinda comforting having them near me. I feel protected.

"All right Babe," he answered, "I'll get a few people together and that's exactly what we'll do."

"No darling," she said, clinging tightly to him, "just you 'n me. I don't want anyone else knowing about this shit, till I find out what's happening to me." She pushed him back as she pulled her gaze away from the now smiling demon and looked intently at John, "Okay, darlin'?"

"Sure babe," he answered as he held her close to him, "if that's the way you want it, that's the way it'll be."

Professor John Poston had an exceptionally hectic schedule at this particular time. His Saturdays and Sundays were even occupied for awhile, so Brandisha agreed it would be best to wait a couple of weeks, until his schedule allowed a few days off, before conducting the séance. "I don't want a mind full of students and their silly chatter when we try to contact these demons."

Brandisha knew he was right, but she still had anxiety about the wait. She was aware that it took very little lately to bring on the flashbacks. The last time it had been the picture of a little girl holding her father's hand. *That's the kind of daddy I wanted.* She stood in front of the shop looking at the photo of the happy couple. She was suddenly filled with rage; no direction—just rage. She resisted an impulse to smash the window and grab the photo, so she could tear it up. The small bag of groceries was flung to the sidewalk and she stormed away.

The one before that came after hearing a country song with a line, "There was always love in daddy's hands." She looked at the middle-aged bartender of the small beer bar she'd stopped in for a draft and a burger. "Can you turn that shit off?" She glared at the surprised man who had served the normally pleasant young lady many times. "What the fuck does some silly little cunt like that know about **daddy's loving hands**?" She emphasized the last three words with such venom that he walked to the far end of the bar and ignored her.

"Drugs," he said quietly to his friend on the last stool eating the last of a hamburger, "even the nice ones are eating that shit these days."

"You know what really happens in daddy's loving hands?" Brandisha was standing now and almost screaming the words, "They hold you down as dear ol' daddy sticks his dick in you."

The other customers were watching in alarm, because of her sudden outburst. Three stood up and walked to the rear of the room near the pool players who had stopped to see what the commotion was all about. Two girls headed for the lady's room, while one older man moved swiftly toward the men's room.

Brandisha knocked the half-full beer mug over as she hastily grabbed her change, leaving most of it on the bar. Before leaving, she yelled at the bartender. **"You shove that radio up your ass, then you'll know how I felt as daddy's loving arms held me down while he shoved his dick in me."** She tore a fingernail off on the third try to open the glass door. She was about to leap through the glass when a customer arrived from outside and turned the knob. He jumped back as she yanked it open and pushed him aside, "Get the fuck outa my way, you filthy old bastard."

There had been several other incidents, all triggered by similar insignificant events—insignificant to all but Brandisha. To her they were beginning to resemble a movie playing in slow motion in her head. *The story of my wonderful youth*, she said to herself many times since it started. She often buried her head in a pillow and screamed a mournful, pleading wail to no one listening but a faded image in her tortured mind—a specter—a demon.

A sound of cornered-animal fear and hate and surrender and defiance—like the last sound the treed and shot and falling animal makes as the dogs get him—when he finally doesn't care any more about anything but himself and his dying.

Ken Kersey.

* As Brandisha wailed her misery into the down of a dead goose, another young girl was facing demons of another kind. They were all as black as her and possessed all the hate and power of Brandisha's demons. They were human demons—replica humans, and they had the pregnant young girl trapped on a lonely stretch of highway. These demons had conspired with her boyfriend to set her up. She was pregnant and would soon have his baby. The rising young star athlete didn't want the burden of supporting a baby as he climbed the ladder of success. He was driving ahead as she followed, but he suddenly stopped. She was forced to stop also and abruptly another car pulled beside her. It was full of demons. Replica humans, imposters, man-made demons; posing as men.

The quiet road was instantly echoing with gunfire. Bullets entered the young black girl's body barely missing the child inside her womb. Mortally wounded she struggled to call for help on her cell-phone as the human demons roared off into the night. After help answered and assured her an ambulance was on the way, she said to her temporary link with life, "It was my baby's father that did this to me."

Miraculously the baby survived. The young woman's struggle to keep her life ended quietly a few weeks later. Many are wondering if she was carrying the seed of one more monster demon? One more of Satan's Dark Angels to join the millions of others that are taking control of our beautiful blue planet?—Time will tell?

Rick Magers

To ignore an enemy is to openly invite death and destruction. Invite the enemy into your den and leave him there—forever.

An observation.

Brandisha suffered greatly during the weeks she waited for John to find time to conduct the séance. The flashbacks were coming more regularly. "It's like the gates of hell have been opened and a million of my nightmares are trying to get out." They weren't nightmares though; simply memories from a nightmare-like childhood. She could now remember specific events that her mind had sealed up to protect her. As one repressed thought came forth, another two or three would surface.

She struggled through her college classes, often missing them entirely as she lay at home in their apartment, crying alone. Often screaming, "**Why did all of you do these terrible things to me?**"

The demons were her only companions as she suffered through the lonely days. They sat in the corners or hung from light fixtures, never saying a word; simply smiling—watching.

"Lets have that séance this Saturday night, babe."

Brandisha almost leaped into his arms when she heard his words. "Oh yes darling, I've gotta get some answers or I'm gonna go crazy."

On Saturday she sat quietly at the Japanese table John had arranged in front of the fireplace. His instructions were, "Do not say a word until I have brought the demons forth." She had become accustomed to following his lead without thought or debate; he was her friend, lover, and mentor. She silently watched as he lit the many candles positioned around the room, and on the table she sat cross-legged in front of on the rug. When he sat across from her and reached his hands out to her, she took them.

"Oh mighty Beelzebub," he began in a hushed and haunting voice, "ruler of the darkness, prince of the damned, sovereign over mankind's demons, we call on you to present yourself to us that we might understand your wishes. You have sent your emissaries to this young woman. She wishes to speak to you, so that she might understand your desires mighty Satan; master of the underworld." He squeezed her hands then nodded and said quietly, "Speak to him."

"Please help me," was all she could say at first. When she saw the candles on the small table flickering, she glanced around the room. All of the other candles were flickering too, and suddenly she had a strong feeling that they were being watched. She turned her head in all directions to see if someone had entered their apartment. She saw nothing, but smelled a familiar odor, one she smelled each time a demon visited—sulphur.

'I am here.'

John was startled at the sound of the voice coming from the fireplace—filled with logs and blazing. He turned back to Brandisha and saw a look of pleasure and contentment sweep across her face. It had been a long time since he had seen her appear so peaceful.

"Yes I know," she responded, "I felt it when you arrived."

'Are you prepared to give yourself to me, body and soul?'

John was surprised at how her voice now sounded.

"Oh yes, my Lord, yes, yes."

John had only seen the look in her eyes immediately prior to them making love. He turned away when he heard the sound of the fire crackling as it suddenly roared. He silently watched through his drug filled vision as the voice from the fire materialized into a pulsating mass of black. The apparition's skin was charred and alive with worms. Within the festering skin glowed eyes so red they hurt his brain to watch, so he turned back to Brandisha. She was aglow with love.

'Then come naked to me.' The voice now had a commanding tone.

John watched as she stood and removed the only garment, a pullover dress she was wearing. His eyes were riveted to hers as she walked past him. When he turned he saw her lower herself onto a handsome young man lying naked on the rug. He watched as she began riding the man just as she rode him to ecstasy when they first met. He turned back to the table and spread a large amount of cocaine in front of him. When he finished with the razorblade, turning it into several long lines the width of a pencil, he turned back to the writhing couple on the floor. The man turned his eyes to him and the burning red glare caused him to turn away. He pulled the hundred-dollar-bill from his shirt pocket and snorted half of the first line. He placed the rolled bill into the other nostril then finished the line of cocaine. The numbing effects of the drug helped block out the sounds coming from the couple on the floor behind him.

Although she feeds me bread of bitterness
and sinks into my throat her tiger's tooth
stealing my breath of life. I must confess
I love this cultured hell that tests my youth!
Her vigor flows like tides into my blood,
giving me strength against her hate.
Her bitterness sweeps my being like a flood.

Claude Mckay.

An hour later, John lifted his head from the table. No Brandisha across from him. He listened as his drugged mind cleared. The sounds of passion at its peak became clear. He turned as Brandisha climbed from the top of the young man.

When the man was standing, john saw the huge penis hanging down between his legs. As John marveled at its size, the man suddenly changed into Satan. His horns were not as John had seen in pictures but were wide and pointed. He intuitively knew that these were weapons that could impale a man and throw him across a room or field. Satan's tail did not have a pointed barb at the end but resembled a cat's tail. It was in constant motion, swishing back and forth then coming up to flail the air behind him. His long arm raised slowly as he pointed at Brandisha.

'You are now one of my Dark Angels.'

That's how a lion would sound if it could talk, John thought.

'I will rid your mind of thoughts from you past as a child,' Satan continued. 'Follow the instructions I have placed in your mind, and you will enjoy a peace for eternity that few on this earth will.' He leaned forward to address John. 'If you are one of us then follow her, and help defeat the enemies that have harmed her.' His voice lowered to a growl-like snarl as he continued looking at John. 'I will make you a General in my army. Soon we will fight the followers of God' He let his head fall back as he howled like a crazed wolf. He looked again at them both then said, 'And my Dark Angels will defeat and devour them.' He suddenly burst into flames as he went into the fire again.

John and Brandisha watched as his red eyes glowed even brighter than before. As the fire raged around the charred head a smile crossed its face—then the head was gone. The fire returned to a bed of coals and the candles went out one by one. "I must go home to see mama and daddy Coolidge."

John turned from the fireplace and said, "I'll take you."

Rick Magers

Turn up the lights—I don't want to go home in the dark.

O. Henry. (His last words)

John pulled the car into the driveway, then waited while Brandisha went to the door of her adoptive parent's house. When she waved at him, he climbed from the seat and headed toward her.

"Mama, Daddy" she said, "this's my professor and friend John Poston. John this is Marlene and Daryll Coolidge." After shaking hands they all entered the small, plain, tarpaper and shingle covered house sitting on a twenty-acre farm far from town.

Daryll Coolidge was a Pentecostal preacher that struggled to keep enough money coming in from the small farm. He and his wife had been childless and were thrilled when the agency accepted them to be parents to the little girl abandoned by her mother. Marlene reinforced her husband's Christian beliefs with long hours of bible teachings for their new daughter. Neither had ever laid a hand on the little girl and tried to raise her with Christian understanding and love.

Daryll knew he had failed when he saw the front of his wife's face blown off from the bullet fired into the back of her head at the dinner table, later that first night. He had only a split second to accept this realization before his daughter turned the gun toward him and fired.

John had no idea what Brandisha was going to do, so all he could say was, "Holy shit." It was the final statement he would make on this earth. He was watching the old man die with his head lying in his supper, so he didn't even see her pointing the gun at him. He barely heard the noise as the bullet sped down the barrel toward the side of his head.

Brandisha retrieved the small kerosene can used to start the morning fire in the potbelly stove and sprinkled a little throughout the house then struck a match and lit all of the curtains in every room. Then she returned to the dining room and stood looking at the three corpses. "Your Christian God didn't help you, did he?" She looked from her mother to her father. "You were just waiting to molest me, weren't you? Well all the others did too, and we're also gonna teach them a lesson."

She squatted in the middle of the burning living room and waited.

'Very, very, good.' She turned to see Satan standing behind her. 'You will soon be rewarded for your obedience, my darling. You will be a queen among my Dark Angels when the war begins.'

THE END

Brandisha was born June 8th-------------GEMINI.
The Professor was born November 7th-----SCORPIO.

The only demons and devils in the innocent minds of children are those placed there by adults.

An observation.

Rick Magers

Satan's Baby

Brenda Lassiter could remember seeing glimpses of strange creatures when she was very young. She informed her mother but was always told, "Oh Breny that's just your imagination working overtime." She couldn't understand why no one else could see them. She also could not understand why her mother wouldn't believe her; she had never told her a lie.

After a few more encounters with the strange little demons, she stopped telling her mother about them. As the years passed she saw less of the creatures and she found herself actually missing them—they had become her only true friends. All of the kids at school made fun of her crossed eyes and protruding front teeth. Several of the boys would greet her with the same line whenever they approached her, "Nyaaaa what's up doc?" She hated the boys, and she hated the teacher for not making them stop. She also hated the other girls who laughed with the boys, but most of all she hated Bugs Bunny.

She told her mother what she wanted for her thirteenth birthday present. She always got what she wanted, so she began making preparations. Her father was always happy to help his daughter. He was painfully aware that she was an ugly little mud hen, but treated her as though she was a beautiful peacock. They worked together all day Saturday in preparation for her birthday wish. Just before dinner they stood back and looked at the wire and wood cage. "Pretty good job for a lawyer and a princess, if I do say so."

Brenda raised her hand with all five digits extended, "Damned straight pappy, gimme five."

The diminutive attorney didn't have to lower his hand to meet his daughter's; she was only an inch shorter him. He put his arm around her shoulder and together they headed for the house. "Bwing on the wabbits, we're weady." She laughed gleefully and snuggled her head against his shoulder as she thought about all the things she was going to do with (to) her new pet.

"Whatcha gonna name it," her father asked?

She looked up with an evil grin—he only saw the smiling face of his princess. "Bugs Bunny, of course.

8

DARK CHILD ANGEL

I am Misanthropos—and hate mankind.

                  Shakespeare.

Brenda Lassiter was born with a severely twisted, misarranged strand of DNA that set her on a path of hatred and destruction—A Bad Seed. For the many who cannot believe such a thing possible, there is evidence of it every day—many thousands of times over. We have been programmed to believe that humans are born pure and ignore all of the obvious signs. We do not want a finger pointing at our own possibly flawed selves. Our secret is safe as long as we ignore the strange and cruel acts of the little monsters that slithered from our loins. In our hearts we always know that there is something not quite right with 'little Joey,' or darling 'little Suzy.' Rather than dig for the problem when they are young and attempt to help them deal with their problems, it is easier to say to fat, dimwitted little Joey, "You're such a smart little boy—have another donut." To little Suzy, with Dumbo ears protruding from a long, thin head advertising a bulbous nose holding up eyes too close together, we find it easier to say, "You're such a beautiful child—we're going to get you a pony." Easy way out for the parent, but Suzy and Joey will carry those lies on their shoulders for a lifetime…ignored and the child always pays.

      Tough love is true love.

        Rick Magers

Truth hurts—only a moment—replaced with understanding by loving parents. Lies last a lifetime.

An observation.

Several people saw Brenda hitting her dolls in the face repeatedly when she was less that a year old—all ignored it. By two she was plucking the eyes from her dolls; giggling as she attempted to stuff them into their mouth—ignored. At three the cross-eyed little girl with protruding teeth and her mother's homely features, would stand and stomp her favorite doll for a full five minutes. If anyone thought it strange—they ignored it.

The bright, ingenious, seven-year-old built a trap from scraps of wire in her father's workshop and caught the family cat, which would not go near her—cats know. Before the Saturday sun was barely over the horizon Brenda was out checking the trap that only she knew about. BINGO! Hhhiisssssstttttt. The cat intuitively thought it was in trouble—it was. It lunged repeatedly at the wire as it hissed at the little girl.

With the cat and trap in the potato sack she brought with her from the garage, she headed toward the creek a short distance away. She emptied the terrified cat and trap onto the bank, and then tied the short rope she'd carried around her neck to one end of the wire trap. Each time she got her hand near the wire, the cat tried to bury a claw into it. "Too slow Bozo, way too slow to catch me." She grinned malevolently at the cat as she reached for the stick she'd picked up along the way. "Not too early for a swim is it. Heh, heh, heh." She chuckled wickedly as she shoved the trap toward the water. She watched as the frantic cat tried to eat it's way through the wire while the trap sunk. "Shoulda been nice to me you bad puddy tat." She mimicked one of her favorite cartoon characters as she watched the gagging, gasping cat. "Hold your bweath you bad puddy tat, here we go again." She shoved the trap into the water again. The cat still snarled and chewed at the wire as the trap sunk.

"Hey puddy tat," she said as she dragged the trap from the water for a third time, "you wanna sit on my lap now? Oh, too tired," she jabbed the stick through the wire and into the exhausted cat's side. "All I wanted to do was pour my daddy's battery acid into your eyes to see if I could fix those silly blue things. They're too straight."

"Look out Captain Cat," she said just before the sixth return to the water, "there's an enemy ship and you gotta get your sub outa here; dive, dive." She shoved the hapless family pet into the muddy river again then watched the sunrise a full ten minutes before pulling the trap back onto the bank. "Too slow Captain, the enemy gotcha. C'mon let ol' Doc Breny take a look atcha." She untied the wire holding the end shut and dumped the dead cat out. After beating it hard a dozen times with the stick she said, "Nope, you're gone. The enemy was just too smart for ya. Well Captain at least you get a burial at sea. Ha, ha, ha, ha, ha." She laughed quietly and lay back on the grass, and looked at the blue sky a moment before sitting back up. "Lovely day for a funeral," she shoved the carcass into the water, "unless it yours. Ha, ha, ha." She giggled as she watched the cat float away and begin bobbing in the moving water.

Brenda stood and was about to throw the trap into the river but stopped and looked at it. *That was fun; bet I could catch one anytime I want to.* She wrapped the rope around it and stuffed it back into the sack. She headed back home with it over her shoulder thinking, *sure I can, and there are plenty of hungry cats all over this neighborhood.*

Several people noticed the disappearance of not only their own cats but also the strays that normally came around for something to eat. None of them would ever think that the homely little girl with the bucked teeth and horribly crossed eyes could be behind the crimes—"She's so sweet."

Her mother did—she knew. She knew Brenda hated their cat, plus she had always had a strange feeling that there was something wrong with her little girl. Permissa had learned early in her marriage not to admonish her daughter. Her husband Dillworth decided early to shower the ugly little girl with love and gifts. He went into a rage at any attempt to discipline his daughter. Permissa had learned with bruises from her husband to be very careful when probing for information from Brenda.

"Have you seen Bozo, darling?"

Brenda knew her mother didn't like her, so she didn't try to hide her disdain. She emphasized her crossed eyes as she answered her mother, "Sure mummy, I saw all twelve of him just a few days ago."

Permissa also had a caustic side to her personality, and it came through when she answered, "Were they all still alive?"

"Oh I knew it, I knew it," Brenda cried as she flung herself onto her bed sobbing, "you think I had something to do with him leaving."

Permissa could always tell when Brenda was acting. The girl had never cried in her entire life—even as an infant. She turned and left her daughter's bedroom. Before she had taken three steps along the hall she heard the TV come on in her daughter's room.

Rick Magers

*Just a few miles from where Brenda sat watching cartoons on her big screen television, a private petting zoo funded by the donations of concerned citizens, was having a night visit.

Several teenagers and a dozen demons that had been with the two leaders for a long time, were entering unseen. "Everybody got their ball bat?" The five-foot-tall leader of the gang that called themselves AVENGING DARK ANGELS spoke in hushed tones to his followers. "Good," he answered, "then let's get started."

The pimple faced leader turned his cloudy gray eyes to his second in command and said quietly, "Take your guys 'n start over there. We'll meet right here in twenty minutes, so check your watch." The demons that had been with the two boys since they were toddlers danced with glee as the bloody carnage began. The other boys never knew who their General and the Colonel were talking to, when they each rambled on to unseen ghosts, but all were too frightened of the two leaders to ask. To them it was simply, some kinda spooky stuff Jimmy and Danny have dreamed up to scare us.

To Jimmy and Danny the demons were as real as the bloody bats they now held. "You're the only person I've ever met that can see them too." That was the bond that glued the two diminutive, physically unattractive, dumb boys together. That was also the glue that kept them together to the grave—which wasn't far away.

The demons danced among the many dead sheep, goats, and other animals as the boys departed from the scene of their heinous crime.

Man and the animals are merely a passage and channel for food—a tomb for other animals—a haven for the dead—giving life by the death of others—coffers full of corruption.

Leonardo da Vinci.

Brenda's eleventh birthday party was a great success. Of the many children gathered on the huge lawn, not one liked the skinny, overbearing, redheaded girl, but each knew her parties were the best of any they would ever go to. "Her goofy looking dad's a famous lawyer, and always has gifts 'n all kindsa neat stuff for everybody."

She thanked each for the gift they brought, but when her mother brought out the box with the birthday rabbit in it she was absolutely ecstatic. "She's really weird," one of the young guests said quietly to her friend, "all of the fabulous gifts she got and which one does she go nuts over? A stupid rabbit."

They couldn't possibly have dreamed what pleasure their host was planning to get from the unfortunate animal.

The melancholy young girl was already scheming and planning the future of her new pet, when she returned to school from Christmas break. Several boys led by her main tormentor, approached Brenda. The tall, dark haired, handsome boy that she had fallen madly in love with when he arrived the previous year from out of state sauntered toward her. The homely, cross-eyed girl's obvious affections for him made him the brunt of jokes from his first day at school. He put a stop to it in a very easy way—he began ridiculing her. His coldhearted treatment of Brenda made him a champion with his buddies—he was now their leader. "Hear you got a new little brother for your birthday, Fireplug." He knew she hated her red hair and detested the nickname he had given her. He had a double dig going this day as he leaned toward her, "What was his first words?" He leaned forward and crossed his eyes then glanced back to be sure his gang saw the gesture, "Nyaaa what's up, sis?" He had planned the entire thing, so when he pulled the carrot from his pocket and began chomping on it dramatically, his buddies howled with laughter.

A group of demons danced around Brenda as she walked away—anger showing on her scowling face. 'Let's put him in a big cat cage,' one of the demons said as it flapped its wings and flew backwards in front of her. 'Let's burn him at the stake,' another screamed.

"I intend to take care of him soon," she said aloud as she passed by her schoolmates. They heard her talking to unseen people before, so they silently watched. They were all afraid of Brenda. The handsome young boy with the carrot still in his mouth should have been. It might have saved his life.

Brenda spent a great deal of time with her new pet, feeding it treats of carrots, lettuce and fruits along with the rabbit food her father provided. It grew rapidly from a small bunny to a huge, plump white rabbit. "Breny sure takes good care of that rabbit," her father mentioned one morning after watching his daughter carrying fresh carrots to it.

His wife only nodded. She had noticed how the rabbit backed into a corner whenever her daughter approached. Her husband would never see the cruel side to Brenda, but Permissa had seen it from the very first. She now maintained a constant vigil for signs.

Brenda looked forward to the times her parents were away from the house. She always checked to see what the maid was doing before going to her rabbit cage. She had a stick hidden nearby that she used to torment the animal. "Hey fatso," she said as she poked it into the side of the rabbit that she named Bugs Bunny. "Wanna play jump 'n bump?" She giggled with sadistic delight as the animal jumped each time she jabbed him. It bumped its head so many times against the wooden top that a sore began to develop. "Oh, poor Bugsy got a sore head?" She crooned as she manipulated the stick to rub the wound.

Brenda learned that rabbits bite when it was just a bunny, so she took great care to stay away from the large teeth. By summer the rabbit was huge and Brenda was ready. She had located a piece of heavy vinyl material in her father's workshop that he used to recover the foam on his weight lifting bench. She also found his large needles and thread, so within a few days she had fashioned a hood with a drawstring and waited. During the sewing, and the tormenting of the rabbit, her demons were never far away. As she grew older there was never a day that they didn't visit her at least once. The young girl's dark sinister urges were growing with her.

"Yes," she said loudly as her mother drove away.

Permissa approached her daughter earlier that morning. "Breny, the maid's not coming today. She's going to a doctor and I simply must be at a meeting of my Orchid Society, so you'll have to hold down the fort all alone for the day." She grinned at her daughter, "I hope you don't mind."

Brenda didn't mind at all. She had been preparing for just such a fortunate event. It would be a very unfortunate event for Bugs.

"Hi Bugsy, you big tub o' shit," she said as she held the rabbit against the wire with the stick until she could grab it behind the head. "I know this heat's killing you so I'm gonna help you." She pulled the immobile animal to her, then slipped the hood over its head and tightened the drawstring enough so it couldn't get it off. She held the rabbit up by its neck fur and with two swift blows from the stick she broke both of its back legs. "Ain't goin' no place now you naughty wabbit."

Demons danced and howled encouragement as Brenda slipped the rope noose down over the animal's head and front paws. She soon had it hanging from the rear wall of the workshop with the noose tightly around its upper body; suspended from a nail. The rear feet hung limply down as the terrified creature's body jerked.

"You're gonna feel so much cooler," Brenda said as she held up the sharp knife, "when I get that heavy fur coat off. The young girl's face was a mask of evil as she made the first cut just below the rabbit's neck; taking great care not to make any deep cuts into it's body. Her demons howled. 'Yes! Yes! Yes!' When she had the fur severed from the neck all around, she slid the blade beneath it and cut down the back as she pulled the skin out then worked it beneath the rope. When Brenda reached the tail she tossed the knife on the ground and grabbed the fur with both hands and pulled down until it was all beneath the rope. The fur rolled down over itself, exposing raw flesh. With the entire fur hanging from the broken rear legs she reached up and removed the hood. "There now Bugs ain't that cooler? Ha, ha, ha, hee, hee, heeeeeeee." She squealed so loud that she drowned out the howls of the demons. "Hey," she said as she poked the rabbit with the stick, "you oughta feel much cooler and boy-oh-boy are you ever slim now, Bugsy."

She stood back and watched the mutilated animal's eyes as they bulged from their sockets; it's body twitching and jerking as she stood smiling in front of it. "Hey, I see what the problem is," she said grinning, "that's too big a load you're carrying." She picked up the knife and severed the rear feet, then yanked the fur the rest of the way off. After removing the rope it was hanging from she threw the animal to the ground, "You can go ahead and go pway now you wascally wabbit."

Brenda kicked the rabbit a few times as she giggled and looked at the demons, jumping all around her and the rabbit. "I guess I'll hafta jump start ya," she said as she jumped on the animal's back. She used her stick to turn its head so she could look into its straight blue eyes. The terror she saw in the twitching animal's eyes made her feel warm and good inside. "Well Bugs, if you don't wanna run and play let's go for a swim." She picked it up by its bloody neck and walked the short distance to the river. "Have a nice day Bugs," she yelled as she threw it in the river and watched it try to paddle with its front paws until it sank from sight. She returned for the fur and threw it in also, then used the hose to wash the blood from the wall of her father's workshop.

After checking the area good to be certain nothing remained to give her away, she picked up the knife and headed toward the house.

When her father came home from his office, she ran to meet his car. Through eyes made red by pouring salt water in them, she said, "Oh daddy, my lovely rabbit got out of its cage and I can't find it anywhere."

He went with her immediately to the rear of the house to look at the cage. "Looks like the latch wasn't secured properly."

Brenda started crying, "Oh daddy, I feel so bad. It musta been me that didn't close it right."

"I don't see how that could be, darling," he said as he looked around. "you come out here every day and you've never done it wrong yet." He put his arm around his daughter's shoulder as they walked slowly to the back entrance of the house, "Has your mother taken anything out to the rabbit's cage lately?"

I hate and I love. Why I do so, perhaps you ask. I know not, but I feel it and I am in torment.

Gaius Valerius Catullus.

Rick Magers

*As Brenda was working her magic on her weak father, a group of men were gathering in a barn in the Carolinas. Several had brought their sons to watch what they called, 'A real man's sport.' They all moved to the large enclosure with five-foot-high wooden sides. The very young boys had to find crates to stand on so they could see into the arena. All bets had been made and they waited impatiently for the contestants to enter.

Muzzles were removed and a panel on each side was lifted. The two snarling pit bull dogs rushed at each other in a fury brought on by starvation and metered abuse. Men screamed in delight, as children yelled with pleasure, and many demons howled from the rafters. Satan stood silently in the corner and watched. When He finally spoke, his words came as a whisper on a chilling wind rushing across the crowd of real men—no one noticed. They were all to busy watching one dog tear the throat from the other.

'My kind of people,' Satan said then disappeared in a swirl of dust. The demons remained and screeched from their perches overhead, especially when one ten-year-old boy's face was covered with blood from the unfortunate dog being shook by the victor in the 'sport.' The child proudly showed his father his new badge of manhood.

. . .

"Yes," Brenda answered her father, "she carried some lettuce or something out yesterday I think." She hadn't planned things this way, but it was working out perfectly. She hated her mother, because she knew she was aware of many of the sinister and devious aspects of her daughter's personality. *She'll be in shit up to her straight blue eyes now*, Brenda thought as she followed her father into the house.

An hour later, Brenda listened at her slightly opened bedroom door as her father stood waiting for her mother. "Where in the goddamned hell have you been all day?" The young girl smiled as she heard her mother stammering to answer.

"What in the world are you talking about, Dillworth?" She knew only too well what the outcome of her diminutive husband's temper could be if allowed to get out of control. She had pins in her shoulder from a beating with a ball bat. "I've been meeting with my orchid society on the last Friday of the month for years."

Brenda could hear her father huffing and puffing. *You're up shit creek now mummy dearest, and you don't have a paddle.* She pressed her ear closer to the cracked door.

"Well where was that damn Indian?"

"She's not an Indian Dillworth, she's from Guatemala and she asked for the day off a week ago."

The sound of his palm hitting the side of her mother's face made Brenda smile wickedly. *Knock her fuckin' eye out daddy*, she thought as she held her breath, not wanting to miss any of it.

"Don't talk back to me you worthless bitch." The crack made Brenda grin widely. *That was a good punch*, she thought, and then heard the sound of her mother falling into something.

Permissa lay in the corner on top of the broken antique table and the shards of pottery. "Oh," she moaned as she rubbed her jaw. Her daughter grinned as she looked down at the demon standing below her. "What in the world have I done?" she said through tears and sobs.

"You let my daughter's pet rabbit out of its cage, you dumb cunt." He never referred to Brenda as our daughter—always my daughter.

"But I haven't been," she didn't finish the sentence, so Brenda knew her father was beating or kicking her mother by the sobs and moans. "Don't back-talk me or I swear I'll send you to the hospital again."

'Yes!' The demon wrapped around Brenda's leg screamed, 'Kick her fucking brains out.'

Kick her again daddy. Send her back to the hospital. She looked down at the little demon and said in a hushed voice, "It'd be nice around here with her in the hospital again for awhile."

She eased her door closed and lay on the bed, and then looked at the grinning demon sitting on her dresser. *Couldn't have worked out better if I had planned it this way.*

Celebrity-representing attorney, Mr. Dillworth Jacobson Lassiter buried his tiny size six Gucci zipper boot into his wife's groin then turned and stalked away, leaving her crying in the corner of the foyer.

*Foolish men who accuse
a woman mindlessly—
You cannot even see—
You cause what you abuse*

Juana Ines de la Cruz.

Rick Magers

*A few short blocks away, in a home similar to the Lassiter home, a five-foot-tall wife was being stabbed to death by a six-foot-tall husband while in a PCP altered state of mind. After a short stay in a drug re-habilitation hospital he was declared cured. He began searching for another wife. (And a new supplier.) His demons howled joyously as he walked free.

*On the other side of town, a dark-haired, black-eyed, beautiful Mexican woman was being hacked to death with a machete by her live-in-lover—after only a few months together. Her three young children huddled in the corner of their apartment and watched in terror—they would soon be next. His demons screamed and laughed as he took the first swing with the machete at the two-year-old child. 'Yes, yes,' the demons yelled, 'cut 'em to pieces'—he did. His state appointed attorney showed the jury his client's lifetime dependency on hard drugs. He pleaded for treatment rather than punishment. The following year with all appeals exhausted his client felt a sharp pain as a needle was inserted into his vein. It had been a long time since he had felt a drug-rush. He knew this would be his last as he looked at the faces of the people on the other side of the glass. The room began getting darker and he felt himself falling. His was an easy death.

Every few minutes, similar acts are being committed all around the world. Always in attendance are demons. They carry with them the odor of death and destruction.
    Few notice—Fewer care.

Oh true apothecary! Thy drugs are quick.

Shakespeare.

Brenda's mother didn't need hospital care, so the little girl was disappointed. She had hoped for a little time alone with her father. At the breakfast table she sat beside her father, watching her mother limp around the kitchen. Her crossed eyes gleamed as she asked, "Are you gonna buy me another rabbit, daddy?"

"Yes darling," he smiled down at his ugly little girl, "my little princess gets whatever she wants." He looked at his bruised wife and said, "And you are not to go near that cage, Permissa." He waited for an answer as he kept his eyes on her. He didn't see the grin spreading across his daughter's face. "Do you hear me?"

"Yessir," his wife responded through loose teeth, emitting a slight whistle where one was now missing.

Brenda knew what was causing the odd sound coming from her mother's mouth and loved it. She felt great as she ate her breakfast. The demons felt great as they surveyed the scene of their destruction.

'You will soon have another Dark Angel, Mighty Satan.' They howled—unheard by human ears, for the great battle that was coming. Brenda heard them and smiled.

A few days later, Brenda was enjoying the warmth of the sun as she leaned on a heavy walking stick she had found laying beside the overgrown trail that led to the river. She moved ahead to her favorite spot to sit and watch the river flow by. *Sometimes I wish I could just get in a boat and let you take me wherever you're going.* Thoughts had always ran through her confused and warped mind, with nothing determining their content. *Wonder where ol' Fatso Catso is these days? I gotta get daddy something really nice for his birthday. I wish mommy woulda died from the beating he gave her. I'm gonna do something real nice for grandma Lassiter when I see her; she's so sweet. I think I'll burn this new rabbit as a sacrifice.* Her thoughts came out much the same as an ancient ticker tape in a stockbroker's office—click-click-click.

Brenda's thoughts were coming through at a rapid rate when she heard a noise to her right. Her breath stopped and her heart skipped a couple of beats when she saw who was walking along the narrow trail on the riverbank. Her initial feelings for the dark haired, handsome boy she had fallen in love with had changed dramatically. Since he had mocked and shamed her in front of everyone, just to impress his friends, she thought only of ways to pay him back. As she watched him walking slowly along she thought, *maybe today's the day I pay you back, you rotten bastard.*

From her perch thirty feet up the slight hill, she could watch him unobserved. She knew each and every nook and cranny in this entire area. It was her favorite place in the entire world. A place where she could be alone and think her thoughts without being disturbed. Her demons always came with her, but never interrupted her thoughts or bothered her with senseless chatter like people did—even her father.

When the handsome boy stopped just below her and sat down, she watched as he let his head fall down between his knees. After a full ten minutes without moving his head she was curious. Brenda stood and used her walking stick to approach him. "Hi Brett, I didn't see you sitting here."

The boy had thought he was alone, so was momentarily startled by the sound of her voice. He turned to her, "Oh hi, Brenda." His tone was very gloomy, and he turned back to watching the river with his head down.

Brenda was already a master at reading people's moods, so she asked, "You seem down in the dumps, what's the matter?"

After a long pause he finally said quietly, "All my buddy's are going over to Lake Brandy and they said wasn't any need for me to come along, 'cause I can't swim."

The ticker tape was going at full speed as Brenda looked quickly around. She knew there was only one place someone could see the two of them so she looked hard in that direction—no one. "Gee," she said sounding very concerned; "I can help you there."

Before the boy could respond he felt the heavy walking stick hit the side of his head. A split moment later her foot was on his back pushing him into the swift running water. She was able to give him one more good, hard blow before he disappeared beneath the water. Brenda looked around to be sure there were no people watching—no one.

"Hey asshole," she said quietly, "if you see my cat or that stupid rabbit, tell 'em I said hello."

When she returned to the house a while later the maid said in broken English, "Meece Brenna, hew louk more happy chew deed in theece morning." Her smile was always sincere and the young girl liked the dumpy, middle-aged little woman.

"You're right Alenna, I've had a great day already, and it's not even half over." She was whistling as she continued toward her bedroom. The demons that had jumped with enthusiasm at the river accompanied her now, and were howling—screeching—laughing.

Time is a sort of river of passing events, and strong is its current—no sooner is a thing brought to sight than it is swept by and another takes it's place—this too will be swept away.

Marcus Aurelius Antoninus.

*Thousands of miles away, children were having their legs busted by their parents wielding long, hard sticks. They screamed in agony into the rags wrapped around their mouths so their noise wouldn't disturb their neighbors, as their broken legs were tied in unusual angles behind their bodies. They were then thrown into a corner of the hovel they knew as home. During the next few weeks they were fed very little. "If she lives we will have a strong beggar," the father often commented casually, "if she dies we have plenty more." Demons danced in every hovel in all of these countries. If the woman was unable to produce more it was not a big problem. A child could be bought for less than a meal at an American Burger Basket.

. . .

At the end of summer, Brenda eavesdropped on a conversation between her father and her mother, and it shocked her. She was very upset to see them sitting on the couch with their arms around each other, and talking quietly. Brenda silently slipped along the wall nearest the couch, where she wouldn't be discovered and listened intently.

"It's been the pressure of this Handlemeir deal, darling." Dillworth spoke in a subdued tone, but loud enough for Brenda to hear, "And now that it's settled I'm gonna show you how sorry I am for the way I've been treating you. How does a month in Europe sound to get our love back on track?"

"Oh yes sweetheart," she heard her mother say, and it made her stomach do flips. She strained to hear as her mother continued, "What about Brenda? She'll be going back to school soon."

"She's a big girl now," she heard her father reply, "and we'll have the agency position a temporary butler and maid to live here every day while we're gone." Brenda heard her mother sigh loudly and she couldn't resist the urge to sneak a careful peek around the corner. When she saw her father and mother kissing passionately, she flattened herself against the wall again and had to fight to control her breathing. She thought she was going to pass out until she was finally getting enough air. *Goddamn traitor, he's loved her all the time, and I thought he was all mine.* She silently slipped back into her room.

As Brenda's parents were petting and re-confirming their love for each other, Brenda was laying on her lavishly decorated Cleopatra Canopy Bed; watching her demons hanging from the framework overhead.

'He deserted you—He never really loved you—He only acted like he loved you because you're so ugly—He's like all the others.' She turned her attention from one to the other as they spoke. 'Let's kill both the bastards. Yes, they all began to chant. Let's kill them—let's kill them—let's kill them.'

As Brenda's eyes began getting heavy with sleep she was thinking about her father's disloyalty to her. *Sure! Why not kill them both; they sure as hell don't give a shit about me.*

Rick Magers

*In a small town up north a teenage boy was getting madder by the minute. His robust, overbearing, perfection-demanding mother had been following him from tree to tree for an hour, as he manipulated the roaring chainsaw through the branches of her miniature fruit trees.

"Jesus H. Christ. Denny I told you on that last one, that you're cutting the branches too close to the main trunk."

The boy slowed the speed of the engine, and screamed. "What are you hollering about now?"

"Stop cutting the goddamn limbs so close to the trunk."

He didn't answer her for fear of what he might say. He simply squeezed the throttle and continued cutting.

"Stop, stop, stop," she screamed at the top of her ample lungs. When he slowed it again she screamed louder. "**Look! You moron.**" She then grabbed a limb, "right here's where you cut 'em." When the boy looked where his mother pointed, he could easily see that he was cutting them almost exactly where she was indicating on the uncut limb. He shook his head and kept cutting.

When she stepped forward and grabbed his arm he slowed the engine again. "You stupid shit, you're as dumb as that ignorant father of yours." Denny loved his father and knew he wasn't dumb at all. *He was smart enough to leave your fat ass, you big sow.* He thought. He revved the engine and prepared to cut another limb, so he could finish and get going to the ballgame. Her hand on his arm caused him to stop again. "Gimme that fuckin' saw you ignorant asshole."

Instantly his mother's red face blended in with the rest of his world, which had suddenly turned blood red. "I'll give you the saw you fat pile of shit," he screamed and depressed the throttle, then thrust the roaring saw into his mother's face. She screamed and threw her hands up then turned and ran. Denny threw the saw on the ground and also ran—In the opposite direction. Several demons that had been with him since his father left Denny and his mother alone ran with him. No one else had ever seen them, but they had been with the boy for a long time. 'We'll soon have another DARK ANGEL' one said, and the others all began hooting—dancing—screeching. 'Yes, yes, yes, yes.'

His mother survived, but what was once a human face, even though it was swollen to the size of a small pumpkin from the daily pizzas, jellyrolls and dozens of other snacks, now resembled something out of a cheap horror movie. Her guttural mutterings now came from a mass of scar tissue with a hole in it. She continued bitching at everyone about everything.

Denny continued to run and would for several years—He had plenty of company. The Demons knew they had a good one and weren't about to let him get away.

My mother was accursed the night she bore me, and I am feint with envy of all the dead.

Euripides.

The following day Brenda waited until her father left for work and her mother was on the phone for one of her hour-long calls. She slipped into their bedroom and got the revolver that she knew her father kept in the bottom drawer of his nightstand. He let her shoot it a few times when they went target practicing together, so she was familiar with it's operation. Back in her room she opened the chamber to be certain it contained an unfired bullet in each hole. Satisfied, she closed it and put it in the special hiding place behind her dresser.

She went to her new rabbit and reached in to grab it by the loose fur behind its neck. She hadn't had time to spend with it, so the pet didn't fear her. It gave her no trouble as she carried it to the rear of the tool shed, where she picked up her heavy walking stick before laying the hapless animal on the ground. With her foot heavily holding the small rabbit to the ground she began beating it with the stick. When it finally quit struggling she removed her foot so she could use both hands on the stick. When she tired a few minutes later, there was little left that could be called a rabbit. After tossing the carcass in the river she washed her stick and laid it against the shed. Brenda replaced the lock, but neglected to place the latch over the piece that the lock went into. *If anyone looks, it'll look like I just didn't close it right and it got out.*

She lay awake that night thinking out every detail of her plan. At two o'clock in the morning, she was satisfied that her parents were sound asleep. *Coulda went in at ten, because they both sleep like dead people.* She grinned as she thought about her choice of words. *They'll really be sleeping like dead people in a minute.*

Rick Magers

Brenda walked silently to her father's side of the bed and put one bullet into his head. When her mother started to rise, still sleep-drugged, Brenda first put one bullet in her head then another in her father's bloody head. She calmly walked around to her mother who was laying half on and half off the bed. She placed the barrel a few inches from her forehead and shot her again. Returning to her father she shot him two more times in the head then unlatched the window and raised it.

Back in her room she retrieved the pair of her father's shoes that she had taken from his room earlier. Brenda left the house and walked in the dark to the river to throw the pistol, after wiping her prints from it, as far out as she could. She then carried the shoes to a spot near a stand of trees next to the road in front of their estate. She slipped her feet into them and walked straight to her parent's bedroom window.

Using the small pocketknife her father had given her, Brenda slit the screen enough to allow entry. She walked the same route she had awhile earlier then went back out the window. She walked to the same stand of trees then stepped into the road and removed the shoes. She used a dead branch from a tree that she had picked up while at the river, and brushed away all signs of her bare feet, then returned to the river by another route. She threw each shoe and the branch as far as she could out into the river, then returned to her room. *Those shoes'll be a mile from here by noon.*

Brenda slept soundly until about ten that morning. It was Saturday, so she knew no one would be expecting her father at his office. She stood in their room and surveyed the scene with cold emotionless eyes. *Wiped my fingerprints from the window sill,* she thought, *any good hit man would wear gloves, so the police won't be surprised that there isn't a print.* She calmly looked everything over while standing there. She watched as one Demon lapped blood from her mother's neck while another sat on the headboard grinning at her. She grinned back, "Looks like I did a pretty good job, huh?" She turned and walked to the kitchen for a glass of milk and some fresh donuts her mother made.

After calling the police, Brenda prepared herself for the role she would play for them when they arrived.

Through sobs she told the detective, "I didn't expect them to get up early on Saturday, but I finally decided to knock on their door to tell them what time it was." She looked up at him with red eyes that had been drenched with salt water before they arrived, "We were all gonna go to town shopping this morning." He could barely understand her through the sobs. "I knocked a little harder then a lot harder, 'cause I was getting worried. They both sleep real sound, but were never hard to wake up. I finally tried the doorknob and opened their door, and, and, and. . .

Rick Magers

She couldn't continue, so the detective said soothingly, "That's all right kid, I'll get someone to help you." He placed his arm over her shoulder and escorted her to the living room, where a female officer waited.

A cursory investigation revealed facts that most of the detectives already knew. Dillworth Jacobson Lassiter was deeply involved with organized crime. They quickly closed the case, labeling it a hit by rival underworld leaders. His books were done with such expertise that the authorities could not touch his fortune, so Brenda Elaine Lassiter not only inherited the family fortune, but also the assets from two multi-million-dollar life insurance policies.

She lived alone for many years in the same house near the river where her parents died. Brenda spent a great deal of time raising rabbits. No one ever saw demons, but Brenda had a lot of company for the rest of her long enjoyable life.

THE END

Brenda was born Dec. 23rd-----CAPRICORN.

Author's note: All events proceeded by the *asterisk were taken from local and world news. None of the characters are imaginary. The author based each character on a person he met, or read about in world newspapers.

. . .

How long must we hide in our houses from these human demons? No more evening walks on our quiet streets—No more picnics near lovely isolated streams—No rest along the highway as we travel—Fear as we watch our children go off to school—Fear as we search for our car in daylight—Fear as a policeman approaches our car at night—Fear, fear, fear. We now know that demons are everywhere. In a uniform—In a dress—In a suit—On the ball field—In the classroom—Behind the stethoscope—Above the dentists drill—Beneath a parent's smile—On the pulpit—everywhere! Can we, with God's help; do battle with these Dark Angels of Satan? Have we waited too long?

Rick Magers

BEGINNING OF THE END

~ As it might very well happen ~

World War III ended in 2022, as did the lives of most of the people on the once Beautiful Blue Planet. By the year 2033 Planet Earth was a spinning cauldron of hopelessness and despair. Birth deformities from the stockpiles of nuclear waste were much more common than the birth of a normal child. It was estimated that one in every three humans was afflicted with some form of cancer due to the nuclear waste; found in every major country on earth, and resembled high mountains: with one exception—nothing grew on or near them.

The warlords were warned many times by their informants, "The next war will not be like the others. All nations now have terrible weapons and will not hesitate to use them."

The Generals did not listen. Killing was what they lived for—dreamed of.

Killing has always been:

THE SPORT OF GENERALS

Death rained down in a manner far worse than had been expected, by the people who simply went about their tasks on a day-by-day basis. They had been lied to for years. "Only smart bombs will be used on the big cities. This time they'll only kill the people and not destroy all that has been built. When we are in control we're going to use nuclear energy to save mankind." Each country had its own lie.

When the world's people accepted the fact that war was inevitable, the great exodus to the rural areas, far away from the center of the cities, was like no other in the history of mankind. The same was true in the suburbs. Farming areas were confronted with thousands of city people moving among them to escape the war, that all thought would come and go as all the others had. "And then we'll return and begin our lives again."

The great cities of Earth were quickly emptied of all life except a few entrepreneurs who dreamed of incredible profit, and vast wealth—nothing else mattered.

Those ever present men-of-vision purchased land away from the cities and spent fortunes building survival complexes. Their crews threw together flimsy apartment buildings with hundreds of tiny apartments. Heavy fences surrounded them; each with gun-turrets located in strategic areas. They waited for war and dreamed of even greater wealth.

Many refugees begged farmers to rent them space on which to build temporary shelters. Soon, farmers were converting their barns and buildings into apartments, and began constructing shacks on every square inch of farmland. As more people arrived, the cost of anyplace to live went up like skyrockets. The same thousand dollars, that only day's earlier in New York City would purchase dinner for two plus a two hour, VIRTUAL VACATION HOOK-UP, now secured an abandoned automobile for one week. A family of four was thrilled—a place to get out of the weather and hope that the war would soon come and go, so they could get back to their homes.

Soon, for every person living in anything that would put a roof over their head, there were thousands of people building lean-to shelters anywhere they could muscle their way into—Muscle often being the only way.

Entire families were slaughtered and thrown into rivers and canyons so the killers could occupy their living quarters. A decades old derelict delivery van, a mud and grass hovel with a leaky sod roof, a constantly sinking boat requiring daily pumping—anything livable.

Farmer's wives spent hours, sewing small tents from any material they could find, while the farmer cut tent poles and whittled tent stakes. At fifteen thousand dollars each, the desperate people buying them didn't care that they were not waterproof; it was a place to live until the war came and went—as all others had. "Then we're going home."

When all, even the thinnest blankets and sheets, had been sold as tents; farmer and family shivered beneath mattresses rather than upon them—but they were getting rich. "When this's over we'll live like kings."

Similar scenes were in every country. Herds of humans—millions searching for any place to weather the coming war; while others searched desperately for wealth, which until now had eluded them.

Soon, black market entrepreneurs began arriving with waterproof canvas, stolen from the few functioning factories remaining throughout the world. A piece of canvas large enough for a family to construct a small tent cost the buyer a fortune. The only gasoline available was in the hands of the black marketers. Often, a new luxury car, which the owner and family lived in, was traded for enough canvas to build a tent large enough to survive in until the war passed—"And then we're going home."

Capitalism had crept into even the smallest countries. It was at its finest hour—its philosophy of supply and demand had crept into every crack and crevice of every country on earth by the time the planet was ready to self-destruct.

In Russia a child's shoes would get the bartering entrepreneur three bottles of vodka. "He vill zoon be dead anyvay." The live child itself, especially a girl, with or without shoes, would bring as much as two cases of vodka.

In China they realized their population was still twenty times what the land could support. They implemented a program that paid a week's lodging with food in a state run apartment, for every pair of matching hands brought to the Center for Population Control. The government's position was that if the previous owner of the hands didn't bleed to death, they would soon die without the use of them. Often those who exchanged hands for food and lodging awoke as their own hands were being severed.

India thought the Chinese were onto something, and began the same program. Sacred cows were eaten. Hunger like they had never dreamed of began to touch even the most religious of the population. Soon, entire carcasses could be seen turning above pits of glowing coals by emaciated children. As they struggled to turn their meal they grinned hungrily at the carcass, and often wondered why it didn't have any hoofs on its front feet.

Similar situations existed in every corner of the world. And then it happened—not as they had been told. It was more like they had seen in old movies of previous wars—magnified many times over. Missiles struck the east and west coast of America with such precision that it was felt a thousand miles away. Incendiary bombs were then dropped with incredible accuracy, and soon the winds generated by the blazes were causing flames to run with unbelievable speed. Within hours of the first strike, most of the United States was on fire. More strategic strikes with both incendiary bombs and nuclear missiles completed the cycle of deadly destruction.

Spies have plied their trade since the beginning of mankind's efforts to eliminate all earthly species, even his own. Soon every nation with war capability had the same technology as its neighbor. When the first nuclear strikes began, missiles rained down on almost every nation on earth.

The warlords knew the effects of incendiary holocaust following their initial nuclear strikes. Within hours of the first strike, most of Planet Earth was on fire. Half of all the humans on earth died within the first twenty-four hours of World War III. By spring 2052 half again had died of war-related events. People were dying of hunger, insanity, environment, wounds, murder and the one that took many lives—cannibalism. Humans were hungry like never before.

AND THEN THEY CAME

Rick Magers

The first to come over the hill was Alaine Catrich. His head was still shaved except for the row of long red spikes of hair down the middle. He was in his black leather boots with knives in sheaths attached to each. He now had a bandoleer of ammunition for the assault rifle he carried. His eyes glowed with the fire of the righteous. He was now no longer a nothing little freak—he was a leader of soldiers...one of Satan's Dark Angels.

Beside him strutted little Bradley Morrison—zits and all. As he limped along in his friend and mentor's wake, he felt good. He knew that he was now among his own kind. All around him the hideous demons that had plagued him his entire life screamed and screeched as they ran in and out of the multitudes who had come to fight for Satan. They no longer frightened him; they were his kind—his brothers.

. . .

Another battle zone was being formed many miles away. Preston Childers marched at the front of several thousand of Satan's Dark Angels, as they began forming the formidable army that would soon confront the army of believers, which was also forming in the distance. The Dark Angels came from every corner of the land. They could be seen oozing up from the fields—slithering from the rivers, lakes, and oceans—emerging from the bark of forest trees. Three-hundred-pound Preston stretched to his six-foot-four-inch height and watched his soldiers arriving. He smiled in anticipation of the battle to come. "I knew I was born to be a leader of men in a great battle." The smile that spread across his black face was one of total confidence. He had been deceived since birth. 'You ain't worth the few pennies the wine cost to create you.' The final lie came from Satan himself, but it was the lie that Preston had wanted all of his short life. *You will be somebody*. He was now a General with hundreds of thousands of troops about to embark upon a great battle—a battle like no other.

~ The last great battle to be fought on Planet Earth ~

Similar leaders were taking command of their troops on every continent. The soil was alive with emerging soldiers. Trees withered and died as soldiers stepped from the bark of their wooden bodies then shook like dogs, and re-incarnated soldiers stepped from the piles of bark in their previous human forms to join the ranks of Satan. Waters everywhere boiled as gelatin-like creatures slithered onto the land to be transformed to their original form. They too followed the masses ahead of them—eager to begin the killing. The moment in time had arrived.

They were Satan's Dark Angels.

Yorda Poleski and Baileen Darden were once again joined, as they shared command of the millions of soldiers gathering around them. A short time earlier Baileen emerged from her earthly grave, as Yorda slithered from his watery domain. both stood upon the beach and resumed their human forms— together they would assume control of the soldiers that were coming by the thousands, every minute that passed. Baileen's dark, Jamaican face glistened with a radiance she never had before. She had reached out to Satan and he took her to him. He had touched her heart as no man on earth could—she now felt warmth she thought had forever been denied her. She was one of Satan's most devoted Dark Angels. Yorda had no idea who or what he was and didn't care; he was with Baileen. He was prepared to follow her wherever she led— the perfect soldier.

. . .

Charles Holden was still the mild mannered little man he had been in life. He stood among the many soldiers and held his lover, Morrison Hemp's hand as they looked up to the top of the building where Ruben Ostermyer and James Pruitt stood in the elaborate uniforms of Generals. Leaders in life, they were also leaders now in Satan's battle for the souls of the remaining people of Earth. Each being as ruthless as the other, they shared the command equally. They stood as Caesar had centuries earlier, and looked out over the heads of millions of soldiers awaiting their signal. Their orders had been the same as every other chosen leader across the globe. Satan's voice thundered as no other ever heard by man.

You will know when the time has come. Attack the heathens and tear them apart. Their brothers will watch then join us. Accept them as your brothers. Together we will stomp God from mankind's mind and then send Him into a deep dark chasm from which he will never return. When all have gathered watch the horizon for my sign.

* * *

Shirleen Davidson took great pleasure at seeing the faces of her previous crewmembers, mixed in with the masses of soldiers assembled beneath the balcony on which she stood. She had dressed herself in the garb of an Amazon General, and leaned on the five-foot-long sword she intended to wreak havoc on the males she came in contact with. Millions of Satan's soldiers stretched as far as her eyes could see and more were coming. A million demons danced among them—eager too for the great battle. Beside her stood a small boy with the face of her father and the body of Satan—a black smoldering mass, writhing with worms. She looked away from her soldiers a moment to let her eyes feast on the child. "You will one day be the leader of all you see, my son."

The boy did not hear a word. He was obsessed with the masses gathering beneath him. His eyes glowed red with the hatred that was his birthright, as he observed the demons dancing about among the men, women, and children. Mortals could not decipher his thoughts—dark and sinister, his tiny mouth opening and closing, much the way a shark's did in the days before the oceans were depleted of all living creatures.

* * *

Sheldon Hamilton III was only one of many that Satan had placed in the sky prior to the start of the great battle. His bomber carried an arsenal of nuclear weapons of immense destructive capabilities. His orders had been burned into his brain, and he was now approaching the place where he was to begin dropping his bombs. He glanced to the rear and looked at the demons that sat waiting for his orders. Sheldon returned to his navigational gauges. He thought about Satan's orders. *When you reach your target, circle and watch the horizon. You will know when the time has come.*

* * *

Brandisha Omahasha Candide marched slowly ahead of an army that stretched to the horizon behind her. John Poston followed slightly behind. Nearby, her mother Alma marched beside the many foster parents who had molested her little girl. They were all united in one large group to do Satan's work. Alma turned as a young man moved in beside her, and was pleased to see the Native American Indian who was the father of her daughter—now the leader of this mighty army. She looked around at nearby faces, hoping to see her black lover, Chester. He was not in this army, because at heart he had been a good man and was now a soldier in Gods army. Daryll and Marlene Coolidge were also missing from these assembled soldiers. With all of their faults the two old people were sincere, God-loving Christians. They were far away, gathering with the millions of other remaining Christians who were ready once more to do battle with Satan for control of Earth.

Brenda Lassiter was one of the few child leaders of Satan's army. The evil, that had permeated her mind since birth, had placed her in Satan's highest esteem. 'You will be a leader among my leaders.' His voice thundered as he carried her with him through the air to the top of the hill above the mass of people gathered below in all directions—awaiting their orders.

She stood now and looked across the heads of her army. They could all feel the evil and hatred radiating from her, and knew they had a General worth following. She thought of her mother and father as she drew the razor sharp knife from its sheath on her side. She was aware that they were on the other side, with God's White Angels. She could see the Christians in the distance and thought, *where are you mommy? Where are you daddy? Your sweet little Dark Angel's coming to see you.*

If we win here we win everywhere. The world is a fine place and worth the fighting for and I hate very much leaving it.

Ernest Hemingway.

The great multitudes that formed the two largest armies ever assembled on Planet Earth had converged simultaneously in thousands of places. The living and once-dead were ready to fight side-by-side—each knowing that this was the last battle between God and Satan.

Blood flowed across the parched earth, as water had not for many years.

Sheldon Hamilton III and the other pilots in Satan's bombers saw their master rising large on the horizon like a new sun. They each knew it was the sign to begin. Sheldon turned to the demons behind him. "Our master stands before us—It is time." The Demons pulled the lever to open the bomb bay and screamed with joy as the bombs departed, carrying nuclear death of such magnitude that it would be the end of all but the most microscopic life on Planet Earth.

Mushroom clouds of destruction ascended toward the heavens all over the world. Fires raged as nuclear winds tore across the land. Still the battles went on. When guns were empty, swords were drawn, and the slaughter continued.

    The first to see it was a young girl who was leaning on the huge sword with which she had been hacking a wounded old woman. She leaned on the great weapon and looked at the sky. It was so odd to see a young girl standing quietly, amid such carnage, looking at the sky. Soon others were also looking up.

    At first it was only the suggestion of a face. Eyes were added, and they took up almost the entire sky. Then came a nose—a mouth far below—an arm was now rising slowly as the mouth opened. When the face in the sky spoke, the words came with a force never heard by mankind.

I gave you my most beautiful planet in the heavens. I sacrificed my only son that your wounds would heal. You have inflicted more hurt on each other than my son ever saw. I thought I had planted seeds on a wonderful planet that would grow into beautiful beings but I was wrong. You have defiled the grace that I allowed you, time and time again. You did not worship me. You worshipped yourselves as you built larger and larger ornate temples to celebrate your own greatness. I failed, and now scatter you to the roaring winds of time from which you will never be released.

    The arm in the sky was now drawn back—holding bolts of lightning that were flashing across the entire heavens. Gentle people on other worlds saw them and smiled. They knew God—had felt his wrath; in a time before they had put aside their petty jealousies and wars. When the arm came forward and released the lightning bolts, everyone on Planet Earth was standing still.

    Another voice roared across the sky as Satan lunged to grab the bolts of lightning…**Nooooooooooooooooooooooooooooooooooooooooo.**

    Satan screamed as he grabbed one bolt—then another—and another. All watched as God thrust a flashing bolt into Satan's heart, and then grabbed the bolts from his weakening grip; thrusting them into the blue planet.

    Planet Earth was still wobbling from the thundering speech, when the first great bolt hit. Others followed it, and soon the planet began splitting apart. Torn from its celestial orbit, Earth began to wobble uncontrollably. When the two pieces collided there was an explosion of such magnitude that beings in other solar systems, beyond the mind of earthman, heard the sound for years and saw the flash for decades.

Rick Magers

The heart of man is the place the devil dwells in—I feel sometimes a hell within myself.

Sir Thomas Browne: 1605-1682

The fantastic Blue Planet Earth was no more.

It was

THE END

Rick Magers

Other books

By

Rick Magers

THE McKANNAHS
~ A western novel ~

• • •

DARK CARIBBEAN
~ A novel based on a true story ~

• • •

LADYBUG and the DRAGON
~ biography——FREE at www.grizzlybookz.com ~
Book II available in 2007
Follow Katia's progress against the Dragon
http://caringbridge.org/fl/katia_leukemiapage

• • •

THE FACE PAINTER
~ short stories for young readers ~

• • •

A FATHER'S VISIT
~ 80 short stories ~

Rick Magers

IN PROGRESS

THE McKANNAHS
~ together again ~

Four McKannah brothers arrive to help Jesse *right a wrong,* done to his Native American friends. Corrupt Politians and others will wish they'd never heard of The McKannahs.

Their hair now has gray streaks running through it.

Steel gray
~ The same color as the steel running through their bodies ~

. . .

AMERICA
~ Western, Indian, and other short stories ~

. . .

ASHES and MEMORIES
~ biography ~

. . .

CARIB INDIAN
~ warrior / cannibal ~

The first novel ever written about these ferocious South American Indians who ruled the Caribbean Sea for centuries.

Available in 2007

Rick Magers

WE HOPE

...

The biography of Dolores (DEO) Fisher…

widow of the author's friend; world famous treasure diver

Mel Fisher.

Many years prior to locating the $400,000,000. sunken treasure of the Spanish Galleon Atocha, not far from Key West Florida, Mel would have been the first to say that the greatest treasure he ever found was in California…it was

DEO

Together they roamed the world in search of adventure and sunken treasure…they found plenty of both.

BUT

With the many books written, a feature film, and numerous TV specials…this will be an untold side of the story. Stunning, movie star beautiful, Dolores was not window dressing…she was a full time diver who went down through the sharks like all the rest…often bringing up treasure.

Check www.grizzlybookz.com to see when it's available.

Rick Magers

BOOKS BY

RICK MAGERS

ARE AVAILABLE AT:

Amazon.com
Borders.com
Target.com
Waldenbooks.com
Alibris.com
Abebooks.com
BooksInPrint.com
GlobalBooksInPrint.com

Made in the USA
Charleston, SC
02 March 2016